Digger's Moon

Digger's Moon

John W. Heird

*To: Dusty Richards
With warmest regards!*

John W Heird

John W. Heird
2423 GristMill Rd.
Little Rock, AR 72227
(501) 221-9171 * jheird@comcast.net

iUniverse, Inc.
New York Lincoln Shanghai

Digger's Moon

All Rights Reserved © 2003 by John W. Heird

No part of this book may be reproduced or transmitted in any form or by any means, graphic, electronic, or mechanical, including photocopying, recording, taping, or by any information storage retrieval system, without the written permission of the publisher.

iUniverse, Inc.

For information address:
iUniverse, Inc.
2021 Pine Lake Road, Suite 100
Lincoln, NE 68512
www.iuniverse.com

ISBN: 0-595-28387-X (pbk)
ISBN: 0-595-65780-X (cloth)

Printed in the United States of America

For my wife—she is my Katherine.
Strong, resolute, loving and true.

Killing a man is rough business. I guess you all know that. Here in the Territory, we are about that rough business, every day. Not a soul in the Territory is unaffected by the life here. Men and women live rough, they talk rough, and they die rough. When the great minds in Washington designed to take all the Indians and turn them loose here, they forgot there is a civilization to build. There is no civilization here, at all. It's a rough business.

—John Robert Singleton
United States Marshal
Fort Smith, Arkansas
September 2, 1875

Contents

Preface xiii

PART ONE: TWENTY-FIVE YEARS BEFORE THE CAPTURE OF THE MISSIONARIES 1

Chapter 1 3
Chapter 2 11
Chapter 3 17

PART TWO: SIX MONTHS BEFORE THE CAPTURE OF THE MISSIONARIES 29

Chapter 4 31
Chapter 5 43
Chapter 6 54
Chapter 7 61
Chapter 8 73
Chapter 9 83
Chapter 10 92

Part Three: Three Months Before the Capture of the Missionaries 101

Chapter 11 103
Chapter 12 108
Chapter 13 116
Chapter 14 120
Chapter 15 141
Chapter 16 156
Chapter 17 169
Chapter 18 176
Chapter 19 184

Part Four: The Capture of the Missionaries 197

Chapter 20 199
Chapter 21 207
Chapter 22 212
Chapter 23 220
Chapter 24 223
Chapter 25 233
Chapter 26 239
Chapter 27 252
Chapter 28 262
Chapter 29 269

EPILOGUE **281**

About the Author 291

Preface

This book is a work of fiction. Many tales of the Old West are a mixture of fact and myth. This, in kind, is such an effort. Researched for accuracy, some characters portrayed in this book are based upon actual persons, and some events, places and incidents described herein are taken from historical fact, and myth, surrounding the lives of those persons; but in actuality, all events, places and incidents relating to the characters are used fictitiously, or, are a product of the author's imagination.

That does not alter the fact that the Indian Territory of 1875 was a dangerous place. That is documented history. Years of research have borne out the facts contained in countless stories—all testifying that the dying was easy; the hard part was the living. Life was a cheap commodity on the border. Reports of atrocities were so commonplace that such cruelty was just another day's event in the lives of the citizens.

Federal Judge Isaac C. Parker punctured this world of crime and vengeance by establishing a hard hand of justice to deal with the lawlessness. His bench was the point of no return for many outlaws. The condemned filled his jail from wall to wall, calling that cold, dark and dank place *Hell on the Border*. Eighty-eight souls met their doom on his fabled gallows as the *Hanging Judge* determined to bring an end to the reign of bloodshed.

No event was more cruel or shocking than the one put into motion by the capture of a group of missionaries traveling in the Choctaw Nation on February 12, 1876. That day, the savage outlaw band of renegades and killers who had terrorized the Territory unabated, unleashed their vilest fury. These *Men of Blood* set in motion an evil plan to bring the full force of violence and mayhem to the lives of many in Fort Smith. Their actions portrayed the hatred and vengeance in the hearts of those bent upon disrupting life and civility. The response of Judge

Parker and his Deputy Corps was quick, decisive and final. Their actions were those of retribution, redemption and a nobler human spirit. This is that story, as it might have happened.

—John W. Heird

Part One

Twenty-Five Years Before the Capture of the Missionaries

Chapter 1

New Moon, October, 1850
The Llano Estacado, Northwest Texas

For Six Claws, the young Kiowa lad so named because he was born with six toes on both feet, life was hard; his was harder than most. The extreme cruelty that forged his life was the topic of often told, and retold, village stories. His father, Walking Bear, saw to it that the boy adhered to a drastic discipline of duty. A duty black and dark. A life of violence and brutality. The father molded the son into his own forbidding image. A legend to the Kiowa people, Walking Bear was the perfect warrior, hunter, and keeper of the old ways. His prowess as a killer was known throughout the Plains tribes. He was a no-nonsense man with no patience for error.

It was in the shadow of this legend that Six Claws grew up. While most Kiowa boys endured tests of manhood at the age of twelve, Six Claws had conquered the initiations at the age of five. Taken to the mountains and forced to survive for a week, alone and frightened, the boy had never wavered. He never laughed. He never enjoyed boyhood games and experiences. He never cried. Not in the recall of any in the village was there a memory of Six Claws ever shedding a tear. Not in pain, or in fear, or in sadness.

Six Claws had watched the cruelty of his father, Walking Bear, while the man would beat the boy's mother, Hand Over Mouth, as a matter of daily life. He needed no reason. He beat her with leather strips, animal bones, rocks, sticks, logs, and gun butts—anything in reach. Her name, Hand Over Mouth, was given to her because she always used her hands to hide the bruises and wounds on her face. Walking Bear also beat his two other wives, but not as often, or as savagely as Six Claws' mother. The young boy always sat and watched, never saying a word. The cold, black stare that always kept his enemies uncertain of his next move was being burned into his character. Often, after a day of raiding or hunting, his father would not only beat his wives, but Six Claws also. This demonstration built the character that he wanted in his son. Six Claws was being transformed into the image of Walking Bear.

This new moon ushered in Six Claws' fifteenth birthday. Walking Bear, angry because his young daughter did not bring his deer meat fast enough from the serving being prepared by Hand Over Mouth, struck the girl with a burning log and broke her leg. The scream pierced the village. Six Claws and his mother ran to the girl's side.

"I am sorry, Father. I am sorry," she said. Her sobbing was taking her breath. She could not speak in coherent sentences, but everyone gathering at the scene could understand her plea. "Please, Father, I am sorry."

Hand Over Mouth picked her daughter up and tried to carry her to the lodge. The weight was too much for her and she dropped the girl. The pain was so great, the daughter screamed even louder. Six Claws scooped her up into his muscular arms and turned to his father. Their gazes locked. Walking Bear sneered and spat upon the ground as Six Claws carried his sister into the lodge. The crowds stood in silence as the young warrior returned to where his father was sitting and sat beside him. Six Claws' eyes went void of color and feeling. As if moved by some primordial sense of violence, he grabbed Walking Bear's prized bone-handled, forged-steel knife—taken from a captive mountain man—and shoved it so far into his father's heart that none of the blade was left exposed. He then withdrew the knife and chanted curses aloud to the new moon.

Howling Moon, the wise old spiritual healer of the tribe, stood over the body of the slain man. He spoke to the people.

"When a father molds a son in anger, that son will rise in anger against him. Take no revenge for the murder." He then wept and chanted loudly in a spirit of deep lamentation. "I sense our end as a people," he said sadly. "We will be tossed by the wind to a place from which we will not return. The great evil of Walking Bear has spawned a greater evil. The darkness of this night will not pass. It is our end. Fold our camp in your hearts, because it will perish soon."

It was evident to everyone that Walking Bear had trained the one to take his spirit from him. The people avoided Six Claws that night. No one would even make eye contact with him, because of Howling Moon's prophecy.

"You must leave for the edge of the camp, and stay there. Your mother and sister may attend you; but you must not walk before our faces," Howling Moon said.

The boy moved through the crowd, eyes downcast, and walked slowly to the end of the camp near the bend of the river. No one followed, except his friend Two Snakes, who had gathered meager belongings from the lodge and brought them to Six Claws.

"I will stay with you tonight," Two Snakes said.

Six Claws did not answer. He looked at the full moon and thought about things a dark mind ponders. He was alone except for the half-Kiowa boy Two Snakes, so named because he always carried two rattlesnakes inside a pouch tied around his waist. Six Claws had no other friends, and he wanted none. He tolerated Two Snakes because of an act of bravery years ago.

Once, in the past, Two Snakes had come to Six Claws' campfire at the challenging of the other boys in the camp. Six Claws took the two snakes from the boy's pouch and bit their heads off. He then beat Two Snakes with the reptiles' lifeless bodies until the boy broke away and ran back to the place from where his friends had been watching. The boys ran into the village and made no further attempt to invade the territory of Six Claws, who had lived in the lodge of Walking Bear. Except one. Two Snakes, covered in blood from the snakes and from his own cuts, walked fearlessly back to Six Claws' lodge. The village watched in amazement as the young Kiowa courageously picked up the snake corpses, lifted them up to Six Claws and began to chant to the Snake Spirit as he turned and slowly walked back to his own lodge. Two Snakes, who had been heckled all his life by the young boys in the village because of his half-breed heritage, never again experienced their torment. Six Claws never bothered him again, either. Even though there was no compassion or respect for anyone in his stone-cold heart, the brave act of young Two Snakes that night long ago had elicited the closest thing to admiration for another human being that Six Claws had ever experienced.

Tonight, at the full moon, following the savage murder, he accepted the company of the boy. As his friend? Even Six Claws was incapable of knowing that. Two Snakes, however, chanted to the Snake People to protect the young warrior, now without family or home. There were no words spoken between them. They ate an evening meal brought by Hand Over Mouth, but Six Claws stared into the darkness as the two sat by the fire. Two Snakes did not try to invade the thoughts of the vanquished youth. He felt a strange premonition of a reign of terror that was about to be unleashed into his life, and all the camp. A dark foreboding and sadness gripped him. The prophecy of Howling Moon seemed to smother the night. Two Snakes chanted as sleep overtook him. Six Claws stood and watched the passing clouds cover the full moon.

The next morning, Six Claws left the village forever and began his part of the prophecy. As he left, he placed a parting gift beside the still sleeping half-Kiowa boy. Two Snakes awakened to find Six Claws gone, but the knife used to kill Walking Bear was beside his blanket.

After the murder of Walking Bear, life had not been the same in the Kiowa camp. There was a sense of life without constant fear of being brutalized by the warrior, but the laxity made the villagers lazy. The spirit of Walking Bear had been a driving force on their hunts and raids. Without that leadership, they had become without vision. Howling Moon had warned of the doom that would follow the departed Walking Bear. He sang and chanted of the good and evil forces and the necessity to keep balance in life. He warned that the force of evil had disappeared with the murder of Walking Bear. Evil was necessary for courage and skill in battle; it was a complement to good, and without it the people would perish. The people, however, were glad to have the tyrant removed from their lives. Besides, they reasoned whatever evil dissipated with the death of Walking Bear, Six Claws, though gone, more than made up for in spirit.

Howling Moon lamented that the evil of Six Claws did not complement its counterpart, the good spirit. His evil was too far from the dark side of the spirit world and would not help in the balance of life. The people did not understand and did not care. They were happy with just hunting, raiding Comanche camps and living an uncomplicated life, far from the days of their constant fear of Walking Bear.

Six Claws was now almost forgotten. By the end of the new moon, there was no need for evil to balance the good. The people liked the life of the good spirit. Howling Moon stopped trying to convince the elders and the people that disaster was coming. He sat, refusing to eat and awaiting death, hoping to avoid witnessing the tragedy of a people whose life had lost its desire to honor its ways. To him, the village was no longer Kiowa. *Something like the young warrior Two Snakes, they were only half-Kiowa*, he had thought repeatedly in his prayers. Howling Moon died a week before his prophecy was realized.

Now, on the last night of the full moon, Two Snakes, like Six Claws, would be forced to be a man before his years. The thunder of Indian ponies exploded through the camp. The fat and lazy village was caught unaware as the Comanche war party, under Heavy Eagle, rode into the village and slaughtered the people under the moon's ebbing light. Every person in the camp was herded together; the raiders employed unimaginable torture upon the Kiowa village.

Only one Comanche brave was lost. The raid would be talked about in the same breath as the great raids of Quanah Parker and legends of the old chiefs who terrorized Texas and Mexico for two generations. Details of Heavy Eagle's raid into the placid Kiowa camp this night were added to these great stories.

"Run," shouted Running Elk to his family. His wife, Winter Fawn, a Cherokee princess—the most beautiful woman in the village—and their son, Two Snakes, had been awakened by the violence and screams.

Two Snakes grabbed his prized knife, the steel that ripped Walking Bear's heart, and his pouch of rattlesnakes and leapt to his feet. He took his terrified mother's hand and ran toward the tree line by the river.

"Hide here, Mother," he said as he pulled brush around her. "I'll be back." He ran to find his father, but was struck by a heavy blow to the head and knocked unconscious. He was dragged, along with all the remaining men and boys, and tied to a stake. When Two Snakes regained his senses, he was faced with a horrifying sight. Every baby and small child was thrown into the river and used as targets for the Comanche arrows. Their small screams filled the night. Every woman was brutally raped in public view. One by one, the women were cut and eviscerated from the thigh to the heart.

The dust raised by the ponies running through the village was so thick that the captives found it hard to see or breathe. The cacophonous mixture of screams, galloping horses, Comanche war cries and the sound of terror was deafening. The smell of burning lodges, and the rancid odor of blood flowing and bowel parts tossed about from scores of fallen Kiowas, hung over the village like the putrid stench from an open sewer. The heat was oppressive. Even on this cool evening, the fires were not a comfort, but an inescapable inferno. Whatever torture the men endured, it was nothing compared to the unimaginable horrors the women suffered. Their violation was so inhuman that no amount of tears, screams and prayers could remove the taste of death in their mouths. Each prayed for a swift death. Each prayed that Howling Moon's prophecy would pass quickly.

It was then that Two Snakes saw his mother, Winter Fawn, being led to the center of the circle. Tonight, she was especially popular among the Comanche raiders. The half-Kiowa boy sat with his father, bound hand and foot, and watched her violation. She caught a glimpse of her husband and son and from that time closed her eyes. The Comanches jabbed firebrands to her eyes to make her open them, but she never did and her eyes were soon burned out. She was one of the last to be cut and have her intestines pulled out and fed to the dogs. The men and boys tied to stakes were beaten and killed, one at a time with the rest looking on, awaiting their turn. Two Snakes felt the blood from his father splatter his face. It was warm and thick and ran down his cheeks like tears. He did not cry; the drops of red from his father were the only tears he had.

For hours, Two Snakes had chanted to the Snake Spirit to come to his aid. He chanted to have the gift to take one Comanche with him on his death journey. For a young man to kill his first Comanche as he himself was being killed would bode well in the spirit world.

The Snake Spirit heard his plea. As the Comanche executioner faced the boy, Two Snakes' hands slipped free from the ropes behind his back, and in a motion faster than the Comanche could see, reached into his pouch and threw a rattlesnake into the Comanche's face. The warrior's scream rose above the noises in the camp. Somehow, it was different. Everyone knew it was Comanche, not Kiowa. The snake had bitten with such vengeance that the warrior was on the ground when Two Snakes loosened his foot bindings and stood with the other snake in his hands. There was dead silence in the camp as everyone watched the boy standing over the dead Comanche. Two Snakes looked around the circle and shook the snake again at the gaping Comanches. He picked the snake off the face of his enemy and waved both snakes at the group, chanting loudly to the Snake Spirit.

Heavy Eagle slowly approached a defiant, yet confident, Two Snakes.

"This is a warrior," he shouted, pointing to the boy. "He is not a Kiowa dog like the rest. I will take him for a captive."

Two Snakes swiftly threw both snakes at the war chief, who deflected both vipers. His short, fat arms reached down as he struggled to make the move. His heavy body made it difficult to bend over with any swiftness. He finally grabbed the snakes from the ground by the heads, and spread their mouths wide as he turned to his men.

"See, he even tries to kill me—Heavy Eagle—with his little pets. But I am greater than his magic," he said. "Take him with us to our village, I will teach him Comanche ways and he will be a good death to bring upon our enemies." He laughed loudly—a silver tooth sparkling in the moonlight—as rolls of fat shook around his girth. "He is a warrior," he said again, looking at Two Snakes. The boy looked back with a cold, dark stare. Heavy Eagle lost his smile and his good nature. It was as if he sensed a bad omen from the Spirits about this Kiowa boy. *Maybe he should kill him,* was his first, immediate thought. But he had already praised the boy—in public. It was of no matter. The night was successful. No time to think of such thoughts from the Spirit People.

"Let us go now, and return to our home and dance and rejoice at our victory," Heavy Eagle said, laughing with his raiders. He looked one last time in the direction of the Kiowa boy. It was not good. Somehow, it was not good.

Two Snakes, like his friend Six Claws, now found little to laugh about in life. The boy was taken from his village in the Indian Territory, across the Red River, into the staked plains of the Llano Estacado. He had been forced to walk, sometimes falling, as they dragged him behind a horse all the way into the Comanches' village where his captors treated him with exceptional cruelty. His special skill and power of handling snakes had earned the Comanches' respect, but not their hospitality. He was kept outside in the camp and tied to a stake in the middle of a corral. There they brought him food and water once a day and allowed him infrequently to go, under guard, to the river to bathe. The only reason he was alive was to be an object of sport for the Comanche.

The Indians wagered on the outcome of battles between him, armed with his rattlesnake, and a challenger armed with a knife. In the two weeks he had been at the camp, he had killed sixteen people in the corral fights. So accurate was he with the toss of the rattlesnakes that none of the Comanche braves dared to challenge him. Live captives brought in from raids were substituted as challengers. Since the raid on the Kiowa village, it had become the rule not to kill any human, if possible, in the many attacks on settlers, farmers or enemy Indian villages. With live captives available, more gambling sport could take place. The Comanche brought women and men alike against him. One by one, he was forced to unleash his rattlesnake upon them and allow it to make a fatal strike. He had killed more people for the wagering sport than any of the Comanche braves in the camp had killed in battle. After each contest he chanted loudly and reverently to the Snake Spirit; praying for the spirit of the one he had just killed and that he would be released from captivity. Many times this ceremony had amused the Comanche crowd more than the actual battle.

Tied to the stake in the light of another full moon, the third since the slaughter of his village, he was praying to the Snake Spirit until the half-light of the morning. The Snake People heard his prayer. A large rattlesnake crawled into the corral and up around to his hands, exposed through the knotted ropes tied around his wrists. The rattlesnake had come to give its life for the boy. As if by the leading of the Spirit, he gripped the serpent with his hands and squeezed it until the blood and fat ran from its body. The lubrication caused the dry leather strips to become supple and his hands slipped through the knots. He untied himself as the village slept. He lay prostrate on the ground for a while and chanted silently to the Snake Spirit. As he walked out of the corral, two large rattlesnakes came across his path. He picked them up and stole quietly into the lodge of Heavy Eagle. The warrior's wife awoke immediately as the Kiowa walked inside. She sat up startled, stared at the boy, but said nothing. Whether from fear, or at the prompting of the Snake People's spirits all around the lodge, she remained silent, reclined and closed her eyes. The boy knelt in front of Heavy Eagle. The warrior chief stirred. He did not struggle.

"You have come to claim my spirit, my little Kiowa dog," he said. "Then get on with it."

Two Snakes lifted the rattlesnakes over Heavy Eagle, chanted softly, and shoved their open-fanged mouths at his throat. The Comanche's eyes stared wide in horror as the poison entered his blood stream. He did not scream. The warrior only whimpered slightly and stopped breathing. The boy, now a man, stepped over the lifeless body, walked out of the lodge and into the horizon toward home. No one came after him. No Comanche would dare quarrel with so powerful a spirit. After his escape from the depravity he had suffered, nothing could erase the memories of the prophecy of Howling Moon and its fulfillment. Two Snakes also could not erase the memories of Six Claws, who was part of the prophecy and of his life—for good or bad. The young Kiowa set out on a journey unknown to him; only the Spirits were there to guide him.

Chapter 2

▼

April 23, 1855
The Guadalupe River between Austin and San Antonio

Robert Buford Johnson was the only child of Captain Tobias W. Johnson and Elizabeth LeBeaux, the daughter of Gaston Boone LeBeaux, a ship's Captain and avid treasure hunter from New Orleans. Tobias and Elizabeth had met while he was in New Orleans acquiring supplies and arms for Sam Houston's Army in the effort to defeat the Mexican dictator, Santa Anna. Even given the urgency of his mission, Elizabeth had been a stronger priority. They married and he returned to Galveston, not only with the supplies, but also with a new wife. Robert Buford was born some years later. Life never had a dull moment for young Bob, with his father serving as a Republic of Texas Army officer, and later as a trooper and Captain with the Texas Rangers. One post followed another and the adventures in life that involved Mexicans, Indians and outlaws never left a doubt the path in life chosen for young Bob. He was born with a gun in one hand and a Comanche scalp in the other, Tobias would tell his troopers on the many long forays into assignment after assignment. How young Bob would be the most renown Ranger in history was a statement that always worked its way into the conversation. Long days and nights on the trail of some bandit or Indian band afforded a great deal of time to think about family and home and dreams of his young boy's future. Tobias could talk. His son Robert would inherit this trait honestly. From the day he was born in 1844, Bob Johnson was his father's joy. When most fathers returned from a journey, they would bring their children some rock candy, a wooden toy or some-such trinket found in the general store. However, when Tobias came home from an assignment, young Bob usually was the recipient of a captured Indian bone knife, hatchet, occasional scalp, or firearm. By the time he was three years old he could lay claim to ownership of half a dozen black powder musket loaders, as many sets of arrows, bows and quivers, knives and even a Colt Navy Percussion pistol. He was the best-armed three-year-old in Texas. He also had a sizable collection of old hanging nooses, blood-splattered Indian clothing, and a few unidentified scalps that Elizabeth insisted be kept in an old seaman's trunk stored in the shack behind the house.

Once, when grandfather LeBeaux had made one of his very infrequent visits, he was pleased to see the collection in his old trunk. He promptly added a shrunken human head he had gotten in the South Seas, and an eye patch complete with a glass eyeball he had taken from a cardsharp named Happy Jack in Tujajue's saloon down in the Vieux Carre. Captain LeBeaux had caught Happy Jack cheating, and knocked him unconscious with the butt end of a heavy Colt pistol. When he fell, his glass eye had popped out and LeBeaux took it, the patch, and everything in the man's pockets. Tobias thought the items added greatly to young Bob's collection and encouraged his father-in-law to deposit anything of interest. Such things horrified Elizabeth but she had followed her own mother's resignation: accepting the unusual items brought home from the sea by her husband. Elizabeth now had the same lot in life from Tobias. Her duty was to keep that trunk from Bob for as long as she could. Later, when she finally allowed Bob access into his treasure trunk, he considered the glass eye his favorite of the lot. He would often hold it in his fingers and think about the story his grandfather had related of the incident. Trying to picture this fellow, Happy Jack, would always amuse young Bob. *I'll bet he's Sad Jack or Mad Jack now, or even one-eyed Jack,* he would say to himself and laugh. Bob carried the glass eye with him from the day he mounted up to ride as a Texas Ranger. It was a source of fond memories—a much-needed diversion in the wild and dangerous times on the plains.

Now, in April 1855, young Robert Johnson found it increasingly difficult to contain his impatient restlessness. It was his first official ride with his father, Texas Ranger Captain Tobias W. Johnson and his troop. Robert could not take in everything fast enough. He did not want to miss a thing. Elizabeth was reluctant, but Tobias convinced her to allow Robert to accompany the troop on a routine prisoner transfer. The boy did not sleep a single full night, fidgeting in anxious anticipation. Since his earliest memory with his father's duties as an army officer and Texas Ranger, Bob had been ready to go on this adventure. Every conceivable necessity had been packed and repacked for the trip from Austin down to San Antonio and again back up to Ranger headquarters in Austin. Tobias allowed Bob to bring his big Hawken rifle taken from an outlaw and given to the boy on his tenth birthday. It was a good foot taller than Bob.

The Alonzo Pierce gang had been captured near San Antonio by a local group of citizens. It was a lucky event. The three outlaws, Alonzo Pierce, Eli Barnes and Jake Standing Owl, a half-breed, had been drinking all night in their camp after raiding a small ranch and killing the family for the few meager possessions they owned. The gang butchered the entire Hobart Walton family, only a year out of Louisiana, including the husband, wife, two children and an old grandmother. The killers had scalped the family to make it look like the work of Comanche raiders. The outlaws tied the scalps to a tree limb near the horses. Dangling in the breeze was the white-haired scalp of the eighty-year-old grandmother, still crimson with blood, when the posse rode in. The posse caught the killers drunk and asleep, and subdued them without a struggle. The rancher's goods were scattered around the camp. The posse took the killers to the San Antonio Sheriff, who then dispatched the Rangers to take them on to Austin. It was a routine job and Tobias felt that it was the perfect time for Bob to make his debut on the trail. Tobias was proud of the boy and eager to give him a taste of the life of a Ranger since there would be little chance of danger. Normally a job that the Captain and two men could handle, Tobias took four Rangers along just to quell Elizabeth's fears. Robert was thrilled. A few birthdays had finally promoted him from mama's little darling to pa's Ranger assistant.

After an uneventful ride toward San Antonio and a day's look at the sights for young Bob, the Rangers had securely tied the three prisoners to their mounts and pointed back north to Austin.

"Son, see what you can do tonight with the bacon and biscuits," Tobias said to Bob at the camp that night. The boy was thrilled with the assignment—or any assignment for that matter. "I'll put these potatoes and beef together for some good stew while you take care of that, and these boys will have a good meal for once."

"I'll do it, Pa," beamed Bob. He quickly set about slicing off some thick slabs of bacon and warming the biscuits in the iron pot set into the hot coals. Some of the ladies in San Antonio had sent along the biscuits and some sourdough bread for the return journey. Bob knew what he was doing. Elizabeth had seen to that aspect of his training. He laid the quarter-inch slabs of pork into the hot pan and the delicious aroma filled the evening air. Tobias, also no stranger to Elizabeth's cooking instructions, filled a pot with water, beef, potatoes, and various vegetables the women had sent along.

Noah Parnell, just a few years older than Bob, usually pulled the cooking duties for the troop, and did an acceptable job of it. There was never much complaining except he rarely salted anything enough for the troop's general taste. He was, however, heavy-handed with the other spices, especially the Mexican chilies. Most enjoyed the taste, though, and would always look for second and third helpings. Noah was watching Bob with an approving eye and the scene convinced him that the boy would do all right by the bacon and biscuits. He was hungry and the enjoyment of just relaxing after the day's ride was a novelty. He could get used to this. Maybe he could mention to the Captain that young Bob could come on a few more trips and cook. It would be fine with him.

Tobias ladled the boiling stew on their plates along with the crisp bacon and tender biscuits. The cool spring water from the Guadalupe made excellent coffee, and then that clear water mixed with a little sugar and some wild blueberries Bob had picked near the river made every man full and contented. Even the outlaws, who were being fed, relished every bite and were asking for more. Bob was an asset to the troop, as the Rangers saw it. He was an eager and well-tempered young man who, like his father, enjoyed talking, and he asked more questions on the short trip than they had heard in a dozen similar jaunts.

They had already fed two of the three prisoners, one at a time, while under guard by alternating Rangers. It was standard procedure that an unshackled, single prisoner be allowed to eat unfettered while a guard held a shotgun on all of them. It was held that if one tried to escape during the meal, both barrels would not only drop the escapee, but also wound or kill those shackled near him. This was a double incentive not to try.

Among the three, they fed Jake Standing Owl last. Everyone naturally understood that the white men were to be fed first. As the Indian was finishing the last spoonful of blueberry syrup on his plate, he lunged from his crouched position toward Ranger Billy Davis and drove the handle end of the spoon into the young Ranger's left eye. A roar of laughter, coming from the other Rangers sitting around the campfire, had momentarily distracted Billy. He had looked away for just a second. Jake Sitting Owl had been waiting for just that opportunity. Billy fell to the ground screaming as blood shot from his wounded eye. Jake immediately grabbed the shotgun and leveled down on the Captain and the three other Rangers. Every man went for his pistol, but the threatening motion by Jake with the shotgun convinced them to stand down.

"I'll kill all you goddamn Rangers," he said. "Don't a one of you move." He walked closer to them as if to emphasize that he could get all four with the blasts. "You," he said. "Loud talking Captain. Get over here and unshackle my friends. And be very careful."

Billy Davis began to scream even louder at the pain coming from his wounded eye. The noise irritated Jake. Without looking away from the Captain and the rest of the Rangers, he kicked Billy, violently and repeatedly in the head with his heavy, metal-studded Mexican boots. "Shut up goddamn you," he shouted. Blood began to pour from the trooper's mouth and ears, and he went silent.

There was not a sound from anyone. The Rangers looked on in shock and startled anger. The good turn of events stunned even Alonzo and Eli.

However, the sneer on Jake's face turned to a horrified grimace, as a .50 caliber bullet passed completely through his chest and heart, and exploded into the tree behind him. He looked down with an incredulous gawk at the fist-sized hole in his chest, lurched backwards and then fell dead to the ground.

Bob had been removing his night gear from his horse when Billy had screamed. Without hesitation, as if by instinct, he slipped the huge rifle from his saddle scabbard, laid it over the horse's back, pulled the big hammer back, and aimed dead-on at the Indian. In the frenzy, everyone had forgotten about the boy. When Jake had begun kicking Billy, the boy had hesitated. But when the Indian had looked at the Rangers with that demonic smile after Billy died, Bob had not hesitated. He pulled the trigger and held the sight steady, just as Tobias had shown him a hundred times. Bob still had his Hawken rifle to his shoulder as the blast recoil knocked him to the ground.

Tobias scrambled to lift Bob up. He held the boy firmly at arm's length and stared into his eyes. He felt surges of fright and relief, and he was proud. Very proud. He wanted to hug the boy and just cry. But Bob was no longer a boy. He was a man as much so as anyone else in the camp. He slowly released his grip on Bob's shoulders, grasped Bob's hand and shook it firmly.

"Thank you, son," he said slowly. "You saved all of our lives."

The Rangers, still grief-struck at the events that had resulted in Billy's death, each walked over to Bob and shook his hand. Noah Parnell, just eighteen, broke tradition. He hugged Bob anyway and said nothing. He fought back the tears.

Tobias made the decision to pack up, go on across the Guadalupe, and ride on to Austin. The Captain swore everyone to the oath that none would reveal that Bob had killed Jake Standing Owl. He himself would inform those who needed to know—those who should know. But Elizabeth would never know. Every troop captain, and the major, would hear the tale from a proud Tobias. The governor met with Bob to express his sincere gratitude on behalf of the people of Texas, and promised that when the boy reached eighteen he would personally administer the oath of a Texas Ranger to him. But Elizabeth never found out. This event forged Bob into the individual who would meet destiny with two other young boys in the future. Years of midnight dreams of the sight of that large caliber bullet crashing through the Indian invaded the rest of his childhood.

During those nightmares, there was no consolation available from an understanding mother. Just the unspoken respect and admiration of a very proud father. The event forged young Bob into an individual who learned, masterfully, to mask his pain and feelings with a good nature and lightheartedness. But when life demanded a strong response, he was just as much to the task. He was never at ease with his emotions since that night on the Guadalupe. He tried as best he could to work it out. It was a lifelong task.

Bob Johnson enlisted in the Texas Rangers when he was eighteen. He spent the next dozen or so years serving and ranging with troops all over Central, South and West Texas. Comanche raiding bands, Mexican outlaws and bored cowboys, for whom an exciting adventure or two had gone wrong and deadly somehow, kept him busy. Riding from the Gulf to the Indian Territory, across the Llano to Mexico and back, and all points between, filled his dozen years with adventure and boredom, terror and death, all a daily portion of life.

Most of those assignments were with his father's troop. They made a good team. Tobias had taught him well. Bob could joke and outwit the best of them, but when it came time for life and death tactics, he was as capable as any. He never shirked his duty when laughing-matters needed to be put aside. Bob could, and often did, captivate the younger troopers with one of his yarns. Then in a flash, he could fire his rifle and pistols with deadly accuracy if the need arose.

He did not enjoy killing as some of the young troopers did; yet, he would kill without hesitation, almost with an innate sense that it had to be done. He had done so often in his years on the Texas plains. Still, Bob could always bring the troop back to happier thoughts with his wit and personality. *Now, boys, let's don't let a little blood and a few hours diggin' graves get us down,* he would always say. Tobias would let his son take the lead. The son had out-mastered the father. Tobias was proud.

CHAPTER 3

▼

May 7, 1861
Tyler Plantation near Helena, Arkansas on the Mississippi River

William Timothy Tyler was born in Nashville City, Tennessee, and in 1856, at the age of ten, moved with his family to the black-dirt delta in Eastern Arkansas. The Tyler family worked hard. All nine of them. They turned their dream of a cotton plantation into a reality within five years. William—called Will by everyone but his mother—was the fourth in line of four boys and three girls born to Franklin and Dora Tyler. Franklin had married Dora Singleton on her sixteenth birthday, much to the dismay of her father, U.S. Marshal John Robert *John Law* Singleton, the most feared and respected lawman ever to come out of Eastern Tennessee. In fact, the reality that Franklin Tyler was courageous enough to win her hand and the apprehensive approval of Marshal Singleton was a feat of renowned history. It did not take long, however, to win the solid support of John Law once the grandchildren started coming. Some say the Marshal retired at the early age of fifty—not because of the half dozen bullets and numerous other life-threatening events that had been part of his long career, but because he had taken up the full-time job as a doting grandfather. Franklin, Dora, and those seven kids were his life now. Some thought it was a waste of good law-enforcement talent. Most thought he'd earned it. Just carrying the nickname *John Law* was tough enough. Upon hearing the name, most thought immediately of the infamous Scottish financier, gambler and land speculator who caused such misfortune during the time of the French-controlled Louisiana Colony. John Singleton cringed at the sound of the name, but soon wearied of the task of explaining that the nickname was not of his doing—just the title given him by an adoring and grateful citizenry. The nickname stuck, and the land scheme innovator, who carried the original name, was soon forgotten.

When Franklin pursued his lifelong ambition to be a successful cotton farmer, quit his career as a banker, and moved his family from that fine two-story home with the porch that wrapped around it from front to back, it was no surprise that John Law had come right along for the adventure. He was always in the ready for an adventure, and he sure as hell was not going to be separated from those grandchildren, not even for one day. It was a unanimous decision. Dora was ready for a life away from the blue-blood society of Nashville—ready to go to a place where her children could grow strong and free and put down roots away from the rigors and expectations of a banker's family. She had been a free spirit with a pioneer heritage from her father and her grandfather, who was a famous lawman, soldier and Indian fighter. She would often argue with herself, especially after an afternoon meeting of the Nashville Ladies Literary Society, about how the granddaughter of Captain George Singleton who fought Colonel Tarrolton at the Battle of The Cowpens, and was present at the surrender of General Cornwallis, could be satisfied as a banker's wife.

She was satisfied, of sorts, because she loved her life with Franklin Tyler. Now, however, she was overjoyed with the prospect of going west, even if it was just to Arkansas. The children were excited too. The prospect of open spaces and a vast land to explore, compared to shoes, socks, stiff collars, teas, and society functions—why, there was no comparison.

John Law was content with thoughts of sitting on the porch of some fine rustic palace the family would build, and drinking his buttermilk churned from the milk of a couple of fat cows that would be in his charge. He thought of sitting with his rifle, now and then, just in case some desperados were to come looking to take him on. Of course, his most recurrent dream was sitting and telling his grandchildren story after story of thirty years of pursuing, capturing, and hanging if needed be, some of the worst outlaws and killers in Tennessee and Kentucky. He had enough tales for those seven grandchildren and then again for seven more.

However, Dora had told him that seven children in ten years was her absolute best duty she felt to populating America. Franklin was no help either. Every time the old man would broach the subject of another grandchild, Franklin would have to set him straight. "Now, Marshal, I sure don't feel like a scrap with Dora over that subject. If you can convince her then I'll be glad to do my part to bring it about. But the hell lies in the convincing, not the doing."

The children were ready, Dora was anxious, John Law said he could be packed in less than a half-hour and Franklin, the man with the dream, was soaring with the possibility. He had worked in his father's bank for almost twenty years, saved, and invested his money. The enterprise was ready—more than ready. The only one that was apprehensive, and so much to the point that he had threatened to cease all contact with Franklin and his family, was James H. Tyler: Franklin's father, successful banker and son of professor Matthew Tyler, late teacher of classical languages at Harvard college. As Dora had wondered about her misplaced station in life, James Tyler, just as ardently had wondered about his own. He insisted that the son and grandson of Harvard-educated and Boston-encrusted society barons in the Tyler family could never be a dirt farmer and pig chaser in Arkansas.

It was a time of sad farewells when they departed. James Tyler relented and had seen them off, and even had promised to come and visit some day, to which John Law told him to be sure and do that, and he'd share a glass of his cool, freshly churned buttermilk. James Tyler, who preferred the taste of fine brandy and had probably never had a glass of buttermilk to his lips in his life, ignored the comment. The two men tolerated each other—and that just barely.

Will Tyler was blessed with a mixture of all the personalities that surrounded his life. He had his father's vision and desire to do something new. He inherited from Dora a restless spirit that would not let him be satisfied with things if they did not suit him. From his grandfathers he received a mixed bag of traits. From James Tyler he got a desire to learn and appreciate subtle pleasures of life. From John Law he got the biggest portion of his ways. He had a respect for law and justice. He learned from the Marshal to adapt to the rough side of life as easily as to the pleasures in life touted by Grandfather James. He learned the value of adventure and the necessity of a good, true partner and friend. Many of John Law's stories drove home the point of that. Will Tyler also took from John Law some innate ability to show proficiency with horses, frontier strategy, weapons, guns and survival. He was a crack shot with a rifle and deadly quick with a holstered sidearm—the two most important traits that allowed him to live his full life.

John Law had given Will his great grandfather's old musket when he was only eight. He talked an apprehensive Dora—only with the support of Franklin—into allowing him to trek off on a short hunting trip to the north of Nashville City. After being assured the boy would be back before dark, and with John Law's promise that all the Indians had long since departed that part of the country, she had relented and let William journey off. The challenge was important to the young boy. John Law and Franklin saw the importance in the adventure. James Tyler, however, agreed with Dora. "Damn foolish and dangerous nonsense," he had said. After they said and did all, however, Will had left for his one-day hunting expedition with his old musket, some water, some roasted chicken, and fresh cornbread lovingly packed by Dora.

"Why, when I was packed off for my first hunt, your grandfather sent me off with nothing but that musket and some advice: 'shoot you something to eat first, so you'll be fit for the rest of the adventure'," John Law had told Dora when they were discussing the matter. She still tried to ignore his advice, but reluctantly relented.

So, young Will Tyler set off for his one-day adventure.

He returned four days later after the worried family had dispatched half of Nashville City to find him. He found his way back, much to the joy of Dora, who was furious that Franklin and John Law had talked her into the 'damned foolish nonsense'. Franklin, too, was worried but John Law had some serene sense that the boy was all right—a foolish boy and damned insensitive to the point—but all right.

The boy, only thirty minutes into his trip, had taken a small, hand-hewn raft that someone had abandoned on a nearby river, in hopes of finding good game away from the settled area. He floated much farther than his inexperience could reckon, and found himself nearly fifteen miles downriver before he steered to the bank and trekked on the other side. None of the searchers could have imagined that a young, small boy could have gone so far. Then again, they did not know about the raft. Their search pattern was off to the east, settled side of the river—not one of them thought to look more than two miles down the river and certainly not across the river on the north shore.

The boy had not been off the raft and into the brush more than two hours when he saw the bear. It was a large, mother black bear with two cubs in a small clearing. When the bear saw him, she reared up on her legs and roared so ferociously that Will peed on himself. However, he had the reflexes and wits about him to immediately climb a big oak tree by which he was standing. He amazed himself with the speed and agility with which he scurried up the tree. He dropped the bag with his provisions and the old musket rifle on the way up. He had no time to think about it, however. The mother bear's razor-sharp, three-inch claws swiped his leather boots at the last second and gashed his ankle to his heel. From a branch twenty feet off the ground, he watched the bear prance, snort and growl as her two cubs sat peering out from under a bush. They scurried out, though, to devour the roasted chicken that flew from the ripped sack as the mother bear tossed it back and forth in her huge teeth. Inside the burlap bag, the sheep bladder full of water burst into the bear's face, making her angrier. She tore the small bag into pieces.

The bear attacked the musket on the ground so fiercely that it seemed she knew that guns had killed many of her fellow bears and creatures. Will watched intently from the branch. The bear tore the hickory-wood stock handle off and reduced it to splinters. She gnashed and tossed the fine metal barrel so furiously that teeth dented the metal and made a ten-degree bend in the barrel.

To Will's dismay, the mother bear stayed under that tree for three full days, waiting and watching for any opportunity to get to the boy. If it had not been for those seven robins' eggs he found in a nest, eight or ten grasshoppers, and the occasional rain shower that allowed him to drink from little puddles of water trapped on the leaves, the boy might have died. Nevertheless, on the fourth day, when the mother bear gave up the vigil and departed, Will climbed down the tree, walked back to the raft and made his way back to Nashville City.

Five pounds lighter, covered in dirt, limping from the gash in his right foot, and dragging the piece of musket barrel behind him, he strolled down toward the two-story house at the end of Washington Street. Awaiting him were a frantic mother and father, brothers and sisters, half the town's folks standing, cheering and scratching their heads, and one proud grandfather. John Law took the broken barrel later, had it put in a finely polished walnut wood case with a metal sign that read, *Kilt by a Tennessee Bar*. Even James Tyler appreciated the wit and irony in that trophy which John Law proudly displayed and told to anyone who would listen.

Now, five years later, in April 1861, settled and successful in their endeavor on the Tyler Plantation, all was well for the family. The three oldest Tyler boys had joined the fight that was brewing—Blue against Gray, North against South—and had left for Washington City just the week before. The matter of the abolitionists' cause was a deep conviction in the Tylers' hearts. John Law and Franklin had encouraged them to rally to save the Union from a mournful scar. Young William was extremely distressed that Dora had forbidden him to even discuss enlisting. It was bad enough that the three older boys had left with the encouragement of her husband and her father! Will would stay home where it was safe.

Josiah Cranford Holcomb was never a patient man. Patience was a virtue that he could not afford. The cotton business was not for the weak of heart. It was full of highs and lows, successes and disappointments, and situations that took a firm and often times ruthless hand. His thousand-acre plantation near Helena, Arkansas was successful because he looked to business and dispatched negative elements quickly and ardently. He was the third-generation Holcomb to own and operate the plantation. People feared, respected, and obeyed him, just like they did his father and grandfather before him. The two hundred slaves it took to run the farm were his pride. He could boast that in the fifty-eight year history of the farm, since its land-grant beginnings following the Louisiana Purchase, there had never been one successful runaway attempt by slaves. Several had tried. All had died in the attempt. Their deaths were of such exceptional cruelty that the word was out: any runaway was a dead man, and his whole family with him. Holcomb believed that the expense of a few extra slaves from the runaway's family, killed to make an example, would be a good investment. This policy proved him right. In the three attempts he had lost eleven slaves, including two children, by beating and execution. Eleven in fifty-eight years was an excellent record. There had not even been an attempt in more than twenty years. All of his actions of this kind were just conjecture between the other plantation owners and the general white population. Judicial authorities brought no legal investigations or charges. It was just so much rumor and speculation—except among the slaves. They knew firsthand.

Holcomb was the unchallenged King of Cotton in Eastern Arkansas. He knew what to do and he got it done. His way of life changed, however, in the summer of 1856 when a family from Eastern Tennessee—Yankees at that—bought the old Williamson Farm and turned it into a viable, competitive cotton plantation. Old Jacob Williamson had been at odds with the Holcombs since the beginning. He and Josiah Holcomb's grandfather, Elijah Holcomb, bought identical thousand-acre tracts, twenty-five miles apart on the banks of the Mississippi after the land acquisition. They had never been friends, and the hatred between the families was passed from generation to generation. The Williamson farm never enjoyed the success of the Holcomb operation, and was near bankruptcy several times in the decades that followed. Each Holcomb generation had tried to purchase the land from old Jacob several times but was met with contempt at every offer. However, Josiah Holcomb was determined to wait until the old man died and just buy it up at an auction for taxes. Williamson had no heirs and was habitually in arrears for taxes to the county. But then, suddenly, he sold the land to Franklin Tyler from Nashville.

"Tyler is a damned Yankee banker," Holcomb had said at every occasion where he mentioned Tyler's name. "He knows less about cotton farming than I do about kissing niggers," he most always would repeat with a smile. Holcomb's hatred for Tyler grew as the Tennessee family began to make a success of the farm. Tyler had received support and money from his father in Nashville, who had become a partner in the operation. So, the lack of resources that had once hindered Williamson was not a problem for Franklin Tyler. Another thorn in Holcomb's side was a crusty individual who lived on the Tyler Plantation. John Robert Singleton, Tyler's father-in-law, made it his business to irritate Holcomb at every turn. Singleton thought that Holcomb was a maniacal beast, and he let the old man know publicly that one day he would pay in full for the way he treated his slaves.

The Tyler Plantation had no slaves. Every man, woman and child, bought as slaves, was freed and drew a good wage for their work. Compared with other plantations throughout the South, the Tyler farm was unique. It was setting progressive precedents that many felt could be dangerous to the entire economic base in the Mississippi Delta.

"Your niggers are setting bad examples for all our niggers," Holcomb had spewed at Tyler at the monthly Cotton Cooperative Board meetings.

"I don't like that word. If you can't refer to these people as Negroes, then I will leave this meeting," Franklin Tyler would respond to Holcomb.

"That's exactly what I'm talking about, they get these goddamn ideas about freedom in their heads and they will be hard to control, because you do things like—call them Negroes and not *niggers*," Josiah would shout. He dared Tyler to head to the door.

"Get your Yankee ass back to Nashville before your stupidity ruins us all. There is enough of this talk going on all over the place, and we don't need it here in Arkansas. Mark my word...there will soon come a day when Yankees like you will destroy this Union and split us apart," he growled at Tyler. "You, sir, will not survive the trouble that you, and those like you, have bred."

Franklin Tyler never took his father-in-law to those meetings. John Singleton would have shot Holcomb on the spot. Tyler was convinced that his way was the right way. With good business and management practices, plantations could not only operate and survive, but flourish without slavery. That conviction was costly.

The struggle and clash of determination and tempers reached a pitched climax in a matter of weeks, on May 7, 1861. Franklin Tyler and Dora, and four of the seven children (William, age fifteen; Maggie, age thirteen; Martha, age eleven; and Zora, age nine) were sitting at the supper table in the dining room listening to a particularly good yarn being told by John Singleton. The thunder of horses and riders approaching the main house interrupted the story.

The entire family went to the front porch and saw two dozen soldiers in new gray uniforms with gold trim sitting astride their mounts on the front lawn. Josiah Holcomb, arrayed with Colonel insignias, spoke loudly, shaking with anger. "Tyler, I am here to inform you that the State of Arkansas formally seceded from the Union at eleven o'clock last night and has aligned herself with the Confederate States of America. As commander of the Phillips County Volunteers, I place you under arrest for treason." His voice cracked and his face was blood red. Five years of pent-up hatred and hostilities between himself and Franklin Tyler were hard for him to conceal under the restraint of military protocol.

"You have no authority here, Holcomb," shouted John Singleton. "This is private property, and we are violating no law—Confederate or Union."

"Now, now, Josiah, why don't you just leave?" Franklin asked in an attempt to cool tempers. "You're scaring the children. We can talk about this tomorrow at the courthouse."

Out of instinct, John Singleton reached for his Henry rifle leaning against a porch post. A young soldier reacted and fired at Singleton, striking him in the chest. He fell to the ground as the children screamed and Dora leaped to the ground to aid her father. The wound was not fatal, but blood soaked his white cotton shirt. Dora shrieked in anguish as she cradled him in her arms.

The entire company was in disarray. Holcomb, who was visibly shaken but energized by the sight of his nemesis on the ground, called for order. "We've been attacked by the enemy, by traitors to the cause. Arrest everyone here and hang the men," he cried out, the blood vessels bulging on his neck.

Four soldiers quickly dismounted and subdued Franklin, who was reaching for the fallen Henry rifle.

"But Colonel sir, there's only Mr. Tyler here and one boy," his young aide, Lieutenant Galard Haslowe said. "Shall we hang the boy, too?"

"How old are you, boy?" Holcomb shouted to Will.

A terrified Dora left John Singleton on the ground and rushed to embrace her son. "He's only twelve. He's only a child," she shrieked.

"I'm fifteen, sir," Will said in a strong, steady voice. "Hang me instead of my father, and let my mother and sisters go."

"My God, aren't you a brave little Yankee bastard. I think I'll just let you watch and see what happens to those who betray the cause," Holcomb said with a snarl. He turned to his men holding Franklin. "Hang that traitor," he said, pointing his shaking finger at Tyler. "And one of you go over to the worker's houses and get two niggers to hang in the boy's place—one man and one woman."

The soldiers tied three ropes to a big limb on a large oak tree in the front lawn. Franklin Tyler, Joseph Creed, and Bessie Rison, with their hands bound behind their backs, were set astride horses. Old Joseph, as everyone affectionately called him, had been on the plantation for over fifty years. Jacob Williamson himself had bought him in New Orleans and brought him upriver to Helena along with a dozen other slaves acquired at the market. Joseph was popular from the start, even-tempered and neighborly in most matters. He seemed to accept his lot in life and tried to make the best of it. He was the peacemaker in disputes among slaves and acted as a representative in most matters between the Master and the slaves.

When Franklin Tyler had bought the farm, he had given every slave his freedom, and none had left. At the prompting of Old Joseph, everyone had stayed with the farm to see how this grand experiment would turn out. For his loyalty, Franklin had rewarded Old Joseph by making him a foreman. He was well liked by the Tylers and, on occasion, was a guest at their table. Young Will Tyler and his sisters had spent a lot of time around Old Joseph and listened intently to his many stories and tales—especially the ones about his boyhood in Africa. Old Joseph never failed to entertain with his dramatic rambling about life in that mysterious land. Bessie Rison was his granddaughter. She had Old Joseph's pleasant disposition and always sported a wide smile. Maggie, Martha and Zora often spent hours in play with Bessie, and as much as culture allowed counted her as an equal and friend. She had gone out of her way to speak to, or to be spoken to by Mr. Will. She liked him. She loved him, and she acted as girlish around him as any other fifteen-year-old smitten with a young man. Will realized this and would blush every time Bessie would take an opportunity to speak to him—which was ever more frequently lately.

The soldiers led the three horses under the limb and placed the ropes around the necks of the condemned. The wide-eyed soldiers forcibly held back Dora and the girls as they struggled to get free and go to Franklin. The conscripts were in horror at what was about to happen. Nevertheless, no soul was brave or stupid enough to argue with Colonel Josiah Holcomb. Every soldier there knew that this was not war-related. It was common knowledge that Holcomb hated Tyler. This was a vendetta. Murder in the name of the Confederacy. Every man just did as he was told.

"Prop up that old son of a bitch Singleton. I want him to see this," Holcomb said. Two soldiers did as they were ordered and brought John Singleton to his feet, and held his head erect toward the tree.

"Now, you brave little Yankee bastard, come over here and give these horses a whip," Holcomb said to Will. "I want you to understand the cost of your daddy's actions as you send him to hell."

"Holcomb, you're a murdering bastard, you have no jurisdiction to do this. Where is the warrant? Where is the military court? Surely you don't think it's possible for *even you* to get away with this." Blood was pouring from John Law's mouth as he strained to speak.

"Your Yankee laws don't apply here. This is Arkansas, by God. The Tyler family should have stayed in Tennessee," shouted Holcomb with glaring eyes.

"Get over here, boy, and whip these horses, or I'll make your little sister do it," the Colonel said to young Will.

"No!" shouted Dora. "No!"

"Now, boy, or I swear I'll make the little bitch sister do it," Holcomb repeated with even more vengeance. "I'm sure you don't want to see that, or are you not as brave as I thought?"

Will stepped forward and took the whip from Holcomb's hand. He looked at it intently as he clutched it tightly in his fist. Holcomb always carried the short, black-leather riding whip. He used it frequently on his horse and slaves, just as it had been used by three generations of Holcombs. When they whipped a slave on the Holcomb Plantation—a frequent event—Josiah would finish the damage done by the foreman's bullwhip by inflicting the last lash with his prized riding whip—"to keep the leather soft and oiled," he would always say with a laugh. Will had always admired the look of the whip when he had often seen it in the old man's hand around town. The whip was a thing of fine workmanship, with gold inlay on the handle. It had now lost its beauty. For Will, it was a thing of ugly revulsion.

He looked up at his father. "It's all right, Will. Be a man and save your mother and sisters. Be brave. Always remember, I love you son," Franklin Tyler said. Tearfully, he turned his head and looked up at the star-filled sky.

Old Joseph squinted through watering eyes at the boy, whom he knew to be bewildered. "Mista Will, you remember the story I done tol' you about the little lion. That's you, sir," he said as he shook his head approvingly with the big grin that made everyone love him. "God bless you, son." Will had always liked that story of the lion cub that lost his father and grew up to be the protector of the lion pride.

Bessie looked away. She could not force herself to look at Will, even for the last time. Every ounce of her soul screamed for her to do so. Will looked at his grandfather. John Singleton wrenched one of his arms away from the soldiers and gave a crisp salute to Will. "Be a good soldier, boy," he said. It was the first time he had ever seen John Law cry.

"Now, goddamn you, now!" Holcomb shouted at the boy. Every soldier was standing at strict attention. No one moved. No one breathed. Not even Dora and the girls.

Will, with a blank stare coming from his dark, tearless eyes, pursed his lips, gritted his teeth as hard as he could, drew the whip back and hit his father's horse first, as if to end the suffering quickly. He then whipped the other two horses in rapid succession. The condemned died quickly. The silence filled the night, except for the creak of the ropes, taunt on the limb, and the cricket's serenade.

All eyes were on Will Tyler.

Lieutenant Haslowe turned to Sergeant Tompkins. "Herman, I'd sure like to salute that young fellow too, just like Mister Singleton."

"I surely would too, Galard. I can't hardly keep from it. But, you know the Colonel."

"I know," Haslowe said, fighting back the tears as he watched. "I know."

The terror of the event so occupied everyone that no one noticed Dora break loose from the hold of the soldiers. She ran toward Holcomb, screaming at the top of her voice. She stumbled as she ran, tearing her skirt from her body. The guards tried to help her up, but she broke loose again and attacked Holcomb. As she beat his leg with her fists, the Colonel's mount became frightened and reared up. To everyone's shocked amazement, with its front hooves suspended, the horse came down on Dora's head with a crushing blow. She fell dead just under the hanging body of her husband.

Will, stunned, took the whip in his hand and struck Holcomb repeatedly, as hard as he could. For the first time in his life, Will cursed aloud—vehemently and with his words sharp and understood. "Holcomb, you goddamn bastard! You goddamn bastard! I'll kill you!"

Holcomb drew his Dragoon pistol and brought it down across the boy's head, dropping him unconscious to the ground.

Surveying the carnage, Holcomb gave the order to ride. They were down the road in front of a thick dust cloud before Will struggled to his feet. He ran for the Henry rifle and pulled off ten shots at the distant dust cloud. John Singleton staggered to him, took the empty gun from his hands, and hugged him with all his strength. Young Will Tyler stared blankly past the tree, the bodies, his screaming sisters, the crowd of farm workers, the dust cloud, and the luminous sky. He stared past his own emotions. He had none. No tears came. No expression. No feeling. The boy clutched the whip tightly in his hand.

Part Two

Six Months Before the Capture of the Missionaries

Chapter 4

▼

August 23, 1875
The Mississippi River Delta, Eastern Arkansas

The Mississippi River cut through the black delta land, moving silt and mud along with its steady current. It was nearly a hundred degrees on this August afternoon, unusually hot for late summer. The sloping bank was on the Arkansas side of the river, but it could just as easily have been in Mississippi or Tennessee. No trees for shade, just short wilted grass in the long stretches of open fields. The sun was high and bright.

Will Tyler, wearing long johns, was bathing in the river. Bob Johnson rode up slowly from the west, pulled a pistol, pointed it at Will, and yelled with a surly and deliberate voice. "Tell me where your money and goods are, or I'm gonna rip you another asshole."

Two Snakes stood up from his resting spot behind a bush on the bank. He had noticed the rider coming and had thought little of it, but now instinctively began to reach for the leather pouch around his waist.

"Awright by God, I see you, you damned red savage. Drop your weapon or I'll plug you, too."

"No weapon; just my food," Two Snakes said.

Bob's horse slipped in the soft mud of the sharp slope, and with the bandit's gun firing in the air, the horse tumbled into the river. Will Tyler scurried out of the water and jumped to the bank as Bob stood up in waist-deep water, his arms flagging in the river.

"Get your ass back in here and help me find my damned gun," an embarrassed Bob said with a deep sense of irritation. "You too, Indian."

Will looked incredulously at Two Snakes as he pulled his pants on over his lanky, muddy body.

"Two Snakes, have you ever seen a sight like that?" Will asked, struggling with his boots.

"He sure is one bad desperado, ain't he? He's lucky he didn't shoot *himself* another asshole with that pistol." He looked at the bandit in the river. "What's the matter with you, fellow? Your manners are the worst I've seen in a long while," he yelled.

Bob reached wildly in the muddy water for his gun. "If I hadn't fallen off that horse I'd have plugged the both of you," he shouted back.

Two Snakes reached into his leather pouch, pulled out a three-foot Diamond Back rattlesnake, and shook it at the wet marauder. While Bob's attention was diverted, Will picked up a good half-pound rock and threw it at the tall, thin, Texas bandit. It found the mark right between the eyes with a loud crack. Bob reeled around, blood streaming down his face, and splashed head first into the river.

Bob Johnson lay face up on the ground. Suddenly, he stirred and sniffed the smell of coffee coming from the campfire. He tried to sit up but fell back with a loud thump. He grabbed the back of his head, squinted his eyes, and smelled the coffee aroma again.

Will Tyler blew into a tin cup; the hot steam rose into his face.

"It looks like the fish we caught is alive and flipping," he said loudly to Two Snakes.

Two Snakes sat and looked at the Texan and said nothing.

Bob peeked up at Will and squinted at the sun.

"What the hell happened? Where's my damn gun?"

Will waved the gun toward Bob. "Oh, this rusty old piece of iron. I'll just keep it until we get this little set-to figured out," he said.

"Old piece of iron!" Bob said indignantly. "I'll have you know that is the deadly Colt .45 caliber six-shooter. It ain't no rusty old piece of iron."

"You must be proud of it. We found another one just like it, all oiled up and still in a paper wrap in your saddlebags," Will said. "And those." He pointed to a collection of rifles and weapons leaning against a nearby tree. "A Winchester repeating rifle, a Sharps .44.70 breach loader, a Henry .44.100 long arm, a ten-gauge, short-barrel shotgun, that heavy, big-assed Dragoon cap and ball pistol, an eight-inch knife, that ancient Hawken, and enough ammunition to put a hole in every standing tree, signpost and outhouse between here and St. Louis—what the hell were you planning, boy, a war?"

"Well you forgot this one, by God," Bob said. He reached quickly into his soiled and wet denim jeans' back pocket. He found the pocket empty. Now, he was even more exasperated.

Will Tyler retrieved a Sharps' four-barrel *Pepperbox* pocket pistol from the ground. "You mean this pea-shooter?"

"Pea-shooter hell. I have you know, that is the favorite boot-weapon of none other than Frank James."

"Well, Frank still has his, I guess. But you don't."

Will surveyed all the guns again and shook his head in disbelief. "I don't see how your horse can carry all that and you too. You need a pack mule just for your weapons." Tyler looked closer at the Texan's horse. "She sure is one beautiful animal you have there. It's hard to keep your eyes off her. Too much prized horse-flesh for the likes of you. Where did you steal her?"

"Never you mind, by God," Bob replied with a snarl. "You keep your damned eyes off my *Molly*. She's damned sure my horse and I intend to keep her that way." He squinted through the sunlight and a blaring headache. "You sure know a lot about weapons. I guess you're plannin' on stealin' all my fine arsenal? Just keep your hands off that property."

Will, sprawled under an elm tree, pointed to his horse tied to a low branch. "Just you look at my *Sky*. He is more than enough horse for any man; more than I deserve for sure. I'll admit your Molly is one grand looking lady, but my Sky will be the one I keep."

Both horses were indeed grand animals. Sky was a magnificent Big Gray Stallion with a shimmering silver mane and tail. He was large and muscular with dark piercing eyes. Will Tyler dressed him impeccably. He sported a fine, black-leather, hand-tooled Mexican saddle with silver trim and inlay. In the evening half-light, as the big Gray stood against the glowing sunset, Will Tyler often thought that Sky was a vision out of some Norse legend that his mother often read to the children. *Odin's own Sleipnir*, he thought.

Bob Johnson's Molly was equally striking. She was a large blood-red mare with midnight-black forelock, mane and tail. There was not a spot of any other color upon her. She stood seventeen hands high and weighed three-quarters of a ton. She turned heads; everywhere, crowds would stop and notice her ballet-dancer entrance gallop. She sported a polished red leather saddle with an extra high cantle in the rear—*for comfort*—Bob Johnson would say. Two double, polished saddlebags lay over her muscular rump and twin-matching scabbards that held Bob's various rifle armaments completed the impressive array. If ever there was a horse that would be worth a hanging risk for stealing, it was Bob Johnson's Molly.

Bob Johnson was looking with pride at Molly and with an approving nod to Sky. "If'n the Almighty ever put me in a choice for a decision between my beautiful wife in Texas and my Molly, well, I'd have to give it some thought."

Will Tyler changed the subject. He pulled his pistol from its holster with his free hand. "Now, back to your weapons, I am good enough a marksman that I only need one side arm. This Model 3-Schofield pistol made by Mr. Horace Smith and Mr. Daniel B. Wesson is all I need," Will said, artfully releasing the frame latch with his thumb and swinging the barrel down on his knee to pop the six cartridges to the ground in one swift movement. "I can reload that on the run in less than ten seconds," he said, holding the pistol between his knees. He then retrieved six .44 caliber shells from his vest pocket and masterfully dropped them into the cylinder, swung the barrel closed, spun the pistol in his hand and pointed it toward Bob. "I'll admit that I do own one of these Colt pistols just like yours here," he said, waving Bob's gun in his other hand. "In fact, it's in my saddlebags next to my carbine."

Bob looked at the Schofield, and at his own Colt, now pointed at him. He decided this fellow might not be the fool he initially thought he was. Then suddenly, he remembered the Indian and that rattlesnake. "Where's that snake?"

"That snake is under the control of my partner here," Will said, pointing to Two Snakes. "I suspect that you'd better treat him with a little respect too, just like you do these two fine pistols."

Two Snakes tossed a stick at Bob and hissed loudly. Bob flailed on the ground, trying to escape, while Will and the Indian laughed aloud at the Texan.

"Don't you do that again, you damned Indian," Bob said with a scowl painfully displayed upon his bruised and swollen face.

Two Snakes made another sudden move with his hand and Bob jumped again, instinctively throwing a handful of dust in their direction. He glared back and forth between both of them.

"Who are you and what are you doing riding up here with that unfriendly attitude and disturbing my cool dip in the river?" Will continued.

"You're just a lucky skunk that you still ain't in that river face down with one of my bullets in your head," Bob growled back.

"You sure do talk a lot of noise for someone who has a knot the size of a peach on his head—and come within a stitch of drowning, to boot," Will said, peering over the pistol at the Texan. "Seems as though you're the lucky skunk. I ought to let the hot air out of you with this Colt that you're so proud of. If I hadn't pulled you out, those Mississippi gar would have had you for supper by now. I still ought to feed you to one of Two Snakes' friends." Will pulled back the hammer on the pistol, pointed straight at Bob's head.

"I suppose the right thing to do would be to haul him up to Fort Smith and let that new Federal Judge hang him. But being out of his jurisdiction here on the Mississippi might get him off, so maybe I'll just shoot him right here and get it over with," Will said to Two Snakes, leveling the pistol to a spot corresponding with the nose on Bob's face.

Tyler pulled the trigger. The loud snap from the empty cylinder got Bob's full attention, as he instinctively dodged to one side with his arm covering his face.

"Well, looks like a misfire. You'd think you could expect more from this fancy new gun. So, I guess I'll be sociable. Want some coffee?" Will reached for a spare cup. "It's probably a might stronger than these wet cartridges of yours." Bob stretched for the cup, knocked it away, and grabbed Will's arm, trying to throw him over. Will picked up the pistol with his free hand and cracked Bob across the head. Bob fell back, shook his head and grabbed the wound.

Two Snakes just looked on, almost as if disinterested.

"Damn you! I wish you'd stop whopping me on the head. Damn, that hurts," Bob snorted.

Will cracked him again on the head with the pistol.

"What the hell was that for? Damnation!" Bob yelled.

"That was for all that cussing," Will responded in a low, but steady voice. "I don't abide it particularly. Say one more unfriendly word and I'm really going to make it hurt this time."

The Texan fell back holding his head.

He mumbled. "Just my luck to try and rob a crazy son of a...." He stopped suddenly. Seeing the displeasure on Will's face, he mumbled the rest of the sentence under his breath. He looked at Two Snakes, whispered inaudibly, put his hand over his eyes and sighed as if content. He slept.

Will took another a sip of his coffee and looked at Bob. He was trying to figure this Texan out. He struggled with the whole matter of the attempted robbery. It just did not set with his impressions of the stranger.

Tyler was sipping coffee again as a bright moon replaced the retreating sun. Cool night air blew gently across the open fields. Grass swayed with a soft rustling noise. Prairie crickets serenaded the vast landscape with their evening song. Occasionally, a catfish slapped the water near the bank in search of a juicy bug.

As Two Snakes chewed on a piece of prairie hen that they had roasted, Bob slowly sat up, wrapping a blanket around him.

"Damn, I must have been out all day," he said, rubbing his aching head.

"Yep. Maybe you were tired from all that robbing and shooting. Or maybe those bumps on your head helped a bit," Will said.

"Awright, you sidewinder, I get your point," Bob said, peering at Will and then to the Indian. "I've already tried to tell you that I wasn't gonna rob nobody. I was just tired and bored and saw you two hay shovelers and decided to give you a thrillin' adventure that you could tell your plow-pushin' grandkids about. I don't need to rob nobody, hell, I got money—and plenty of it."

"Yeah, we also found about three hundred dollars in your poke," Will said.

"Well, that settles it. Now, give me my money, guns and horse and I'll just ride on out of here and forget all about that pistol-whippin' you gave me. Unless we meet again."

"Still the tough hombre, huh? Boy, who put that *Texas goat head* under your saddle?" Will asked.

"Look asshole, don't give me none of your guff. My damn head hurts," Bob responded.

"What did I tell you about that goddamn cussing?" Will asked, growing more agitated with the lanky intruder as he waved the pistol again at him.

"Hell, reverend, pardon me. I forgot," Bob said sarcastically. "Where I come from, airin' the lungs ain't no crime."

"Well, start remembering. I told you I don't abide that. You've had me to using the Almighty's name in vain here. My mother taught me that cussing is for extreme times. And you may be one of the most extreme individuals I have ever seen; but that don't matter. So, when I tell you to stop that damn cussing, I mean it. Before you get me started using them unnecessary, unfriendly words."

"I got one thing to say," Bob said indignantly. "You are, without a doubt, the most peculiar one person I ever saw. It don't pain you a bit to whack a fellow over the head, but it sends you into a fit to hear one *damn, shit or hell*."

"Those are my rules and if you're going to ride with us, you follow them."

"Ride with you! Why, you poor, tetched soul, I wouldn't ride with you if twenty-dollar double eagles was falling outta your ass. And I especially wouldn't ride with that damned Indian cuss," Bob said, making an exaggerated hand toss toward Two Snakes. "Now to mention that, why is he feasting on that range chicken and here I am damned near starving to death? Ain't you got no compassion for a white man?"

Will stood and faced Bob. He was a good half-foot taller and his voice a full octave lower than the Texan's. His wavy black hair was neatly combed back over his ears. He rubbed his short, trimmed beard and looked at Two Snakes. "I'd trust him a sight more than I would you," he said. "I'd sure share my grub with him first. He's part Cherokee and part Kiowa. He has tracked for the Army for years and stopped more desperadoes with those snakes than any three other men with repeating firearms. He's been my friend and ridden with me for two years now. Two Snakes saved my scalp more times that I care to remember; our friendship was solid from the first day we met while chasing the same deer near Fort Worth."

"Well, ain't that a homey story, I'm damned near to tears," Bob said with a sarcastic smile. "Why do you call that rascal 'two' snakes? I only seen one."

Quicker than Bob's eyes could focus, Two Snakes held two rattlers in his face.

"Goddamn, get them things away from me!" Bob screamed as he shuffled backwards.

Will continued with some delight in Bob's discomfort. "I've seen him throw those things quicker than a hawk's dive, and they'd wrap around some poor soul's neck and fill him full of poison before he could even think about his gun, much less draw it. One unfortunate Choctaw brave down near Vicksburg tried to rip them things off his neck and tore his jugular right out. The blood squirted everywhere. He just lay there in a puddle of blood, ankle deep."

Bob did not move. He stood and looked at Two Snakes. The Texan was hardly breathing. That image made an impression on him.

The Sisters of Loretto had educated Two Snakes in their small convent school on the Arkansas River, at Plum Bayou Landing, near Pine Bluff. He spoke perfect English, when it suited him, and sometimes quoted Shakespeare with some skill. He preferred to dress and smell, like a wild, desert Apache. The Indian always prayed to the Spirits that ruled the world—to the Sun, Moon, Water, and Fire. Without fail, he would remember the spirit of the Snake People, and then say a *Hail Mary* before bed at night. Since he had stumbled into their convent when he was fourteen, Two Snakes (or Andrew Peter as the sisters called him) had worked around the convent, helping the nuns in return for their care. A bad experience with his people had caused him to run away. He had made his way from the Indian Territory across the Ozarks, the Mississippi River, and finally down to East Arkansas to Arkansas Post. Traveling back up the Arkansas River, he met the nuns. He never talked much about the experience that had caused his exodus from the Territory—even to Will, who from his experience with Indians, knew that private thoughts were kept private. When they were revealed, it was for a reason.

Two Snakes had never been bitten. To his mind, it was because of his reverence for the ancient Snake People. An old Kiowa legend, told to him by his grandmother, said that the Snake People swam from the great water, crawled on the land, and protected the Kiowa from enemies. This was because Coyote called to the first Kiowa man to come and help the Snake Man who had come up from the water and could not breathe. The Kiowa man breathed air into the Snake Man and he came to life; the Kiowa man was not bitten from that day. All Kiowas could live in peace with snakes if they respected the snakes and did not harm them. They could, however, use the snakes for food if they were starving. Two Snakes not only used them as deadly accurate weapons, he also carried two of them in case he was starving; he could eat one until he captured a replacement.

The nuns made him keep the snakes outside in pens during his years at Plum Bayou. Nevertheless, he would sneak out often and sleep beside them on the ground, singing and chanting an old Kiowa song about the Snake People. He even showed his snakes to the bishop once when he was visiting the faithful at Pine Bluff. The bishop, being a transplant from New York, and a fine Irish gentleman, took no fond interest in the boy's pets. In fact, Two Snakes liked to report that the bishop had said, that, although he was fond of all God's creation, snakes could have just as easily been left out of the Almighty's plan.

"I'm going to bed," Will said, reaching for his bedroll. "I suggest you do the same, and if you ask real nice, Two Snakes might give you a wing or something off that bird carcass."

Two Snakes extended the rest of the hen to Bob, who took it without hesitation and began to chew it, bones and all. Bob peered at Two Snakes. "At least it's something. But you could have left me a little meat!" He pointed the gnawed bird leg at the Indian. "By the way, if you ever throw that damn snake at me, I'll shoot his head off and then I'll shoot your head off."

"If I throw a snake, you won't be shooting anything but your foot as you hit the ground dead," Two Snakes replied stoically.

"Damned, uncivilized, heathen rascal," Bob said, his eyes squinting at Two Snakes. "You'd better be careful one of them rattlers don't crawl out and up your britches and bite your privates some night, then you'd be in a mess of trouble."

Two Snakes took a small twig he used to stir the campfire and threw it at Bob. The Texan threw his coffee up in the air and tripped as he scrambled to his feet and rolled into the fire. "Damn you, I told you about that," he yelled.

Will rolled over in his blanket and looked at them both. "If you two don't shut up and let me get some sleep, them damned snakes is going be the least of your trouble."

"Loco Indian bastard," Bob said. He stood and dusted the hot coals off his britches and limped into the woods to take his nightly shit.

"Be careful, one of my snakes' brothers might be in that brush waiting to take a bite out of your privates," Two Snakes said softly and menacingly.

Bob turned, glared at Two Snakes, kicked swiftly but carefully at the bushes around him, and squatted, never taking his eyes off the Indian. "Crazy son of a bitch," he muttered softly under his breath.

Will was up first and was breaking camp when the other two joined in. He pointed Bob's pistol at the Texan as he prepared to mount. "You going to ride with us?" Will asked.

"I dunno. Y'all are a mighty strange pair if I do say so. I might be in some danger with you bastards," he replied.

"Suit yourself, then, walk," Will said. "I guess I will just finish the job you started. Except I'm going rob you of all you got. You can just sit here and catch one of them wild Arkansas pigs for breakfast, if they don't catch you first."

Bob looked at Will, then at Two Snakes, rubbed his head and began to pack his horse.

"Well, on second thought, maybe the quality of your company might improve after a few miles on the trail. Anyway, if I let you out of my sight I will never get to repay you for your hospitality; who knows, sometimes I might favor some cooked rattlesnake. It's mighty tasty, and I'll know where a meal is at all times," he said, knuckling his thick, red mustache at Two Snakes, who just grunted and mounted his horse.

"I guess that settles it." Will stretched out his right hand. "Just come on, and I'll be delighted to give you another whopping anytime. Just let me know when you're ready. By the way, I'm William T. Tyler. My friends call me Will. You can call me Mr. Tyler."

Bob took the handshake and the gun by crossing his hands. He grinned as he looked at the pistol.

"Why, thank you kindly, *Willy*. I'm Robert Buford Johnson. You can call me Mr. Johnson."

Will sported a wide grin, the first Bob had seen. "Okay, *Buford*, if you want your bullets for that firearm, they're in the river."

"You can call me *Aaron, a Moor*," Two Snakes said with a haughty air to Bob. "If ever one good deed I will have done, for you, I, in advance, do repent of it with my very soul."

"What the hell does all that mean?" Bob asked.

"It's just some of his Shakespeare that those old nuns taught him," Will replied.

Bob just shook his head. He could not reconcile in his mind the thought of an Indian talking like any other savage in one breath, and like an eastern professor in the next. To his mind, those Catholic Sisters had done the world a poor service. An educated Indian—what good was that? He turned his thought to the gun in his hand and looked at the river, pondered about the bullets in the water and decided that any conversation about Will holding him with an empty gun all night wasn't worth the effort. The three mounted their horses.

"I'll say, Shakespeare. I never had the pleasure of meetin' the gentleman myself and from the sound of him I'm glad I've been denied that particular adventure." Bob paused and looked at the two of them staring at him. "Well, Will, and *Aaron* whatever, this is gonna be one interesting enterprise. Where are we headin'?"

"Fort Smith, and then into Indian Territory," Will said.

"Fort Smith?" Bob questioned with emphatic disagreement. "Who in their right mind would want to go to Fort Smith, at least of their own free will? Hell, there ain't nothing there but a couple of whorehouses, some pigs and goats and such, and a whole hell of a lot of Indians. It's just one big mud puddle."

"Two Snakes and I are going to sign on as Deputy U.S. Marshals under Judge Isaac Parker," Will said to Bob. "I hear that he is determined to clean up the Indian Territory of all that riffraff that blows up from Texas, and he's going to hire individuals of exceptional aptitude for assistance. That qualifies me and Two Snakes." He paused, waiting on some smart remark from Bob, but the Texan just looked on without saying anything. "My family raised me in lawman ways," continued Will. "I guess I've decided that I've roamed enough and would like to be in on the adventure of capturing a few outlaws and renegades. Two Snakes is the best tracker and companion I could want. So, we are off on a grand adventure."

"I'm from lawman stock myself," Bob said defensively. "In fact, I probably know more than both you skunks put together about chasin' outlaws and killers, and I'll tell you for sure it ain't no grand adventure. In fact, it's dirty, nasty work and I had my fill of it. Hot, scorchin' days, freezin' nights out in the open; meals not fit for a mangy dog, and if you're lucky you might scrounge up enough of your measly pay to save a twenty-dollar gold piece once a year. Yes, sir, that's one grand adventure awright."

"I'm determined to try it before it's all gone. Before I'm sitting on some porch drinking buttermilk and telling a passel of kids to shut up so I can sleep," Will said with a nostalgic tone. His outburst reminded him of home and a life that was, in his memory, unsatisfying and unrewarding now; it just might be what he wanted some day, just like his father and mother had wanted, and loved until they lost the struggle. "I just want to feel the frontier and that jolt of danger every once in a while, before all the Indians are quoting Shakespeare and the screams of the train whistles on the prairie replace the screams of the eagle. Hell, it's 1875!" Will looked off at the distant fields and the sun rising on the river. "I just want to be a part of it, like my grandfather and my great-grandfather were," he said. His thought and gaze were interrupted by a noisy paddle steamer belching its way down the river.

Will Tyler's words touched Bob. In fact, he was silent for the first time since they had met. He found a lot of truth in what the man had said. In fact, in some sense it was exactly the way he felt. It was just that those matters that mixed emotions with experiences, were awakened at odds with each other. Still there was something to be said about the grand adventure that he wanted. Two Snakes, too, felt that they were fine words—full of meaning and truth. The three men sat on their mounts and looked at the sunrise for a long time, pondering what they had just heard, each in his own way with his own memories and dreams, intruded upon slightly by the sound and billowing smoke from the streamer's stacks.

"Sounds like an adventure to me, I guess. Now, whether it will be grand or not, you'll have to show me," Bob said. The steamboat's loud whistle brought him back from the trance. "I'm in with you, amigo."

"The last fellow who called me an *amigo* all the time, was eaten by a bear on the Missouri. So, you better choose your words sparing like," Will said, strangely pleased that Bob had agreed to ride with them. There was something about the Texan that he had liked from the first time he threw that rock at him in the river.

"Hell, I'd a wound up eatin' the bear for lunch," Bob said; now back to his usual self. "So, I'll just keep repeatin' *amigo* in hopes one comes along. Then I'll shoot him, let Two Snakes cook him and we'll have a dandy feast. I'm hungry, amigo. That chicken leg was not very fillin' last night."

"Just remember one thing, no cussing," Will said.

"I promise, Willy," Bob replied with a grin. "Not one goddamn cuss word out of me."

Will looked at Bob and shook his head. Bob grinned and tipped his hat to Will and Two Snakes. Will Tyler shook his head again and gazed at the vast flat lands. "I'm gonna regret this." He paused and took a deep breath. "Let's ride."

The three galloped off with Bob remarking about when they stopped for camp, he'd like to discuss his plan with them about finding that old Spaniard's treasure. That was the main reasoning his mind had used to sooth his restlessness to up and leave Texas for a while.

"Treasure?" Will asked. "What treasure?"

"Spaniard?" Two Snakes asked. "What Spaniard?"

"You know, that old explorer De Soto," Bob said. "He buried a bucket load of it somewhere between Fort Smith and the Missouri border."

"That's a whole lot of somewhere," Will said.

"Huh," muttered Two Snakes.

Bob kept talking. They kept riding. Two Snakes kept one hand on his leather pouch.

Chapter 5

▼

**Dusk, August 30, 1875
Campsite, two days from Fort Smith, Arkansas**

The three riders covered more than two hundred miles that first week, traveling steadily west and north. Will Tyler was glad to put the distance between him and Helena. He had made the trek with Two Snakes, up from Louisiana. He still did not know if he ever intended to go by the old plantation. Most likely not. He did not have the courage to revisit the memories. In all the years of absence, a dozen trips had been started in that direction. None was ever completed. This time was the closest. *A damned close escape*, he thought as they rode.

The trip had been six days of riding, sweating, and enduring sparse meals of rabbit, squirrel, and an occasional range chicken. Although they had money, and could have ridden by any number of settlements and towns for food, the three somehow never considered the alternative. Two Snakes and Will Tyler had also endured a nightly litany of stories and legends that Bob Johnson rolled out about lost gold and silver and treasure that his granddaddy or one individual or another had told him over the years. Those stories had convinced him that early Spanish explorers had left vast fortunes buried, and was certain that they could at least find some of it with a little effort.

As evening fell at the end of their seventh day together, they made camp in a pecan grove near a small lake. It had been a humid day and breathing was difficult after the temperature had reached more than one hundred degrees. The horses were exhausted even after being watered and allowed to graze freely for several hours; and the men, too, felt the rigors of the long hot day. Two Snakes' meal was the only redeeming event. It was the best Bob Johnson had experienced in a long spell and he kept repeating its praises to his two companions. He was partial to fish. The Indian had caught two dozen hand-sized sun perch in a small net he always kept in his saddlebags for such occasions when coming upon lakes or ponds. He thanked the Fish Spirit for the gift, cleaned them expertly and then roasted them over the fire. The three of them quickly devoured the whole catch. Plenty of coffee and an amazing treat of a can of peaches that Will had been hoarding for two months made the meal even better. They finished off the feast with roasted pecans that had been put on the open coals. This made for an evening of attitudes that were becoming progressively friendlier. Will Tyler had noticed that even Bob's temperament and cussing cooled to a tolerable level, though his constant talking and cocksure attitude on most any subject had not subsided—if anything it had steadily increased as they began to know each other better. As the hour approached nine o'clock, the men were full and contented. Two Snakes, quietly and thoroughly, gathered up all the fish bones, took them to the lake's edge, knelt and placed the bones, a handful at a time, into the water while chanting a song to the Fish Spirit, assuring favorable fishing on another occasion.

"Fine meal, Two Snakes," Bob said, stretching his arms over his head and yawning widely, as Two Snakes approached the campfire and sat. Bob thought better of saying anything about the strange ritual he'd just witnessed with Two Snakes and the fish bones. Nevertheless, he continued the conversation. "I still don't see how you knew exactly where that school of fish was laid up in that little cove. You went right to them without missing a step."

"I heard them talking to the Fish Spirit," Two Snakes said. "They were saying what a fine meal they would make for their hungry Kiowa brother, and then they said to me, 'come and enjoy us for a good supper.'"

"Well, I doubt they was intent on committin' suicide as you say, but that brings to mind another thought I have," Bob said. "You Indians are all alike; every one of you I've come across, Comanche, Kiowa, Apache, even the Sioux and all them Plains Indians—you're all always talkin' to animals and such. This spirit said this, and this spirit said that. Dogs, alligators, chickens, goats—anything. Why can't a white man like me, who sure has more intelligence than all you Indians, talk to them animal spirits? Why, if I could, I'd say, 'Hey antelope spirit, tell me where the hell is the nearest fat doe that I might shoot with this Spencer rifle and have a juicy meat-steak off of tonight,' or something like that. Explain that to me."

"Because you don't listen," Two Snakes replied. "You must listen with your heart and with your ear. White men don't do that."

"Just be that one way or the other, all I know is that the ear is for hearin', and my main job with my heart is to keep some red scoundrel from puttin' an arrow in it. But speakin' of hearin' and such, I don't doubt your ability to hear things," Bob said with assurance. "I've noticed all week how you had your ear turned to everything and could hear something before I could hear it, see it or smell it."

"His hearing is the best I've seen on any man," Will interjected. "Many a time, I swear, we'd have gone to bed without a meal if his hearing didn't find us supper."

"I knew a fellow like that down on the Brazos, south of Austin," Bob said. "He scouted out those renegade Comanches, under Red Eagle, who kept raidin' and murderin' between Austin and Mexico during the war. He rode with Captain Holder and his Ranger troop for a long time after I knew him. I swear he could hear a mouse piss on a cotton boll at a hundred yards."

"What happened to him?" Two Snakes asked, who thought this was the most interesting thing the Texan had said all week. Natural senses always fascinated the Indian. Sight into the horizon; tastes that awakened new pleasures in eating; the feel of the earth to the body as you lay against her in the dawn; the sound of creation communing with itself—it was part of his spiritual past, before the Catholic Nuns had tried to convert him. He remembered the stories that the village elders told about gifts of exceptional senses that the spirits gave to men. No matter how much the Sisters of Loretto had taught him, some things he learned from the *Old People* still made sense, even more so than other explanations he had found in the Catholic catechism.

"A war party captured him, as he was scoutin' ahead for the troop," Bob said in answer to Two Snakes' question. "It seems that his fame had spread to all the tribes in that area and this was a great catch for them. An old Kiowa woman showed up in Austin with him later and told the story that those Comanche were afraid of him because of his close ties with some sort of spirit ghosts so they didn't dare kill him. But they felt confident that puttin' scorpions into his ears would not incur any spirit's wrath. So, that is what they did. After puttin' the scorpions in his ears, they held his head under water so the scorpions would put up a death struggle and sting with their last vengeance. They let him go after a few days of that torture, when he had recovered from the poison. Then he wandered into that band of Kiowas somewhere west into the plains. The last I heard he still lives in a little shack on the river, and just sits all day and stares at the water with cool mud stuck in his ears. That old woman stays there and takes care of him and changes the mud when it dries."

Two Snakes nodded. The Comanche could get rid of an enemy that the spirits had blessed without making the spirits angry. Their wrath would be on the scorpions.

Will had been listening intently also. Those Comanches were a nasty lot, and it sounded just like something that they might do. "There are Comanches and Kiowas in the Indian Territory where we are heading, and plenty of other desperados west of Fort Smith. Texas don't have the corner on torture and lawless types."

"I never said it did, Will," Bob responded. "Things just seem to event themselves on a grander account south of the Red River."

"What I don't understand is why you ain't bellyaching to head toward Texas. For a Texan, you don't seem very home-sickly," Will said. He knew would get Bob started—it had been the pattern at the evening meal all week. "Besides that, you fit in up here just like the rest of these dirt farmers and hillknobbers. Just like you were born and raised in the cotton fields, or them Ozark hills. Where's your spunk to fill our ears with the joys and golden memories of that fine land? I ain't never met a Texan that wouldn't."

"Well," Bob said, pondering a moment like he was about to say something very profound. "It's not that I ain't proud of my status as a brought-up Texan. Why, that is one of the Almighty's favored gifts to man. No, I just wanted to see what else is out here. I left my wife in the bosom of my mother and just struck out to clear my mind a bit. I have to admit my forays through Arkansas has been more disappointin' than I anticipated." He didn't miss a beat. "It's like God took a short spell and let some lesser angel do the creating north of the Red River. To my mind, that angel was a slacker. Pitiful work he did here, and I 'spect that they tossed him out of Heaven on his ear when the Boss saw the mess he made." Bob paused with the same air of deep pondering, as he looked away from a squint-eyed Will Tyler, who was now sorry he had even started the conversation. "You're a religious man, Two Snakes," he started again, looking at the Indian. "And as such, you ought to agree with my assessment of the Creator's handiwork, especially with regards to Texas as laid up against *this* poor excuse for a country."

Two Snakes stared at Bob, as he usually did, with a blank look of disinterest. He was beginning to like Bob, sure enough, but his general assessment of the Texan was that he was hard to listen to on any subject. More than once in the past week, the temptation to reach in his pouch and throw his friends on the constant babbler was difficult to resist. He had begun to think of the necessity for a third snake, defanged but mean, just to scare the hell out of the Texan, as needed.

Seeing he was not going to get any conversation out of the Indian, Bob turned his attention back to Will Tyler. "Anyway, as I was saying, I'll never find any place that will match Texas, but I'm determined to keep lookin', just in case. Besides, it takes a mighty strong and dedicated individual to be a Texan. It's rough down there. Life is cheap, and livin' is costly. It takes a lot out of a man just to make it from sun up to sun down. Not like here in Arkansas, where all you do is eat, and then shit yourself a bucketful, then get up with the chickens, with your whisky jar, and lop-eared hound dog there on the front porch where you been sleepin' and ponderin' deep subjects such as, what a fine shit that was. Then you go and pick up your wife and daughters that morning as they was gettin' off from their all-night jobs down at the whorehouse."

Will finally spoke. "The only whores in Arkansas I know of are ones that washed up from Texas."

Two Snakes could stand no more. He got up quickly and decided that he would rather listen to the crickets and the spiders crawl along the ground as he squatted in the bushes, than to listen to that damned Texan ramble. Besides, it made sleep difficult as his mind reeled with the ignorant and useless words the man spouted off each night around the campfire. To his mind, the Texan knew more about nothing than any other man he ever met.

Will sat staring even more blankly at his worrisome and talkative companion. He should know by now not to get him started so close to bedtime. Two Snakes had often threatened to put a snake in each of their bedrolls if it ever happened again. Even Will, after a talkative sprint by Bob, thought about checking his roll every now and then before sticking his feet in—a task that Bob not only did every night, but sometimes two or three times, all the while looking at Two Snakes and cursing under his breath.

"Yeah, it's rough down there," Bob reemphasized. "Take them Texas Rangers for instance. Why, you get caught with a stolen horse, you'll be swingin' before that horse can do his next droppin'. No mercy. No questions. Just you, a tree, a crow or two, the dust from their departing mounts, and a fresh horse turd, still smokin'."

"So, what were you doing on a stolen horse?" Will baited with a tone of sarcasm.

"I wasn't on no damn stolen horse," Bob said, irritated by the inference. "I was just talking as a *what-if.*"

"That wasn't a what-if back there on the Mississippi. You were fixing to rob us if your horse hadn't slipped. I guess we'd just caught you and hung you from some Arkansas oak tree for that banditry," Will said.

"I told you already a dozen times I was just bored that day, and saw what I thought was a dirt-clod hillbilly in the river, and intended to show you a real Texan. I wasn't intendin' to take your horse or nothin'. It was more like an enjoyable way to smooth over my anxious feeling of ridin' and ponderin' why I was up here so far from home and such. And even if I did take a couple of dollars, it woulda been fun to let some dumb Arkansas bumpkin buy me some bacon and biscuits for breakfast in the next little town. I'd have left the change there with the fellow and told him to give it to you when you came after me," Bob said with a sincere grin. "Hell, if you'd acted half way sociable, I'd a given you money for breakfast, just for the conversation. I was just seeing what you fellows was made of, in case I decided to let you ride with me after that breakfast," he continued. "Can I help it if you and that damned snake charmer can't take a little joke? You sound just like my little wife back in Texas, acts like she never heard of a joke."

"I don't recall that you felt that those knots that I put on your head were much of a joke," Will said. "In fact, I thought that they would made you see a bit clearer. But I guess it'll take a lot more than a couple of whacks on the head to get you thinking and your talking more in line with the rest of us."

"Now, Will, why in hell would I want to think—or talk—like you and that damned Indian? It's plain to anyone that what I say has a lot more value. Why, you don't say hardly anything at all. You been sittin' here moody and starin' off all the time. You're a gloomy fellow to be around. Not to mention that heathen is always talkin' in circles about spirits and dreams and some such that some dead John Bull Englishman wrote before you, or me, or any of us was here. Now, I ask you, don't the voice of experience that I have particularly, especially from my vast adventures as a Ranger in Texas, make a lot more sense than anything else you've heard around these campfires for a week?" Bob asked, looking at Will for affirmation.

"Now here's another, *what if*," Bob continued. "Suppose them Rangers catch you with some scalps hangin' across your saddle. They'd sure better be some red Indian's or Mexican's hair and not some white man's, excepting that he was from Arkansas, of course," Bob said with a slight grin. "That's a sure way to shit your pants while swingin' in the noon-day breeze. Yeah, life's cut and dry in Texas."

"I've notice that you Texans are sure preoccupied with bodily functions and such. That's about the third or fourth reference you'd made to that subject in the last hour," Will interjected quickly, before Bob could state another 'what-if'. "But I guess us ignorant people north of the Red River just ain't caught on to the importance of that particular subject. What we tend to do is deposit them and walk off, never giving them another thought. I guess you Texans have found a value in such that we just haven't seen yet. Yep, we sure have got a lot to learn from y'all."

Bob Johnson, not as slow and dull-witted as his speech presented him to be, immediately caught the sarcasm in Will's remarks. It made him smile, though.

Damn that Will Tyler, he thought, *just once I'd like to get the last word on any subject with him.* Will was good when it came to fast-witted conversation, Bob was thinking as he enjoyed a rare cool breeze that blew across the lake and invited him to a good night's sleep. Leaning against his saddle, he pulled his hat over his eyes, and thought more about it. Will was quick with his mind and remarks, no doubt, but Bob was determined to keep trying until he prevailed with his own wit over Will.

"Two Snakes, hurry up and get back in here and let's talk about that load of silver up near the Missouri border that I was tellin' you and Will about this afternoon," Bob shouted at the general direction that the Indian had gone into the brush.

All this left Two Snakes with a desire to stay longer in the brush, depositing on the crickets and spiders. With Bob around, he began to spend more time burying insects than he did listening.

Bob nodded and fell asleep, waiting on the Indian. He dreamed, as usual, about his hard and violent life in Texas. Tonight, screams of Indian horses and pounding hoofs revisited him, and blood puddles replaced cracked, parched dirt.

Dreams vivid; dreams violent; dreams unwelcome, invaded the men's sleep that night.

Bob's dreams caught him up in the vision of one of his last assignments. The assignment that had finally set his mind and spirit north, away from Texas, to find life elsewhere. The massacre at Palo Duro Canyon was haunting him. He was there, a year ago, in September 1874 when his unit under the command of Colonel J.A. Mackenzie participated in the defeat of Quanah Parker and the last great Comanche tribe. The troop herded two thousand Comanche horses into the canyon after they had captured them from Quanah Parker. Soldiers, Texas Rangers and volunteers lined the canyon rim and fired randomly with their rifles, killing the corralled horses. Bob's Henry rifle was so hot he had to pour water on the barrel to make it cool enough to handle. The scene revolted him. He vomited until his sides ached. All the troops stood in horror as they looked down at the carnage. Bob decided then to take leave for a while, to some place where life and living were not so cheap, where a good story and a pleasant outlook were of more value than turning the earth into one big graveyard, where he could recapture the joy of life with a loving and beautiful wife and, someday, some children.

Bob had married Rebecca Fontaine when he was twenty and she was eighteen. They had known each other in Austin since they were small children, and if he would admit anything that resembled a true emotional feeling, he loved her very much. He just did not know how to show it sometimes. It was lucky for him that Rebecca understood this and had a great deal of patience with him and his ways. The same restless spirit that sometimes controlled his father, and especially his grandfather, Captain LeBeaux, also plagued him. Elizabeth taught Rebecca a great deal about the trials and the extreme joys of being life-partners with Johnson men. It was worth the work and the heartache. They were good men, easy to love, just hard to live with when that mysterious restless invader possessed them. Rebecca and Elizabeth were a comfort to each other during those long absences of the Rangers.

When Bob left Texas for Arkansas to satisfy an unsettled urge to find something, under the guise of chasing Gaston LeBeaux's treasure stories, Rebecca remained with Elizabeth and Tobias. She was not just a daughter-in-law; she was more like a daughter. And a saint, too, Elizabeth would often say, for her loving patience with Bob. Just as she had for Tobias, who understood his son's decision. Rebecca, even though grieved at his departure, also understood the Texan's restlessness and the need to stretch his legs a bit, as Bob had said. That event on the canyon rim and all the dying and killing in general had caused even Tobias to rethink his life's work and its worth. He entertained the thought to go with his son, but quickly abandoned it as he saw Elizabeth's familiar I'm reading your mind look. It was a powerful tool, and she was teaching it to Rebecca. But for Bob's sake, both women knew that he had to make this one journey. As Bob had left the next day for anyplace out of Texas, Tobias felt a deep depression. He did not grieve necessarily for his son's leaving, but for the realization that he had led his son to a life and destiny that had somehow caused this profound unhappiness. The firm handshake of his father, the warm hug of his mother, and Rebecca's tender kiss were fond memories and keepsakes, but not enough to keep him from leaving. He felt destiny's tug; he just didn't know to where. Bob rode north out of Buffalo Gap, Texas and did not look back.

Bob slept on. His dreams blazed with screams, and flared nostrils. His sleep was alive with stallions, mares, and colts falling to their death. The smell, the dust, the colors were vivid.

Two Snakes lay prostrate on the ground with his ear pressed to the dirt listening to the earth breathe, unaware of Bob's fitful dream. Will Tyler rolled over on his blanket and faced away from Bob. *That fellow sure does like to talk*, he thought. Bob Johnson decidedly reminded Will of old John Law in the talking department. The thought of old John Law, the only name by which he had ever referred to his grandfather, John Singleton, brought a smile to his face, and a warm, nostalgic feeling to his tired and sleepy body. *John Law.*

Will awoke and stood up to stoke the campfire. It was a very warm night, but the fire helped him somehow. It was a comfort he could not explain. He liked the light, the smell, and the leaping flames. He looked at Two Snakes, motionless on the ground, and at his new friend Bob Johnson, tossing and turning. Perhaps he was dreaming, too.

Will did not like tobacco particularly, but the nostalgic feeling of his dreams made him yearn for the long-forgotten smell of John Law's cigar. He got up and retrieved an old cigar, several times water-soaked over the journey, and lit it as he sat back down. He thought about his family more as the blue smoke curled in the moonlight.

The first indictment that assailed him was that it had been fourteen years since he had left home to escape the horrific May night on the front lawn of his home in 1861. His reasoning had been to right wrongs dealt him at the hands of the Confederate killers, then to travel and find adventure. However, the surrealistic nightmares about his father and mother, and Josiah Holcomb, haunted Will. Time had spanned a distance between that event and now, but the cacophony of thundering hooves, little girls' screams, and cracking horse whips never left his senses or memory. Will was strong, but he felt a profound sadness at any remembrance of John Law, and at the thoughts of Maggie, Martha and little Zora. Time had tempered the overbearing hatred for Josiah Holcomb somewhat, but a strong nostalgic moment about his family would rekindle those boyhood dreams of killing Holcomb.

After the murder of Franklin and Dora, Holcomb had seized the plantation and the Tyler family had fled. John Law had taken the children to James Tyler in Nashville, where he accepted a Brigadier's commission with the Union Army of Tennessee. He had a successful and distinguished career, participating in several important battles, including the capture of Vicksburg. He became friends and able assistant to General U.S. Grant, a relationship that would surface again in Will's future.

When John Law left for the war assignments, news soon followed that Confederate raiders had killed the three older sons of Franklin and Dora Tyler early in the war. James Tyler decided to take the remaining children and return to Boston. It was a wise move, John Law had thought. It would be much safer for the children, and they could reunite after the war. The loss of Steven, John and Robert was almost more than James Tyler could take. "This damned South," he would often say. "I'll never stain my feet with its wretched soil again."

Will, then sixteen, went along, but refused to stay in the comforts of Boston. In July 1861, he packed his horse with a few supplies, a Henry rifle that John Law had given him, and rode out to join the Union forces of the Nineteenth Massachusetts Regulars to fight the Confederacy. It was his attempt to take his vengeance against Holcomb; but sadly, it would add further chapters of darkness and death to his young life.

Will Tyler never saw his family again, although through some infrequent letters and an occasional telegram he had kept in touch. The horrors of war had so sated him with an uncontrollable sense of gloom that he could find no comfort in anything—even his family. He had become an uncle three times, twice by Maggie and once by Martha. Zora was the social darling of Boston. Her beauty was stunning, and a mirror image of Dora's.

After the war, James Tyler had reclaimed the Tyler Plantation and had been awarded the Holcomb Plantation in reparation. Colonel Holcomb had fled the state after John Law had begun efforts to have him tried for war crimes. The new Tyler Farm was the most successful in the state. Grandfather James Tyler had hired capable managers and with his annual visits and frequent telegraph communications, had continued to operate the enterprise from Boston.

Will Tyler was in reality a wealthy man. The trust had deposited his inheritance in St. Louis, where he could draft funds as needed during his travels. He very seldom did so, preferring to live off his own abilities. His most painful regret was his fourteen-year absence from John Law. He missed the old man and had thought about him a lot lately. Will had not heard from him, or about him, in years. The last he heard, his grandfather had returned to Nashville and had become the U.S. Marshal again. John Law also had declined several administrative appointments from President Grant. He preferred the action of a lawman, although he was in his late sixties by now. He had understood Will's need to ride off to war at the age of sixteen, although hearing the news was hard to take. He was proud but realistic about the dangers the young man would face. The old man knew, though, from first-hand experience, the powerful urging that sometimes moves a young man to just get up and go. He also understood the hatred that drove young Will. That same urging had pushed him as a young man along the same path, and deep down he still could feel the gnawing of fires yet burning in his soul. That same hatred now drove him against the Confederacy, Holcomb's Confederacy. Now, years later, the family could not understand why Will Tyler had abandoned them, save the few brief letters. That, more than anything, haunted him. More so than Holcomb, and the horrors of the war that followed.

Will went to his saddlebags and dug out a tattered letter that he had wrapped in a leather cover. He had kept that one letter. It was the letter from John Law that Will had received in the Army hospital in Washington City. He returned to the fire and began to read.

John Law had lamented the heavy burdens and misfortunes that had been Will's lot. He agonized over the demons the boy must be facing. He imagined he knew the demon to be, in part, *the horsewhip* in Helena. He knew, too, unknown by the sisters or anyone else, of another demon. He confided that he had been notified that Will was one of the soldiers released from Andersonville Confederate Prison, and that he was going to let Will have time to work out his tortured life.

Will Tyler had the closing remarks of that letter burned into his memory. He leaned back and recited them from his heart.

Son, I know that one can never fully understand the horrors of that God-forsaken prison in Georgia. So wretched was that place, I will not even mention it by name. May its memory be cursed in God's eternity! Even more of God's damnation is on that night in Helena. This, on your young shoulders, was the single most worthy demonstration of courage I have ever witnessed. I can only imagine the hell you have seen, and I know that you need the time and distance to heal. As did I. I cannot bear, however, the possibility that we might never see you again. God grant it not to be so. Your sisters pray for you every day. I think of you with all fondness in hopes of a reunion someday. Your grandfather, John Law.

Chapter 6

▼

2:00 a.m., August 31, 1875
Campsite, two days from Fort Smith, Arkansas

Will Tyler, finally asleep again, was deep in memory, in happy places and in sad, of John Law and his sisters, when he felt the searing pain violently stab through his body. The bullet caught him in the fleshy part of his left upper arm. The impact, however, was powerful enough to spin his body completely over.

The second shot that exploded in the night came from Bob's pistol. The first blast had awakened him; in an instant, he sprang to his knees, pulled his Colt, and fired at the shadow in the brush. The bullet tore through the shadowy figure's right shoulder, causing the shooter to drop his pistol and scream violently. Two Snakes quickly had one of the snakes in his hand, turning in a circle looking for another marauder.

"Goddamn! The bastards have shot me," the wounded man cried.

"What did you expect, you son of a bitch?" Bob shouted. "Two Snakes, check on Will," he said quickly as he kept the cocked pistol on the man who had now fallen to his knees, screaming.

Bob glanced toward Will. "Are you hit bad?" he asked.

"No, it's just through the flesh," Will said.

"If he had shot three inches lower, it would have pierced his heart," relayed Two Snakes, who was binding the wound with a strip of the bloody shirt.

The wounded bandit continued to scream.

"Shut up, damn you or I will put a matchin' one in the other shoulder," Bob growled. He suddenly became aware of a rustling noise coming from the brush to his left. "Awright, you son of a bitch. I'm going to give you just one chance to come out in the open. Now! Damn you. If you don't, I'll light up these woods with a fire so bright they will see it in Fort Smith."

A voice came from the dark. "Don't you shoot! I ain't armed."

"By God you won't even be breathin' if you don't come out, and come out right now," Bob said.

"Get down, Bob, you damned fool. You don't know how many are out there," Will shouted, pulling his pistol.

"At least I'm going to take this one with me that's rattling that bush. Come out, and I mean now. If you don't, I'm going to fire, and this time I'll aim for the heart," Bob shouted at the noise in the dark.

"Awright, I'm coming. Don't shoot. I ain't armed," the voice from the brush shouted again.

"Kill that son of a bitch, Elton," yelled the wounded bandit. "Hell, he can't see you. Kill them all. The bastard shot me!"

Will pulled the trigger without aiming and drove a .44 bullet from his Schofield into the man's other shoulder. He fell to the ground, face first.

"Thanks. I told him what would happen if he didn't shut up," Bob said.

"Awright, goddamnit, here I am. Don't shoot me," the second man said. Immediately, he threw his pistol on the ground near Bob. "I guess you done kilt my brother," he said as he walked into the clearing with his hands in the air.

"No, but he'll be needin' some help to take a piss for a while," Bob said. He then approached Elton and swung his pistol down hard on the man's head, behind his ear. Elton fell to the ground with a loud thud.

"Why did you do that?" Will asked, surprised. Two Snakes looked on, caught off guard by Bob's quick move.

"The son of a bitch lied to me," Bob replied in a slow voice. "He said he wasn't armed. I can't abide liars."

Two Snakes finished wrapping Will's arm and stoked the smoldering campfire. He then tended the wounded man's shoulders and Elton's bloody head, and dragged both of them to the tree line around camp. When Elton regained consciousness, he had been tied to a tree with his brother, Samuel, semiconscious and bound to him at the feet. "Sam, you dead or alive?"

"He ain't dead," Will said, sipping on fresh coffee Bob had made. "But if we don't get some answers quick to some questions, we'll bury you both, where you sit. Who are you, and, why did you shoot at us?"

Sitting by Two Snakes, Bob looked on and drank his coffee. Will, to his mind was a sight better with words and could probably get some answers. He had learned a little about Will Tyler's background from the week they had been together, and he wanted to see if he had picked up any of his granddaddy's lawman's skills. Even down in Texas, Bob had heard of the exploits of Marshal John

Law Singleton. Not that any eastern Yankee lawman could match even a green recruit Texas Ranger, of course, but John Law was, in legend at least, a tough individual. Maybe Will took after him.

"Answer the man," Bob said with a loud snap. Will looked at Bob as if to remind him that he was still in charge, and had been, since he threw that rock at him in the Mississippi River a week ago. Bob just nodded his head to Will as if saying, *go ahead, sorry for the interruption.*

"I asked you who you were," repeated Will. "Your friend called out to you as Elton. Elton who? You called him Sam. What's his full name?"

"None of your goddamn business," snapped Elton, his eyes blinking the blood running down his head. "I ain't saying nothing to none of you sonsabitches," he said, glaring at Will.

Bob felt he had been patient beyond what was reasonable. He could not control his anxious nature in situations like these. Never had been able to. He slowly rose to his feet, walked over to his saddlebag, retrieved something and walked toward the outlaw. Will wondered what Bob was doing, though in their short time together, he had learned that the Texan was a surprising individual. Anticipating his next comment or action could be difficult. Will decided to let the situation play out. If Bob killed the man, well, even if it was in cold blood, it would not be an overly sad occasion. That bandit was as about as obnoxious and mean spirited as he'd seen. He probably deserved to die for several things. Two Snakes just watched. All his life he had tried to understand white men and their actions. He was beginning to think it was a hopeless quest, especially regarding this Texan. Nevertheless, the paradox within the man was intriguing. One minute, Two Snakes was ready to throw a snake on him; and the next, Bob would say or do something that Two Snakes found admirable. This man is worth my study, Two Snakes surmised.

"What do you want, you bastard?" spewed Elton, looking up at Bob. He then rolled up a good portion of saliva in his mouth and spat it on Bob's boots. He looked back up toward Bob with a surly grin on his face, exposing his broken, black teeth. "You lookin' for me to polish your boots?" he asked in a slow, sarcastic drawl.

Will and Two Snakes thought the bandit had drawn his last breath.

Bob ignored the remark and continued with his firm expression as if on a single-minded mission. His countenance cooled Elton's attitude. The bandit's expression changed from confident contempt to genuine concern. "My partner asked you a question, and you were very rude in your answer. That didn't set particularly good with me, so I decided to come over and see if I could persuade you to be a bit more polite," Bob said, holding his large eight-inch skinning knife at his side. Bob never carried a knife, but Two Snakes had seen this one in his saddlebag at the Mississippi river. He thought then it was a handsome knife with an exceptionally sharp edge. It was one of the things in the list about Bob that Two Snakes had in the admirable column. A man who cares for his knife has good sense and can be trusted, went the old Kiowa saying. Both Will and Two Snakes looked on with anticipation.

"I guess a little demonstration is in order, to show my determination in this matter," Bob said, bending down quickly over Elton's wounded brother, Samuel. As a stunned Elton looked on, Bob made a quick cut at the right eye of the unconscious man. With blood flowing all over the man's eye and face, he pulled his hand back with a bloody eyeball nestled in his blood-soaked palm.

"Goddamn! Goddamn! Goddamn!" screamed Elton. Two Snakes stood up quickly, and Will, even in severe pain from his arm wound, lifted himself up to his feet.

"Now," Bob said as he extended his bloody hand to Elton. "Maybe you can see your way clear to answer a few questions, or would you require another eyeball from your brother to help your decision?"

Elton was in near shock. With his gaze on Bob's hand and its ghastly contents, he began to talk in a loud and rapid tone. "I'm Elton Crabtree and this is my brother Samuel."

"I know of you. You're the two that's been robbing and murdering those farm families on the Missouri border," Will said.

"They've also been busy down in Texas and over in the Territory," added Bob. "They rode with some Comanche and Mexican killers down on the Canadian. We chased them into New Mexico and lost them in the flats last year. I saw what they did to a little family near El Paso," Bob continued. "I can hardly believe that these two peckerwoods are those bad killers. They ain't smart enough. These two act dumber than dirt."

Elton glared at Bob with disgust. "Are you some damned Texas Ranger?" he demanded, snarling his mouth. The outlaw looked again at Bob's bloody hand, and looked away quickly in disgust. He wanted to look at his brother, but he could not bring himself to witness the gaping hole that skinning knife would have left in his eye-socket. They may have been murderers and thieves and even worse, but he had cared for and supported his younger brother since they were boys, and dreaded the thought of them mutilating him.

"You have the honor sir of being skulled by one of the best Texas Rangers that ever ranged that great land," Bob replied. "Your asshole of a brother there has the honor of one of my bullets—not to mention one of my partner's, to match."

"Why did you fire on us?" Will asked.

"We been hounded by a posse out of Clarksville until they gave up and went back. One of them was on us for a week, but we lost him last night. We saw the campfire that had smoldered down and thought we'd just kill you for some of your bacon and coffee, if you had any. And if you didn't we'd just kill you anyway," Elton said with the same contempt he had shown toward Bob. "What we didn't know was that there was three of you. We didn't see the Indian at all, and that damned Texas Ranger was in the dark. So, Sam just shot you," he said to Will. "You, we could see, laying there sleeping like it was some fine Sunday morning. He should have killed you. He don't usually miss a killin' shot."

"I suspect his aim was off that time," Will said.

"Just bad luck on our part," hissed Elton. He was getting angrier. "Go ahead, cut his other eye out—cut mine out, you Texas bastard, I don't care. If I was free of these ropes, I could take on all three of you stupid sonsabitches, cut your hearts out and shit on your graves. And then I'd go find your mother's graves, scatter their bones, and shit on them." Two Snakes had been staring at Elton throughout the ordeal. He never said a word. His constant staring made Elton even more infuriated. "Especially you—you goddamn red bastard," Elton said, spitting toward Two Snakes.

Will looked at Bob as if he could read his thoughts. "I ain't seen him in action yet," Bob said to Will. "How about a little demonstration?" Both looked at Two Snakes and nodded.

Two Snakes had already retrieved one of the snakes and now threw it toward Elton's right leg. It bit with a violent frenzy deep into the outlaw's flesh. Not only was the Indian quicker than the eye with his release, but also he was very accurate about which body part he intended to have the snake strike. This had been a non-lethal throw, but Elton did not realize that. He sat incredulous at the sight of the rattlesnake biting his leg. He had never seen or even imagined anything like that. If the shock of seeing Samuel's eye cut out could be topped, this accomplished it.

"Damn, Two Snakes," Bob said. "Remind me to stay on better terms with you. That is the most amazing feat of bandit stopping I have ever seen. Damn," he repeated in amazement at the sight. "Damn!"

"You better retrieve that snake," Will said to the Indian. "Open that wound and bind it so the poison can flow out. I want to take these two to Fort Smith and let that Judge Parker take care of them. Two Snakes grabbed the snake by the head; before pulling it from the man's leg, he pressed it hard into the flesh so the fangs were as deep as they could possibly go. He then kissed the snake on the back of its head, went to the lake and scooped some water, poured several drops into the snake's mouth and slowly slid it back into its pouch. All the while, he chanted the song to the Snake Spirit.

Elton was comatose and just looked off into the night. Samuel was still unconscious, bleeding from two bullet wounds and a gash to his right eye.

"Damn," Bob said again, his eyes wide. "Damn." Two Snakes returned and sat again as if nothing had happened. Bob reached for his canteen, poured water over his hand and washed the eyeball. He then held it up with Will and the Indian looking on. "I'll bet this would be a tasty morsel." Bob casually popped it into his mouth. "Kind of salty, but not bad," he said.

Two Snakes thought this was truly the most amazing and unpredictable thing he had ever seen a white man do. He was more determined than ever to study this Texan. Much was to be learned from this man.

"Goddamn," Will shouted. "Bob, goddamn!" He was speechless.

"Oh you mean this thing," Bob said, spitting the eyeball into his hand. "Why, this is a glass eye that my granddaddy took off some pirate down on the Gulf. It's one of my prized possessions, and I like to show it off every once in a while to fellows like Elton there."

"But I saw you cut his eye out," Will said, pointing to Samuel, tied to the tree. "The blood is still gushing down his face."

"Oh, I just nicked him a little over the eyebrow, it'll stop bleeding directly, I suppose," Bob said, walking over to his saddlebags and replacing the glass eye into its little leather pouch. "Besides, where else could you fellows get a show like that west of St. Louis—and for free at that?"

Will fell back down on his blanket, propped his wounded arm over his forehead, and began to laugh. "You sure made a fool out of that damned bandit. He damn near shit his pants."

"Now you watch your cussin' there," Bob said sarcastically. "That's the second or third time I've heard you say something like that tonight."

"Well, being around you, a fellow hasn't got a chance in hell to keep his language pure. So, I guess my missionary work is over. The sad fact is that it looks like you have converted me, instead of the other way around."

More had happened that night than the event of stopping the two Missouri killers. Deep respect and friendships were forged among the three. Two Snakes and Will Tyler saw that Bob Johnson was more, a lot more, than the babbling prankster he pretended to be. He was a man they could call a partner in every sense of the word that counts. Two Snakes, Bob saw, was the first Indian who was as likeable, good as and smart as, if not better than, most white men he had known. Bob saw in Will Tyler a strong and brave individual with whom he could face life and sleep with both eyes closed in the camp, confident that he was dependable. But Bob perceived a dark shadow looming in Will's mind. He would often just stare off and say nothing. Bob determined to give him room on that. Lives were bonded that night.

Chapter 7

▼

7:00 a.m., August 31, 1875
Campsite, two days from Fort Smith, Arkansas

For the next few hours, Will had a fitful night. The wound to his arm was not serious, but it hurt him considerably. The action and strange events had kept his mind reeling. He slept only a few minutes at a time. Bob, however, snored loudly the entire night, another distraction that kept Will from resting. Nothing disturbed Two Snakes' rest. If dangers were present, he could stay alert and at the ready for days. However, his mind and spirit were always at rest even at those times. Still, he thought it curious that Bob would sleep so soundly after all the happenings of last night. He was a very strange white man. He would think about him some more.

Two Snakes had built up the fire and was cooking bacon and making coffee by the time Bob stirred. He had already tended to Will's injury and checked the wounds on the two Crabtree brothers. He un-hobbled the horses to graze, caught two fat field mice for his snakes, and was picking up around the camp, when Benjamin Colbert walked into the edge of the clearing.

"Hello in the camp," he shouted.

Two Snakes, not normally startled, but edgy after the previous evening, dropped the frying pan piled with bacon into the fire when the stranger announced himself. Bob jumped up, pistol already in hand, and swung toward the sound. Will, almost simultaneously, had his Schofield in hand and was looking toward the tree line from where the voice had come.

"Easy now, fellows," said the big, burly Colbert, his hands raised in the air. "I definitely come in peace." Colbert was a mammoth man. He stood well over six feet tall, weighing nearly three hundred pounds, and looked like a grizzly bear as he walked slowly into the camp. He was dressed in buckskins, and wore a buffalo hide vest over his large chest. Streaks of gray accented his full beard, and his hair under his big black hat was flowing down to his shoulders. A large leather pouch hung over his left shoulder and a Henry rifle was strapped to his back. Two Snakes thought that these last two days had produced many wonders. This was another. He thought the man was a spirit, for he had seen many like him in dreams—mountain men who killed and depleted the animals for their skins. He was a bad spirit in the dreams and this might be the man of the spirit, and that would be very bad. The Indian reached for his snake in the pouch.

"Now hold it there, sir. If you would please, keep those snakes fettered in that bag. I ain't partial to being bit by no rattlesnake, especially before breakfast," Colbert said. He lowered his hands and smiled. "I apologize for disturbing your sleep so early, but the smell of that bacon was more than I could resist, and now it looks like it got dumped into the fire, damnation," he said, looking hungrily at the flaming bacon.

"Just stand there, mister," Bob said as he walked toward Colbert. "Take that Henry off your back and lay it here on the ground." He obliged, and Will walked over and took the rifle.

"I swear, it's damned near impossible for a fellow to get any rest in this damned Arkansas country," Bob said. "Bandits are either shootin' at you out of the woods or some mountain man comes loping in here and scares the cook and spoils the breakfast. Not to mention I was awoke from a right comfortable dream about this little whore down in Sweetwater."

"Damn, Bob, shut up," interrupted Will. "Nobody cares about your Texas whores right now. Who are you and what do you want?" he asked the big man. "Things are a bit high-strung around here presently, so I'll be direct and to the point."

"I don't blame you a bit," Colbert said. "I witnessed most of what went on here last night. Damned if I wouldn't be high-strung too, er, Mr. Tyler," he said in a friendly tone.

"How do you know my name?" Will asked.

"As I said, I watched everything last night from just beyond that stand of trees," he said, pointing to a cluster of bushy pecan trees. "I saw everything that happened. It was the damnedest series of events I have ever witnessed," he continued with animated gestures. "When Bob, excuse me for being so rude, I'm Benjamin Colbert," he said. "When Bob put that glass eye in his mouth I thought sure you would hear me because I damn near shouted from amazement."

"What was you doing out there Mr. Colbert?" Bob inquired sternly.

"Well, I…excuse me, but I didn't get your full name in all the conversation I was listening in last night. I heard Will Tyler, and Two Snakes, and Elton and Samuel Crabtree, but I only heard Bob for your name," he questioned. Colbert talked fast and without breathing. This amazed Two Snakes. Too much babble was coming from this man, he thought.

"The name's Johnson, Robert Buford Johnson, and I swear Mr. Colbert I believe I've found a man that can talk as fast and as much as me," Bob said with a smile.

"We will get to the pleasantries when we get the facts settled here," Will said, showing his irritation with not being able to get the story. "Now Colbert, what's your story?"

"Oh yes, Will…you don't mind if I call you Will do you? Well, I have been following those two skunks for a week," he said, pointing to the Crabtree brothers, still tied to a tree. "They killed a couple of farmers on the river up by Russellville, and I came by the place and the wife told me that these two had killed her husband and son, over a gallon of whisky. I knew from her description that they were the Crabtree brothers, so I started tracking them to collect on the reward. A small posse chased them for a while, but they got tired and went back home. I chased them up to your area last night but they gave me the slip for a few hours and I guess they decided to rob you." He took a breath and continued without stopping. "So, I arrived at your camp just as they started shooting. With all that hell going on I decided that I better wait until morning until I showed myself, what with the agitated state and such you fellows were in. Bob might have shot me if I had even breathed hard. That was the most amazing bit of pistol shooting I ever seen. And that snake toss by Two Snakes, why hell, that ought to be in a dime novel somewhere, 'Two Snakes and his Killing Friends'," he said, gesturing his hand in the air to show the point. "…So, I just put myself on down and went to sleep. You fellows had everything under control, and I just waited for daylight so we could talk in a more friendly manner. By the way, Elton would not have got a shot off at you when he was hiding in the woods after you shot Samuel," he said, glancing to Bob, without taking a breath. "I had my Henry trained on him and I would have dropped him before he could shoot. But I knew he was a coward, he can't do anything without Samuel. I knew he would give up. Still, don't underestimate him. He may be a coward, but he's a stone cold killer, and a sadistic son of a bitch, too. He's a mean one. Almost as mean as Samuel. Why, the things they did to those farmers would make…."

Will interrupted him in mid-sentence. "That's enough Colbert, I think we got the story," he said, handing him back his rifle.

"Why, hell, I was enjoying that talk," Bob said, surprised at Will's disruption. "I'll bet Benjamin here could tell us some adventures that would make a jackrabbit stop and listen. Let's sit here and enjoy some of Two Snakes' coffee and bacon and talk about this matter."

Two Snakes had prepared more bacon and thrown some hard biscuits in the pan when Benjamin had started his long-winded story. He could not believe that now there were two white men there with tongues that never ceased. As the four sat and ate their breakfast, Samuel Crabtree stirred back to consciousness and began screaming. "What the hell happened? Where am I?"

"We tied you up like a hog ready to be put on the spit," Bob said. "Now stop that screaming and I'll see about getting you some coffee and bacon here."

"Go to hell, you rotten son of a bitch," he shouted back, and then realizing the pain from his two bullet wounds and the gash over his eye, he began screaming louder.

"Suit yourself then, go back to sleep," Bob said as he got up, walked over and cracked Samuel across the head with his revolver. The bandit fell back, out cold. "Damn," Bob said, wiping the blood off his pistol butt. "If one of these bandits causes me to break my new pistol on their heads, I'm going to be real mad." He returned to the others at the fire. "Pardon the distraction friends, but that fellow is the densest son of a bitch I've ever met. He don't seem to learn nothing. Go ahead, Benjamin, tell us your story."

Colbert continued. "I was roaming around sometimes trapping, sometimes bounty hunter, sometimes army scout. I guess it was just the Lord's good graces and my good luck. Now, I ain't saying that whisky was my downfall, but it sure put me down many a time. Neither was women. Too much trouble. Besides, I smelled like a grizzly most of the time. I know I looked like one. If it hadn't been for them squaw wives I had in the Territory, and them whores scattered across my travels, I guess I'd never even talked to a female. And I can't blame it on a larcenous attitude, even though I been known to be ornery a time or two. But I never stole anything that didn't need stealing, or killed anyone who didn't need killing. It was just a hard life I reckon. Hard land. Hard times. Never saved more than fifty dollars at one time. And if I did, some jackass woulda stole it anyway. But I seen it all. I near froze to death in the Yukon in fifty-two. I been snake bit on the Brazos; shot in the leg in Matamoras; in the back in Austin; and in the rear side in New Mexico—not to mention the various arrow holes and knife scars that decorate my torso. I fought a grizzly bear over a deer carcass I shot in the Montana Territory—he won. I walked a hundred miles across the salt flats; and I damned near had my scalp lifted—twice—worst time was on the Platte. I would have, too, except I wrestled that knife away from that red scoundrel and vented his spleen in that cold mountain water. That was close. I couldn't wear a hat for near on three months. Hurt like hell! To this day I think about that Comanche son of a bitch ever time I put a comb to my hair."

He paused briefly to take a bite of his biscuit and bacon, and continued as he chewed. "No, my problems began in fifty-eight when I lost my partner to a group of army regulars that raided an Ogallala camp in the plains," he continued. "Hell, he was just there with his squaw sitting in a little hut and them damn Federals massacred the whole lot of them. That set me back in my simple outlook on things. So, I traveled a while with some plains tribes trying to make sense out of life and bemoaning the fact that life as I knew it in the frontier was gone, and gone forever. The beaver was gone, no more deer to speak of, why, hell, they done nearly even killed off the buffalo. Would you have ever thought that we'd live to see that? The buffalo gone—why, there was millions of them. It was damn depressing, I'll tell you, damn depressing. But, what a time we had…"

The four looked into the fire without speaking. Colbert's words reminded Bob of the eloquent speech Will had made on the Mississippi a week ago that had inspired him to ride with him and Two Snakes.

"So, I just started here and there, and roamed," Benjamin said, breaking the silence after the pause. "You wouldn't believe it, but I've been a schoolteacher of a kind, tried being a lawman, an explorer—I went with John Wesley Powell down the Colorado River into the Grand Canyon. Looked for gold in the Dakotas and tried my hand at cattle raising in New Mexico…"

"Hold on, a *schoolteacher*?" Will interjected.

"Well, not much of one I guess, it stopped inspiring me—and that was a lifetime ago," Colbert said, looking uncomfortable, like it was a distant, forgotten subject. He finished his talk by speaking softly as he leaned back. "I've been bounty hunting, mostly. Been in these Ozarks looking for one thing or another of late. That's why I'm here, at this moment, I guess."

"For my part, you can share in the bounty on those two," Bob said, pointing to the Crabtree brothers. "You drove them in, we just corralled them and shut the gate. Besides we owe you something for that damn amazing story."

"I reckon I agree with that, Colbert; fair is fair," Will said. "We're going on in to Fort Smith to deliver these two and see about signing on with Judge Parker as Deputy Marshals. You're welcome to come with us and try your hand at it, if you like. There is plenty of bounty and plenty of adventure left in the Indian Territory."

"I've pondered that ever since they appointed Parker in May," Colbert said, stroking his beard. "It sure was a mess under the old judge and his marshal. A lot of corruption. Both of them damned near went to jail themselves. But this Judge Parker is cleaning up from the get-go. Why, he's going to hang six at one time in a few days there in Fort Smith. Now, that's getting off to a good start in my way of thinking."

"Damn, six at one time," Will said. "We need to get there to see that. That's a marvel." Will had made the statement more out of reaction than conviction. Since Helena, on that night in 1861, hangings drew him into his dark depression.

"We hung four Mexicans, two at a time, down on the lower Brazos, but six legal hangings, all dropping at the same time, with a gallows and everything—I'll admit, that might be a marvel," Bob agreed.

Will nodded without saying more. He had seen three die at one time by the rope. He began to stare blankly past the group.

Two Snakes pondered the thought of six evil spirits being released at the same instant. He had heard of hangings where the head would snap off when the body dropped. This would make an evil spirit even more powerful in the Kiowa way of thinking. He was not sure he would want to be near that event. He would have to think about that.

"Yes, a marvel at that," Colbert said, looking pensively into the morning sun. "I guess I will ride with you boys. At least until we get the reward money. Then I'll see what Judge Parker has to offer," he added with a nod of affirmation.

"Benjamin, being a man that shows an interest in money, what do you know about some of that old Spaniard's treasure up here in these hills?" Bob inquired.

"That's what I've been doing in my spare time in these hills. I've heard my share of reports, I reckon. I been looking into one rumor in particular, but I gave up," Colbert said.

Bob sat up straight. Colbert had his full attention. "Rumors! Hell I've got more than rumors," exclaimed Bob.

Will stirred from his depressed stare. "Are we going to have to listen to more of this?" He asked. "I've heard enough of those tales this week to last me a lifetime."

"Well... *Willis*, if you'd pay attention to some of what I been saying, maybe you'd just stumble over a big box of that gold or silver, and then, you'd really be grateful for my stories," Bob said with a tone of irritation.

"You know, there are plenty of folks who believe these old legends. Some have spent their whole life looking," Colbert said.

"But, has anyone ever found a five-cent piece worth of anything?" questioned Will. "Anyone is a fool that believes those lies."

"Hell and damnation, you sure are a depressing individual," Bob said. "You got to have a little faith in the fact that you just might be the one to come upon the very cave or hole in the ground where they hid it. I feel it in my bones that it's out there just waiting for me to come and get it. My granddaddy LeBeaux made half a dozen trips up the Mississippi and into Arkansas looking for some of that treasure. His information is straight from pirates and such in New Orleans. He ain't no fool. If he thought it was real enough to come all the way up here to this hellhole, well you can bet your last biscuit that there's something to it. I left the love and comfort of my little wife back in Texas, rode off from a promisin' career as a Texas Ranger to investigate some of these stories. I'm sure as hell ain't no fool."

Two Snakes could not believe that he was sitting there listening to this conversation. He got up and started picking up the camp. He, too, had heard rumors all his life about treasure and gold left by the Spaniards. All Indians in the Ozarks knew that there were silver veins running through streams and limestone caves. But these just attracted more white men. So, they were best left alone. Indians did not have the ability to undertake large-scale mining. And if they showed up at a trading post with a saddlebag full of raw ore, they would more than likely never return with a second bag full, for a number of reasons. Mostly bad.

"What particular rumor was you following here lately, Ben? By the way Benjamin is a mouthful, I'll just call you Ben." Bob awaited the response with a critical squint.

Colbert looked at Bob with a slight hesitation. "Ben's fine, but I dunno if I should be giving anyone the particulars on my rumors."

"Hell, you ain't never heard a rumor that I dunno better, and I probably have four or five maps to boot in my saddlebag. My granddaddy has told me everything and given me maps and eyewitness reports to all these accounts. I just recently left him in St. Louis and I got a whole new retelling of those stories. He probably started half the rumors himself," Bob boasted.

"Yeah, they're probably like that glass eye he gave you, just a fool's trick," Will said.

"No, I myself have heard about Captain LeBeaux and his forays into these hills to find the treasure. Bob might have some valuable information," Colbert said.

"So, what have you heard?" Bob inquired again, ignoring Will's comment.

"I have been on the trail of the *Madre Vena* cave," Colbert said carefully, as if relinquishing a deep, dark secret.

"The Mother Lode treasure." Bob replied.

"Why, yes," Colbert said, somewhat surprised.

"That's a particular favorite of mine," Bob said. "Old Miguel Alarcon and some Mexican miners found some of the old abandoned Spaniard mines and dug out a ton of the gold. They hid a mess of it in a cave on the Missouri border and started diggin' more, when old Miguel bushwhacked his three partners and sealed up that cave and rode away. He wandered around guardin' it for years and went loco," Bob said with animation. "On his death bed, he babbled on about the cave up there in the northwest part of the state. No one has found it yet. But I believe it's up there. Spanish curse and all."

"Spanish curse?" inquired Will, who for some reason had been listening to Bob's story with more than usual interest.

"Yes," Colbert said. "It goes that De Soto himself will drive the person mad that disturbs his gold. It cost the lives of the four Mexican miners in the end."

"How could there be a curse of some Spaniard that died over three hundred years ago? That's just plain ridiculous," Will said.

"His body was buried in the Mississippi River and his spirit swims up the Arkansas to protect all his lost and hidden gold," Two Snakes said. He had tried to ignore the conversation, but his keen hearing betrayed his best efforts.

"There you go, even Two Snakes believes the legends," quipped Bob.

"All I can say, that's a hell of a swim, all the way up the Arkansas to these Ozark hills from way down there on the Mississippi. Seems like that spirit could just call on his ghost pals and carry it all down to the Mississippi once and for all and save all that damned swimming," Will said, now more amused than intrigued by the story.

"That's the most outrageous thing you've said. Well...hell, everybody knows he'd have to get aholt of some ghost horses and some ghost wagons and such to do that. It seems a whole lot easier just to take an unhurried swim upriver ever once in a while and scare off a few prospectors. I know for certain, if that old son of a bitch come out of that water at me, I'd give up my treasure huntin' ways on the spot," Bob said sarcastically, answering Will's irreverent attitude.

Two Snakes had been giving a serious possibility as to the Mexican's madness and for the murder of his partners. Every Indian knew that the spirits of powerful men, buried in water, have free range of the waters and can move at will. The ancient Spaniard De Soto had been the chief man spirit on the Mississippi for generations. Two Snakes was even more irritated when Colbert burst out in laughter at the verbal exchange between Will and Bob. No white man ever took matters like that seriously enough for Two Snakes. Spirits were not a laughing matter.

"This is going to be a very enjoyable adventure with you, Bob," Colbert said.

"And some day soon, we'll have to go look for the *Madre Vena* without these two naysayers," Bob said with a wide grin. "Or, we could let them come along to do all the hard diggin' and loadin' while we do the countin'."

"Seriously, we do need to compare thoughts on some of these stories of Confederate gold buried up here during their retreat at Pea Ridge. That could be a real bonanza," Colbert answered.

"Why don't you two just compare thoughts all you want to as we ride to Fort Smith," Will said. "Just make sure you stay back out of ear shot, because I don't want to hear it."

"I'll wager you'd be plenty anxious to hear about it if old Ben and I staggered on a big strongbox full of Yankee twenty dollar gold pieces that some fine bunch of southern boys put in the ground," Bob said.

"The only thing you'd be hearing is a hearty *thank you* from the Army when I handed it over to them," Will said.

"See what I have to endure Ben," Bob complained. "A cheerless cuss that don't have a game thought in his skull and an Indian that talks like a college professor and smells like something the professor stepped in."

They finished their breakfast and packed up the camp, loaded their prisoners on their horses, tied them securely, and rode west.

Two days later, the four riders and their two prisoners reached Van Buren, on the north shore of the Arkansas River as it runs through Fort Smith. It was the tenth day since they had left the Mississippi River near Memphis. They had never laid out a real plan and there was not much reason to hurry. The trip had been uneventful since the Crabtree brothers had attacked them at that small lake. Two Snakes had, in his usual manner, said very little about that night. He had, however, thought a great deal about it. He thought a great deal about everything. He listened, evaluated, and acted in concert with his reasoning. To him, that was the way to live. As they rode into the edge of town, stopped on the eastern ledge, and looked at the Arkansas River ahead, Two Snakes broke his silence.

"I have given it much thought. I will give you a name from the language of my people," he said, looking at Bob. "You will be called *Kahwenah Ath.*"

"And just exactly what does that mean?" Bob asked with a furrowed brow. He was somewhat surprised that Two Snakes had spoken to him directly and without warning. In the ten days they had been traveling, he could count on the fingers of one hand the times Two Snakes had directed a comment to him.

"It's hard to put into English," Two Snakes replied. "But it means, Sleeping Gun." He looked at Bob and nodded as if giving a profound affirmation of the value of the name.

"Why, thank you, Two Snakes, I guess," Bob said. But if I ever got an Indian moniker, I would have thought it would be something like Charging Bull, or Stalking Lion, or Growling Bear, or some such as that," he exaggerated with pronounced inflection. "This Sleeping Gun, it's good though?" he asked.

"Very good," Two Snakes said. "You were asleep and then firing your gun at the same time. I saw it. It was like a dream—like the spirit of the gun took your hand and fired the pistol for you."

"I'll vouch to the soundness of that name. From what I saw that night, the name is very good," Colbert said.

"*Sleeping Gun* it is then," Bob said. "What about a name for Will? What's the Kiowa name for Sleeping Log? That would fit him. He damned near slept through the whole scrape."

Bob's persistent irreverence at any subject annoyed Two Snakes. He had thought about the gunfight repeatedly and he was sure that Bob was spirit-blessed with a keen awareness that allowed him to keep his wits in a dangerous moment. He had known Indian warriors with that ability. They were spirit-blessed. He had pondered his recollection of a particular Kiowa named Six Claws, before the warrior had become the renegade and killer that struck fear in every heart from Texas to Arkansas to the Indian and New Mexico Territories. Reports also had him raiding as far as Missouri and Kansas—murdering, raping, stealing and torching everywhere he rode. Six Claws, having six toes, was touched by the Spirits. Two Snakes remembered as a boy, trying to steal glances at the warrior's foot in hopes to see this marvel. He tried to befriend him on the tragic night that the warrior left his people forever. That saddened Two Snakes, but the warrior's stature and feats made him immortal in a young boy's mind, no matter the tragedy or his killing ways later in life.

Six Claws, however, was renown not only for the extra toes, but also for his ability to know when danger approached. This was one way he and his band of killers had avoided capture all these years. He could tell by the information given by the Spirits when death was near or how to react one way or the other in a situation that required a quick decisive move. When Two Snakes was a boy in the same camp with Six Claws, wonderful stories were told at night about that young brave standing firm in front of a charging buffalo, and moving right and left, forward and backwards, until the moment he thrust his single lance through the eye of the beast. Hearts pounded and breathing was heavy around the campfire as stories like that were told and retold. Two Snakes had wondered, during his deliberation, if perhaps the Texan had six toes also. Maybe this would explain his ability to shoot a gun and hit his mark from sleep. He thought to himself that at the next opportunity when Bob would wash in a stream or river, he would count his toes.

"Yeah, Sleeping Log. That will do just fine for you, Will," Bob repeated.

"If you're through with your babbling, let's get on with taking these Crabtree brothers on over to the sheriff in Fort Smith. If Colbert is right, I suspect that there is a sizable reward out on these two," Will said, not impressed with Bob's constant reminder that he had been shot in his sleep and Bob had shot back while asleep.

They had tied the Crabtree brothers to their horses for two days, and hobbled the horses at night with the riders still securely bound to the saddles, hand and foot. Samuel moaned and wailed constantly, complaining about the pain from the bullet wounds in his shoulders. He would scream at Bob to let him off the horse so he could lie down and rest. Bob invariably responded that he would have plenty of time to lie down once Judge Parker put him in a grave. "Now shut up, you whining son of a bitch, you're beginning to disturb my thinking," Bob would say. "Why can't you just sit on that horse and keep quiet like your brother Elton there? He ain't said a word since Two Snakes' pal took a bite out of him."

Elton Crabtree just sat astride his horse and stared straight ahead. To feed him for those two days, food had to be put into his mouth, which would just fall to the ground. He made no attempt to chew or swallow. His leg was swollen twice its size from the snakebite and had turned a deep dark purple. "His mind was with the spirit world," Two Snakes had said. "The part of the soul that thinks and talks has been sucked out by the snake."

Now on the bank of the Arkansas River, looking over at Fort Smith, Samuel Crabtree began cursing and screaming again. "You bastards let me off this horse long enough to shit at least," he said. "I ain't shit in three days."

"I thinking that Judge Parker will allow you that opportunity there before he hangs you. Now, do you think he'd want you leakin' in your pants when your neck broke and soilin' his fine hand-carved gallows?" Bob replied. "I heard they give them a fresh coat of paint before every hangin'. Hell, come to think of it, they might just decorate it up with ribbons and all sorts of finery for important bandits like you two. Why, they wouldn't surprise me if they build a special stand there for a brass band to give you boys a grand send off, flag wavin', hymn singin', and everything," Bob continued with a loud, sarcastic tone.

"Bob, please stop talking to that man. Between his screaming and your carrying on with him, I can hardly hear myself think," interrupted Will Tyler. "And you, Crabtree, stop your yelling and crying."

Samuel was still screaming and jerking around on his horse as they loaded on the ferry to cross the river, and Will pulled his Schofield and cracked him across the back of the head. Samuel Crabtree slumped forward in the saddle.

"Thanks," Bob said. "That damned guy was beginning to annoy me greatly."

"Just let it be a reminder to you what I am capable of when a fellow talks too much," Will said.

"I'll sure remember that little demonstration," Bob said.

"As will I, sir," Colbert said.

CHAPTER 8

▼

Noon, September 2, 1875
Fort Smith, Arkansas

The sheriff at Fort Smith was amazed at the motley riders outside his office. He stepped into the street. "Can I assist you men?" he asked with his right palm resting on the butt of his holstered gun. He was not sure about this group and was not going to take any chances. He motioned to his deputy, seated on the porch and holding a shotgun, to join him. "I'm Sheriff Jack Hainey," he said. "What's the situation?" He looked over the group and saw two intelligent looking, but not particularly well groomed, white men—well armed; an Indian; the biggest, burliest mountain man he had ever seen, with a Henry .50 slung over his shoulder; and two bound men who had been shot up and beaten. The deputy looked on nervously, raising the shotgun a little toward the mounted men.

"I'm William T. Tyler," Will said, pointing to the others. "These are my partners, Robert Johnson, Two Snakes, Benjamin Colbert. He continued in a louder voice. "These two are the Crabtree Brothers, Elton and Samuel."

"Jumping Jesus," exclaimed Hainey. "The Crabtree brothers! My Godamighty. Marshal Singleton and Judge Parker will be glad to see this," he added. The deputy joined in the celebration, walking over to look at the two bandits and smiling broadly. "Uncle Jack, that's them all right. It sure as hell is," he said with enthusiasm.

"Get on down boys, and let's get them locked up. Does anyone need medical attention?" Hainey asked, noticing their wounds.

"Will, there, took a bullet through the arm but we bandaged it on the trail. He might better see a doc." Bob pointed to the two outlaws. "I 'spect them other two will live to hang, but you might have that big ugly one's leg looked at, he tangled with a rattlesnake and hasn't said a solitary word since. That other little scrawny bastard up there with those matching bullet holes, he's been yellin' and screamin' for two days. We had to whack him a few times to shut him up."

"Looks like he's had a bad cut on the face," the sheriff said.

"I would like the pleasure of telling you about that little fact over a couple of shots of Tennessee Mash," Colbert said as he pushed his hefty frame off his horse. "That is an amazing story, well worth the price of a bottle."

Hainey remembered Will's wound. "Mr. Tyler, do we need to go to Doc Sweeney's office first?"

"No, we'll wait," he said. "Two Snakes' poultice is doing the trick for now. I'll drop by later."

"Let's go then. We'll all have a drink over this," the sheriff said. "But first, let's get them secured and start the papers on 'em, and get over to Marshal Singleton's office at the courthouse. He'll want to hear about this."

The first time Jack Hainey had mentioned Singleton's name, Will felt the weight of a well-placed blow to the stomach. But the second time he heard it, a deep well of emotion started churning violently within him. It knocked him breathless. He was afraid to ask the question swirling in his brain, but he had to.

"This Marshal Singleton," he said slowly. "Who is he?"

The sheriff thought a moment before he answered in an almost indignant tone. Why, everyone knew Marshal Singleton. What kind of backwoods idiot was this man with such a question?

"God, Mr. Tyler, where have you been that you don't know John Robert Singleton, the most famous United States Marshal that ever lived? General Singleton—the hero of Vicksburg. John Law. Hell, everyone has heard of John Law," he said, showing his pride in even mentioning his name. "He was appointed by President Grant himself after accepting the invitation of Judge Parker to leave Tennessee and come help clean up the Territory. He's only been here three months and we are already going to hang six murderers tomorrow."

Bob Johnson looked at his friend's face, drawn and colorless. Will had shared his story on the week's journey from the Mississippi, and Bob knew what John Law meant to Will.

"Hell, yes, he knows who he is," Bob fired back in defense of his friend. "This man is John Law's grandson."

"Grandson?" Hainey said with a startled voice. "William Tyler. Well…yes, of course. John Law has told about you often. You're the one that got chased up that tree by the bear in Tennessee. He's got a old musket mounted over his desk that tells the story," he said with a wide smile.

Samuel Crabtree screamed. "One of you sonsabitches get me off this goddamn horse. I'm dying up here!"

"I'll be glad to oblige you," Bob said as he angrily pulled the ropes from Crabtree and yanked him by one of his wounded arms off the horse. He fell to the ground screeching in pain.

The sheriff and his deputy took Elton from his horse without any struggle at all. Elton still had not said a word. They were locked in separate cells in the county jail.

The walk was less than half a mile to the federal courthouse at the site of the old Fort Smith garrison barracks. As Jack Hainey and the four walked, there was a lot of talk about the capture of the Crabtree brothers. Will, however, said nothing. He was consumed by his powerful love for John Law, fourteen years of self-imposed absence, and the memory of the look on his father's face when he had swung the whip. These unresolved conflicts were now coming together in the span of a half-mile walk. When they reached the main building with the outside steps to the basement office of the U.S. Marshal, Will's breathing was labored and his legs felt heavy as he descended the stairs.

The marshal was talking to Valentine Morgan, one of the court's best deputies, when the group walked in. "John Law, have I got news for you," Hainey said with great anticipation. He motioned with a sense of pride for the others to follow him up to the big oak desk, with a framed piece of musket over it bearing the words, 'Kilt by a Tennessee Bar.' The sheriff could hardly contain himself. The four men were standing just behind him as the marshal scanned them quickly and then locked his eyes on Will.

"I hope, Jack, that it is not bad news," John Law said, still staring at Will, whose eyes were locked intently on his grandfather. John Law feared that the sheriff now had his long-absent grandson in custody for some reason.

"No sir, it's decidedly good news," he proclaimed proudly. "I have in my jail those murdering Crabtree brothers, brought in by none other than Mr. William T. Tyler and his partners," he said, putting his arm around Will. "I think you know this fellow, Marshal."

For the second time in his life, Will saw tears well up in John Law's eyes.

"Why, yes, I do," John Law said, his voice weakening. "Yes, I do," he repeated and slowly moved to Will and put his big hand on his grandson's shoulder. He embraced him trying to hide the tears streaming down his face. Will Tyler also wept. John Law finally spoke, as every man watched with an embarrassed but empathic gaze. "Sheriff, why don't you and Valentine take these men over to Birdwell's Saloon and buy them all the whisky they can hold. Put it on my tab, and consider yourself off duty so you can join them," he said with more strength of tone. Noticing Two Snakes, he composed himself and remembered his place. "Of course, sir, you will not be able to drink, by law."

"Sir, I don't drink whisky by law or for any other reason, so perhaps I can be served some cool buttermilk," Two Snakes replied. Hainey was shocked to hear such refined speech from an Indian.

"Why, I'll be honored to drink buttermilk with you," he said.

"It's settled, then," John Law said. "Go on, and I'll stay here for a moment to chat with Mr. Tyler…" his voice broke as he continued…"and then we'll join you and see the judge to inform him of the capture." His eyes never left Will's face.

It was a good reunion. The two hours of catching up, and explanations and confessions were a healing time. It was long overdue. They talked about demons and blessings. They talked about Andersonville. They talked about family, alive and healthy. Will learned that little Zora had finally married, and he was about to be an uncle for the fifth time. Maggie had given him a third niece. John Law broke the news to Will that James Tyler had died, and had asked about him often. The plantation had been sold and the shares were in probate in Boston but would soon be divided among the heirs. Even John Law had been allotted a substantial bequest, enough to retire in great comfort any time he wanted.

"Let the girls have my share. I have more than I need in the bank in St. Louis from the money that Grandfather Tyler deposited there years ago," Will said. "Almost five thousand dollars."

"But, son, this will be ten times that," John Law offered.

"I don't care," he said. "Would you see that it is given to the girls or to my nieces and nephews? I don't want anything that was spawned from the damned Holcomb land." The thought of Holcomb drove him into a deep depression again. "What have you ever heard about that murderer?" Will asked his grandfather.

"I've exhausted every lead I've every had. He was too well protected by the Southern establishment, and after the war he went underground. Your Grandfather Tyler had the Pinkertons on the case for about two years and even they were not able to turn him," he said with a dejected look. The wrinkles on his face were new to Will, who remembered a solid, stone-faced man with the look of strength and determination. The years of worry and depression over losing half his family had placed a heavy toll on the old man. He was still capable and able, but just not the giant that Will remembered. Will was struck by the guilt that he himself had added to that worry, but he was glad to see him as happy as he had been in fourteen years.

When John Law and Will joined the rest of the group in the saloon, both expected to see the results of two hours of whisky drinking. To their surprise, all five men were drinking buttermilk. They had finished off nearly two gallons, and the bartender had to send over across the street to the Garrison Street Restaurant for more. Bob Johnson and Benjamin Colbert had started on rye whisky, but after one bottle decided that they'd better not get drunk if they were going to meet the judge. So, they joined Two Snakes, Valentine Morgan and the sheriff in drinking the buttermilk. Colbert especially enjoyed it, and if measurements had been taken, he had probably consumed a full gallon by himself.

"John Law, come over here and hear this story of the Crabtree brothers. It is the most amazing thing you will ever hear," Valentine said when he saw the two enter the saloon.

"My grandson here filled me in," John Law said with a powerful grin. "I'm particularly impressed by your ability with a side arm, Mr. Johnson. I know your father from reputation, so I guess you've come across that ability honestly."

"My daddy had a lot to do with it, but it was mostly hard work and the fact that a thousand old cans and bottles gave up their lives for me in my practicin' years," Bob said, wiping the buttermilk from his rusty red mustache.

"Is he still Rangering?" John Law asked.

"No sir, he sort of retired about a year ago and took up working a little spread down by Buffalo Gap that he and my mother bought."

"That was about the time of that Palo Duro mess," John Law said. "He was there wasn't he?"

"Yes," Bob replied, in a subdued tone. "So was I. And mess ain't the word for it. It was a *goddamn* mess."

"Well...it's hard to second-guess things like that," John Law said. He could see that this was a touchy subject for Bob. "Ranald MacKenzie probably thought that if he couldn't catch the Comanche, he could stop them just as sure, and most likely for good, if he killed their horses. It's hard to say which way was right. A lot of human lives were spared the Comanche arrow by the sacrifice of those horses," the Marshal concluded.

"I agree," Valentine said. "It was not as cruel as it seems, because the better good was served. Bob, you're to be commended for your gallantry in that situation."

Valentine Morgan was always the diplomat. He had been a U.S. Deputy Marshal for five years and many said that he was the steady force that had kept the scandal of the former judge from being even worse. All in all, he was well liked by the deputies and never said a hard word against anyone, except the outlaws he brought in.

Bob liked Valentine immediately. Maybe his fortune was changing. Since he found Will Tyler and Two Snakes on the Mississippi River, he had met one congenial fellow after another. Valentine was just the type of partner to help boost his spirits. Bob had heard every rationale possible on the Palo Duro event, from dozens of people. But somehow, coming from John Law and Valentine it lessened the guilt of that day. Just a little. And for that he was grateful.

The group talked for almost two hours about the lawless region. John Law told them about case after case of murders, thefts, rapes, arson, and every crime imaginable committed by Indians and outlaws alike in the Territory. They were awestruck as the marshal related the story of how Valentine had brought in nine men single-handed. Only one shot had been fired in the entire adventure. True, some problems were being handled by the tribal police and courts, but more and more frequently, violence and mayhem involved non-Indian outlaws, non-reservation renegades, and settlers, who became the jurisdiction of the Fort Smith court. The war had a very serious effect on the Indian Territory. Tribal feuds had surfaced between those who had supported the Union and those who had supported the Confederacy. Disorder was rampant. Fugitives from other parts of the country were taking advantage of the lack of lawmen and were taking refuge in the Territory. Now the railroads had begun making headway across the region, bringing more troublemakers and problems. A backlog of warrants and unsolved crimes, some notorious, had resulted from mismanagement and corruption by the former U.S. Marshal and District Judge. Relatively few cases had been tried, and administration costs had reached almost a half-million dollars in the past year and a half. The six men they were to hang the next day was just one shy of the entire number executed in the prior fourteen months. A clear message had been sent to the criminal element all over the West: the days of coming to the Territory to practice banditry and mayhem without worry of interference from the law were over!

Marshal Singleton needed help. He had commissioned nearly two hundred deputies to bring lawbreakers to justice, but the task was still overwhelming, especially since most of the new lawmen were poorly trained and inadequate for the job. The pay was just enough to be sneered at—two dollars and a half for successfully serving a warrant plus mileage and trail expense was not a way to get rich. It was not enough for some to even make a living. If they did not find the outlaw, or had to kill him, they did not get the warrant voucher or the expense money. And, deputies had to personally pay the burial expenses for the dead prisoners they brought in.

"Why, hell," Bob said, who had been listening intently. "What fool would bring the bandit in after he killed him? That ain't good economics. I'd leave the son of a bitch out there for the buzzards to feast on."

Valentine smiled and nodded toward Bob. "Yeah, I suspect there is a lot of bones scattered across that land out there that would probably match that stack of old warrants at the office. But, of course, there are state, federal, and sometimes private reward bounties that still make it a worthwhile proposition to bring them in, even if you had to kill 'em in doing so. I always find it better to bring the body in."

"Absolutely, we don't want any bodies littering the countryside," Singleton said. "Bring them on in and we'll figure out the particulars."

Still, it was seventy thousand square miles of uncivilized hell that Marshal Singleton had to tame. It was his job and he relished the opportunity. Will sensed his grandfather's excitement. This was the John Law he remembered before the night on the front lawn in Helena. Will could see the quest for adventure and the thirst for one more bout with the outlaws while there were still some around. He felt this, too. He wanted to feel the excitement rushing through John Law's blood. The meager pay meant nothing. Even if he did not have a cent, he would still do it for the doing.

"John Law, if you'll have me as one of your deputies, I reckon I'm up to seein' what the hell all the fuss is about across the Poteau River there," Bob Johnson said. He had beat Will to the draw and he knew it. He had only known Will Tyler for a week, yet he could tell by watching his face during John Law's lengthy discourse that he was busting to get deputized right then and there—at that saloon table, buttermilk glasses and all. He was determined to beat him. "And I swear I'll bring them all back, but you better get me a couple of sharp grave-diggin' shovels, I 'spect I'll need them," he continued, looking out of the corner of his eye at an exasperated Will Tyler.

"By God, that's just what I need, someone who don't give a damn about the sparse pay, but craves the action," John Law replied.

"Well, now, I didn't say I didn't give a damn about the money. I intend to make a fortune on them stupid bandits. I calculate that at two or three dollars a head, I could make a good fifty or sixty dollars a week," Bob said, rubbing his chin boastfully.

"If you're serious sir, then you can join my grandson here in standing before the judge to be deputized," the Marshal said. "I know him, he was ready before I got three minutes into my speech."

Will looked at Bob and smiled. Bob looked back with that same expression he had every time Will Tyler got the last word in one of their many verbal duels over the past week. "What about you boys?" Bob said to Colbert and Two Snakes.

They both nodded.

"I can sure use a man that's good with a Henry," John Law said to Colbert. "I think you'll find this as satisfying as anything you've found in the mountains. The flats have something in their favor, too." He turned to Two Snakes. "Will has told me some about you over at the office. And for some reason my gut tells me by just watching you here that you are an able and trustworthy man. But, I'm concerned about a couple of things."

Two Snakes had sat silently for almost four hours since first entering the saloon with and some Morgan, Sheriff Hainey, Bob and Colbert. During that time there had been many words, laughter, and some exaggerations and lies, he perceived, passed around the table. His way was to listen. He could learn very much that way. And he knew from the start that John Law was a man to be respected and honored. He saw a lot of Will Tyler in the man. That was good. Two Snakes counted Will Tyler as his closest human friend. And the Texan was gaining ground in his favor, but he still had a ways to go. He might find being a lawman a good thing, if Will Tyler was a part of it. There had been several Indian deputies commissioned by the District Court, usually the best candidates were the ones that had served well with the tribal police. Indians made good scouts and could help with the language barriers, so a few had been chosen and all had proven capable. Jim Roundtree and Charlie Barefoot had served bravely until their death recently near Fort Gibson, when Six Claws and his killers had murdered them. Roundtree and Bearfoot had been killed in an exceptionally savage manner. Their bodies had been butchered and partially fed to wild boars the outlaw band had with them. When the bodies had been found, one of the pigs had been killed and put with the deputies' corpses so their fate might be graphically displayed. Six Claws hated any Indian, of any tribe or nation, that helped the white man or the Federal soldiers. Army Indian guides were especially leery when scouting alone in territory where Six Claws had been rumored to be. So, Indian deputies were hard to recruit. Especially with killers like Six Claws, Broken Mantooth, Limping Wolf, and other renegades running freely in the Territory and back and forth to Texas and New Mexico.

"What concerns are those?" Two Snakes asked respectfully in response to John Law's statement.

"For one, I'm not sure those rattlesnakes are an appropriate weapon for these desperados that we'll be pursuing. Can you handle a gun?"

"I learned to shoot on an old smooth bore musket my grandfather had," Two Snakes replied. "But I guess I can learn the ways of a carbine without any trouble."

"From what I have seen, I'd a lot rather he bear down on me with a fully loaded Winchester than one of them damned snakes," Bob said. "I'd have a fightin' chance that way. Ask that Elton Crabtree about his druthers on that subject. I'd wager he'd agree one hundred percent."

"Sleeping Gun, tell'm heap big truth," Two Snakes said in exaggerated broken English with the first smile that Bob Johnson had ever seen on the Indian's face. *Damned amazing*, thought Bob. *This Indian is a damned amazing fellow.* Bob's admiration of Two Snakes grew by the day.

"I'll sure as hell drink to that. I'd choose a rifle in his hand against me any day after what I witnessed," Colbert said in a loud voice, as everyone laughed. He lifted a glass full of buttermilk and downed it without stopping. Valentine drank his down and slammed his glass to the table, beating Colbert soundly. They smiled at each other with the milk dripping down their beards.

"And your second concern, Marshal?" Two Snakes asked.

"My other concern is the most important one," the Marshal said with a deliberate, official tone. "Your buckskin pants and those moccasins are close enough to being considered appropriate dress, but the fact that you don't wear a shirt brings up a potential problem. There must be a place to pin that heavy badge. Hanging off your teat might be decorative and maybe even a marvel, but I'm afraid it will be a mite painful."

Two Snakes spoke above the loud laughter around the table. "You are a very wise man Marshal. I'll take a shirt along with that carbine."

"Now hold on a minute, Two Snakes," Bob said. "You might ought to reconsider that move. Why, if you ever get tired of that Two Snakes' name, you could switch to *One Teat*. And just think of them outlaws that would give up without a fight when they saw you, tough as an old bear, swagger up to them with that badge hangin' off your teat and blood squirtin' everywhere. Why, hell, half of them would fall down and beg Jesus for forgiveness and the other half would faint dead away," he said, shaking his head in admiration.

If anyone could bring Two Snakes into the fold as a certified member of the group it would be Bob. His constant irreverence and lighthearted outlook was beginning to soften the tough veneer of the Indian. He thought the remark was funny and even began to laugh, a little.

"Just to make sure you boys understand what you're going to be up against, I want to just say a final word," John Law said with a tone that immediately stopped all the laughter and reverie.

"Killing a man is rough business. I guess you all know that. Here in the Territory, we are about that rough business, every day. Not a soul in the Territory is unaffected by the life here. Men and women live rough, they talk rough, and they die rough. When the great minds in Washington designed to take all the Indians and turn them loose here, they forgot that there is a civilization to build. There is no civilization here, at all. It's a rough business."

The men looked intently at John Law. They were, to the man, used to life on the rough side. He just hoped they were ready for how rough and mean it could really be.

"Well…it's been that way for a long time down in Texas. I reckon I will be feeling right at home," Bob Johnson said.

There was no smile at his remark. Everyone felt the weight of the moment.

"Let's go get sworn in then," John Law said.

Chapter 9

▼

4:00 p.m., September 2, 1875
Fort Smith, Arkansas

Judge Isaac C. Parker was a man for the needs of the Territory. As a lawyer, Civil War veteran, former Congressman from Missouri, and a man committed to the dignity of the law, he was ready and capable to bring law and justice to the outlaw-ridden territory west of Fort Smith. But his firm belief in the principle that those guilty of crimes should pay, and pay heavily, branded upon him the reputation of a staunch disciplinarian, and in the words of half the bandits in the Indian Territory, a vile and sadistic bastard. He sent his deputies out in relentless pursuit of every lawbreaker that could be named in a warrant from his Western District of Arkansas Court. Those captured and returned to Fort Smith by one or more of his nearly two hundred deputies covering the Indian Nations at any given time, were tried, sentenced and punished to the fullest penalty allowed by the law. In his twenty years on the bench, he would sentence more than five thousand individuals for various crimes and sent over eighty men to the gallows.

There was another, more human side to Judge Parker, although this was never perceived by those whose only mental image conjured by the name Isaac C. Parker was that of twitching, writhing bodies being dropped through the drop-away floors of the Fort Smith gallows. He was more complex than the public notion of a stern-faced, goatee-bearded man, six feet tall and weighing two hundred pounds, standing by the open window in his office, overlooking the gallows and rigidly giving the signal for his hangman, George Maledon, to proceed.

There was a popular song sung by half the populace of Arkansas and the Indian Territory:

Old Judge Parker, I bid you, watch him well,
for if he gets you, he'll send you straight to hell.
Many a poor boy, having felt his wrath,
awakened down deep in a brimstone bath.
Like little Willy Croaker, for only a sneeze,
was sentenced to swing in the morning breeze.

Judge Parker, to those who applauded having the *Men of Blood* sent to hell, was a man of high integrity, worthy disposition and even a friendly spirit. He was a loving husband and father, having brought his wife, Mary O'Toole Parker, a devout Catholic woman from a fine eastern family, and their two children to this wild and desperate outpost of civilization. Parker was a dedicated, civic-minded man who served his community on several boards and commissions, including the school board. Even though he was not formally attached to any particular religious belief, he did accompany his family to regular Mass at the Church of the Immaculate Conception at the end of Garrison Street. He was well thought of there and had become close friends not only with the pastor, Father Cafferty, but also of Bishop Edward Fitzgerald, whom Judge Parker always found time to visit when the cleric was in the city.

When Marshal Singleton and the soon-to-be deputies came into the outer office of Judge Parker, the bishop had just concluded his visit and was preparing to leave. It was not a coincidence that he was in town on the eve of the mass hanging. He had seen the judge to officially present his plea for a stay, so that some commutations or pardons could be worked on. The bishop knew it was to no avail. The doomed men had originally numbered eight; all the legal moves had been exhausted for the remaining six after two had successfully avoided the approaching spectacle. One's sentence had been commuted; the other had been shot in an escape attempt. Judge Parker was cordial and courteous, but faithful in his determination for justice to be served. Tomorrow, at nine-thirty in the morning, Daniel Evans, William Whittington, James Moore, Smoker Mankiller, Samuel Fooy, and Edmund Campbell would all meet their dark fate together, at precisely the same instant. Parker knew their names as well as his own. He was acutely aware that six men would breathe their final breath on his order. But it was his duty not only to the law, the citizenry and justice, but also to the men, women and children who had been tortured and murdered at the hands of these six. Even though he did not consider himself a religious man, he did give the killers a final blessing, of sorts. "May God have mercy upon you, and upon me," he said each time he nodded the approval for George Maledon to pull the latch handle. The sound of the falling trap doors and the gasp of the gathered crowd likewise never left his conscious thought when, by purpose or by casual glance, he would look at the gallows beneath his window. A visit from the bishop was a welcome diversion, even though today carried with it a reinforced reminder of his grave responsibility. A circumspect and respectful man, Bishop Fitzgerald liked to hear and relate good stories, especially those of Irish humor. Parker, too, would revel in these few minutes of laughter and often write down favorable stories he heard, and save them for his friend's visit. The appointment had been official and bleak. The two came into the outer office not enjoying a laugh as they usually did. The bishop, however, did begin to smile when he saw John Law and the others in the room. He liked the lawman, and remembered that he could tell a story as well, or better, than the judge.

Marshal Singleton greeted the bishop. "Good day, Bishop," he said with a smile. The capture of the Crabtree brothers was occasion enough for a cheerful attitude, but the addition of four experienced men, including his grandson, to his staff of deputies was a circumstance of rare, good fortune. John Law's smile was good for the room.

"And a good day to you Marshal," the bishop replied. "I just wish my visit could be of a more joyous nature," he said, looking at Judge Parker.

"Now, bishop, I wouldn't dare to quote the Bible to you," John Law responded. "But I believe that our actions tomorrow could find justification in that good book." John Law was, as most of his family, a Congregationalist, and he held to a staunch conservatism in the matter of morals and justice. He did not particularly mistrust Catholics in the strict since, but his lack of understanding their doctrine made him wary of any theological debate. He felt there was enough about his own faith that he did not understand—he did not need any additional confusion. Besides, he genuinely liked Bishop Fitzgerald. He knew also that it was his duty to speak for the condemned men, so he changed the subject. "Tell me Bishop. Did the judge tell you the story of why God invented whisky?"

"Why, no, he has not," Fitzgerald replied, warily. "Perhaps you can enlighten me on that bit of fact."

"The way I understand it," John Law said with a very serious countenance. "The reason God invented whisky was so the Irish would not rule the world."

The bishop's two-hundred-fifty pound body shook with his laughter. He was genuinely amused. Judge Parker, also humored and delighted that the somber tone had been taken from the meeting, laughed aloud.

Marshal Singleton, in an official yet brightened manner, reported the basic details of the capture of the Crabtree brothers to Parker and introduced to him the men to be deputized. He related a little about each man and was justifiably excessive in his praise of his grandson. Judge Parker knew the story of young Will, as a boy, and the horror of the night in Helena with the whip and Colonel Holcomb. He had always admired the courage relayed in that account and was delighted to finally meet the boy who was now a man. Judge Parker shook their hands and spoke briefly with each.

"Mr. Colbert," he said, turning to the giant mountain man. "If any desperado gets away from you, well, he's probably too big to be supported by the gallows anyway." He smiled broadly.

"Professor Colbert, is that you, sir?" Bishop Fitzgerald interrupted Judge Parker and approached Benjamin with his hand out-stretched. "It can't be."

Colbert responded with a decided change in speech and mannerisms. "I'm afraid sir, that you have me at a disadvantage," he responded.

"It is you. Dear God. It has been reported for years that you were dead. It is you. Professor Benjamin Colbert. I am dumbfounded. Where have you been for all this time?"

"Well...it seems that I have been discovered. Unwrapped, even with my frame expanded by corpulent excess, my hair matted like a flax field in the spring deluge, and my skin darkened and cracked by the celestial onslaught of summer's rays. I have been exposed," he said, tipping his hat to the bishop.

"Sir, again, and pardon me for my incredulity, but I am astonished to see you like this," the bishop replied.

"No reason to be alarmed, my dear Bishop, I assure you that I am in good health both physically and mentally. I have found the essence of life that I espoused so long to have known so well." Colbert finally reached and took the extended hand and shook it firmly. "I deduce that you were a former student."

"Student, admirer, devotee, sir I am honored to see you again. I attended many of your lectures at Harvard and was all but mesmerized at every word...."

Bob Johnson interrupted the exchange. The entire group had stood fascinated at the conversation of the two. The perfect diction and proper tone that came from the bearded and buttermilk-stained mouth of Colbert was cause for attention.

"Professor?" Bob exclaimed, puzzled. "What kind of double-dealin' is this?"

Bishop Fitzgerald, still firmly shaking Colbert's hand, kept his gaze on the mountain man and responded to Johnson without a break in stride. "I assure you sir, there is no mistake here. Professor Benjamin Colbert is the world's most renowned anthropologist. His insight into the history and condition of man and humanity is unparalleled."

"*Former* anthropologist, Bishop Fitzgerald," Colbert said with a smile as he loosened his hand from the bishop's grip. "I left the stricture of parchment and ink and sought the reality of the answers to the plight of humanity in a universe filled with contradictions and injustices. I assumed the role of primitive man to find the corporeality of primitive man. I sought to discover the genesis of our being, but in the acquisition I was captured by the verity of the answer."

Bob Johnson was motionless, his mouth wide open but silent. Colbert turned and looked at the stunned Texan speaking slowly and deliberately. "I found that what I was, was what I became, and what I became was that, that I was. And besides, if memory serves me, I *did* say that I was a schoolteacher, *of sorts*."

Bob shook his head rapidly and started to speak, but stopped in mid-thought with his mouth agape.

"I'm sorry for any problems that my ruse might have caused," Colbert said. "But the man I sought found me, and I decided to follow him."

"But I thought you was a real-life mountain man," Bob said in disbelief.

"Well, I am. Ain't nothing but, for the last twenty years or so," Colbert replied with a wide smile as he slipped back into his backward speech and mannerisms, slapping Bob hard on the back. "My days of starched collars, snooty women and afternoon teas, boring faculty discussions and even more, the bored faces of privileged students, are long past. No disrespect meant, Bishop," Colbert said.

"None taken, I assure you, Professor." A thoroughly delighted Bishop Fitzgerald tried to continue the conversation. "Do you realize the value of your lectures now, after you've lived the experience of your scholarship? Why, you would have tremendous insight into the evolution of man and his coping with life. You could..."

Judge Parker stopped the cleric in mid-sentence with a quick move toward Colbert. He sensed the need to rescue the man. "Yes, Bishop, how true. How true. Glad to have you with us, Colbert," the judge said as he turned to the Indian. "And you, Mr. Two Snakes, I'm afraid you'll have to leave those weapons of yours outside when testifying before the bench," he said, pointing at the pouch around the Indian's waist. "I suspect that we'd have a difficult time seating a jury on those days. I suppose that those who are brave enough to come into the building would be paying more attention to what might be coming out of that pouch than what was coming out of your mouth."

Moving down the line, the judge turned to Bob. "Glad to have you in my service, Mr. Johnson. A man of your experience will be invaluable to our work. I have always had the highest regard and respect for the work of the Texas Rangers. Thank you for agreeing to join us."

Will waited anxiously to receive the judge. "Mr. Tyler," Parker said, as he gripped Tyler's hand firmly. "I feel as though I know you already. From the stories John Law has told me, and if you are cut from any of the bolt from which he came, then, I welcome you."

Judge Parker administered the oath of office to the four men as United States Deputy Marshals for the Western District of Arkansas. He handed each new deputy his badge and thanked him for his allegiance. He then introduced each man, again, to Bishop Fitzgerald, as a matter of courtesy. He was somewhat embarrassed that he had forgotten his guest and his manners.

The bishop was still thinking about his encounter with Colbert. It had been a quarter-century since the distinguished Harvard professor, literally in the middle of the night, had left Boston for the wilds of the West to find answers. No one had seen or heard from him in all that time, though myriad rumors had circled through the years. It was quite a shock to have the answer to an often-discussed mystery unfold before his eyes.

"We'll talk more, Professor. I have many questions," Parker said, as he moved with Bishop Fitzgerald to the next man. When the bishop reached to shake Two Snakes' hand, to everyone's amazement, including the bishop's, the Indian genuflected to one knee, reached for his hand, and kissed the emerald ring on his huge finger.

"Excellency," he said. "May I have your blessing?" It had been a dozen years since Two Snakes had seen or spoken to a priest. After the war, there were fewer than ten priests in the entire state. It had been over two decades since he had seen a bishop. To meet a holy man was a spiritually good thing. Not in a Catholic sense, but in meeting any holy man. Receiving his blessing could not do him any harm, and could only help.

Bishop Fitzgerald blessed him and bid him to rise. "Are you Catholic?" he asked, somewhat astonished. He was aware that there were hundreds of Indian converts in the state and in the Territory, but he had met very few.

Two Snakes told him briefly of his contact with the Sisters of Loretto. All eyes and ears in the room were on the two of them and their conversation.

"Great day," the bishop exclaimed. "I read in my predecessor's journal about a young Indian convert that cared for rattlesnakes, but I never imagined that I would meet him." The bishop peered slowly at the pouch around Two Snakes. "Is that where you keep them?" he asked cautiously. His big, bushy eyebrows were raised in surprise. "I have never seen one of these famous western rattlesnakes. Do you think I might be allowed a small peek?"

Two Snakes accommodated the bishop and swiftly produced one of the large snakes from his pouch. The visual reply caught the bishop so off guard that he almost fell into Judge Parker in trying to maneuver his large frame backwards. Parker alike was startled, but Bob, Will and Colbert looked on without flinching. They were used to it. Marshal Singleton instinctively drew his pistol, but just as quickly replaced it into the holster, somewhat embarrassed and hoping no one had seen his reflex.

"Jesus, Mary and Joseph," shouted Fitzgerald, trying to regain his balance. "I'll say. I'll say," he repeated. "If the serpent in the garden was anything like that fellow, it's a wonder that Adam and Eve came out alive at all."

"Thank you Mr. Two Snakes. You may replace Cleopatra's dagger back into its sleeve," the judge said, amused at his own wittiness. "There will be no doubt in my mind, that criminals will be trying to go in the opposite direction of you when the word gets around."

Two Snakes slowly slid the reptile back into the pouch, looked up slowly at the judge, and quoted in perfect meter:

> *Is this a dagger which I see before me,*
> *Handle toward my hand?*
> *Come, let me clutch thee.*

"I know of no other man, white or Indian, that can hold a vile, prehistoric villain like that snake in one hand, and quote the Bard with the other," Parker said in admiration. "Mr. Two Snakes, you are a man to be watched."

"You've got that sentiment right, Judge," Bob said. "I do watch him regularly. And that sir, is my religion—keepin' snakes and arrows and knives and bullets and such out of my body," he said, looking at the bishop.

"And of what formal faith are you Mr. Johnson?" Fitzgerald asked, as he looked jovially at the Texan.

"I guess, sir, after the eye-openers of the past few minutes—a college teacher turned mountain man and a Catholic Indian—I dunno that I have much faith in anything," he said, giving a wry glance at Colbert. He was going to consider this subject a lot more. He liked Colbert too much, even so early in their relationship, to start disliking him this soon.

"No, I mean what is your religious background?"

"Well, Padre," Bob continued with a slow drawl. "My mother and her father, Captain Gaston LeBeaux, are Catholics down from New Orleans. I believe I was baptized as a baby in Austin. She tried to teach me the way and I went to a lot of them Mexican churches down there in Texas, but I couldn't understand a thing they was saying. I could make out some of the Mexican, but then he would go off in Greek or Latin and I was completely lost, so I mainly just left it to them that understood it. Now, my father was a dyed-in-the-wool Texan," he continued. "And I guess you'd call him a country church man, when he went—and I don't recall that sight but a couple of times, at his mother's funeral and such. But I guess you'd call me a Duck Water Protestant, you know where they take you down to the river and duck you under the water and they come up shoutin' and hollerin' and jumpin' and clappin' their hands and such like a snappin' turtle had got aholt of them down there in that water." Bob paused and looked at the bishop, who was incredulous. "When I was about ten or twelve I went down with a friend to one of those duckins' on the Red River. And before I knew what was happening, all those old women was singin', shoutin', and pushin' me toward that water. It took three growed men to grab me and carry me into that river. Why, when they took me to that preacher I was kickin' and screamin' and hollerin' as hard as most of them did when they come out of the water. Mainly I dunno what all the commotion was all about, because I didn't pay much attention. I had spied a big old cottonmouth snake coiled up on that bank, close to where we was, and I had my full thoughts on him, just in case he was the one that was causing all that hell-raising in the water." Bob paused and looked at the bishop, who had his gaze firmly on the Texan. "I never did go to another meetin' with that group, even though I guess, legally, I been rebaptized into their membership, if there is such a thing. I mostly now just admire God from outdoors, among all his handiwork, breathin' his good clean air, drinkin' that cool stream water, and lookin' at that morning sun come up over the hazy plains. So, I'll just talk to the Almighty, and think how good it is to have my horse, my gun, and my life from all them dozen scrapes that could have killed me, and sometimes just blow on my hot coffee and look into that sky and at that new day ahead and say, *Good work, Sir.*" Bob sighed with a puzzled look on his face. "So, Padre, what would *you* say I am?"

Bishop Fitzgerald smiled. "A lucky fellow, I'd say. A lucky fellow."

Judge Parker was stunned at the Texan's rustic eloquence. He had not heard a better sermon in any of the churches his wife Mary had led him to. And certainly, it was as much or more inspiring than the forty-minute talks delivered by Bishop Fitzgerald when he was in town speaking at the Catholic church.

The bishop thought he had found a man in Bob Johnson who could out-talk and tell a better story than Judge Parker and John Law combined.

Then, as the bishop turned to Will Tyler, Bob Johnson wrangled Colbert to a corner and began to question him about his genuineness as a mountain man. He did not understand the situation at all. The animation of the two amused Two Snakes and Valentine Morgan, who looked on as if watching a stage show.

Chapter 10

▼

9:00 a.m., September 3, 1875
Fort Smith, Arkansas

In less than an hour from leaving the judge's office where he and his partners were sworn in as Deputy United States Marshals, they began a night's activities of settling in. It had been only a day since the full festivities of bringing in the Crabtree brothers and catching up with John Law, but now, the next morning, Will Tyler had another life-changing surprise in store.

"Now, aren't you a picture in that shiny new badge?" Will turned to see who had spoken to him, and looked into the face of most exquisite creature that he had ever seen. Her beauty stunned him. She stood smiling at him with her deep blue eyes flashing and her long auburn hair laying gently upon her shoulders. Her smile was mesmerizing. He stood, his mouth agape, staring at the whitest, most perfectly sculpted teeth he had ever seen—coming from that beautiful mouth or any other.

"Well, can you speak, or must I ask one of your friends there to interpret for you?" she asked with another engaging smile. Bob Johnson and Benjamin Colbert were slightly behind Will, but just as dumbstruck. The three of them had just come out of the bank and were heading back to John Law's office when her voice had stopped them dead still.

Somehow, Will summoned the strength to speak. "Are you speaking to me Ma'am?" he asked with the voice of a small child, then clearing his throat, restated his response. "Yes Ma'am, what can I do for you?" He rubbed his neatly trimmed beard with his one good hand. Doc Sweeney's work on his wounded arm was evident and it lay comfortably in a new sling. Bob and Colbert continued to stare at her.

"I was hoping that you are Mr. William Tyler. I asked about you yesterday when I saw you and your friends arrive with those killers. I hope you'll forgive my forwardness, but when I found out you were Marshal Singleton's grandson, I just had and speak to you," she said in a cheery voice. She had been thinking of nothing else since she had seen him ride in. She was smitten by the tall, handsome man with the cold, dark eyes. She had stared at him for a long time, embarrassingly long, she thought later. But she could not help herself.

"Yes Ma'am, I am William T. Tyler. And you are?"

"I am Katherine O'Reilly, and I've just recently arrived in Fort Smith myself. I am a surgeon and am going to work with the Sisters of Mercy in the Indian Territory," she said. "I cannot believe that I have met the big brother of Zora Tyler, now Zora Ashcraft, of course. We were the very best of friends in Boston, where I am from. She talked about you all the time." She looked at the tall deputy with an inquisitive gaze. "Just what have you been doing with your life for fifteen years, Mr. Tyler? You have had everyone so worried."

He did not answer that question. He turned away and she felt the uneasiness immediately. Whatever his life had been, he clearly was not willing, or able, to discuss it. She quickly changed the conversation back to the happiness of a few seconds ago.

"Yes, little Zora. Little Zora," she said nervously.

Finally, Will returned to the moment. "Zora," he said with a nostalgic smile. "Little Zora."

"She's not so little now," Katherine said. "She's a full-grown beauty, with a little boy that, I'll bet, is just a picture of you when you were a baby."

Will's face blushed a deep crimson color. For his life's sake, he could not take his eyes off her.

"Why, I've embarrassed you," she said with a girlish laugh. She then noticed his arm. "Why, forgive me Mr. Tyler, have you been hurt?"

"No, Ma'am, not really, I just took a bullet catching those Crabtree Brothers. Doc Sweeney cleaned it up and wrapped it proper," he said, watching his shifting boots on the wood plank walkway.

"And that does not qualify as *hurt*?" she asked with a reproving look. "I have rendered aid to countless people with gunshot wounds, and I have never seen one that didn't *hurt*," she said, then smiled approvingly of his heroic characterization of the matter. She knew that it damned well *did* hurt.

"I'll agree that I didn't exactly feel any comfort from the experience, but my partner, Two Snakes, worked his magic on it."

Bob Johnson regained his senses from the sentimental reflections of his Rebecca back home on the fledgling Johnson Ranch north of Buffalo Gap. He did not want to dwell on those memories. They were becoming increasingly painful. At night, he would sometimes question his sanity for being away from her. *It was damned selfish,* he thought often, this quest for the unknown, mysterious something that lay just beyond his reason. He poked Colbert in the side with his elbow. "We're going to head on back to the office now, and leave you to your catching up with the young lady," he said to Will. "Take your time, but remember the hanging is in less than an hour. Excuse us Ma'am."

Will paid no attention to his two friends as they walked down the muddy street toward the courthouse.

"Little Zora," he repeated, searching for something to say and finding nothing else.

Will Tyler was standing and talking to a woman surgeon in 1875 Fort Smith. That was a rarity beyond description. There could have been a hundred things he could have asked her simply out of curiosity, but he was stunned speechless by her beauty.

Finally, he spoke again. "And Martha and Maggie, are they well?"

"Happy as they can be. Naturally, they miss their family, Marshal Singleton and you, of course. We must find time to talk and I will tell you all about your sisters and your nephews and nieces. I just wanted to meet you and say hello," she said with that same infectious smile beaming from her face.

"Yes, thank you Ma'am. Thank you Ma'am, very kindly," he stuttered, again at a loss for words. "I'll be looking forward to a real nice conversation." Realizing that he still had his hat on, he quickly took it off and nodded to her. It was then that he realized that Two Snakes was behind him. The Indian had just finished his business in the bank a moment before. "Oh, Two Snakes," he said happily, as if discovering an ally in an enemy camp. "I would like you to meet Miss Katherine O'Reilly, a doctor with the Convent of Mercy here."

Two Snakes nodded and smiled slightly. He never thought that white women were particularly lovely in appearance, especially when compared to a tan-skinned Kiowa maiden. But this white woman was lovely and pleasing to look upon.

"Mr. Two Snakes, I am delighted to meet you. I have heard so much about you and your exploits. You are the talk of the town. Just now, William was telling me of your healing powers."

Will interrupted, seeing Bob Johnson and Colbert down the street looking toward him with hands on their hips. "We have to go now, Dr. O'Reilly. I'll be looking forward to our conversation." He could not keep from smiling. He felt like another person. His concealed, dark and sad mood that usually accompanied him was supplanted by this bright vision of beauty and elevated spirits.

"As will I, Deputy Tyler. And, by the way, you should smile more often, it becomes you," Katherine said as she turned slowly and walked back up the street to the Convent of Mercy.

Will shouted toward her as she departed. "Call me Will. It's what all my friends call me. Call me Will, Ma'am," he said, flushed. His voice trailed off at the end as if he had asked a big favor of someone.

She turned and smiled. "Will, it is then. I certainly want to be counted as one of your friends. Please call me Katherine. Doctor and deputy are so formal."

He stared, hat in hand. "Damn, Two Snakes, now that was a wonder. I don't think even six hangings is a wonder like that," he said as he watched her depart through the massive crowd that was moving in the opposite direction toward the courthouse. "That *is* a wonder," he repeated softly.

There were an estimated two thousand visitors in Fort Smith for the spectacle, almost matching the town's entire population. Press representatives from all over the country were present. Housing was at a premium. Bob Johnson had rented his bunk in the barracks to a New Orleans reporter for fifty dollars and had given him an earful of wild stories to boot. Two thousand extra people presented all sorts of problems. Fort Smith was on the verge of being, but had not yet attained the status of, a comfortable city. Bob Johnson's description of the town as one big 'mud puddle' was fairly accurate. But today, it was the center of judicial news. Judge Parker was sending six men to the gallows.

In 1819, when Arkansas had become a Territory, there was no defined western boundary, and the territorial court had jurisdiction over the Indians. The early court had been replaced by the Federal District of Arkansas when it became a state in 1836. Split into two judicial districts, eastern and western, the bench for the western district had been established in Van Buren, five miles down the Arkansas River from Fort Smith, and acquired Indian Territory jurisdiction. Congress had moved the seat from Van Buren to Fort Smith in 1871. A large red brick building, a former soldiers' barracks within the old garrison complex, was chosen for the court and jail. From the beginning, corruption was pervasive and the court soon lost the respect and trust of the area. Very few cases were tried and court costs reached unheard of levels. In the next fourteen months, only seven men were sentenced to death and executed. When Isaac Parker came to the Territory as Federal Judge, within four months he sentenced eight men to death, of whom six were about to hang. There was no appeal from Parker's court. The only hope for a condemned man was a presidential pardon. The jails were full. Many times hundreds of prisoners crowded the basement rooms of the old barracks. Young, old, first offenders and condemned murderers were all thrown together in the small rooms. Horse thieves, whisky runners, killers and rapists all waited their turns before the aggressive judge. Parker was determined to expedite the passage of swift justice into the Territory. Opening early in the morning, the court often worked late into the night trying cases and making room for more outlaws. There would be six fewer in a few moments.

Will, Bob, Colbert and Two Snakes stood close by the gallows in a special section reserved for lawmen. They looked at the mammoth crowd. The noise was almost deafening as the horde milled in the ankle-deep mud and shouted for the hanging to begin. John Law stepped on the gallows platform and let two blasts from his ten-gauge shotgun ring in the air. The silence that followed was amazing, concluded Two Snakes, shocked to go from a thunderous roar, to dead silence in a matter of seconds. He must remember this sensation. Given his acute hearing, this was a great experience for him. He relished the sensation.

"Ladies and gentlemen, this is a solemn occasion," John Law said with great determination. "I want to remind you that we are about to send six men to their deaths. It is not a circus, or a Sunday picnic. Be respectful. I have been authorized by Judge Parker to arrest any citizen making a nuisance, and you will be promptly fined fifty dollars and forced to leave town. I have two hundred deputies among you to carry out those orders."

Bob Johnson thought of the two-dozen or so hangings he had witnessed on the Texas plains. Any tree or rafter would do. Justice was swift and certain there. But this was a first-class way to do things. He turned to Will. "By God, I feel ever bit a lawman as I ever felt. This is what justice is all about. Proper and exacting."

Will also was caught up in the emotion. "You're right Bob, but it kind of makes you think that given the rotten breaks, it could just as easy been me, or even you, about to go up there. It makes me want to do my job right and proper."

Bob Johnson agreed, but kept his silence. He, too, was determined to give his best.

At 9:30 a.m., the six condemned men were led by two priests and two preachers from the dark, dank basement cells and into the light of the morning sun. Three white men, two Indians and a Negro prisoner, all in white-pressed pants and shirts, were followed by twelve deputies, carrying Winchester rifles. The condemned were led up the steps by John Law and placed shoulder to shoulder on the platform. Then, each was positioned over his respective trap door. The first was Daniel Evans, who had murdered a teenage boy and stolen his horse. Evans had shot the youth in the head and left him stripped bare in a small ravine in the Creek Nation. He was wearing the boy's boots when caught. The second was William Whittington. He murdered his friend in the Choctaw Nation and robbed him of one hundred dollars. When he was apprehended the Bowie Knife that he used to cut the victim's throat was still coated with blood. James Moore, the third man, had killed eight men including Deputy Marshal Bill Spivey near the Red River. Smoker Mankiller had brutally murdered Billy Short in the Cherokee Nation with Short's own Winchester rifle, and bragged up and down the Territory about his deed. Samuel Fooy, also a Cherokee, savagely killed a schoolteacher on the Illinois River near Tahlequah. The sixth man on the gallows was Edmund Campbell, who, in the Choctaw Nation, had senselessly killed John Ross and his wife in cold blood for no reason.

The crowd watched in silence as the Marshal read the death warrant for each man. Mankiller's and Fooy's were also read in Cherokee.

"Do you have anything to say?" John Law asked Evans. The man dropped his head low and sobbed softly. He shook his head slowly to show that he had nothing to say. The marshal moved on to the next condemned man.

"Mr. Whittington, have you anything to say?"

"Yes, sir," he replied in a weak voice. He looked to the crowd. "I never had any religious upbringing. My pa showed me how to get drunk and lie and cheat. My little boys down on the Red River won't have no pa to show them right, either. I hope they don't fall in no bad company. I hope Jesus will help them. Jesus help me. Farewell. Farewell."

"What did he say," a voice shouted from the crowd. "Tell the bastard to speak up." Immediately the man was grabbed by a deputy and dragged through the streets toward the courthouse. The crowd cheered.

John Law stepped to the next man. "James Moore, do you have any last words?"

"I've lived like a man and I will die like a man," Moore said. "But I can see plenty of sonsabitches in this crowd that done worse than me!"

"Then if you name them and their crimes now, I promise you won't hang today," John Law said, looking up to the window at Judge Parker who nodded his affirmation for the marshal's offer.

"Get on with it, goddamn you, I'll give their names to the devil," Moore shouted. This amused the crowd below, prompting laughter and applause from the group. John Law wheeled around and gave the group a cold stare. There was immediate silence.

"Smoker Mankiller," the marshal said in the Cherokee's language, "do you have anything to say?"

"I am innocent," Mankiller replied, and looked away from John Law.

John Law moved to Samuel Fooy and repeated the question in Cherokee.

"I am anxious to get out of this white man's world," he replied. "I am ready to join the Old People."

Two Snakes, who was half-Cherokee, chanted silently that the spirits would come and take the man to the Old People, and that his spirit would not haunt him for watching the hanging.

The last man, Campbell, spoke loudly and without any emotion as the Marshal approached him. "I am at peace. I am ready to die."

The hands and feet of the six were bound tightly and a black hood was placed over their heads. James Moore cursed the hangman as the hood was put over his head. "I don't want that on me. I want to look these bastards in the face when I die!" he cried. George Maledon shoved the hood down over his face. "Sorry, but the judge insists that all prisoners wear them."

"By God, then, I'll meet you in hell, Parker," he said, thrashing his head wildly.

Maledon placed the noose with a perfectly tied large knot over each man's head and laid the knot just below his left ear. James Moore jerked his head and threw the knot off his shoulder. Each time the knot was replaced, Moore shrugged it off. Maledon replaced the knot a fourth time and reached over and whispered in Moore's ear. "I personally don't care how much you suffer. In fact, I wish you a painful exit. But if you don't leave that knot where it is, then you will choke to death when you fall. The others will not feel a thing because their necks will snap like a dry twig. But you will be screaming, and no one will hear you because your air will be cut off and you'll just hang there for about five minutes until your chest explodes from the struggle. Make up your mind. This is the last time I'm going to place the knot."

James Moore stood silently. "Jesus save me," he cried softly.

John Law looked at Judge Parker's window. He then nodded to Maledon. The trap doors swung open and all six men fell with a heavy jerk that broke their necks. They were dead, instantly. Maledon was a craftsman.

"Damn, what a sight," Colbert said.

"A wonder," Bob said.

Two Snakes chanted to the spirits.

Will Tyler had not watched anything for the last five minutes. He had caught a glimpse of Katherine O'Reilly in the crowd with two nuns. They had rosary beads in their hands and were praying all during the event. Will was hypnotized at the sight of Katherine. It was surreal to him that such a beautiful creature could be standing in the midst of such an ugly circumstance. He could not take his eyes from her. He did not know what true love was. He had been shown the example by his father and mother, but that was a lifetime ago. He was sure, though, that he loved Katherine. Without a doubt. He had cringed at the sound of the falling trap doors, but Katherine kept her vigilance, undeterred. She never once took leave of her prayers. If there was any good thing in Fort Smith on this day, he thought, it stood there with rosary beads in her hands. He loved her. He was determined, after having known her for an hour, that he would marry her.

Bob Johnson saw it in his friend's eyes and soon forgot the wonder of what he had just witnessed. It made him think again of his beautiful little wife in Texas. Nostalgia had tempered the excitement of the hanging.

Part Three

Three Months Before the Capture of the Missionaries

Chapter 11

▼

November 2, 1875
Circle J Ranch, North of Buffalo Gap, Texas

Rebecca Johnson had walked up the little knoll about a half-mile from the house. This was her favorite place on the ranch. Here she could sit under the oak trees and see for miles in every direction. The ranch was just over two thousand acres with plenty of good water and grazing land. The governor himself had helped Tobias acquire the spread as a gesture of gratitude for the Ranger's faithful service to the people of Texas during the Indian wars. One or two good poker hands had helped Gaston LeBeaux to chip in a sizable purse towards the ranch. He had said that there would come a day when his sea legs would have to be land-locked and Buffalo Gap was as good a place as any, so he bought in. Bob and Rebecca had given what they had in their savings and the proceeds from the sale of the Fountaine General Store she inherited in Austin at her father's death.

As Rebecca looked around, she could see some of the thousand head of cattle in the lower north pasture as they were being moved to the east pasture by the ranch hands and her father-in-law, Tobias Johnson. She often wondered what the cattle were saying to each other during their constant bellowing. She thought about many things there in her little sanctuary, but mostly she thought about Bob.

They had been married almost ten years now and his absence was especially difficult for her this time. Over that decade, his duties with the Rangers had kept him gone a great deal. But this was different. He had been melancholy when he left. Restless and unguided. She had been the same way, early in their life, when she lost their two little babies, stillborn. Still, she hadn't packed a saddlebag, mounted up and just ridden away—even though she had felt like it. But her love for him made her call up patience and a stalwart resolve. Somehow, if Bob thought it was necessary for him to leave, it was necessary for her, also. What Bob didn't know was that she was three months pregnant. This time, it felt right. But she had not told him before he left. She wanted nothing to stand in the way of his healing. Besides, Tobias and Elizabeth knew, and their joy was just almost enough.

She missed her husband terribly. That is why one of his letters was so important. It whisked away every particle of depression. Today was such a day for the euphoria. Torres, the foreman, had brought the letter from Buffalo Gap just moments ago. As always, Bob wrote two letters, one for Elizabeth and Tobias, and one for Rebecca alone. She loved that. Even on the trail as a Texas Ranger, he always was considerate enough to write a letter just for her. It was private and the closest thing to having him right there. She held the letter in her hand for a moment and just relaxed in the cool afternoon breeze. It was a good life on the ranch. Elizabeth and Tobias were more like her parents than in-laws. They always took her side in any disagreement with Bob, which was seldom. And when she lost the babies, they were devastated. It took Elizabeth months to recover from the grief. In fact, Rebecca had to comfort her, instead of the other way around.

She began to read. Tears, as always, began to flow as soon as she saw his scrawled handwriting. She knew also that there would be tears of laughter soon to follow; Bob was the most humorous letter writer she'd ever seen. Sometimes she'd re-read them just to feel good all over again.

Rebecca, My Love,

I trust that this letter finds you well and happy. I know it finds you beautiful, because that's the case at all times. Your sweet face is the last thing on my mind at night and the first vision I have in the morning. Then, I have to look at the faces of my two partners and I give thanks for your pleasant image still in my brain. Not to say that they are hard to look at, but they ain't easy either. Their names are Will Tyler and Two Snakes. You have most likely guessed that the last one is an Indian. There is one other fellow, Benjamin Colbert, who is a mountain man. Words cannot describe how bad he looks. It has been past two months since we met up after I left St. Louis and rode down the river to near Memphis. Then we met Ben on the road to Fort Smith. I must say he is a refreshing break from them other two fellows. They are gloomy and don't say much. But Ben can talk a blue streak. Almost as much as me. Of course, he don't know half as much as me, so he repeats himself a lot. Got in a gun battle a few days out of Fort

Smith and I had to shoot one of the Crabtree brothers. Pa will be glad to see all about that in his letter. We chased that pair clear to New Mexico Territory one time and never did catch them. Here they just fall into my lap. I got a seven hundred fifty dollar reward out of the deal. The money is in the First National Bank of Fort Smith and it's in your name too, so I'll be drafting it to home soon and you can put it into our funds in the Cattlemen's Bank there.

Rebecca, My Love, I am genuinely happy with my new partners; they are men who can be trusted. I know that your heart is broken by my leave, but I am sad also and hope to see you soon. I signed up for a short stint with the U.S. Marshal here to do a little deputing, and after I put a few more dollars in savings, and scratch a few more itches, I will be back to Texas and to your loving embrace. I'll join Pa in the work and maybe fate will give us leave to grow old and happy.

As I wrote you from St. Louis, my visit with Granddaddy LeBeaux was fine. He gave me a few more maps and hints on all of that lost gold up here, and I plan to find some as soon as the time comes. Except for my heart hurting for you each day, I am at peace. I will see you soon, I hope.

Your Loving Husband,

Bob

"I hope so my darling. I hope it will be soon. Very soon," she whispered to the letter.

That evening at the supper table, Tobias was reading his letter from Bob for the third time.

"Goddamn, the Crabtree brothers. What do you think of that?" he asked in a loud and pleased voice. "Why, we couldn't come within fifty miles of those scoundrels and here they come in right to his camp and say 'take us to jail' almost." Tobias was proud. Anything Bob did made him proud. He had only been gone a little over a month before capturing those two killers.

"And this Will Tyler is the grandson of John Law Singleton, and here they both are deputies for him and that give-em-hell Judge Parker. By God, what do you know?"

Rebecca was already a little irritated by the length of Bob's letter to his father. It was at least five pages long and her letter was barely a page.

"Don't fret dear," Elizabeth said softly to Rebecca as Tobias read and commented. "As much as those two used to talk to each other, I'm surprised there's enough paper and pen in Arkansas to supply his needs for all he *could* say to his father." She looked at Rebecca. She understood. After all, she had been abiding Johnson men for three times as many years. "Besides, there's not one use of the word love or any heart-tenderness in that letter, and I'll bet yours is good enough to put under your pillow and dream on," Elizabeth said, trying to reassure Rebecca.

Rebecca smiled and tried to hide the tears as they welled up in her bright blue eyes. Elizabeth always knew the right thing to say at the right time.

"And this Two Snakes fellow, damn I'd like to see him in action. That would be something to behold, all right. Something to behold," Tobias continued. He read on, mumbling phrases and smiling from genuine pride. His boy—a Deputy United States Marshal under General Singleton and Judge Parker—that was impressive. "Six at one time," he muttered, as he read. "Why, they ain't a tree limb in Texas strong enough to hang six at one time. Damn."

"Why don't you put that away dear?" Elizabeth suggested. "You can read it again tomorrow. I'm sure you'll want to take it down to the saloon and the sheriff's office to read it to all the boys. They will be mighty proud of him catching those outlaws."

"Yeah," offered Tobias, still beaming. "Sleeping Gun. Why, I never knew a Johnson that earned himself an Indian name. It don't sound very ferocious, but the boy says that it is a powerful name in the Kiowa tongue. I've killed many a Kiowa, myself," he continued. "And I doubt that they was calling me anything but some devil name as they departed, and here old Bob's done earned a big name. Sleeping Gun, I'll say."

Elizabeth reached over and put her arm around her husband. Rebecca got up and hugged him around the other shoulder. If anyone loved Bob more than them, it was Tobias. It made both women love the old man even more, if that was possible. He sighed as he folded the letter and got up from his chair. "I guess we'd better start thinking about building another place around here. When that boy gets back, I don't know if I could stand his constant jabbering. Yep, we're going to have to build him and you a place near by," he said to Rebecca. She could swear she could see tears in his eyes. At the very least, he was misting up. She hugged him again.

"How does your grassy knoll suit you, for a house? Right beside that stand of oak trees," he said, looking off in the other direction across the room to hide his watering eyes.

"Papa Toby, that would be the most wonderful place on earth," she said. "I couldn't be happier anywhere." Rebecca was the only person that called him Toby and got away with it. Not even Elizabeth would dare call him that name. His older brothers, as they shouted *Toby, Toby, dopey, dopey*, had teased him as a child. With that, he learned to fight at an early age at the mention of the nickname. From Rebecca, however, he relished it.

"I'll go into town tomorrow and see about what we'll need to get started," he said. "We'll sit down, plan the house, and get it started before Bob gets here. We don't need his stubborn opinion and long-winded talking messing up our plans."

"Bob mentioned the reward money and we have more in savings, so I'll help with the costs," Rebecca said, agreeing with her father-in-law to let Bob return to a finished house. As much as he talked around things, it would take twice as long to build. *Especially with two stubborn talkers involved, counting Tobias,* Elizabeth thought, and Rebecca silently agreed as she read her thoughts.

"That house will be my gift," he said, almost as if his pride was wounded. "It is a gift to Bob for bringing you into this family, and it is a gift to you for that grandson of mine you're carrying," he said proudly, gently patting her stomach.

"Or granddaughter," Elizabeth said. "All we need is another Johnson man on this spread."

"That, my dear, is an impossibility," Tobias said with a wide smile winking his eye at both women. "There will never be too many Johnson men. Why, the Almighty Himself, when he saw what a good thing he done with those he made, said, on the eighth day, after he rested, 'Let us now make plenty of Johnson men.'"

Rebecca thought how much that sounded like something Bob would say. She often wondered who taught whom between those two. She loved them both. She was happy. *Dear God,* she thought, *bring him back home. Soon, and alive. I love him so.*

Tobias loved him also. He was very proud of his son—as proud as he was on an April night on the Guadalupe River, when he picked up a twelve-year-old boy from the ground, with a big Hawken rifle still in his hands.

Chapter 12

▼

11:00 p.m., December 8, 1875
Fort Smith, Arkansas

Birdwell's Saloon had become, more and more, a home for Bob Johnson on his moments away from the posse trail. It had been three months since their arrival in Fort Smith, and it was beginning to seem a damn sight too long. His moodiness darkened and broadened over his separation from his Rebecca; and watching that love-sick damned fool Will Tyler moon over Katherine O'Reilly didn't help matters any—in fact it was making things very irritating.

It had become a common event that Edgar Birdwell had to point Bob to the door early in the mornings so the establishment could close for the night—long after the last sensible drunk had left. The Texan could handle his whisky sure enough and never really became inebriated to the point of being at a loss of senses, but it had become a comfort to drown his thoughts away from the pits of depression where he found himself more and more. The cheap rye whisky that Edgar peddled had become Johnson's choice of drowning liquid. "You damned fool," Will Tyler would say. "Any idiot knows that stuff makes it worse, not better. I thought you Texans had some sense at least, but I am beginning to wonder."

Benjamin Colbert had not been much help, either. Even though he was genuinely trying to cheer up Bob, his nightly presence with the sorrowful deputy at the saloon just gave him support of a different kind—someone to talk to, on, and on, and on. No matter the subject, it always got back around to his Rebecca and the ranch and his ma and pa and what an asshole he was for leaving, and on, and on, and on.

Valentine Morgan would often join the two. It was help in some sense. After all, Valentine was considered the voice of reason in the troop. Maybe, just maybe, he could be a stabilizing force in Bob's spiral into his doldrums.

Tonight was such a scene. Will Tyler was, as usual, absent. Everyone knew he could be found in the huge front parlor of the convent or, as of late, in some more secluded place. Bob Johnson, Benjamin Colbert and Val Morgan were at their usual table in the rear; it was strategic to see all the goings and comings at the place. Three empty bottles of Marker Brothers' Rye Whisky and a fourth, about three-quarters down, littered the scarred and heavily graffiti-marked table. A half-dozen cigar butts, tobacco juice drippings and an occasional dead fly or two also were present. The three had been sitting for nearly four hours swapping lies and expounding various views on just about every subject their weary minds could conjure at eleven in the evening. Colbert, by virtue of his expansive classical education and extensive experience on the plains of adventure, usually knew what he was talking about. Val Morgan, even though a slight enigma to the new deputies, especially Two Snakes, who distrusted him more and more every day, seemed intelligent but had a reserve that kept him just at arm's reach. But his advice was usually sound and his opinions agreeable and friendly. Bob Johnson, on the other hand, absolutely thought himself to know everything about anything, no matter the event or discussion. If he ran out of steam on any given topic, he would just resort to his trademark dodge of changing subjects quickly, without dropping a beat, and continue on in the former pace. However, he had become increasingly withdrawn. He mourned the absence from his wife and regretted the fact that he had ever begun his grand adventure to seek answers of all the accumulated years of killing and murder and hardships and sorrow as a Texas Ranger. The irony, however, and Will Tyler brought this to his attention many times, was that, he'd seen more killings and depravity in the few weeks as a deputy than in a good bit of his years as a Texas Ranger. And all the while, he was without the comfort of his beautiful wife.

"A damned fool of extreme measure," Colbert said. "He always surmises that chasing the dream to find Paradise will surpass the treasure already stored at the beginning of the quest."

Bob looked into his empty whisky glass and began twirling it on the table. "Damned fool don't begin to describe me at this point, boys. I sure miss that little girl and all her comforts. It's a damned straight fact that all the whores at Miss Emma's place can't even begin to make up for it." Bob looked up from the spinning shot glass and seemed to seek confirmation from his friends.

"That just goes to prove that life and love are a damned sight more than the fleshly matters," Valentine Morgan said thoughtfully.

The profound statement impressed Bob. He began to think about its far-reaching implications, which confused him even more. He was silent for a long time as Morgan and Colbert looked on in a sympathetic sort of way.

"Yeah," responded Bob, picking up his glass and gently rubbing it against his unshaven cheek. "I am beginning to believe that very fact, more and more. I guess a fellow can change. And I guess that sometimes he damn sure needs to...." His voice trailed off pensively.

Seeking to diffuse the morbid morass into which the conversation was sinking, Colbert slapped Bob on the back. "Why don't we go down to Miss Emma's anyway right now and give it one more chance? You never can tell; it might strike an unexpected chord. There are three new additions that arrived today," he said in a low voice, leaning over the table as if to keep the information secret. "Miss Emma said they were not going to be ready for service until the weekend, but maybe we can talk her into a trial ride. One..." he said, even softer and more secretively, "...is a fine Asian girl, according to Miss Emma."

Bob looked up as if interested. "Chinese?"

"Could be, or some exotic delight from the South Seas," he said enticingly. "I'll even pay for your favors to get your mind off that wife in Texas."

"Well then, buy me another shot," he said, looking now at the fourth empty bottle. "Then we'll just see!" Immediately, he felt a twinge of regret. Going from talking about his beautiful Rebecca in one breath to talking about seeing some Chinese whore in the next, things had to change. And they would, but not tonight. To make sure he did not fall back into the bad mood, he pulled up a smile. "What about you, Val?"

"No, you two go on. I'm heading to bed. I'm on the trail early in the morning."

"Hell, it *is* early in the morning," Bob responded. "You might as well hit the saddle with a grand experience in your pants—with that tenderness fresh in your mind—as opposed to a few hours of tossin' and turnin' on that damned ol' lumpy mattress down at your house."

Valentine was looking over Bob's shoulder and seemed distracted. He did not answer Johnson.

"What do you say?" Bob repeated.

Morgan continued to be preoccupied. He looked serious and withdrawn. Both Colbert and Bob finally noticed his demeanor and turned to see what Valentine was looking at. All they saw was a scraggy, weather-beaten saddle bum walk up to the far end of the bar.

"You know that fellow?" Bob asked.

"No. No.... No," repeated Valentine slowly, still preoccupied.

"He for sure caught your attention. I thought it might be some desperado that you recognized that was stupid enough to swagger in this saloon full of deputies."

"No, no," reiterated Morgan. "I don't know him."

Valentine seemed too nervous to Bob. He was becoming suspicious; something was not right here. "I'll think I'll check him out anyway," Bob said, looking back at Morgan with a strange glance.

"Oh, don't bother with that tramp. Let's go to Miss Emma's," Val said with a renewed, exuberating tone.

Bob was now very suspicious.

Morgan and Colbert watched as Bob Johnson slowly walked over to the small-framed, dirty, disheveled figure at the end of the bar. As he approached, the tramp turned away from him as if aware he was approaching.

"Hey, mister. New to these parts?"

No answer. Just a noticeable slump in the shoulders, and a hand movement under the ragged duster.

"Hold on there, fellow," Bob said as he unhooked the leather strap on his pistol hammer and pulled his Colt. "Don't move 'til I tell you to." He moved to turn the stranger around and reached inside the duster to find the gun and disarm him. He reached around the chest, and, to his shock, grabbed handful of breasts! Women's breasts! "Goddamn fellow, I'm a bit perplexed here," he said, eyes bulging. It was then that he got a good look at the face shadowed under the tattered, broad-brim hat. The face was unmistakable. Bony, hatchet-faced, and mean. Bob's face showed his astonished recognition.

"Hello, Bob. What did you recognize first, my face or my tits?" asked the raspy voice coming through the crooked mouth splattered with broken teeth.

"Why, Maybelle Shirley," he said. "It's damn sure a small world. Ain't it?"

"I'd say a damned sight too small, if I have to be here with you handling my tits in one hand and a gun in your other."

He immediately moved back a step and took his hand from her body, but the gun stayed in a ready position. "Why don't you just find that firearm yourself and hand it over to me?"

She reached into the back of her trousers, pulled a small, .31 caliber Wells Fargo agent's pistol, and handed it to Bob. "How long has it been, Bob?" she asked. "It must be nigh on ten or eleven years since you crawled into my bed down there in Scyene," she said with a wide, sarcastic smile.

"Now, that's one night I damn sure want to forget. I was drunk and out of my mind. *Goddamn*," he spewed. "I'm lucky that didn't end my life right there."

"It wasn't a whole night; more like five minutes and I'll tell you the God's honest truth, it was so unremarkable it's a miracle I can recall it at all. I guess it was just that. The unremarkable nature of the thing that keeps it in my mind. *Goddamn* is right. I'm lucky it didn't end *my* life right there—*being bored to death*!"

"You're still the foul-mouth bitch you always was, but I got you now," he said, raising both guns toward her.

"I do not have a warrant out on me—here or anywhere else, you stupid son of a bitch. So, give me my damn gun, and leave me the hell alone."

Bob was taken aback for a moment. It never entered his mind that she could be warrant-free. He had chased her and the countless outlaws she supported all over Texas and into the Territory. But that was some years ago, and as her notoriety and craftiness grew so did the missed opportunities and manpower to catch her with something that would stick in court. She had beaten them all. "I'm sure there is some paper out on you here in Fort Smith, we'll just check."

Valentine Morgan and Benjamin Colbert had joined them at the end of the bar. In fact, every person in the house was glued to the scene. Every ear was straining to hear the comments.

"Give her the gun back, Bob. She's clean here," Valentine said.

Bob held on to her pistol. "Why, hell, Val, don't you know who she is?"

"She is Myra Maybelle Reed, Belle Reed, noted outlaw, Dallas socialite, accomplished piano player and reputed seducer of many eager men," he said with a glib tone.

"Thank you, Deputy. I don't recall. Have you been one of those *eager* young men?"

"No, I'm happy to say, I'm not a Belle Reed conquest. But, I am sure that we could probably look around the saloon for a moment and find a few who have succumbed to your accomplished wiles." Valentine said, tipping his hat to her.

It was a battle of sarcasm. Colbert recognized it as such and was eager to join in.

"I, too, am not in that number, but I have ridden many a dusty mile in hopes of seeing your face and taking your hand. Of course, I would have put it in shackles at that happy event," he said.

"No doubt, I guess you are right, sir—not having been one of my suitors, that is. I would have certainly remembered any event like that; trying to breathe under the weight of your fat ass," she shot back.

"By the way, my condolences on the death of your husband, Jim Reed. A more deserving bastard of an ounce of lead I can't imagine," Colbert said, stung by her comment. "I only wish it was me that shot him dead. He was one ruthless son of a bitch!" Colbert was unusually vehement. "You may not have any standing warrants, but I assure you there are dozens unknown that you are deserving of," he said, his face growing increasingly red behind the full black beard. "Do you still have the thirty thousand dollars you and that husband of yours stole from Watt Grayson in the Choctaw Nation?" he asked with eyes widening. "I wasted four months hunting you down and sorting that thing out."

"I was never charged with that, and I know nothing about it. And neither did Jim," she replied, spewing spit at Colbert.

Valentine intervened. "I said she is not wanted here, so let her be. Bob, give her back the gun," he repeated.

"She's damn sure lost some of her polish on the trip. Look at the way she is dressed. It's a ruse so she can rob somebody and have it blamed on some ugly, scrawny man," Bob said, half defending his position.

Colbert agreed. "I'd say that if we looked into all the settlement robberies between here and the Canadian, we would find her involvement, dressed just like that."

"We can't. We have more than we can handle, and there is no proof that she has been doing anything in our jurisdiction," Valentine said, pulling the pistol from Bob Johnson's hand and handing it back to Belle. "Now drink up and get back down to your place." He handed her a glass of whisky and looked sternly into her eyes as if telegraphing a warning.

"She's guilty," Bob said. "Guilty as hell of something. Any woman that has bedded the Youngers, the James brothers and enough upstanding citizens to get what she wanted and when she wanted it, has definitely been up to no good. Hell, the sun don't rise or set until she has broken some law. Just the law against being so damned ugly ought to get her thirty days."

Belle threw the glassful of whisky into his face. "I'm going to kill you, Texan. Mark my words. I'm going to blow your goddamn head off, some dark night. Alone. You won't know what hit you, unless they tell you when you wake up in hell." She was shaking with anger. She turned and walked for the doors. The saloon was silent. The piano player's hands and fingers hovered motionless. Valentine, Colbert, and Bob Johnson, with rye soaked into his shirt, watched her exit as she turned toward them once more at the door. Bob Johnson instinctively drew his pistol. Morgan and Colbert had theirs at the ready.

"Alone. A dark night. You are going to feel my ten-gauge pellets tear through your brain," she said, pointing at Bob. She reached for the swinging door and turned once more. "From the back." She left.

The piano player hit the keys—softly at first, and then flourished his volume with some vibrato. He had seen it before. Knew when to play and when not to play. And when to begin again. This time, he swung back into his tune with full volume, anxiously awaiting midnight so he could go home.

The three deputies said nothing for a long while.

"Hell. I guess I'll go on down to Miss Emma's before everyone is in bed, occupied, or alone for the night," Colbert finally said. He looked at Bob. There was no doubt that Johnson was deep in thought about the past few minutes. He had that look about him, that look that said, *what the hell happened?*

"Bob, what about you?"

"Yeah, why the hell not."

Valentine, like the others, did not say a word about what had just happened. "You boys go on, I'm going to bed." He headed for the door and walked to the marshal's office, mounted his gray sorrel, turned the mount hard and rode out of town.

Colbert and Johnson, hats in hand, nodded politely to Miss Emma as she opened the door to her home at the end of Fourth Street. Bob Johnson, however, could not feel any enjoyment or pleasure. He could not go through with it. He paid the girl a twenty dollar gold piece anyway—four times the rate—and left quietly. His heart was now Rebecca's property. The vision of her sweet face had mended his ways. He saddled Molly and rode hard into the cold December wind. His mind whirled around thoughts of Rebecca, and just as quickly he was in a mental fury with the vision of that hatchet-faced outlaw, the so-called 'Queen of the Bandits.' *Goddamn her.*

Belle Reed reined her horse in hard as the shadowy figure came from the stand of trees on the road. She pulled her pistol. "All right, you bastard. If you do not want to die, you had better come in slow with your hands in plain sight." The harvest moon helped her see the intruder's moves.

"It's me."

"I thought you would be following me, Val," she said, lowering her gun. Is there anyone with you?"

"No. Why?"

"Don't know. I just had a feeling there was two of you out there."

Morgan looked around nervously. He saw no movement. He had heard nothing, but the wind had been blowing at a good clip, cold and noisy. He was sure he could have heard a horse at least. He dismissed the thought. "Look, Belle," he said, returning to the reason of his ride on this increasingly cold night.

She interrupted before he could get the sentence out. "I know what you are going to say, 'Stay the hell out of town', right?"

"It's no small matter, Belle. You need to keep out of sight. There are too many deputies on the road. Over two hundred. And now you run into a damned Texas Ranger and a bounty hunter mountain man five minutes after you walk into that saloon. Goddamnit, I can't worry about you and your stupidity. I've got other things that I am tied to—big things."

"By God, we used to do big things when the old judge was in control," she said, stung by his condescending criticism. "I made you rich, you pompous bastard, and don't forget it."

"Those days are gone," he said. "Parker and his men are not as easy to get around. Especially when he brings in deputies like that Texan and his friends."

"I have to live since Jim was killed. I have to do what I can."

"Just don't do it this close to the border. Stay down there at Younger Station. Rob all the families you want to, but stay out of Fort Smith. I do not have the time now to worry with you, and for your information, that Texan will be a damned sight harder to kill than you think. And that goes for his friends, too."

"Kiss my ass, Valentine. I will do what I have to do, when and where I want. Remember, I know enough about *you* to have you hanged!"

"No one could ever talk sense into you, Belle. Go ahead, but don't expect me to jump between you and trouble anymore, and for *your* information, whatever you can say about me will also hang you and you damn well know it. That's my last word."

He turned back to town. She rode south into the darkness. The third rider—on the ground, listening—mounted and left the little stand of trees.

Chapter 13

8:00 a.m., December 9, 1875
Fort Smith, Arkansas

Bob walked into the Garrison Street Restaurant with a rifle slung over his shoulder.

"Must you come, even into here, armed to the teeth?" snapped Katherine. She was clearly annoyed at Bob's entrance.

He had honestly forgotten about the rifle. Just a habit. He thought, *what's all the fuss about, anyway?*

"Why, you never know what kind of *anger* you'll run into—even here," he fired back, hoping she got the point. "I just oiled it up. You can't ever tell when the cook will come out swingin' a choppin' knife cause one of the nigra boys back there et up his biscuits." He was stung and dismayed that she had started in on him so early in the morning. What he had just said was part right. He had been up by dawn, oiling his guns, in anticipation of riding into the Choctaw Nation to track down information on what he had heard last night in the cold, as he hid from Belle and Morgan. He was anxious to tell Will all about it.

"You'll never guess who I had a scrape with last night at Birdwell's," Bob Johnson said, determined to salvage some conversation as he walked up to the table in the corner.

Will Tyler looked up, annoyed. He and Katherine had just settled in for a comfortable breakfast and he was taking his first bite of syrupy flapjacks. That stung Bob even more.

"Mind if I join you for some coffee?" He sat down and motioned the waiter to bring some coffee. He slipped his rifle slowly to the floor as he spied Katherine.

"Hello, Katherine, you look beautiful as usual this morning. Did y'all have a good time last night?" he asked with that wide Texas smile covered by that big bushy red mustache. It was hard for her to stay mad at the friend of Will Tyler. In fact, she was beginning to feel that same friendship herself. That Texan was contagious, for sure. But *damned* irritating at eight o'clock on a Saturday morning as she was enjoying a moment alone with the man she loved. The man she loved deeply. The man who had captured her heart, soul and body so completely in the matter of only a few months.

"Why, thank you, Bob, you look beautiful, too," she replied with a smile and a glance at his ruffled clothing and strong perfumed smell. *Miss Emma's,* she thought, for sure. She took a breath, exaggerating the move in Bob's direction.

He got the point. He began to press down his sleeves nervously, and move his fingers through his hair. He thought of the close calls last night; both the victory over the temptation with the little Chinese girl and the ride in the night air to clear his head.

"Who'd you have a scrape with?" Will asked, calming the situation.

Bob was grateful to Will for rescuing him from a further confrontation with Katherine. He really needed to talk to Will, but this might not be the place or opportunity. *Damn, he needed to talk.*

"Why, none other than Belle Shirley Reed," he said with a tone of pride. "And a whole peck of trouble surrounding it."

"Belle Reed?" Will questioned. "Did you arrest her?"

"No, Val stepped in and said she didn't have any papers up here that were in force. But it was damn sure turnin' into a situation of who drew what first."

"Belle Reed," Will said again as he looked off in space. "I heard she was running with one of those Starr brothers down in Texas just a short while back, after Jim Reed was killed. So, I guess it'll soon be Belle *Starr.*"

"Hell, Shirley, Reed, Starr, Younger, James, Dalton, or Mrs. Abraham Lincoln—whatever damn name she goes by she is still the same mean bitch she always was. Excuse me, Katherine," he said, suddenly remembering she was there.

She did not respond, or even look up from her bowl of berries and milk.

"Why didn't you come get me, Bob?" Will asked.

Bob looked at Katherine and back to Will and smiled a bit. "Yeah, I'm sure that would have been a very popular thing to do. Besides, you were sawin' logs when I got in and I didn't want to disturb you." *Not to mention that Morgan was back in the barracks and was staying there for the night,* he thought.

Katherine, realizing that everyone knew that she had Will Tyler occupied last night, took the point with the marked sarcasm it was intended. She replied in kind. With her lips pursed and set, forehead raised and voice slow and deliberate, she stared at the Texan.

"Bob, we've had this discussion before. I guess I'll have to remind you again. I'll let your friend come out to play after he has finished his chores, and not until." Her voice cracked a bit and she took a breath, setting her head in defiance. "Right now, his chores are centered on taking care of me! And specifically, this is our day to relax and enjoy the time when he is not going to even carry a gun. We are going to picnic down on the river cove and enjoy a lunch away from all this violence and killing. It is our morning!" She paused a moment and leaned over slightly to get Bob's full attention. "And I'll be *damned* if I let you, or anyone else, hinder it!"

Her azure blue eyes were wide and glaring. Her lip twitched a bit, and she looked to Will for confirmation. "And, we will be attending the Sisters of Mercy Winter Picnic tomorrow afternoon."

There was dead silence as everyone looked at everyone else.

Since Will Tyler was not going to respond—with fork, full of flapjack, in mid-air and mouth agape—she continued. This had been a long time coming and she was going to make sure she said it all. She might not ever have the opportunity or courage or *reason* to say it again. Will might be out of her life after this volley; she could not help herself. She loved him and was jealous about the time of her man. It was the timeless tug-of-war between friends and lovers. Katherine could not afford to lose Will Tyler. He was whom she wanted, and she had her reasons for protecting her claim. Bob Johnson, or no one else understood the urgency in her actions.

"So, Bob, it will be a while before you can borrow him," she said. The split-second guilty feeling was supplanted by a renewed sense of advantage. She had Bob Johnson, with his pistol out of reach, in a heated battle. The words stung Bob like arrows. She could see and feel it. Any feeling of remorse was quickly overruled by the same realization lingering around like a blacksmith's anvil that she had gone so far that she might as well, for all it is worth, go the distance. "So, why don't you go on down to the barracks and see if Two Snakes or Colbert or any of those boys wants to come out to play today and go on one of your *grand adventures*, guns blazing and flesh littering the ground." She waited, eyes fixed, for Bob to respond. She felt sick. Bob Johnson did not deserve that. She knew it. But she thought it justified because, somehow, she would be in a lifetime-long battle with that Texan for Will Tyler's attention. So, she might as well fire the first shot now as any. Still, she felt sorry for Bob as he glanced to Will Tyler, still holding that piece of flapjack in the fork definitely wishing he were someplace else. Will, too, had his eyes fixed on Bob, who was hurt and embarrassed in front of his friend. He was also furious with Katherine. Ironically, he also admired her for her courage and directness. And one of Bob's traits that Katherine was coming to admire was his ability to soften any situation with a gentle voice or clown's juggle. This was his finest performance.

"Well, partner," Bob said slowly. He breathed deeply and crossed his legs, reached over, picked up his freshly oiled rifle, and retrieved his hat from the adjoining chair, fingering the brim and mounting it properly upon his head. He looked up at Katherine and then to Will. "I guess you know if her reputation gets out in the Territory," Bob said, throwing a half-hearted hand motion toward her. "There ain't a bandit out there stupid enough to take a shot at you. Why, the fear of Katherine huntin' 'em down with revenge in her eye and a sawbones' hatchet in her hands, ready to cut their *manlys* off and feed 'em to the nearest mangy coyote would put the fear of Godamighty into 'em. Hell, it would be like something out of a child's nightmare. Damn, that's for certain." He slapped one knee in a comic gesture, stood up and smiled at Katherine. "I sure feel like *I'm* missin' a few *manlys* this morning." He tipped his hat to Katherine, reached for her hand, and kissed it gently. Then, still holding her hand, he whispered into her ear. "Darlin', we both love him. And because of that, I guess, of sorts, I love you, too." He kissed her gently on the cheek, tipped his hat at them both and backed out of the room, slowly, with his rifle over his shoulder, hand on his gun—half out of his holster—looking intently at Katherine with a mock snarl.

She smiled with tears in her eyes. *She guessed she loved him too, of sorts.*

Will said nothing. He sure hoped that the rest of the day would be uneventful.

Chapter 14

▼

4:00 p.m., December 9, 1875
Fort Smith, Arkansas

Toward late afternoon, filled with beautiful, loving, and tender moments with Katherine, Will Tyler walked back into the barracks. He was ready for Bob.

"All right, damnit, let's have it," he said.

Bob just looked at him. "Have what, partner?" he asked with a perplexed look.

"You know what I mean. Let's get it over with so I can relax and enjoy the rest of the day and look forward to another night with Katherine."

"Why, I have no idea what you're talking about," Bob said.

Will looked around the room. His abrupt and cocky entrance suddenly embarrassed him.

No one knew what he was talking about, except Bob, and he was damned sure not going to play into this. He held the upper hand and had it over his pal and enjoyed it—but he did need to talk to him and soon. But now it had to wait. As far as Will Tyler was concerned, Bob Johnson had forgotten the incident as soon as he left the restaurant. At least, that is what he wanted Will to begin to think. It gave Bob a peculiar sort of pleasure, in a friendly way, of course. The Texan truly did admire and respect Katherine, and he surmised that the whisper into her ear, really, was not all just his usual way. Bob guessed that he meant it.

"Oh, never mind," Will said, taking off his coat, tie and stuffy, wool vest. He threw off those new boots that had hurt his feet all day and slowly, with comfort and joy, slipped on his scarred and trail-worn boots.

"Feels better, huh?" John Law asked, sitting with Bob, Colbert and Valentine Morgan around the poker table that centered the room. Will was so concerned about the confrontation with Bob Johnson that he had not even noticed the poker game in progress with his friends and his grandfather.

"Yeah, John Law, it surely does," he replied.

"Come on over and join in," Valentine said with a smile. "You're the richest one in the room. We definitely need some new money here."

Will Tyler rarely played poker or gambled in any way. Not that he wasn't capable of holding his own in the game, but the whole process never intrigued him to the point that he would invest hours of time, not to mention the money in the enterprise.

Two Snakes also never saw the benefit in the time spent chasing something white men called *luck*. It was a mystery to him. He just continued to lounge in his bunk, reading a book some eastern fellow had written on spiritual beliefs and magic concoctions of the Plains Indians. He looked up, nodded to Will and quickly returned to the book, which he had labeled in his mind: horse dung. The writer knew nothing about Indians.

"Okay, why not," Will said. "I'll join in for a few hands, it's still early." He walked over to his trunk beside his bunk and retrieved a small sack of silver. "What's the game and what's the limit?" he asked, as he sat down in the empty chair by John Law.

"Why, it's no limit, of course, and the game is seven card with nothing wild but the dealer," Bob Johnson said with a wide smile. It was a rare event to get Will in a card game, and a definite delight. He was relishing the moment. He fanned the table-worn cards in his hand with an exuberant flurry. Everyone smiled.

"Ante up, boys, five-dollars," Bob said, looking at Will with a grin, half hoping to elicit a moan at least, or even a fold out of Will before the first card was dealt.

"Five-dollar ante?" grumbled Colbert. "We ain't started but a dollar all afternoon."

"Dealer's choice," Bob said, glancing around the table. "In or out?"

All five players threw silver dollars and five-dollar gold pieces on the table. There was a definite change in the mood.

"Awright, boys, here we go, and be prepared to lose your shirts." Bob dealt two cards down all around and then followed with the first up-card.

John Law, first to his left, got an eight of hearts up; Will, a three of diamonds; Colbert, a jack of spades; Valentine Morgan drew a queen of hearts, and Bob dealt himself a deuce of spades. Everyone peered at their hole cards and looked around the table, suspiciously.

"Val, you're high with the lady. Whatta you say?" Bob asked.

Morgan looked around the table. It looked calm enough. No high card, except his—and it was a good start on a queen high straight. "I'll make it five," he said, tossing in a five-dollar gold piece that twirled around and fell into the pile.

"Hmm," Bob said with a cautious glance. "What are you so proud of here at the start with a five-dollar gold piece?" He reached into his stack and pulled out a similar coin, looked around, and then picked up two twenty-dollar double eagles. "I'm gonna send the store clerks home early. Your five and forty more." His two kings in the hole made him feel lucky and confident.

John Law, holding two sixes to go with the nondescript eight on his first up-card, thought this was damned ridiculous, but he called with forty five dollars. Will Tyler's ace of clubs and ace of spades in the hole made him get back up and go to his trunk again, carrying another sack. This time, full of gold pieces. He had the full attention of everyone in the room. Will Tyler was no poker player. Was he crazy?

He fumbled in the leather pouch, peering into it as he held it close to his chest. He pulled out three double eagles. "Fifteen more."

Colbert, holding a pair of jacks, could not believe the last two minutes of play. Hell, he hadn't put more than twenty-dollars in any previous series in the last two hours, and here it was sixty dollars to see if he believed in his pair in the hole. Not to be the first store clerk to go, he called—reluctantly.

"Damn," Bob said. "The price of poker sure went up here on the Arkansas this afternoon." The next deal around gave John Law another eight—now two pair; Will Tyler a third ace, matching the two in the hole; Colbert a ten of hearts—no help; Valentine a ten of diamonds—his straight was looking good; and Bob gave himself, naturally as things would go, a third king to match the two in the hole.

"Pair of eights, John Law," Bob said, stunned by the size of the pot so early.

"I'm going to settle things down. "One-dollar," the marshal said.

Everyone was relieved. Those who were holding good, and happy not to tip their hands any more than they had to, called the dollar bet. No raises. No one spoke. But every player looked at every other player around the table. Even Two Snakes, who never played but knew the game, had come over to see what all the commotion was about. The noise of all that clinking silver and gold had removed his attention from that book of lies he had been absorbed in.

The third, up-card, came around and gave no help to John Law's two pair; no help to Will Tyler's trip bullets; a nine of spades gave Colbert two pair, nines and sixes; and, an eight of clubs gave Morgan his queen-high straight. Bob Johnson drew his fourth *cowboy*, four kings! He could hardly hold his water. In fact, if it could have been anywhere in the realm of possibilities, he would have gone to the outhouse.

"Let's just see," Bob said as calmly as he could, looking around the table. "Looks like my two cowboys are high. Wouldn't you know? And from the looks of this table, I don't see a damned thing that y'all were so proud of to get that sixty-dollar scrape goin' a while ago."

"Shut up, Bob," Valentine said, confident of his straight. "Bet!"

"I'll just oblige," Bob said, raising his eyebrows at the outburst. "One hundred American, United States, gold, Yankee dollars." He threw the gold on the table. He dug into his front pocket and brought out a tattered leather wallet. "And a genuine Jefferson Davis twenty-dollar Confederate green back," he said with a smile, tossing the old paper bill to the table. He squinted at Morgan. Everyone looked at the old twenty-dollar note, creased from a dozen years of fold in that old wallet. Laughter broke out around the table. Even Morgan was amused.

"Well...I don't have anything that worthless, except, of course, something from the outhouse—which I don't have the particular possession of right now—so, I'll see when the bet comes around if I can conjure one up to match that old Jeff Davis."

John Law, next in line to call or fold, looked at the stack of coins and paper money in his vest pocket. *Two pair,* he thought. *That damned Texan has at least three of a kind. But I'm not going to give him the pleasure of an easy pull of the pot.* "Here's five, twenty-dollar, United States notes. I don't have anything to say about that Jefferson note, but to pick the son of a bitch up before I light my cigar with it," he said, pulling out one of his fine, dollar cigars.

Bob quickly pulled back his prized Confederate note that he used in many poker games to stir a ruckus. He did not relish seeing it go up in smoke against some Kentucky tobacco. He looked to Will. "Okay, Will, it's time to separate the men from the boys. That's a hundred to you."

"What's the limit again?"

"Now, Will, you know damned well it's no limit. But you sure better get out before you get your butt burned. Hell boy, you ain't got but a three, an ace and a seven showing. I ain't seen a more-nothing-hand in all my poker-playin' days."

Will looked at his bag of gold coins. He counted out sixty-five dollars, looked into his silver dollar bag, and found another seven.

"Will, perhaps you ought to listen to this Texan, this time. Son, that hundred dollars, why, that's fifty bandits to bring in."

"Thanks anyway, John Law, for your concern, but you taught me to play, remember."

Tyler looked at Morgan who sported a fine silver and gold writing pen. His pride and joy. He had affixed his named to many an outlaw's long prison term, and for a few a trip to the gallows, with that pen.

"Val, let me borrow your pen," Will said.

Will reached into his back pocket and drew out some fine linen paper pages that Katherine had given to him so he could write her when he was away on posse duty for an extended time. It had a sweet fragrance of lilac.

"Oh Lordy, don't that smell sweet," Bob said. "But, no promise notes in my deal."

"Okay, then, I'll just make it a bank draft on the Fort Smith National Bank," Will said with a slight air of irritation. "You would agree that I have sufficient funds to cover this?"

"Hell, Will, I was just rilin' you. I'll take your promise note, or your boots, or your horse, hell, even your girl. Hell, I trust you."

"Why don't we keep this all legal and on top of the table. It might get expensive and I wouldn't want any hard feelings," Will said.

Bob didn't know what to think. *Hell, he had four kings.* He hated to take the boy's money, but a cocky attitude sure deserved a proper response.

John Law, however, knew his grandson. He grinned. *That boy has aces wired,* he thought. *Good for him.* He was just sorry it had cost him a hundred dollars before he figured it out.

"Okay, Mr. *Vanderbilt*, what's your play?" Bob was tiring of the way things were going and was anxious to show his four kings and see the shocked faces around the room.

Will tossed the draft on his account into the pile. "I'll pony up to that—and more. There's your hundred and five hundred to boot."

"Jesus," Colbert said. "I thought this was a friendly game. I ain't never been in a game where it was six hundred damned dollars to me. I assure you, boys, I'm out."

Bob picked up the note and looked it over. "Damned if it ain't," he said. He was elated. He was going to take this Arkansas cotton farmer for a ride. *Yee-Ha!*

"Well, Val?" Bob asked, as he leaned over the table with all the confidence of a man toting a Colt .45 at a knife fight. "What do you think about all this high-stakes poker? Don't it just get your pickle a stretchin'?" *It goads me fiercely to talk to you, much more so, smile at you. Sonofabitch!*

Valentine Morgan was a lot of things. Valued deputy, friend of many, lauded citizen and secret, bloodthirsty outlaw-killer, but he was not a fool. But both of these fools were just plain stupid, as he saw it. And he had a queen-high straight.

"Hand me back my pen and one of those fine sheets of paper that, obviously, Dr. O'Reilly has given to you," he said to Will. In order, Morgan tossed a hand-written bank draft for six hundred dollars into the middle of the table.

Two Snakes, who had been watching with interest, was becoming increasingly confused by the actions of the white men. Already there was enough money on that table to feed a good-sized village for a year, and they joked and talked as if it were a fine day's play. He shook his head and tried to analyze each man's expressions. If he were to bet, which he never did, he would do so on Will Tyler. He knew him. Colbert was the sure winner; he had dropped out of this madness.

"*Damn!*" Bob said. "Ain't this a stroke of luck? I ain't gonna have to get outta that bunk for a year after I scrape this pot. You boys have paid for me to have a long vacation."

"Valentine repeated his earlier pronouncement. "Shut up, Bob, and bet or fold."

"May I borrow your pen?" he asked, sporting a wide grin under his red mustache. "And Will, may I also bother you for a sheet of sweet Katherine's paper?"

His intention, as he scribbled his bank draft, was to get Will riled and off balance. "Now, wouldn't that sweet lady of yours just be thrilled as to how you're usin' her gift of this fine writing paper? My God," he said, holding it to his nose. "There ain't a thing at Miss Emma's that smells this good."

"Oh, I guess she can buy a wagon load of this paper with the money I'm going to take off of you tonight," Will said.

Bob ceremoniously put the note for five hundred dollars into the middle of the pot. "I call your raise," he said. "John Law?"

"Not me boys, Will is right. I did teach him to play cards, and if he bets six hundred dollars, I'm out."

Okay boys, last card up," Bob said as he dealt around the table. It was hard to contain his glee. This would be a story that he could tell for a hundred years.

Will Tyler caught a seven of hearts and now had a full house. He liked it more and more.

Valentine was dealt a seven of clubs, and now had a six-card straight. Not that it mattered. Just an extra nail in their coffin.

Bob Johnson did not even look as he dealt himself a five of clubs. Valentine noticed that. *Did not even look.*

"Now, let's see who's high and gets the pleasure of leadin' off this round of blood-lettin'," Bob said. "Will, you got a pair of sevens showing; Val, you got a straight working. Damn, better watch that, and I…yeah, I'm still high with a pair of cowboys."

He didn't even look at that last card until now, thought Morgan again.

"Gimme another piece of that paper, Will."

Will Tyler handed a sheet of Katherine's paper to Bob. The Texan tore it into three strips. He looked up at the table full of eyes watching him rip the paper. "I might need another bank draft or two before this carnage is over. I hate to bother Will for another piece."

He placed another note for one thousand dollars in the pot. "Okay boys, if you can count, that is equal to fifty double eagles." *Damn, he could sure use that outhouse now. No way in hell, though.*

Will looked at Bob with a stern gaze. He reached over and took one of the smaller scraps of paper, and looked for the pen. They had lost place of it. Morgan found it in the pile of paper, gold and silver, and handed it to Will Tyler. A dozen of the deputies in the room had now gathered around the table.

Colbert leaned back in his chair. "I've witnessed games from the refined, polished halls of Boston's finest staterooms to the dingiest shithouse saloons in El Paso, and I have never seen a game like this," he said with an air of authority.

John Law was silent. Grinning, but silent as Will Tyler showed him his hand.

Colbert bounded over for a free glance at the duel of Arkansas and Texas. He pressed his hand to his burly beard. "My God," he said. "I should have stayed in."

"No goddamn showboatin', Colbert. Just keep your mouth shut if you ain't gonna put no money with it," Bob Johnson said, beginning to worry. Some. *Hell, he had four cowboys. That damned cotton farmer only had a pair of sevens showing. No way in hell.*

Will finished his note and dropped it into the pot. "Your thousand and four thousand more."

The deafening silence in the room, filled with twenty men and twice as many cubic feet of cigar smoke, was suddenly and rudely interrupted by a knock on the door.

"Hold on boys, it might be the law!" John Law said. "You know that gambling is frowned on in this town. Judge Parker would certainly be interested in these goings-on."

Every badge in the room broke into a loud laugh. It was a welcome break in the tension.

"See who it is, Jesse," Bob said to Deputy Allen. "It might be some fresh money, angling to get its way into my pocket." They laughed again, but Bob Johnson was looking at the five thousand dollar note with Will Tyler's signature on the table. He knew that he could not cover it. He began to ponder the options.

The sweet voice was unmistakable as Jesse opened the door.

"Hello Deputy Allen. May I speak to Will Tyler for a moment?"

Katherine couldn't stay away from her beloved, even for a few hours. She had thought, since their parting a few hours ago, over and over for some reason, trite and contrived or not, to see him again. She had plans, big plans, for their upcoming evening together, and she just wanted to see him again. To give her courage she needed. Her heart was ready. Her passion was ready. This night was to be the most important of her life. Dark secrets and hopes dreamed of were in the offing. Her mission was set. She was dampened a bit, however, after peering in the room and seeing the rowdy action, cigar smoke, and worst of all, Will Tyler in the middle of it.

"I need to ask him a question about tonight," she said politely, and apprehensively, as she walked in. This was no place to shore up her courage for her quest later in the evening. In any event, she pulled up her courage and walked in as if she owned the place.

The room parted as effectively as if Moses himself had raised his Red Sea staff over the group. Hats leapt off heads and were being held in nervous hands from wall to wall. The sound of the foot-shuffling was deafening. The only smart one in the group, Two Snakes, quietly moved back to his bunk and reclined with his eyes closed. This was a story he could tell for a hundred years. The most amazing monument to white men's stupidity he could have ever imagined. The day a squaw put twenty men on their knees.

"Oh, Gawd," Bob said. "Cross your dern legs, boys. Somebody is about to lose some of his *manlys*."

Katherine ignored his comment. She had heard it before, at breakfast this morning. She did not think it humorous then either. She was in no mood. She wanted to see her *quest*. Alone.

"Not now, Katherine," Will said politely. He was embarrassed. It was becoming a common event. If he did not love her so much and take a peculiar pride in her over-protective attitude, he would have talked to her about it by now. Maybe. "We are in a very uncertain situation here and I really need all my wits about me." Then he saw the hurt look on her face. "Your beauty would certainly distract me to the point of a dangerous mistake," he quickly added.

She saw the pile of money and bank drafts on the table and quickly eyed the one for five thousand dollars. She was horrified. She knew that Will had five or six thousand dollars in the bank, thanks to his transfer from the St. Louis bank, but this amounted to most all of it on one scrap of paper. And, it was *her* paper. The gift she had given to Will!

Her blue eyes shown through like shards of ice, as she picked up the note and examined it. There was no lack of oxygen in that room—even with the tobacco smoke—no one was breathing. She looked, not at Will, but at Bob.

"Now, Katherine, he's a big boy. Don't look at me."

"Don't you 'now Katherine' me, Bob Johnson," she said, her eyes flashing even more. "If you cheat him out of his money, you will have to worry about your *manlys*, for damned sure. And I'll put them in alcohol and display them all over this Territory. In a pickle jar! The ones small enough for midget cucumbers!"

"Cheat!" He was oblivious to the expressions on his manhood, but the one about unfair poker dealings was a serious slap to him.

"Now, Katherine, here, look at my hand," Will said, as he drew her close to his side. She saw the full house, aces over, and looked at Bob's up-cards showing a pair of kings. She smiled at Bob and promptly stuck her tongue full out at him. For the third—and most welcome—time, the room broke out in loud laughter.

"Now, I'm gettin' real irritated with everybody seein' your hand Will, and making such spurious remarks about my inability to compete with it. I think it's time to show my hand to someone." He looked around the room then realized that Valentine still had to call the five thousand dollars. "Val, are you gonna call this fool's raise? That's five thousand Yankee dollars to you."

Morgan looked at his six-card straight. He was not going to be a laughing stock, no matter how much was in the pot. He felt the better plan was to fold and just hide his hand in case it was somehow the winner. He reached over, gathered John Law and Colbert's discards, and shuffled his into the stack. "Hell, no, I am going to let both *you* fools settle this."

"Great!" Bob said. "One smart man in the room. Here, look at my hand." Bob moved to his right and closely concealed his hole cards for Valentine to see. He looked up at Morgan and smiled at the vision of the four kings. Every neck from the surrounding crowd strained to get a look. Johnson quickly slapped them down on the table. "Not on your damned life," he said to the deputies stretching to see. "This is for me and my partner's eyes only."

"Partner?" Morgan queried.

"Yeah, Val. I'm afraid that Will has caught me a bit short. About four thousand short. How's about coming in with me and I'll split the pot with you? Besides, I can use your advice and counsel on these difficult cards coming," he said with a sly glance at Valentine. Bob hurt viscerally during that conversation with Valentine Morgan. He hated every syllable of it. After all, he knew all about Valentine Morgan and Belle Reed! But he had a plan. He hoped that Will just did not get hurt. *I dunno enough yet. But when I do, I'll kill you*, he thought, smiling at Morgan.

Morgan looked at Bob Johnson and then at the pot. He could more than double his money in just a few seconds of play. *Why not?* Even if he hated the Texan and every breath he took.

"Dr. O'Reilly, if you would not be offended any more than you so obviously have been already by these vile scribblings on your fine letter paper, with your permission, may I use one of these last scraps that Mr. Johnson has rent from one of those sheets?" He was diplomatic, genuine and offered concern for her feelings. Will Tyler hated that. *Goddamn*. He should have never pulled that paper from his back pocket.

"I would be honored, Mr. Morgan, for you to use that piece of linen paper that I brought all the way from Boston. You may enter any amount you wish. It will be Mr. Tyler's anyway in just a moment," she said with a cocky smile.

"Goddamn, what a game," Bob said. "I wish my daddy and granddaddy LeBeaux was here to see this. It is a genuine piece of history. And, those two gentlemen of poker-finery have never exceeded this!"

Colbert could stand no more. "Marshal, I know that there is no drinking allowed in the barracks, but I have just got to have a whisky or I'll fall dead away from lack of courage to see this foray to its end."

"Where's your bottle?" John Law asked.

Before the marshal could look around, Colbert had returned from his trunk with an uncorked bottle of Tennessee mash.

"Now that's whisky good enough to break my rules with," John Law said as he took the bottle and downed a full swig. Colbert, impatient, grabbed the bottle and downed three fingers worth himself. The bottle made the rounds of the room, passing happily from deputy to deputy. This was more by-God exciting than the *Hanging of the Six* just months ago.

Morgan finished his bank draft and showed it to Bob.

"*Gawd*damn!" exclaimed Bob. "You are a for-sure committed partner." The Texan, gently and with great ceremony, laid the note on the ever-expanding pile. "Mr. Tyler, there's your four thousand, and my partner and I would like to politely raise you another five thousand." He paused. "There's a nine-thousand-dollar note, right there, by God!" he exclaimed. His dancing around, however, was not all from the glee of the four kings. He could stand it no more. "I'll tell you what. I'll give you a minute to compose yourself and I will step out back so my gleeful jumping won't distract you. John Law can watch the deck and my partner here can guard my hole cards. Excuse me, *our* hole cards," he said, looking at Morgan. Bob ran for the back door. Again, the room erupted with laughter. All knew that the next sound they would hear would be the outhouse door slam shut. *Whack*! A dog howled at the noise. The room once more sounded like a clown's convention at a circus headquarters. The Tennessee whisky bottle had been emptied and replaced by another that was also being passed around the room.

As Bob Johnson hopped back into the room from the outhouse, Will Tyler was looking at the last raise on the table. *What did that damned Texan have in the hole? Speaking of in the hole, that last draft cleaned him out.*

"Let me eye-ball this. That's about five thousand to you to call," Bob said.

Will Tyler looked at John Law. The old marshal just shook his head. Saying, in essence, *boy, you're in it now. You've been chased up another tree, this time by a Texas bear.* He had the money to come to his grandson's rescue, but it began to gnaw on him about that Texan's hole cards. Valentine Morgan was no fool. *It must be four kings in that hand*, he thought. Every heart in the room was beating in unison and every man's full attention was on Will as he looked into space. Suddenly, Katherine leaned over and whispered into his ear. She then kissed his ear and then his cheek, and then full on the mouth. She was having fun. Strangely so. The gravity of the events to come later that evening was suppressed in her thoughts. There would be time enough for that reckoning.

"Where's that pen, please?" she asked, as ladylike as she could. Then she looked at Bob Johnson. "Now, where is that…" she paused sharply as if swallowing the expletive, but everyone knew it was there. She quickly finished. "Bottle?"

Hats flew in the air and the hollering could be heard as far as the courthouse. In fact, it had been noticed. Judge Parker walked into the crowd from the unattended door. His knock had not been heard. How could it have been?

He approached the center of the attraction just as Katherine took a swig from the bottle and grimaced, but held it down.

"Dr. O'Reilly," he said. "I know there must be quite a story here, but for the life of me, I can't fathom its genesis, or, its middle, or, most certainly its end. Perhaps someone can catch me up on the proceedings. I hope it's nothing I will have to hear from the bench. I see nothing but friends here, and that would be a shame."

Silence and half-concealed smirks filled the room. So many cookie jars and so many hands.

"Now Isaac," John Law said, finally. "There is nothing illegal here at all. The only crime is that one of the boys—good friends at that—is about to be separated from a small fortune, along with promissory notes from half the good citizens of this town." He gave the judge a retelling of the events, hand by hand. There were a dozen versions along the dissertation offered by as many witnesses and often in loud unison. Colbert was the referee. But the two bottles of Tennessee mash made it difficult to discern the straight of it. After several minutes of the verbal assault, the judge, who by livelihood, received and gave verbal assaults each day, finally had enough. "I think I have the picture." He walked over to the edge of the table. "Now, as I see it, Mr. Johnson along with his cohort, Mr. Morgan, have set a five-thousand-dollar raise on the table." He looked at Katherine. "Now, Dr. O'Reilly is about to cover that bet with her personal draft. Assuming she can write without the aid of both hands," he said as he took the bottle from her. "And, then, if there is not a further raise, and call, and re-raise, and so on, *ad infinitum*, we will proceed to the dealing of the last card, at which we begin again the vicious cycle of raise, and bumps involving more drafts from various accounts in our good bank." He paused. "Let me raise a point at this juncture. Let everyone make very sure that there are sufficient funds in the accounts I see attested to upon this table. Fraudulent overdrafts will not be tolerated and swiftly adjudicated." He paused again, and smiled slightly, in poker terms, giving his hand away. "In summation, let us proceed with Dr. O'Reilly's decision to commence the omega of this august proceeding, and I hereby sentence the two hands dealt, at the summation, to be framed and hung in this barracks as long as it stands, with proper words of description of this deed!" He raised the bottle. "And, I drink to that!"

No one could remember a louder roar by twenty or so individuals, on any other occasion in Fort Smith or the entire Territory, for that matter, as happened the night Judge Isaac C. Parker, Honorable Magistrate of the United States Court of Western District of Arkansas, raised a bottle of Tennessee Mash and took a drink at the infamous Tyler-Johnson poker shootout at the U.S. Deputy Marshal's Barracks, December 9, 1875.

It was almost ten minutes before the crowd settled down and Katherine placed her bank draft in the pile. "There is your five thousand dollars, we call," she said.

Colbert graciously asked the judge to take his seat at the table so he could witness that last card, up close. The judge happily accepted. It was a little-known fact outside of Washington, but as a Congressman from Missouri, Isaac Parker had acquired quite a skill as a poker player and had taken many of his fellow legislators for a ride with his quick, analytical mind and ability to display a stone-cold poker face. He loved the game. Admittedly, this game was a bit lower class, but none in Washington, or anywhere else held this much excitement.

"Awright by God," Bob said. Then he froze. "I apologize, Judge, excuse my language."

"Oh, that's of no problem that I see, Deputy Johnson. I assure you that you can call on the Almighty as much as you wish at this particular event. But it will be all in vain—you won't find him here, or near here, I'm afraid."

Bob Johnson dealt the seventh card down in seven-card-stud poker. He did not look. There was no need; he was pat with four *cowboys*! He could not improve. Will Tyler was showing a pair of sevens and an ace and a three. All of different suits. *It is impossible for me to lose*, thought the Texan.

Will Tyler looked at Katherine and motioned for her to look at the last hole card just dealt. He had carried throughout the game an ace of clubs and an ace of spades in the hole. It made a full house with the ace of hearts and the two sevens dealt up.

Katherine looked and laid the card back down. Will did not look.

"If you aren't going to look at your last card, Bob, neither am I," Will said.

"I don't have to, my friend," Bob replied. "I don't need it." He took the card and placed it in the discard pile.

"Is that legal?" Will asked.

"Nothing in the rules states that a man has to use his last card, if he is fool enough to throw it away," the judge said.

"Why don't you do the same Will, and make it real interesting?" Bob asked.

Katherine squeezed Will's shoulder hard, her nails cutting into his skin.

Will did not move. But still he felt the pain, and the message to leave his card where it was.

"I'll just keep the card here where it belongs, but I promise I won't look at it unless you have me beat and I have to see if I have any chance." He goaded Bob. "I'll tell you straight, partner, out of our deep and abiding friendship that I hope will continue past this night, you're gonna have to beat a full house, at least!"

Bob bluffed a look of surprise. So did his money partner, Valentine Morgan. "No way you have a full house, you're bluffing! But I will tell you straight my friend, and I hold your sentiments about our friendship to be just as heart-felt and honest, you're gonna have to beat three kings, at least!"

"So," Will said. "You're still high with the two kings. What's your move?" Before Bob could answer, Will Tyler felt a twinge of remorse somehow about the predicament that he found himself in with his new and good friend he had found on the Mississippi River bank just short months ago. Two Snakes had joined Will at his side and, maybe mystically, magically, or with some other Indian spiritual concoction, Will had, on many occasions, felt the same mind with his Indian brother. He looked at Two Snakes before he spoke. The Indian nodded in bond with him.

"I'll tell you what, Bob. Let's both just slide our cards into that discard pile and we will split the pot. We can pay our backers off and pocket a few hundred apiece from the store clerks that abandoned this nightmare earlier."

Bob Johnson looked at Will. Deep into his eyes. He felt a sense of relief. *That, by God, may be the way out*—the way to salvage a friendship that had gone too far to be wrecked in a damned poker game. After all, his contrived partnership with that son of a bitch Morgan was enough to think about. Being at odds with Will was just too much complication.

No one had ever seen anything like this. Judge Parker was spellbound. Colbert searched his vast intellect for a story from literature, classical or contemporary or anywhere in between, that had a plot of irony and jeopardy like this scene. He could find none in his memory. He doubted if there ever was one so written.

"Split it, huh?" Bob inquired with one eye closed and the other squinting, half closed. "And we never know how it would have turned out." Bob continued to look straight at Will. Then he turned his gaze to Katherine, Judge Parker, John Law, Colbert and a half a dozen others, looking for some guidance. Some sign to take Will's offer. He wanted to do just that.

"Yeah," Will said, "I think that is a fine way to end this little game. Remember, two hours ago, I said that I was only going to play a hand or two. Damn, Bob, looks like *one* hand will do it for me."

"Let's stop this horseshit!" exclaimed Valentine Morgan. It was so out of character for him that both John Law and Judge Parker jumped. In fact, the whole room was startled and silent. Morgan's facade was beginning to crumble. "I'm a goddamn partner in this, Johnson. In fact, I am the primary money in your hand, and I'll decide whether we bet, raise, fold or enter into some ignorant agreement to 'split the pot'," he emphasized in a distorted, childlike voice. "I'll be goddamn if we split it with that bastard!"

Bob Johnson stood and reached for his pistol. To his surprise, he was not wearing it. The Colt that he depended on for his very life was on his bed half a room away. He continued anyway. "Like hell you will. I'll decide, by God, what is done here."

Morgan was wearing his Walker Colt. The urge to put a .45 bullet through each of this damned Texan's eyes was almost overwhelming. Something pulled him back from that dark place. The strong arm of Will Tyler had helped. He had instantly reached over, grabbed Morgan's shooting arm, and held it down firmly.

Judge Parker slammed the table hard with his walking cane. "That is enough," he shouted at the top of his voice. It was that tone of authority, heard hundreds of time in court, which grabbed everyone's attention. It worked here, at a five-dollar ante poker game gone wrong.

Parker was stunned at Morgan's attitude and actions. Perhaps it was the prospect of the tens of thousands of dollars at stake on the table. Perhaps it was as simple as aggravation and stress. Perhaps it was something more. Parker did not know, but this was not the place to sort out things of that weight. This situation needed a simple and judicial ending.

"Now, what exactly is your relationship to Deputy Johnson's hand?" Parker questioned Morgan.

"Early in the hand, I agreed to back him with money to cover his bets and raises, and at this point I am already nine thousand dollars into this game, and that is three times or more what this dumb son of a bitch has risked." He paused, as Bob Johnson rose again from his chair, his eyes blood red with rage. Morgan, apologetically, continued. "I am sorry Your Honor...."

Parker interrupted him in mid-sentence. Don't 'Your Honor' me in this sordid place. It is not my courtroom, but I do expect some decorum and decency. Do you understand?"

"Yes, Judge. Again, I apologize for my language, but I am just looking after my investment and bond of verbal partnership and request for counsel and advice on the play of this hand. My investment outweighs his, and therefore, I am entitled to make the decision. Yea or Nay?"

"Sound argument, Deputy Morgan," the judge responded. "And you, Deputy Johnson, what say you?"

"I say you all can go to hell as far as I am concerned. This is my hand, good or bad, stupid or smart. I'll make the move." He was shaking with anger. He looked at Will, knowing there could be no support, yet, in some ironic twist of fate, as he looked to the adversary for assistance. What kind of assistance he did not know. It was amazing and confusing how things had changed in just a few minutes since the judge had arrived and toasted the final card with good humor.

"That will be enough, Deputy. I think I have your viewpoint well in hand." The judge told everyone to sit, whether in a chair, on the floor, on a bunk, but sit.

He looked at Johnson and Morgan. Then he turned his gaze to Will Tyler. He looked into the face of John Law, who had been noticeably quiet during the exchange. The judge surmised that he, too, was taken aback by Morgan's actions. "Unfortunately, Deputy Johnson, I'm afraid that Deputy Morgan has a point.

His investment is greater than yours and you did ask for counsel and advice on the play of this hand. Therefore, by the weight of his monetary investment, I'm afraid that he has the last say in judgment of play." He tapped his cane three times on the wood floor. "That's my ruling. Let's get this thing over with. It's turning out to be real ugly."

Katherine asked Will to step to the corner with her. "Excuse me a moment, Judge, and Bob. I need to confer with *my* partner," Will said politely.

"Will, let's take that bastard for all he has," Katherine said as she held both of his hands.

"I could never do that to him. I promise after you get to know him better, you'll see him like I do. There is something...something I can't put my finger on it. Something that...." She interrupted him with a gentle squeeze to the hands, reached up, and kissed him on the cheek—what cheek that wasn't covered by that hard, prickly beard. *Those whiskers were going to go, and go soon*, she had decided. She just needed to let *him* know about it.

"No, darling. I'm not talking about Bob. I know in my heart that Bob will somehow be a very big and important part of our lives, and I am trying very hard to accept him and to love him like you do. I am talking about Morgan. I hate him. He is evil. I know it. I can feel it. We will give Bob back what ever he loses. And John Law and Colbert. Just Morgan will be hurt."

"Bob will never take anything back, he just wouldn't. I wouldn't in his place," he said, looking at Bob sitting silently at the table, shoulders slumped, clasping his hands tightly together.

"We will make him. *I* will make him," she said forcefully, with a friendly sternness. That was one of her endearing qualities that drew him to her. He liked that friendly sternness. It was a mirror of his character. That quality likewise attracted her to him. She saw the compatibility. But, she had thought often in past days, *what will happen if we come to an impasse? That will be a real tug-of-war.*

She continued to persuade Will to take the opportunity to help everyone, including Bob. "We can up the stakes so high that it will either unmask that bastard or unearth some of the illegal fortune he has amassed over the years."

"Katherine, where do you get that? I've never heard a word against Valentine," Will said, confused.

"You are too close. You can't see the tree for the forest. I've heard gossip ever since I've been here and I have a good sense of character when I meet someone and judge him by his actions and words. I got you, didn't I?" she asked, smiling and hugging him firmly. "Just follow my lead. Besides, it's my money I'm going to invest, and Judge Parker has already ruled that the one with the most invested gives the orders. So, do as I say, my man. My *dear* man," she said with her emotions welling up. The event following the game still had to come about. Everything depended on *that* outcome.

They needed to get back to the game. The whole room had turned its attention to their little corner. "Oh, I forgot to mention," she whispered in his ear. "You can't loose. It's an impossibility."

"You mean...."

"Yes!"

Will's eyes were wide with astonishment. That is why she dug those beautiful—but ever so sharp—fingernails into his shoulder.

"We are ready, Judge," Katherine said.

The crowd reassembled around the table as Will and Katherine took their seats.

"I still would like to offer to you, Bob, that we just leave the cards here where they sit and split the pot," Will said, pleading. She dug her nails into his shoulder again. This time harder.

"You can't beat us. You stupid bastard. When are you going to get that through your ignorant—goddamn—Mississippi-Delta—cotton-farming skull?" Morgan asked, his eyes blazing.

Katherine patted Will softly on his now bruised shoulder, as if to say, *see, I told you so*.

John Law immediately started to rise at Morgan's outburst, but Judge Parker laid a firm hand on his arm and shook his head.

"Let's see how this plays out, John. We may find a wealth of information here. I have a feeling I can't quite put together, but it is disturbing."

"I know," the marshal whispered to Parker. "I have the same feeling. And you're right, it is disturbing, very disturbing. But, if he says one more unkind word against Will, I'll break his neck."

"Now, John. Patience. Young Tyler can take care of himself, and if not then I'd wager that Dr. O'Reilly on his side is worth a whole troop of deputies."

Will was looking—one more time—to help Bob, even at the expense of another attack by Katherine's nails. "So, that's your last word, Bob?"

"I'm hogtied, Amigo. Looks like I put in with the wrong side here. Just bad luck. Bad luck—with the winning hand, of course." Even in this dire situation, he could not help himself. He had to brag on the *cowboys*.

"Let's get it done," Morgan said. "We are high with two kings showing. I'm going to open the bet at ten thousand dollars."

He reached for his note in the pile that he had written for nine thousand dollars. "Here, Judge, I want you to witness this and sign as such on the back. I am changing the 9,000 to 19,000. And the *nine to nineteen*. One digit and four letters are worth ten thousand dollars," he said with a smirk. Suddenly, his head jerked to the side twice. Then three times. It seems as though he could not control it. He turned away for a moment, and then turned back to the group. "Damn," he said to the group. "It's a muscle spasm I've had for some time."

Katherine noticed it, also. It looked to be more than a simple spasm. There was more to it. She could feel it professionally *and* personally.

"So, Tyler, that is ten thousand dollars for our bet. Can you cover that or do you fold? Go ahead, get your girlfriend there to give you a little spending money. Call me, or better still call me and raise me." He wished immediately that he had stopped before it was too late. Morgan's mind began to reel. After all, he was limited to immediate funds he could put his hands on and explain. That bet of nearly twenty thousand dollars was close to the limit he could cover and not raise the judge's suspicions. It might be at that point now, already. Then, also, how much money did that bitch have? Would she raise, just to goad him? But he had the winning hand! He laughed inside. Humiliating these dumb sonsabitches and making a bucket load of money at the same time.

Before he realized it, during his mental journey he had put on quite a head-twitching demonstration. Everyone had been watching in wonder. In shock. In pity. He quickly recovered. "Bad neck muscles." Bob looked at him and shook his head in a mocking fashion. It infuriated Morgan. He found it difficult to breathe. With all his strength, he was trying to control his spasms. He had hidden a problem from everyone for ten years. A doctor in St. Louis had told him it was more of the mind than the body. *Whatever the hell that means.* Every time he killed, or robbed, or lost his temper in any way the spasms would return. He was trying very hard now to ignore Bob Johnson. It was becoming very difficult, if not impossible.

"Ten thousand, Tyler. In or out? Pony up or walk on."

During the exhibition, Katherine was filling out a real bank draft. Not some scrap of paper that had the odor of lilacs.

"I'm the primary investment partner, as the judge has ruled, on this side of the table. We see your ten thousand and raise twenty-five thousand dollars," she said slowly, distinctly, and with that friendly sternness that Will Tyler liked so well. "Here is a bank draft on the Massachusetts National Bank of Boston for thirty-five thousand dollars," she said, handing it to Will for him to add to the pile. "See if *that pony* will ride!" She was gaining more and more courage for later tonight. She would need it.

The buzz of whispers that had permeated the room since the game had down turned from a celebration to a funeral in the matter of a few words, suddenly increased to a level that made it difficult for one to hear. The judge thought about ordering silence, but he relented. *Let the thing run its course*, he thought.

Morgan was stunned.

The Texan, again, as always, was in his Bob-Johnson character. "Thirty-five thousand dollars. *Gawd*damn boy, you better marry that girl. If you don't, I will."

Katherine smiled at Bob and gave him a slight nod of the head.

Morgan grabbed Bob by the arm and pulled him up. "Let's talk," he said.

Bob jerked his arm away. "Maybe, maybe not. I ain't got a goddamn thing to say to you!" He followed Morgan to the corner anyway.

"Listen, Bob. This thing has gotten out of hand. I know I've said some things that have been way out of line today. But, after last night when we were all in the saloon, I had a telegram waiting for me at my house. My mother died last week in Ohio. It has hit me hard. I've been out of my mind. Please don't tell anyone. I am not a man who takes to any pity of any sort for any thing. You are the only living soul I have told or will tell about her death. I just want to have a little time to get over it personally. By myself. Can you understand that?"

Bob could understand, perfectly. When he was twelve years old and killed Jake Standing Owl down on the Guadalupe, he did not want anybody to talk about it. No pity. No congratulations. Just personal time alone, to work it out.

"I'm sorry about your ma, Val." *You lying, rotten son of a bitch*! He thought in the same breath. "But you have been a particular asshole today. A very easy fellow to dislike in a hurry. I really dunno what I can do to help; besides, that's twenty-five thousand more dollars, damn. I ain't got that."

"But we have the winning hand. And all I want to do is end this thing where no one gets hurt. I have offended Dr. O'Reilly so much, I'm afraid she has taken it personally. I didn't mean a word I said. You know me. I never talk unkind to women. Never!"

"I agree that you're in a deep shit-hole if you get that female against you. I'm having my daily scrapes with her myself and don't think I've won a one of 'em."

"If she wins, we are all out everything. That nineteen thousand dollars is every penny I have put together over the past twenty-five years of hard goddamn work." *More like twenty minutes of plugging five stupid army guards and taking a payroll in the Nations last month*, Morgan thought, as he relished the lies he was spinning. *This Texan, how stupid can he be? He is falling for every line of turkeyshit I am throwing at him.*

"This thing is way out of hand," Morgan continued. "We have to stop it and make it right. We know we have the winning hand, so all we have to do is call and win the pot. Then we return everyone's money, tear up every bank draft, and even return the original five-dollar ante to everyone. Do you remember this thing started with a five-dollar ante? Seems like a month ago." He was playing on Bob's sympathy. It was working—he thought. "Bob, Will is our friend. We need to get out of this mess, and him too. So, he will take your promise to put up half of your half of the ranch in Texas. You can say it's worth twenty-five thousand, or fifty thousand. It doesn't matter. We have the winning hand! Then it will all be over and we can go to Birdwell's and laugh about this."

Bob was on the verge of saying, *are you out of your damned mind?* Then he realized that it might work. Everyone would forget the harsh words and it would be a story to talk about for along time. The absolute longest and richest hand of seven-card-stud in the history of the West—won by four *cowboys*. How fitting. He hoped that it would work. His plan had so many angles that he lost track. One thing was certain, however, no matter what the outcome, he would have *given* half of his half of the Circle J Ranch to Will Tyler, just for the asking. Or, not even asking. Just to have him close, as a friend, for a lifetime. There was one more thing. Dead certain. It was not going to turn out like Valentine Morgan hoped, no matter what the finish. That was a *Red River Promise,* as his dad, Tobias, had often made young Bob make.

"Okay, by God, let's do it, Val. Just go easy on the name-calling. Especially to Katherine. She's a damn wolverine."

How could he ever relate this story to his outlaw and killer cohorts and make them believe that it happened? *These sonsabitches don't deserve to live for their utter stupidity,* Morgan thought.

They leaned against a cabinet in the corner and Val wrote the following on the remaining scrap of Katherine's paper:

I hereby relinquish to any male bearer of this note one-half interest in my one-half interest of the Circle J ranch north of Buffalo Gap, Texas. The present value of this one-fourth portion of the Circle J is $25,000 or greater. Robert Buford Johnson, Half-Owner.

Bob Johnson signed the note and the two returned to the table. Bob read it aloud, and placed it on the pile. He had insisted on the word *male* in the note. He hated the thought of being partners with Katherine for the rest of his life if something went wrong here with his plan. After all, this entire plan was being worked on as he went along.

"We call," Morgan said with hatred like an over-flowing dam ready to burst.

Will Tyler picked up the ranch note and looked at Bob. *What is the matter with him? What had Morgan said?*

Bob looked away and would not look at Will or Katherine.

She reassured Will, seeing his uncertainty. "We will give it back to him. Tonight before we meet. Over a supper at the restaurant. It's still early. I promise." she whispered. She meant it. Morgan did not.

Will saw no other way. He looked at Two Snakes. The Indian was smiling. What a rarity. Two Snakes nodded to Will. *All is well.*

"I guess that ends it. I'll accept the note for the ranch on one condition, you show first. I want to see what started all this damned mess, and if I have the winning hand and show first, as I am called to by the rules, you would not have to show me. I got to know." Will looked at Bob straight. Their eyes were locked.

"Okay partner," Bob said. "That's fine by me. I am particularly proud of my hand anyway. Why not?" Bob could not lose in any event. He had been united with Will Tyler throughout the entire two hours of the longest seven-card-stud poker hand in history, not to mention the hundred-thousand-dollar pot. He had the same agenda, unknown to both. He had taken a ride at midnight last night after deciding not to violate his marriage bed again. He had come upon two other riders and had hidden in the underbrush on the little hill with the stand of elm trees. He had heard their conversation. All of it. But not enough to prove anything. Just enough to start watching that bastard at his every move. Morgan would get his due, no matter what.

"Here goes, read 'em and weep like a step-child after a Saturday-night whoppin'," Bob said as he turned up his hole cards, displaying the four *cowboys*.

Chapter 15

7:00 p.m., December 9, 1875
Fort Smith, Arkansas

Following the promised supper that night at the Garrison Street Restaurant, Bob walked out with his friend. Katherine walked on to the convent, after Will promised to be there shortly. It was to be the happiest, or the saddest, meeting of her life. She walked up the front stairs of the convent slowly, almost wishing she could turn and run. Anywhere! When she opened the door to her room, she found the McGready sisters waiting for her.

"What do you two want?" she asked in an agitated tone.

"We were worried about you, Katherine," Mary Margaret said. "Where have you been so long?"

"And, you smell like a barroom!" exclaimed Mary Anne.

"When was the last time you were in a barroom, Mary Anne?" Katherine asked, now clearly agitated. She did not need an inquisition right now. She had too much on her mind. She sat on her bed and began to cry.

Both sisters sat by her side and tried to comfort her. "Katherine, when are you going to stop this?" Margaret pleaded. "You can't continue this way. It has been getting worse and worse for the past ten years."

"We love you like a sister, you know that. But you're getting damned difficult to bear—especially in the last three months," Anne chided.

"Why, Anne, I've never heard you say *damned*. My toughness must be rubbing off on you."

"You're not tough! You just act tough, and you're doing a poor job of it lately."

"She's right," Margaret said. "We fear for your mental health sometimes."

"You just don't understand," she shouted, as she moved away from the bed and faced them. "How could you understand what I'm going through?"

"He will love you! He will cherish you! And if he doesn't, then he's not worth a damn anyway, and good riddance to him!" Anne's face flushed as she vented her feelings. Katherine began to smile at her friend's bold talk. It helped somehow.

Mary Margaret went to Katherine and hugged her gently. "It will make no difference to Will Tyler. I promise you that. I feel that. He is the man you've been waiting on all these years, and God will not disappoint you. You deserve this happiness. Believe me, Katherine," she said forcefully.

Katherine moved over and sat in the overstuffed chair she had brought from Boston. The chair was her place of comfort; it was the place from which she had done a lot of thinking since September, and Will Tyler's entrance into her life.

"I pray that you are right. I'll know for sure, tonight."

"What do you mean?" Anne asked.

Katherine stood and walked to her closet and retrieved a box from the top shelf. She laid it on the bed and opened it. Inside was a beautiful, white, linen bed gown. She held it up in front of her body and smiled through her tears.

"No!" Margaret shouted.

"Why not?" Anne questioned with a sense of *I'm for it!* "It's time we got an answer to all of this. Good luck, sweetheart."

Bob and Will continued their walk to the barracks.

"Finally, I am able to get you alone. If you can keep your mind off that gal for just a minute I need to talk to you—real bad—about Val," Bob said.

"Ol' Val," Will said gleefully. "I will never forget, in my entire life, the look on his face when Katherine turned my cards over. Hell, he may still be sitting there at the barracks, looking at the floor."

"No," Bob said. "This is something else. Something I've needed to talk about all last night and today. I been trying to get you alone and talk this out. It's just what I know, what I heard—nothing I can prove. I've sorted it out in my mind and just let it play out today. But tomorrow, we need to take a ride into the Choctaw Nation. Down toward Younger Station."

"Why?" Will asked.

"Just listen."

They talked. Will listened silently and ashen-faced. They walked back into the barracks.

Over that past three months, Katherine had dominated Will Tyler's every free moment. He was a willing participant in the courtship, and his every thought had been tied to her. He doubted his ability and even his worth at times. *This is insane*, he thought often in those days of anxiety. *What would she see in me? I'm about to make a fool of myself.*

He was thinking about that a great deal as he sat in the bunkhouse, self-absorbed. He also thought about Valentine Morgan, who was sitting just across the room, oiling his big Walker Colt. He had his eye on Morgan especially. After losing nineteen thousand dollars, he might just load that Walker and start firing away. But Morgan had passed the game off as a lot of great fun. "I would not have missed it for the world," he had said. *What a load of lies*, Will had thought in response.

But, of course, he had most of his mind on Katherine. Morgan's traitorous actions—if they were true—would just have to wait.

Bob could not get his friend into a conversation about anything. He was trying. Trying to engage him in some speculation about this and that.

"Hey, Ben. You going to the convent picnic tomorrow?" he asked, trying to start anything. "Will, here, says it's gonna be a grand event. Maybe we ought to check it out."

Colbert was involved in his own thoughts. Even though his loss was small compared to Morgan's, he still lost more than he planned to lose in the game. He was still contemplating the possibility of four kings and four aces in a single series. The mathematics professors at Harvard would have a lot of fun with a probabilities study of that. He just nodded at the suggestion of a picnic.

Bob could see Will's dilemma, or at least he thought he could. After all, he had been in love with his Rebecca since they were children. He knew how it felt. He just did not know how to show it or express it sometimes. He suspected what was on his friend's mind.

"Why don't you go down early to church this evening? It might be just what the *doctor* would prescribe." He smiled and looked at Will, pleased with the subtle humor in his words. Will looked back at Bob and wondered if he could read his mind. Was his completely distracting infatuation with Katherine so obvious that even this Texan could see it? *Why, hell, who was he fooling? The entire damned Territory knew it to be a fact. She didn't try to hide it for damned sure.* Will nodded in resignation to Bob. It had only been three months, but his every thought had been about her. It felt like a lifetime. She was confusing. Her mood was happy and loving, but he could feel something else. It just felt wrong.

The Texan's revelation about Valentine Morgan had been a complete shock to Tyler. Even though others, including Katherine, had reservations about Morgan, Will had genuinely liked the man. He was anxious to get on the trail to Younger Station with Bob in the morning to get to the bottom of the whole damned mess. But first he had his date with Katherine and he knew she was waiting. It was close to sundown. It had been a full day. An early breakfast and afternoon with Katherine; a poker game of legendary status; supper with Katherine again and his good friend—now news of a traitor in their midst—had fairly well exhausted him. Not so much, however, that he was too tired to see Katherine again.

As Will headed for the door, Bob followed close to his side. Seeing his friend's confused mental status, he opted not to talk any more about the trip to Younger Station tomorrow. He concentrated on Will's love life. With his usual demeanor, he proceeded to give him some parting advice.

"Women dunno what they want," he said. "They are just naturally confused creatures. The good Lord gave it over to the man to help these females to see things as they should be. What you have to do is help her to understand what she needs to know. I would go with you, but you don't need me there to hold your hand. All you need is to look her in the eye and say, 'I'm available, and the line is already forming. For a kiss, I'll give you the lead place.'"

As Will stepped away from him to the other side of the barracks, he heard Bob's voice trailing in the background. "If you run into any trouble just fire that Schofield into the air a couple of times and I'll come runnin' to give you some more directions."

"If it was me, hell, I'd forget the whole thing and head down to Miss Emma's Social House ever chance I got," Benjamin Colbert said. He had trimmed his beard and cleaned up considerably during his stay in Fort Smith and was now a durable regular at Miss Emma's. He had lost his grizzly bear appearance, and smell, much to the relief of the ladies at that establishment.

"Why, I'll even treat you to a night there, Will. Hell, it's just less complicated."

Will Tyler fixed his attention on Professor Colbert as the mountain man continued, and he began to listen intently.

"But if you want to really astound her, let me offer a word or two on your approach. I'll write this down as I speak and you can memorize it on the way and get it right," he said as he reached for pencil and writing paper from the desk in the corner.

"Look her in the eyes—don't blink, and say: "You, my dear Katherine, are my Juliet, peering from vaulted window; you are my Aphrodite, atop the Athenian hill; you are my Guinevere, and I, your Lancelot with heart stolen swiftly; you are my Mona Lisa with eyes and smile that have melted my stone heart; you are my Helen of a thousand ships; you...."

Bob interrupted. "Whoa, who is this gal Helen? Someone that rich with a thousand boats—hell—I might be interested in her myself."

Will Tyler, who had been amazed by Colbert's poetry, reacted as a man awakened from a pleasant dream by a shrill scream. "Shut the hell up, Bob, and let the man go on."

"That's enough anyway, Will," Colbert said, folding the paper and handing it to the confused deputy. "If you can just remember those few words they will definitely melt the heart of any female." Will took the paper and thought that he just might do it. He had not heard such genteel words since his mother used to read to the children in the cool evening gatherings on the front porch in Helena—a lifetime ago.

"A thousand boats," Bob Johnson said to Jesse Allen, who was most definitely not listening to—or the slightest bit interested in—the goings-on. "What would a gal do with a thousand boats? My God, that could float all the cotton in Texas."

Valentine Morgan had been listening closely. He had acted like a father figure to the new deputies, and they had reasoned his advice was always on target, before the revelation of his other side. Will glanced at Morgan, who sensed the young deputy's need for some solid words to offset Bob Johnson's ramblings, and Ben Colbert's stoic advice.

"If I might intrude with a comment to offset these two jackasses here, it is very simple Will," he said. "Just love her. Just love her."

"What kind of advice is that, Val?" Bob asked.

"The best," he replied. "The very best." Valentine Morgan never quit with his alter ego. It was who he was. A lying, murdering, son of a bitch. And a good one, at that.

Bob didn't say anything else. Even though he detested Morgan and considered everything he said, and did, to be the actions of a hypocritical bastard, he knew Morgan was right in a very real sense. It made him think about Rebecca. It hurt. Even Colbert was moved by Morgan's graceful words of advice. "I agree sir. Good advice to be sure."

Two Snakes bid him some parting advice.

"Will," he said. "With mirth in funeral and with dirge in marriage."

"Thanks, Two Snakes. I *really* needed that."

"What in the *Gawldernhell* did that mean?" Bob asked.

"Sage advice from the Bard," Colbert said. "Sage advice."

Will thought about Valentine's words as he walked away, but he felt strangely inadequate to fulfill them. *Just love her*, he thought. *Just love her*. Coming from Valentine, what were they worth? Still, they sounded just right. How he wished he could approach Katherine that easily. He kept Colbert's words on the folded scrap of paper tightly in his hand, just in case. Hell, he didn't know what to do. This was turning out to be a very perplexing matter.

He wouldn't admit it, but he had really wanted Bob to come with him. After all, no matter how sound Valentine's advice was, or how poetic Colbert's words were, Bob was a married man with a beautiful wife in Texas, and if his stories were true, the most beautiful woman in Texas. It always perplexed Will as to why the Texan would stay separated so long from someone he loved that much. But Will surmised that Bob was cleansing the same type of demons that plagued his own dark reasoning about what happiness was. In any event, all Bob did was offer his Texas-filtered advice. So, Will ambled on down alone.

Even though he had performed his courting duties—within proper decorum, of course—to her dozens of times since they first met, she was still as frightening as that mother bear that had chased him up a tree as a boy. He could just never get the right words out. She toyed with him and that made it all the more perplexing. Will walked down to the church and waited until she came out. That was when she knew that she had him. His countenance had changed and acquired some courage, or maybe he was drunk. He just acted differently. She was thrilled. His worry and fretting for the past weeks had melted away.

They talked, sitting on the front steps of the church, under the watchful eye of Father Cafferty and the McGready sisters. Father Cafferty watched more out of concern for his young charge. Katherine was the daughter of an old friend in Boston and the priest was instrumental in bringing her to Fort Smith, with her medical skills, to help with the work in the Territory. She was badly needed there. The last thing his dedicated doctor needed was some smitten deputy distracting her from her duty. Mary Anne and Mary Margaret McGready, sisters by blood and nuns by vocation, watched in secret suppressed joy that their girlhood friend, Katherine O'Reilly, had a beau, and a handsome one at that. She talked about him constantly, from the first moment she noticed him as he rode in with the Crabtree brothers. Father Cafferty left the window in the vestibule and went about his duties, satisfied that Katherine was in no danger, at least at the moment. The McGready Sisters continued to hang on to every word they could strain to hear.

The three women had lived on the same street in Boston since they were born. Mary Anne was three years older than Mary Margaret and Katherine. But their bond was as strong as any sisters. The girls were inseparable. Katherine's father, Dr. Dennis O'Reilly, and the sisters' father, Dr. Michael McGready were partners in a hospital they jointly owned and operated in Boston. The girls were happy and privileged. Their only disappointment came when Katherine did not follow Mary Anne and Mary Margaret into the convent. It was just understood that it was going to happen. Katherine, however, had different plans for her life. Her dream was to be a wife and a mother. To find happiness with some man of her dreams, and live with him and their children and grandchildren until a very old age, was her ambition since childhood. Instead, she altered her course and followed her father into medicine, intent on becoming one of the few women doctors in the country. The Civil War had changed her plans and her life. She responded to a call for volunteers to serve the Army wounded. She worked in hospitals at most major engagements and distinguished herself as a capable surgeon's assistant. President Lincoln himself, acting on a recommendation from General Hooker, gave her a commendation for exemplary service. The war, however, changed Katherine in other drastic ways. She lost her youthful naiveté in the field hospitals. The gritty realism of war supplanted any idealistic view of civility that she once thought the norm. Amputated legs by the wagonful, young boys screaming in the night for their mothers, and the cold, blank look coming from the eyes of a dead soldier, who just hours ago was talking and joking with a buddy, all changed her. A darker specter, known only to her closest family and friends, also remained from the war. While serving at the Union field hospital at Gettysburg on July 3, 1863 a tragic, twist of fate struck. It was not discussed, but it shattered her idealism of home, husband and family. Those closest to her had tried for years to help her gain a positive perspective on the tragedy, but Katherine was often thrown into bouts of depression and acts of extreme moodiness that were out of character for her. Sometimes, she had to act tougher than she really was. It confused people. She was a world apart from her friends and what she once thought life was about. The trip to Fort Smith was necessary. Even the ten years that separated her from the horrors of the war and finishing medical college at the top of her class had not diminished her despondency. She had tried to find pleasure through the lives of her friends but nothing helped. She took great joy in the work and ministry of Mary Anne and Mary Margaret. She genuinely tried to find happiness in the marriages and children of her other friends, the Tyler sisters, Maggie, Martha and Zora. But the war, and its cruel irony, had voided any happiness in her own life. She needed to find fulfillment in something. Will Tyler was that something. From the first time she had heard about him from his sisters—about his incredible sorrow for the night with the whip—she felt that he was her ideal. This was a man who could understand her cryptic sorrow—especially now. Hearing that John Law had gone to Fort Smith made up her mind to make a change. Maybe, some day she would meet William Tyler through his beloved grandfather. She felt her premonition of destiny was a divine sign when she had seen the man ride in that day with the prisoners. She fell in love with him, body and soul, at first sight. For the first time in years, she felt the rise of elation and happiness in her body. It was a welcome return to a long-absent feeling. But, sadly, he must know the story. She would not go on dreaming if there was no hope. *She was damn well worth a lifetime of investment on the part of Will. She would make it worthwhile. But would he consider it so?* Tonight, she planned to roll the dice.

"We will be heading out to the Choctaw Nation tomorrow," Will said. "Bob and I have something very important to check out." He said no more about the urgency, or the unsettling information about Morgan. He just left it at that.

"Please be careful, Will," she pleaded. "These are very dangerous men that the court goes after. You have the scars to prove it."

"Dangerous is not the word for some of these men, they go beyond that. But someone has to stop them. So, I'll be satisfied when we are bringing them in to be hanged on the gallows," he said, pointing down the street in the direction of the courthouse. He knew no one would hang from the trip tomorrow. Not yet at least. It was just something to say.

"Haven't you had enough of hanging?" she shouted with tears in her eyes. She was concerned for his safety, and the spectacle of the mass hanging three months earlier still weighed heavily on her mind. But her real thoughts were elsewhere. A showdown with Will and her destiny. She had spoken boldly. Uncharacteristically so to someone she had known for such a short time. But this was no ordinary someone. Her heart told her that. This was the one. The one that would understand. And she was as protective of him as she had been about anyone in her life. She wondered though if she had been too brash. She was growing tired of second-guessing her every word.

"Yes," he said slowly, looking towards the end of the street. "I guess I have seen enough hangings. I guess I've seen enough of just about everything."

Realizing what she had said, and Will's obvious lapse into the nightmarish memory that had plagued him for almost fifteen years, she was at a loss as what to say next. "I'm sorry, I didn't mean that. Forgive me." She had not gotten Will to talk about his life at all since Helena. Where he had gone, what he had done, what he had seen that had so locked him in that dark and solemn place—which he would not talk about. Her mission was to bring him out of his dark place and bring him to her, bright and hopeful. Her problems were going to be enough—if the relationship survived. She tried again, thinking it was all beyond Helena somehow.

"Will, what about the war? Why don't you ever talk about it? I know you were in action for the full time," she said. She was concerned that this held the key to his dark closet where he had locked himself. It was her closet, and she was well aware of its lonely and destructive confines.

"Not much to say. Four years of hell." He continued, looking away from her. "You were there. You saw it."

"Yes, I saw it." She began to weep and fought hard to hold it back. "But I am concerned that maybe you have not turned it loose," she said. *What a hypocrite I am*! She thought.

"I can't."

"Why?" She was exasperated. She had seen the horrors. *But for her sake, move on.*

He looked into her eyes, and she saw in his eyes a dark place. It frightened her.

"What is it, Will?" she persisted.

"Andersonville."

For the first time, she saw him try to hold back tears. He was not very good at it. It tore her soul. She could feel the pain he was going through, trying to forget. Trying not to talk.

Just the word, *Andersonville*, shocked her into revulsion. She had no idea that he had been there. She could not speak. Forty-nine thousand Union soldiers had been held in unimaginable conditions in an outdoor prison camp with no food, no water and nothing of any kind with which to hold on to hope. It was run by Confederate Captain Henry Wirz, the only American ever tried, convicted, and executed for war crimes. Thirteen thousand died, decimated by starvation and disease.

Will Tyler survived for over a year in that *hell*. He survived by thinking of revenge on Holcomb's Confederacy—driven to a will to survive by raw revenge and hate. It had taken ten years to temper that scar on his soul.

Katherine struggled to speak. She could not look at him. She thought again of him—starving, naked and despondent at that prison. She loved him too much. She did not ever want to think of that place again. *Dear God, take that from my mind.*

He saw her pain. Her shock. He wanted to change the subject back to anything else. His first thought was his trip with Bob.

"Never mind," he said reassuringly. "It's just a job that I have to do. We'll do it and be back before you know it—definitely in time for the picnic!" He had wanted to tell her about Morgan, but there had been enough talk about things of that sort tonight. It could wait. He struggled for his next words. He had been practicing them over and over in the bunkhouse that evening. He was amazed at the thoughts in his head. He was more amazed that he vocalized them. Nothing could have held them back. He reached for Colbert's notes and held them to his side as he strained to remember. "Katherine, I have to say something to you. You are my Juliet in the window; you are my Lancelot...er...I mean my Guinevere," he said, grimacing as he tried to read the words, hastily scrawled by the mountain man.

She could hardly hold her laughter back. It came through her tears of Andersonville. She covered her mouth with her hand, but her eyes gave her giggles away. Sweet giggles at his inept attempt at lovemaking.

Will continued. *Damn, why is she laughing?* "You are my Helen...my Helen," he continued slowly peering at the paper. "Oh hell," he said, crumpling the paper up and tossing it to the ground. "Katherine, what I mean to say is that, you.... you are my girl," he said with a pleading in his eyes as if asking for mercy from the ordeal. Her giggle turned to a full broad smile. Her eyes were wide and glistening with tears. It was the tenderest moment she had ever experienced with a man. This was the one! She was ready to put her plans into action. Her plans to make him hers, totally and bonded.

"And when I get back, I'll expect that I'll be marrying you." The word, marry, shocked him. He would never have believed that he could just say it right out. He had known her for only three months. What would she think? He was afraid to even look at her. He was dumbfounded and yet strangely pleased with himself. His self-congratulatory thoughts were brought back to reality by her voice, stern but gentle, forceful but loving.

Her mood changed again. This time back to the pre-war, girlish idealism. Hoping against hope that it might be, somehow.

"Why, William Timothy Tyler, if that is a proposal, it is the worst one I have ever heard of in my life," she said with a face that displayed a frown and a smile at the same moment.

His shocked expression was further confused by the gleeful shout coming from behind the church window. The McGready sisters were embracing each other and dancing around the room.

"Well?" she inquired, looking at a clearly dumbstruck Will Tyler. His own words had been too much for him to believe, but her quick and confusing response was also a shock.

"Well, what?"

"Is that a proposal or not?" she asked, her eyes brimming with joy.

"I guess it is," he responded in a dazed voice.

She beamed. "Then, I accept," she said as she reached down and picked up the tattered piece of paper he had discarded in seeming defeat. She held it close to her heart. It was as important to her and as precious as a copy of the Bible. It would remain in her possession for the rest of her life, she promised herself.

She reached over, placed her lips against his, and kissed him. He was trembling, looking on with his eyes wide open. The last few seconds had been the biggest shock of his life. And now, to be in her arms and to feel her soft perfumed lips against his took his breath away. It was better than a dream. He began to return her kiss as he wrapped his arms around her.

Realizing where they were, and that the she was about to be lost in the swirl of the passionate moment, she gently pulled away from him.

"Katherine," he said. "I think I love you."

"William Timothy Tyler, you'd better know that you love me. For I know, with all of my soul, that I love you," she said softly and lovingly. They lingered in the moment. Not speaking a word. They kissed passionately. Lovingly. She was happier now than she had been at any time in her life. The horrors of the war and the dark depression deep in her soul had fled with that one kiss. Tyler, too, had felt the dark specter in his memory lift slightly. He was experiencing feelings he never thought imaginable. Love was a new frontier for him and he decidedly liked it.

The silence was broken as she garnered the courage to speak the words *she* had been practicing for weeks. The words she never dreamed would be a reality. Her plan was now unleashed. No turning back. It was now her turn to be brave. She must finally have a resolution.

"I am only going to say this once, and then I am going inside," she said.

He swallowed hard. He was completely out of his element here, and he knew it. He had no clue as to what she was about to say. If he had the choice of just plain getting up and running like hell, he would have done it at that moment, at that pause. He looked on as if a child expecting something very frightening.

She took a deep breath, closed her eyes and spoke softly. "Will, I want you to come to my room tonight. Before you have to leave for the Territory," she said slowly. With her eyes still closed, she took a deep breath, and paused. "I don't know what I am saying, but I do know that I am *sure* of it."

Will was in a trance. He was still looking at the spot on the stone steps where she had sat after swiftly retreating into the convent. It was sundown, but her heart blazed as if basking in a noonday sun. His daze was broken by her whispered words as she peered from the slightly opened door. "The door will be unlocked at nine o'clock."

He had walked the streets until he was too restless to just walk. He saddled Sky and rode in the cool December night. The anticipation was an unbearable weight. He whipped his big Gray into a full gallop around the river, until it was time. *Damn. It was time.* He quickly ran into the barracks, put on fresh clothes, and left without saying a word. He imagined every eye was on him. Behind every grin in the room was knowledge, somehow, that something big was up.

"Damn boys, he looked spruced-up like he was going to Miss Emma's," Bob said. "But ten dollars will get you a hundred he ain't." They smiled. They knew.

The brass doorknob gleamed in the bright night as it turned in his trembling hand. The full moon had concerned him. What if someone had seen him enter the door? He quickly dismissed that fear because he was inside now, so it did not matter.

Will Tyler had been inside the Convent of Mercy many times to meet Katherine in the front parlor. Although he had the room memorized, he did not need the mental picture now because the moonlight filtered through the windows like bright lanterns. Only the stairway to the second floor disappeared into darkness, and that was where he must go. Katherine had left the front doors unlocked for him as she promised, so by the same promise, he realized that she was ready and waiting for him in her room just to the left at the top of the stairs. He was frozen at the stair landing, unsure of his next step. He had been in life and death situations without flinching, many times—Andersonville—and some as recent as two days ago in the gunfight with the Martin brothers at the Poteau Landing—yet the act of climbing those stairs left him quaking. Will swallowed the small amount of saliva he could muster in his parched mouth and started up the stairs.

The loud creak of the first step stopped him again, with one leg raised in mid-air. *Sweet Lord*, he thought, *what am I doing here*? The prospect of being caught in the convent was not half as frightening as what awaited him in Katherine's room. He removed his boots with the skill of a circus acrobat and continued up the staircase.

As he slowly opened her bedroom door, his eyes, now accustomed to the darkness from the hallway, were assaulted by the bright moonlight cascading through her open, double windows. The lace sheer curtains were blowing gently around her as the south breeze made its way through the unfastened shutters. The brisk night breeze decorated her skin with chill bumps. She stood, draped in *the* white linen gown, looking out of the window as if in a trance and did not acknowledge that he had entered the room. He watched, transfixed, as she slowly tilted her head back, eyes closed, and let her perfectly brushed auburn hair shift and linger down her back as the breeze tossed its ribbon-laced tips. The scent of the perfume from her hair intoxicated him. His imaginations, visions, fantasies, dreams—none of these—had prepared him for the sight upon which his senses feasted. Her perfect body, white and iridescent, seemed to reflect the moonlight around the room as a multifaceted diamond caught in a firestorm of light.

He was breathless as he looked upon her body hidden beneath the gown, interrupted and accented by the shadows created by the light, and by her natural features that stood out like something from a beautiful dream. Her eyes glistened. Dark eyebrows arched and eyelashes jutted from her pearl-like forehead and cheeks. Lips, dark and shimmering, framed her mouth. Shadows that fell under her breasts uplifted and presented her beauty even more so. He was somewhat reluctant, however, as he stared, believing that he had gazed upon something holy, beyond his right or permission to continue. But he could not help himself. Slowly, she turned her head and peered deep into his eyes from across the room. He felt ashamed. *This was no by-God two-dollar whore*, he thought. This was a vision that deserved more respect than his base reaction, driven by lust. True enough he had come to her room, at her invitation and insistence, to lay with her, to finally have her, to consummate their three-month infatuation—*to give her a good poke*, as Bob Johnson would say. But now he did not feel worthy, or deserving, to violate the beauty that stood before him.

"Well...what are you waiting on, Deputy?" she questioned softly and nervously as she turned to face him with her arms held out, inviting him to her. Her body was trembling. So was his.

He tried to swallow again. This time he could muster no saliva.

"It's just that you're so beautiful. I.....I....never....I mean....I...."

"Shut up and come here, please," she said with a nervous laugh. His boyish actions endeared her. "I am as frightened as you."

Before he realized that he had moved, he was in her arms, kissing her. Inhaling her. He found it difficult to breathe. With their mouths pressed, she began to unbutton his new gabardine shirt. He had selected it at Girley's General Store especially for tonight. She fumbled with the buttons. In his haste at the barracks, he had buttoned them erratically. He finally yanked it free of his muscled shoulders. She gazed upon the long scar on his shoulder still bruised from the Crabtree brother's bullet. She saw a dozen other scars and wounds. *Andersonville*, she thought again. But that feeling was quickly overcome by the strongest passion she had ever felt, as he reached for her. He lifted her gown over her head.

It was time for the truth, she thought.

"Oh, my God. Oh, Jesus. Oh…Katherine…I…." He struggled with his words.

Suddenly, he pulled back in shock.

Her eyes locked on his gaze as he gently reached and softly ran his fingers over the deep, ghastly scar on her lower abdomen.

"I caught a stray bullet that ripped through the surgeon's tent at Gettysburg," she said, unburdening a decade of worry and apprehension. "The surgeon did the best he could in those horrible conditions, but I can never have children." She looked for his expression, it was the moment she had feared for so long. The long-awaited confession—that she was not a whole woman—had finally been faced. An ounce of Confederate lead had destroyed her dream of being a wife and mother.

Will Tyler felt a deep pain of sadness. He had been so self-absorbed with his war-demons that he cursed his selfishness. He immediately knew the reason for her sadness and the answer to her confused moods.

"Will, can you still love me?" she pleaded. The question had haunted her since the wound and botched surgery. Would a man ever love her?

He took her into his arms and gently put his head on her shoulder. He whispered into her ear. "Katherine. Sweet, Katherine. I want you, and you are perfect." He looked deeply into her eyes. "The two of us will be enough for me. More than enough. Thank God you are alive."

He said no more as he lowered her down on the soft, goose-down mattress bed.

Now Katherine knew physically that her heart's decision was the right one. So did he. As they lay together afterwards she whispered softly into his ear. "Will Tyler I love you. I love you with all my life."

"I love you Katherine, with all of my life also."

Will Tyler decided never again to mention the prospect of a childless life. He truly meant what he had said. She was more than he could have ever hoped for. Her love was going to make him complete. He sensed that. He hoped his love in return, could do the same for her. Besides, Martha, Maggie and Zora had given them more than enough nephews and nieces to go around for several lifetimes.

Chapter 16

5:00 a.m., December 10, 1875
The Choctaw Nation, Indian Territory

Will Tyler and Bob Johnson rode across the Poteau River early the next morning. They told no one but Katherine, and all she was told was that Will would be back before the start of the Winter Picnic at the convent that afternoon. It was just a two-hour ride into the edge of the Choctaw Nation to see if any tracks could be found. Bob Johnson promised this with sincerity, and she accepted as she watched them through her sleepy eyes from her bedroom window. If they wanted to ride out at five o'clock on a dreamy Sunday morning, well then, let them go.

"Just make sure you have him back here cleaned, dressed and ready at two o'clock," she said sternly to Bob Johnson.

"Yes Ma'am," he said, tipping his hat.

"I love you," Will Tyler said to Katherine, as she leaned out of the window.

That was all that was needed. Katherine would be satisfied with any request he had made. She replied, more from the heart than from the lips. "I love you, too." She was still in a trance from the night before. Her faced then dropped a bit. "But be sure you are here—and on time!" Smiling, she waved goodbye and closed the lace curtains.

"Damn boy, I must say she is a vision," Bob said.

Will agreed. *More than you'll ever know.* They reined their mounts riding hard, west to the river.

They were only a half-hour into the Nation when Bob noticed that Molly was stepping odd. He dismounted and found a loose shoe on her front right hoof.

"What's the name of that family right over there about a mile past this break?" Bob inquired, pointing north as he squinted in the half-light just before dawn. "You know, the man and his boy. The wife died last week."

"You mean Harris, James Harris," Will replied, looking at Molly's shoe.

"Let's see if he's up and could let me borrow a hammer and a couple of shoe nails. Damn, I can't believe I didn't check her over. Sorry girl," he said, stroking her forehead.

"It's awful early. He's still probably asleep."

"He won't be when we get there. I'm gonna walk, and lead her in," Bob said as he turned and started walking north off the trail. He heard Will mumble that he didn't have all day, something about two o'clock.

When they arrived at the small cabin, they noticed that there was no smoke from the stack. Odd fact on this cool December morning. As the light of the morning sun began to show things a bit better, the men froze as they saw the bodies. Closest was the boy, John. Just twelve years old and his head caved in. The axe lay by his body. Five paces away, his father James moved slightly at the approach of the deputies. He had been shot four times, as best they could tell.

"My God, it's early to be seeing this," Bob said as he lowered to one knee and held Mr. Harris' head in his hand.

Will Tyler covered the boy with an old piece of cloth from the clothesline nearby, and then joined Bob. "It's for sure I won't be going to a picnic today, even if I was back in time," he said, removing his hat and shaking his head. "Is he alive?"

"Just barely," Bob replied. "He's trying to talk."

"Three…three," Harris tried to say, but was exhausted after the effort.

"Hold on now, Mr. Harris. Take your time," Bob said. Will had retrieved a blanket from the cabin and covered the man from the cool breeze.

"Three." He said with a louder voice. "They robbed us. Damn, they kilt my boy." He began to cry with what strength he had left. He coughed as blood ran from his mouth.

Will looked at Bob Johnson. His face was stern and his nose flared. "For damn sure, there won't be no picnic today." He turned again to the dying man. "Mr. Harris, do you know who they were? Did you recognize them? Or where they went?"

James Harris opened his eyes, bloodshot and red, and looked up at Will. "They was three," he repeated. "One was a woman, a woman in man's clothes. You could tell," he strained to get the words out. "One, I seen in town. Wilson. Aaron Wilson. Always down to the Saloon on Fourth Street there in Fort Smith.

The Riverboat Saloon. He talks big a lot. He laughed at me when he shot me. The sumbitch laughed at me." Harris he attempted to rise up. "The woman kilt John," he said. It was his final word.

"Belle!" Bob Johnson stood and looked around.

"Do we want to bury them here?" Will asked with a solemn stare.

"I think we ought to ride," Bob said, pointing his hand south. "Let's go all the way to Younger Station and settle this matter."

"You fix Molly's shoe and I'll put the bodies inside. We can pick them up on the way back and bring them on in to Fort Smith," Will said.

"Leave a note, telling anyone who might come by who did it and where we have gone," Bob said.

Will wrote:

This is James Harris and his boy John. Killed by Aaron Wilson, Belle Reed and unknown assailant. U.S. Deputies, Will Tyler and Robert Johnson have pursued killers to Younger Station in the Choctaw Nation. December 10, 1875.

It was the last sheet of Katherine's paper he had left. He had planned to write her a love note on it for today's picnic.

The deputies were only ten minutes' distance from the Harris settlement when they heard voices and horses in the clearing ahead of them. Will and Bob dismounted and walked to cover in the brush right behind the two men.

"I know I checked the drawers in that storeroom," one of the men said.

"Which storeroom was that?" the other man asked.

"I dunno. The *storeroom*!"

"You stupid son of a bitch, you didn't check, did you?" he yelled, whipping the smaller man with his leather reins. "You didn't check a goddamn thing I told you to. You was too scared. All you wanted to do was run and go," he said, continuing to whip the man with every word. Both horses reared and whirled.

"Now we got to go back. I know that farmer has some gold. He said so, at the Riverboat Saloon. For the sale of his land in Missouri. Goddamn! Now we got to go back and search that storeroom," the large man repeated.

"You ain't going nowhere," Bob said as he stepped from the brush. His .45 was in his hand and cocked.

Will had his Schofield pointed directly at the smaller man's head. "You either, mister."

Both riders reined their horses hard and kicked in their spurs as they pulled their pistols and fired wildly at the two lawmen.

The deputies' guns exploded in the morning calm. The small man lay dead. Shot between the eyes. The large man hit the ground and moaned. He was suffering from the gaping hole in his shoulder caused by Bob Johnson's bullet.

Bob looked quickly at the smaller man that Will had killed. He knew how his friend felt about killing. He did it when he had to, without hesitation. But he still hated it, and took every occasion hard. Bob imagined that here on this Sunday morning, before he even had a cup of coffee, killing a man was weighing heavy on him. So, in his manner, he worked on Will.

"Damn, partner. Now, that was a shot. I was off. I only hit mine in the arm. Damned lucky I hit him at all, the way my hand is *still* a shakin' from them four aces that whopped me last night." Bob patted Will on the back. "Let's get these two back to the Harris place."

Will still had not said a word, and did not at all during the short ride back to the cabin. They put the dead man on the ground and pulled the wounded man off his horse.

"What's your name, Mister?" Bob asked.

"Bastard. You shoot me down and *then* ask my name. Who the hell are you?" the man screamed back.

"We are going to ask you just one more time, fellow. I don't have time for this so early," Will said. "What is your name?"

"Wilson. Aaron Wilson. I work odd jobs in Fort Smith. You can check with anybody," he said, grabbing his wounded shoulder.

"That's all I need," Bob said. He buffaloed the killer. It was his trademark—skulling—to leave a mark from his beloved Colt .45 on any prisoner he arrested. For violent crimes, especially. Of late the Fort Smith Federal Jail housed a large and ever-growing congregation of fellows with matching marks on their heads from in and around the Territory.

They tied Wilson to a tree near the house and laid his killer friend next to him. "I'll not defile the memory of Mr. Harris by having you in his house again," Bob said to Wilson and the corpse. "Just wait here till we get that woman."

Will had already revised the note penned to Mr. Harris.

This is James Harris and his boy John. Killed by Aaron Wilson, Belle Reed and unknown assailant. U.S. Deputy Marshals Will Tyler and Robert Johnson have pursued killers to Younger Station in the Choctaw Nation. December 10, 1875. The bastard tied to the tree is Aaron Wilson and the dead man is the unknown assailant. We trust that Wilson will survive until our return. If not, then we made our judgment to tie him up and go on. We are gone again. U.S. Deputy Marshal William T. Tyler.

They rode again toward Younger Station. This time with more speed and determination. They reached the outskirts of the former outpost just before two o'clock in the afternoon. The abandoned way station in a small clearing, where two small cabins and an old fallen-down livery stable stood, was less than a mile away when they stopped. Bob Johnson looked at his old pocket watch. "Well, boy, it looks like about time for some fried chicken, apple pies, tart lemonade and one mad woman back at the little swimming cove where all the church folks are gathered."

Will Tyler ignored his comment. He was full aware that he was not at the picnic and there would be hell to pay. But there was more important *hell* for someone to pay right here and now. Of course, Katherine's hell had yet to be felt.

"We are still about a half-mile from the Station. I suspect they have a look-out posted closer in," Will said.

"We could tie our horses here and walk in a bit through the brush to see who is where," Bob replied. Before he could dismount, a shot rang out and the bullet caught Bob in the lobe of the left ear and glanced off his cheekbone, shattering it. His face was covered with blood and it hampered his vision. Blinded for a moment, his instinct was to ride—somewhere in the opposite direction.

"I guess we found 'em," he said, turning Molly hard to retreat to safety. Will followed behind, turned in his saddle, and firing in the direction of the shot with his Schofield. A second shot exploded from the tree line at the front of the clearing. The bullet tore through Will Tyler's left leg. Blood splattered all over Sky's silver mane. For a moment, he thought his horse had been hit. Then, he felt the burning pain. "Someone has a Spenser or something trained on us; get off of this road," Will shouted to Bob, who was turning back to aid Will.

"Head for that wash down there," Bob said, looking through his eyes matted with blood. They rode hard down a steep ravine protected in back by a small rocky wall, which held back a swamp. The ravine was dry and afforded a good defense. It was deep enough to protect the horses and graded such that they could crawl up and point their rifles from safety.

"Most unfriendly Sunday outing I can remember in a while, Bob said, checking his face to see if any of it still remained. "How's the leg?" he asked.

"A sight better than your head, I suspect," Will replied. "What's the damage?"

"I think the bullet just bumped my face bone, but I do believe it smashed it a bit—and, of course, the bastard almost took my ear off. I suppose it's a good thing I have gave up whoring. It would be costing a fellow double with my looks now, and free ones is completely outta the picture." He found he could not move his left arm. "I believe that ball went into my shoulder first then bounced out on to my ear, and then ended up whopping my face. Damned efficient use of lead, I'd say." He frowned with pain, trying to raise his arm. *A stoke of good luck*, he thought. *At least it ain't my shootin' arm.*

Another rifle shot got their attention. The bullet exploded in the rock wall behind them, sending shards raining down upon them.

"Damn, that fellow is a crack shot. We better be paying more attention or he'll be addin' a couple of notches on that handle.

"Do you think there's more than one?" Will asked.

"More than likely at this point. But you can bet your last dollar outta that hundred thousand you won last night that there will be more coming from all this gunfire."

"We better see what we got, while we can," Will said as he crawled over to the horses. He tied them under a small tree for deeper safety and pulled the saddlebags, rifles and supplies off.

"Bob Johnson fired a flurry of shots in the direction of the tree line to give cover for Will.

"Hit anything?" Will asked, as he dragged the supplies, and himself, back to the bank.

"Why, hell yes," Bob said. "Three bandits and a unlucky squirrel. Did you bring my silver tea set?"

Will laid the supplies out. They had two Winchester carbines, Bob's Henry rifle, about one hundred and fifty rounds of ammunition, two canteens of water and some ground coffee, sweet cakes and cherry tarts he had left over from Saturday's picnic with Katherine. Immediately he thought of his tardiness at the event now in full swing in Fort Smith. He was saddened by the thought of Katherine standing there, alone, looking down the road for him to come riding up with some excuse.

"I should have brought the bedrolls," he said, looking at the pile of articles.

"I don't expect I'll be doing too much sleeping tonight, if we live that long," Bob said.

Will found an extra shirt in his bag and began tearing it into strips for bandages. He tied one tightly around Bob's shoulder, face and ear, and then tied off the wound on his own leg. "That ought to stop the bleeding for a bit," he said. "But my leg wound is pretty deep. I need to keep an eye on it."

It had been five or more minutes since the last rifle shot and they began to wonder about that. "He's either gone for help, or they've come and are planning on what to do," Bob said.

They looked up and suddenly two riders were at full gallop coming toward them firing Winchesters. Bob and Will each raised up with their rifles and took aim. "You take the one on the right," Will said.

They fired simultaneously. Will's man fell backwards over his saddle and rolled on the ground hard. Bob's target fell to the side of his horse, and, with his foot caught in the stirrup was screaming as the horse sped down the road past the deputies. The man's cries trailed in the distance. "Looks like yours is not dead," Will said.

"Not yet," Bob said. "But that horse ain't gonna stop before he gets to the Poteau River. I guess he'll be good and dead by then."

"That's two," Will shouted to whoever else was in the tree line. "How many more of you bastards are willing to die?"

"It really makes four if you count Aaron Wilson and that stupid-looking one with him back down by the Harris place. Yep, they both dead," Bob shouted toward the clearing as he reloaded his Colt sidearm. He continued even louder. "Killed where they stood, by United States Deputy Marshals William T. Tyler and Robert Buford Johnson. Who's next?"

Two more rifle shots sent slugs that clipped the wall behind them after that last statement. The two smiled at each other. It was a dangerous situation, but never too dangerous for a smile at a genuine Bob Johnson remark.

"Bob Johnson," Belle Reed said with a dark stare. "Son of a bitch!" Then she realized her good luck and the snarl turned to a half-smile. "Now I got you—you bastard!" she shouted toward the ravine.

"That you, Belle?" Bob Johnson asked with shout. "I'm glad it's you. We can just get this thing over right now; come on out."

"I know you both are hit, Bob. I don't miss with this Spenser. Are you bleeding to death?"

"You didn't even come close Belle," retorted Bob.

"You are a black liar, Johnson. I saw the blood on the road. Both of you are hit, and one of you pretty bad. I hope it's you."

"You are mistaken as usual Belle. Why, Will here cut himself shaving this morning that's all—by the way, have you had the pleasure of meeting my friend and partner, Will Tyler, here? Come on out and we'll all get acquainted."

"Oh, I've seen him sashaying around town with that doctor bitch. Been in her bed yet, Tyler?"

"Why, Belle, what an indelicate thing to say. And from such a genteel and refined *bitch* as yourself," Will replied, as he reached up over the bank and took three shots off from his repeater rifle.

"Struck a cord, huh, Tyler. I'll have to remember that," she shouted back with an evil laugh.

"Bob, we need to get on with this. I'm losing a lot of blood here and I am tiring pretty damn quick from this situation," Will said.

A sudden, hot searing pain filled his chest, so much so that he could not breathe. Bob Johnson felt the same intense pain rip across his lower abdomen.

The gunman, who had sneaked onto the ridge of the rock wall from the swamp behind, had shot them both with his pistol. Bob Johnson still had the strength to fire his Colt he had just finished loading. The aim was true. The man fell back dead into the waist-high, moss-covered water.

"Okay Belle, that's five. How many more dumb sonsabitches you got left?"

There was no answer. The loss of Jack Hargett, just then, her beau's brother-in-law, was the sign to regroup and rethink the situation. They rode back to the Station cabin and left one man on sentry.

"Goddamn, Belle, let's just ride the hell on out of here," Sam Starr said. It's just you and me, Eli here, and José down the road. By God, Florence is going to take Jack's death hard."

"No more than he did, I expect," she said. "She'll get over it. I did, many times." She moved right into his face. He swallowed hard. He feared Belle. The answer was as big a mystery to him as it was to the dozen people a day who asked him: *What in the hell makes you want to go around with that crazy bitch?*

"I am not going to let that Texas Ranger slip out of my hands. Not this close! Goddamn, Sam, where's your guts? He has killed five of our men here in one day—and one was your dear sister's husband. Where's your backbone?" She turned to Eli Traskly. "Go back with José and keep those marshals in that wash until we can think of some way to get in there. Now, it's getting dark, so keep your eyes open." She took her Walker Colt and pressed it close to her heart. "It sure is getting to be a hard job to do a simple thing like kill a Ranger anymore," she said, staring at Sam, as Traskly went out the door.

Dusk was making it hard to see, even if the deputies were in any shape to see in any event. Both were wounded badly, if not fatally.

"Hold on, Will, I'm workin' on a plan," Bob said.

Will Tyler uttered a soft laugh; even in all his pain, of losing and regaining consciousness, Bob Johnson still managed to make him laugh.

"If anyone could pull a plan out of this, I believe that you could," Will said.

"What I think we ought to do is rush 'em and kill 'em all, and steal that bacon and coffee I smell comin' from that cabin," Johnson said with a serious look.

Will leaned back against the ground. *Damn, he sure wished that he had taken that bedroll from Sky when he had the chance.* He was cold from the night air and the shock.

"I could sure use some coffee," Bob said.

"Why don't you build a fire," Will said. "I suspect they know where we are. It sure won't give us away. Pour some of those coffee grounds into one of the canteens and lay it on the fire. That ought to quench your craving in a short while," Will said, coughing up blood as he spoke.

Bob Johnson did just that. Moving slowly and awkwardly with his one good arm and the searing pain in his abdomen, he had a small fire blazing with the canteen boiling in just a few minutes.

"Good idea there, Will, we can have some of Katherine's fine pastry to go with this in a minute."

Bob was well aware that his friend was in trouble. More so than himself. He needed to keep him awake. Keep his mind active.

"Hey, Will, do you know any songs?" he asked with a forced smile. "Why don't we have a sing-along?"

Will Tyler opened his eyes and looked at the Texan, supposing that his wounds were in the *head*. They had to be for a crazy thought like that.

"Sing with me, partner. Do you know that well-loved Texas Ranger song?"

"What song is that Bob?" Will asked weakly. He, too, knew how important it was to stay awake.

"Why, you know, the one about the pretty Texas gal—and the ugly Arkansas gal."

Bob began singing. Badly.

I left my gal in Texas,
Prettiest Gal I knowed;
Not 'acause her face, I sayez,
But 'acause her legs was bowed!
Singing, Why, yi-yi-yippie-yi-yay-yi-yay,
Why, yi-yi-yippie-yi-yay-yi-yo;
Yi-yi-yippie-yi-yay,yi-yay.
Yi-yi-yippie-yi-yo!

Will had passed out and was oblivious to Bob, who checked his friend's breathing. At least he was still alive.

"Come on now, Will, I ain't got to the best part yet."

Will stirred and blinked lazily at Bob.

"Now here is the best part..."

I left your gal in Arkansaw,
The ugliest gal I knowed;
It was 'acause her face I saw,
And my beans I just up and throwed!
Singing, Why, yi-yi-yippie-yi-yay-yi-yay,
Why, yi-yi-yippie-yi-yay-yi-yo;
Yi-yi-yippie-yi-yay, yi-yay.
Yi-yi-yippie-yi-yo!

He checked his pal again. Will was smiling strangely. Bob thought that a good sign. He shook Will to arouse him. "Stay with me, Willy. Don't you die on me. By God, I won't allow it." Bob Johnson was becoming more concerned by the minute. He, too, was beginning to lose consciousness, but he had to keep Will awake at all costs. He slapped Will Tyler hard across the face again and again.

"Damn, Bob, take it easy," Will finally said.

"You try going to sleep on me again, I'll give you a full-sized Texas-ass-whoppin'," he said. "And you Arkansas boys ain't never seen a thing like that."

Will smiled again. "Sing that stupid song again. I don't quite have it down yet."

He repeated his song. This time even louder.

Will tried to sing along.

A shout from the trees was angry and just as loud. "Shut that damned noise up. It sounds like a cat-a-hollerin' at a full moon. It's hurtin' my damned ears."

"Okay, then, you bastards, here's something to hurt your damned ass," Bob hollered back. He raised up and exploded a rifle shot in the direction of the tree line.

"Touchy ain't cha? Ya Texas sumbitch," the voice came. "Hey, that come pretty damn close. Hell, I think you hit a hoot owl." There was laughter coming from the two bandits.

Bob leaned back, waited on the coffee and closed his eyes. They were both out.

The approaching footsteps awakened Bob. He moved as quickly as he could and pointed his Colt at the figures coming up the ravine. "Well, here we go boys. This is it," he said. He pulled the hammer back and was within a split second a pulling the trigger when he heard the familiar voice. "Hold on there Bob, it's me, Benjamin."

Colbert and Two Snakes had been sent to look for the men, by Katherine, of course. They had come to the Harris cabin, found the note, and had followed as quickly as they could ride.

"My God, ain't you two a sad sight," Colbert said.

"Never you mind," Bob said. "Just get that canteen off the fire before my coffee boils away into thin air."

Two Snakes was already working on Will Tyler's wounds. He looked at Colbert and shook his head in concern. He went to the men's horses and returned with blankets, covered Will and attempted to cover Bob.

"No you don't," Bob said. "Cover yourself. I got a few more shots to deliver in this scrape."

"You won't be doing any more shooting tonight," Colbert said. He crawled up to the edge of the bank and could see the cabin in the moonlight. "What do we have here?" he asked.

"You got at least two in that tree line and a couple of more in the cabin. We done killed five today."

"Damn," Colbert said. "It's been a usual, peaceful Sunday for you I guess, Bob."

"Belle Reed is one of them. She killed a child back down the road."

"I know. Two Snakes and I found the cabin and your note."

"Is Wilson still alive?"

"Yes, and when we left him, still tied to the tree, he was screaming like a Banshee."

"Benjamin," Bob said with a tone of seriousness—a rare moment for the Texan—"if I die here, or pass out and can't talk later, tell Judge Parker that it was James Harris' dying statement that Aaron Wilson killed him, and Belle killed his boy, John."

"You won't die, Bob. I promise you that. It is a fact." Colbert was becoming emotional. His tough mountain man exterior was weighed down with the sight of his friends lying there with grave wounds. "And, I can't ever imagine a situation where you can't talk for yourself—even from the grave." He managed a short laugh.

Bob smiled back. "That's for damn sure." He winced with pain. The night was beginning to take his strength.

Will began to breathe with short gasps. Two Snakes sat by the fire and watched. He did not cry. Never. But this was as close as he had come in a long time. "I'm going to walk up and see the situation," the Indian said.

"You be careful, my friend. You be very careful." Colbert said with a frown.

"They're crack shots. They're definitely better than the five she sent after us, must be some *vaquero* that Belle hired," Bob surmised. "One has a wide sombrero on his head. Bring it back for me. I fancy that hat as a souvenir," he said. "Go safe."

Bob, as best he could, detailed the events of the day to Colbert.

"I see no choice but to get you back to Fort Smith. We will have to confront these bastards another day," Colbert said.

Bob Johnson did not argue. He had passed out again.

When Two Snakes returned in a few moments, Bob Johnson stirred. "What did you see?"

"There are two in the tree line. Both have long rifles. There are two more in the cabin arguing about leaving and riding on out to the camp."

"Camp? What camp?" Bob asked.

Two Snakes did not answer for a moment.

"What camp?" Bob repeated.

"Six Claws." The spirits were leading Two Snakes to another place. Six Claws was sealed as a journey begun in his past. And that would mean the spirits had plans for the future for the two of them. It was not fear of which Two Snakes thought of Six Claws, only nostalgia and regret that things had come to this. It was a bad sign. He felt his own death for some reason, spiritual or by just common reasoning; he felt that the mention of Six Claws and his camp was a bad sign. A very bad sign.

The persistent Texan brought Two Snakes back to the present reality.

"Goddamnit, Two Snakes, are you listening?' Bob Johnson kept asking. "What camp of Six Claws?"

"I don't know. That's all they said." Two Snakes was only half-present in the ravine.

"Why, every deputy in the Nations and every Ranger in Texas has been trying to find that bad egg's camp. Here we are with information just right up the road. Let's go and beat it out of them, boys," he said, trying to move.

Colbert spoke again, this time even more sternly. "Bob, you're not going anywhere but back to Fort Smith. We will gather the biggest posse in history, return to this place, and then find our way to Six Claws."

Bob tried to argue, but Two Snakes leaned over to him. "Think about William. He is dying." That was the end of the conversation for Bob Johnson. Will Tyler meant more than any dozen Six Claws.

"I will stay and watch them," Two Snakes said. "Benjamin, you take them back and I will be here when the posse returns. We will get your information, I promise," he said, turning to Bob.

Benjamin mounted Will Tyler and Bob Johnson carefully upon their horses, tying them securely and as comfortably as he could. They stole away quietly into to the darkness.

"I'll get you back boys, don't worry. I'll get you back," Colbert said.

"Yeah, but I'll be laying up in some sawbones' bed and miss the whole damn thing. The biggest scrape since *the* poker game, and I'll miss the whole damn thing. By God, what bad luck," Bob said sadly, as he rode close to his wounded comrade.

Chapter 17

▼

3:00 p.m., December 11, 1875
The Choctaw Nation, Indian Territory

When the posse returned to Younger Station late Monday afternoon it was deserted. There had been a hasty retreat by whoever had been there; personal items, clothes, and pictures and letters of Belle Reed were strewn about the first cabin. Even a recent tintype of her and Sam Starr was lying on the floor. It looked as though someone had stepped on it in the shuffle to leave; it was bent by a boot-print, making her distorted face look even more so. While the rest of the posse searched the Station, John Law and Benjamin Colbert rode down to the small ravine and saw the blood-soaked ground—evidence that this was the place where his two deputies had made their heroic stand.

"This is the place all right," Colbert said. If we had not got here in time last night I am afraid we would be coming upon their corpses."

The thought made John Law shudder. He was getting too old for this, and for what time he had left, he damned sure did not intend on using it to bury his grandson.

"Marshal," a voice shouted from the cabin. "Come and see what I found in the fireplace." It was a leather pouch burned with the charred remains of rattlesnakes inside.

Then they remembered. Two Snakes! *Damn, how could someone this important just now enter their minds?* They looked at each other with a common shame and embarrassment. Where was Two Snakes? Colbert looked up the road. He galloped and returned. "Two Snakes' pony is gone from where we tied our mounts last night. I guess at least he was able to ride out of here." Colbert said. "But without his snakes is a bad event." The concern on his face was evident. John Law, too, looked as though he did not want to hear anything more about this. Not another man down.

Colbert shouted from outside the cabin. "Come and look. This is where he was shot."

John Law and the others stood at the spot and saw the blood covering the ground near the outer wall of the cabin. A large-bore bullet hole had passed through the flimsy clapboard siding.

"Looks like a Spenser ball from the inside. A luck shot. But he ain't dead or he'd be laid out here," Colbert said. He picked up the Mexican sombrero near the pool of blood. "It was Two Snakes all right. He had Bob's souvenir with him."

Another deputy shouted from the tree line away from the clearing. "There's two here, dead."

Colbert reached the scene first and looked up at John Law. "Snake bites. It looks like our friend sent two to hell before he left."

The entire group was speechless as they looked at the swollen and pale blue corpses. Eli Traskly had taken the poison especially bad. He was almost black in color.

Each man was revisited by a common childhood fear of snakes. They shuddered under their clothes, all glad it wasn't them, and determined to give Two Snakes a little more respect—and maybe wider room—when they found him.

John Law shouted to the other deputies. "Let's ride!"

The bandits had left no trail. The swamp made it impossible. It could be in any direction, even southeast from where they had come. It looked hopeless.

John Law's recent enthusiasm to *ride* with all dispatch lessened in intensity. He was at a loss as to what to do. Walking blindly through the swamp and dense forest would be a waste of time. Two Snakes' absence was a blow to their plans. His information was what they were counting on. He was not there. It was a troublesome fact for more than one reason. The Indian had become a trusted ally, friend and deputy. *Information be damned.* His well-being became their first concern.

"Let's go back, men. Back to Fort Smith."

"What do we do with these two?" Jesse Allen asked. John Law looked at them for a moment. "They're not worth two dollars for me to even exert the energy to put them on a horse; and they are damned sure not worth the sweat to dig them a grave." He spat a mouthful of tobacco juice on them.

"Get your horse," the marshal said dryly. "Let's ride."

There was an air of disappointment in the group. They rode back silently, every man having his own heart-felt depression to deal with.

Will Tyler and Bob Johnson were settled in a small, makeshift infirmary at the Church of the Immaculate Conception. The Convent of Mercy had been destroyed by fire on the evening of the Feast of the Immaculate Conception—the next night following Will and Katherine's first rendezvous. Bob would later quip that it must have been a spark from the goose down mattress. A remark that Will Tyler dreaded, every time he sensed it coming, on one occasion or the other.

Katherine O'Reilly stood over their beds. Her face was swollen and eyes large with red streaks, evidence of no sleep and long bouts of open weeping. It had been over thirty hours since the deputies had been brought in, multiple gunshot wounds wrecking their bodies. Her fiancé, the love of her life, the man with whom she would spend the rest of her life, had not regained consciousness during all that time. She had stopped the bleeding in his leg—thanking God that the femoral artery had not been pierced—but the chest wound was grave. All her skills had been applied to its repair. Doc Sweeney and Dr. Studdard Thorton, from Van Buren, had assisted her through the hours, but the bullet had done considerable damage. The ball from a Spenser rifle was not meant to do anything else. Bob Johnson, too, still lay unconscious, although several times he had sat up screaming, "where's my damned gun?" and "hold on Will, I hear the Cavalry comin'."

Judge Parker had sat through the day at the deputies' bedside. He had—the first time in memory—canceled Monday's docket, and sat with a blank look upon his face. Judicial protocol, right and wrong, law versus vigilantism all whirled through his thoughts. He had entertained, perhaps secretly to his inner-pleasure, the thoughts of mounting up, with pistol in hand and leading the posse to exact a stark brand of frontier justice upon some individuals. At one of Bob Johnson's outbursts, Parker had laid the Texan's gun by his side—unloaded, of course.

"I don't know what else we can do, Katherine," Doc Sweeney said. "*Please* get some rest. Studdard and I will check Johnson's dressing again. You go lie down. I will call you at the first sign of anything," he said, holding his arm tight around her shoulder. She just shook her head slowly from side to side, seemingly not hearing a word said, and certainly not in any mood to agree to leave the deputies' bedsides.

"It is no use, Doc," Parker said. "I wouldn't expect her to do anything but what she is doing. Let her be."

"Awright, by God, come on out," shouted Bob Johnson as he rose halfway in the bed holding his empty gun in his hand. *What a stroke of divine intervention to unload that Colt*, thought Parker.

Katherine quickly left Will Tyler's side and turned to Johnson's adjacent bed. "Bob," she said loudly, "Bob."

He gazed at her, blinking his one good eye with the grimaced grunts coming from his groggy world. "Katherine?" he asked. "Sweet Katherine. I told that skunk we needed to be getting' on back for that picnic, but he just wouldn't listen," he managed to say with as much of his bullshit he could muster. He fell back onto his bed, still holding his beloved Colt .45 firmly in his grasp.

"Katherine...Will?" he questioned, fearfully.

"He's here, Bob, right beside you. He is alive; and I know I owe my thanks to you. In fact, he has been mumbling some song that *you* must have taught him. Some vulgar song, about Texas women and Arkansas women." She leaned closer. "Thank you, Bob, for keeping him alive."

Tears appeared in the corner of his right eye. The left side of his face was so badly wounded and swollen from the glancing Spenser ball that he could have wept a river full and it would have been dammed up. He held back stifled moans, as long as he could, and then began to cry in earnest. Judge Parker turned away. He, too, was weeping.

Katherine reached down, embraced Bob, and kissed him lovingly.

Since he was a boy on the Guadalupe and killed Jack Standing Owl, Bob had made it a life-long practice to use humor to change the course of any action, event, conversation, or just plain whim of the moment. This was a regal moment of opportunity for his best ability. He was so moved that Will Tyler had survived and that they were in the comfort and aid of Katherine, that tears would come. But, they must be stopped! He had just enough strength to try something.

"Doc Sweeney!" he shouted with Katherine still clinging to him. "Where is Doc Sweeney?"

"Here I am, Bob," responded the town's most beloved doctor, who for thirty years had served the town with the greatest of dedication and selflessness.

"Doc, thank God! You gotta get me outta here and down to your place. Why, if that damn Arkansas pig-chaser over there so much as has toe ache, this woman sawbones will cut my *manlys* off. She done said as much!" He smiled as best he could. "She will blame me for his every scratch. And I told him, and told him, we needed to get on back in time for that lemonade and all the fineries this sweet lady had prepared." He smiled again. "Help me escape, Doc."

Judge Parker, Dr. Thorton, and Doc Sweeney all managed a genuine laugh at the Texan's irreverent spirit in such a dire circumstance. But they all knew him and knew what he was trying to do; what he was compelled to do. It was his nature.

Katherine, however, said nothing. She just looked at Bob, and then responded as any doctor giving the worst case to a patient. "Bob, you don't have to worry about your *manlys* anymore. That last bullet removed them before I got the chance."

Halfway convinced she was just running him—but on the other hand she had turned up a fourth ace the other night and showed him who was boss—he looked at her with eye wide. The left eye was not available for the shocked look.

The silence in the infirmary continued for what seemed an eternity to Bob. Not knowing whether to look away from Katherine and seek some sort of consolation, confirmation, or whatever from another face, he took the best route—his Bob Johnson way.

"I 'spect half the ladies in Texas have done and gone bought 'em a black dress. It is a sad day for sure, and bad luck to a whole passel of 'em that's been waitin' in line for years."

She hugged him again, weeping quietly.

By God, he thought, panicked for a moment, *they may be gone, for a fact!*

Bob Johnson's wounds were serious enough, almost as bad as the damage done to Will Tyler. The Texan suffered some nerve damage to his left arm and would have problems using that side to quick-draw a side arm, though he used his right arm for that task. He could not ever throw a blow with his left fist that would render anyone unconscious; and his lower arm would at times twitch involuntarily. His left ear lobe was gone. His left cheek was shattered and rendered a deep scar from his jaw to his eyebrow. The most serious was his stomach wound. The bullet was a smaller caliber than the devilish Spenser bullet that had so wreaked havoc on Will and him. Nonetheless, it had pierced his left kidney and lung before exiting out the back. He had lost a lot of blood and would suffer the effects of the organ damage.

Will Tyler's leg wound was grave enough to have cost him his life on the ride back to Fort Smith. He had lost so much blood that Deputy Jesse Allen had personally spent hours scrubbing Sky down to get the crimson stain from his majestic gray coat. Will's chest wound was deep and lucky. It missed his heart, but was such a peculiar trauma to his body that it rendered him unconscious for days. His breathing was labored and difficult. His body temperature rose to dangerous levels and he wavered, as Katherine was admitting to herself, between life and death with each breath.

"Two Snakes," Bob said. "What did he find out?"

Parker answered. No one else wanted to. "Deputy." There was an air of official conversation in his tone. Bob felt it and looked more intently at Parker. "Deputy Two Snakes was gone when the posse returned. We judge that he is on the trail of the assassins."

"What do you mean you *judge* it, don't you know?"

"No, not for sure. There were no signs and no tracks out of there. Just a deserted camp." Parker reached to the floor and brought up a bloody sombrero. "He got this for you before they evidently shot him. But we believe he is alive. We truly believe that."

"This blood, is it Two Snakes'?"

"That is what I have been told. It must have been important for him to get the hat for you."

Bob looked at the tattered hat. He was going to weep again. He could not stop. He did not try. He knew that something was wrong. Bad wrong. If it was the last thing he did on this earth, he would find that Indian and just grab him, snakes and all.

It was a week after Christmas when the two deputies were up and out of the infirmary, ready for duty. It had been a grim time. Daily posses had scoured the Territory for Two Snakes and the trail of Belle Reed, Sam Starr and any sign of the fabled 'Fort of Six Claws'. No signs were uncovered. One deputy group under Captain Buck Thomas had not returned; and no news in weeks from them left everyone with the gravest concern. Valentine Morgan had on four occasions spent days searching for the overdue lawmen. Bob Johnson and Will Tyler sneered at those reports.

"Morgan probably killed them himself," Bob said after the deputy meeting where Judge Parker had just praised Valentine for his efforts. "Just wait," Will tempered his friend, "we'll get the evidence on him. Be patient. We can't make a move without some sort of proof. He is too well-liked and respected."

"And besides, he is nineteen thousand dollars poorer," Will added with a laugh. They both laughed. It was some victory anyway.

The month-long recuperation was doubly hard on them both. Each day they wanted to saddle and ride with the men, feeling like they each had a personal stake in the events as much and even more so than any other deputy. Not only the scars, both physically and emotionally, but the loss and uncertainty of the fate of Two Snakes cut hard.

Katherine O'Reilly had not only nursed them to health with her exceptional medical skills, she had mothered them to the point that they had begun to depend upon her. They grew accustomed to her constant attention and liked it. They were her only patients; all others had to see Doc Sweeney or go across the river for medical needs. She was consumed with their recovery; she would have it no other way so no one even dared to speak against it, not even the priests and nuns who often needed her skills for their various ministries. They just made do. Bob Johnson admired her more each day, and she began to accept him and his ways. Will Tyler *loved* her more each day, and she began to spiral deeper and deeper in love with him. He was all she thought about. Along with the constant danger in the Territory and the inevitability that he would return to harm's way soon. She had to relocate their lives and destiny elsewhere. But how? It occupied her every thought, just as Will Tyler occupied her every heart's beat. She had made Will her total property. Absolutely and sealed!

Chapter 18

February 6, 1876
Cherokee Nation, Indian Territory
One week before the capture of the missionaries

The exhausted rider reached Fort Gibson in the Cherokee Nation about seven hours after he had found the badly decomposed remains of Captain Buck Thomas and his posse. The young corporal had been on routine scout duty to the south when he came upon the site of the massacre. Realizing that such a horrific act was more than likely committed by Six Claws and his men, he was acutely aware of the extreme danger he was in if they were still around. He rode as hard as he could with his head constantly turning and looking back over his shoulder. He had not even taken the time to bury them—or what was left of them. He just took his mount north as fast as he would run.

He ran to his sergeant and reported what he had found.

"Now slow down Corporal," the sergeant snapped. "I didn't understand a damned thing you said." It had been a peaceful day at the fort. More than was usual. Sergeant King was irritated that the young corporal had disturbed his fine afternoon of lazily catching up on neglected paperwork.

"Sergeant King," the soldier said, breathing so heavily that his chest heaved. "I was out near the Canadian as ordered, and I came on some bodies."

"All right," the sergeant said, listening more intently now. "What bodies?"

"I counted seven," the corporal continued. "Five white men and two Indians. Two of the white men were wearing Deputy Marshal badges. Looks like they been there about two weeks or more," he said, his eyes wide in his face.

"Here, have a drink," the sergeant said, offering the soldier a cup of water that he had just poured for himself. "It must have been that missing posse out of Fort

Smith that we got word on. How were they killed?" he asked the corporal who had gulped the water down and was looking around the small office for more.

"It was bad," the soldier said as he spied the sergeant's canteen on the desk, grabbed it and proceeded to swallow the water as fast as he could. "It was bad," he repeated. "All gunshot wounds I think. It was hard to tell. They was eat up something terrible. Bones sticking out and all," he said, almost in a daze.

"Hard to tell. What the hell do you mean, hard to tell?" the sergeant demanded forcefully.

"Damn, Sergeant, the two deputies, they was all hacked up and wild animals or something had been chewing on their parts."

"My God. What about the other five, were they eaten too?"

"No, Sergeant, as close as I could tell, they was just killed outright by rifle fire to the head and body. The animals didn't bother them."

"But you said the other two were hacked up. What about the feet?"

"Cut up something awful, bones cut and all, and, I know what you're asking. I made sure I looked. There was a toe missing from the feet. Of course, they was so messed up I couldn't tell for sure. It could have been the animals." He was now breathing at a slower rate and had better recall of the scene.

"I don't know of any coyotes or vultures that carry knives or axes. This is the work of that goddamn Six Claws, the murdering bastard," the sergeant said.

"Yessir, that was my thought. That's the reason I hightailed it back here as fast as I could. I didn't stop to bury the bodies or anything. I just got the hell out of there," he said, almost remorsefully.

"You did fine Corporal, just fine. You're off duty. Go get you a meal and hit the barracks," King said. He was talking to the young soldier but his thoughts were elsewhere. He was thinking of his younger brother and his young wife who had come from Pennsylvania at his urging, to start a new life and prosperity in the West. They had been intercepted by Six Claws and murdered before reaching Fort Gibson. That had been a year ago. A day did not pass that the sergeant did not think about them and the horror that they must have gone through. It was a signature Six Claws massacre. They were butchered and one toe had been cut from each of them. Six Claws always cut a toe from his victim that he killed personally. It was rumored that he had hundreds in his collection which he carried with him in a fine silk bag, stolen from some unfortunate victim before her own toe was put into the bloody group.

Since that day, when the bodies of his brother and sister-in-law had been brought in, Sergeant King was obsessed with Six Claws. His last thought at night, before he went to sleep, was the thought of taking the Indian's head off with his knife and smashing the skull into bone fragments with his rifle butt. This fantasy allowed him the ability of sleeping soundly.

He received permission from the fort commander, Colonel Julius Dixon, to personally take the message to Fort Smith about the posse. The colonel understood the sergeant's obsession, and offered no resistance at the request. He had seen the change in the man's nature in the year since the brother's death. This might be the catharsis needed to exorcize the demons. Dixon suggested, and Sergeant King was brought to near tears at the proposal, that when he arrived in Fort Smith, he asked to join in the posse tracking Six Claws. He gave King a personal letter to deliver to Judge Parker. Even though it crossed jurisdictional boundaries, the Army had cooperated fully with the Fort Smith deputies in every way possible. Colonel Dixon was a good friend of Isaac Parker. Both were Missourians, and he had even campaigned for him in the judge's Congressional race. Dixon was confident the judge would honor his request, and assured the sergeant that he could stay as long as needed. In fact, it was official. The colonel issued formal orders to him saying such.

King was shaking as he packed his gear. His eyes were filled with tears as he pocketed a small, ruby-colored broach that had belonged to his sister-in-law, Lucy King. Six Claws had overlooked the trinket in the massacre and it was the only thing he had of her except his memory of the beautiful young lady who had married his brother. He also took a small tintype of his brother, Marcus, and their mother. "I'll kill the bastard," he said softly as he looked at the portrait and put the picture into his coat flap. "Dear brother, I'll take you with me to let you see his rotting corpse."

He questioned Corporal Jones again about the exact location where he had found the posse, and rode east to Fort Smith.

Two Snakes' bunk was empty. His belongings were just as he had left them the night he and Colbert went toward Younger Station in search of Johnson and Tyler. It was not a shrine, but close to it. The deputies passed by it each day, paused and thought of their lost friend and comrade.

Bob Johnson and Benjamin Colbert were in the deputies' barracks playing poker with three others when Will threw the door wide open. A haze of blue cigar smoke hung in the air like a low-settling rain cloud on a steamy Mississippi River bank. Will choked and winced at the assault to his nose. "Why don't you men smoke those damn things outside?"

"Outside?" What kind of nonsense thinking is that?" shouted Bob. "I guess that is the Yankee side of you. Huh?"

Will ignored his comment and shouted to them as he quickly remembered his mission. "Bob, Colbert, come on. John Law wants to see us, pronto."

The three walked down the street to the courthouse and into John Law's office. The marshal was standing near his desk with a haggard-looking soldier who had evidently been on the trail. Sheriff Hainey was standing beside John Law. He, too, was anxious to join the posse.

"Gentlemen," he said. "I'd like you to meet Sergeant Rupert King. He's here giving us some sad news about Captain Buck Thomas' posse. As you know, they've been overdue for weeks, and our efforts to turn them up have failed. It looks like they met the same fate as Roundtree and Bearfoot a few months ago. Same situation. The news is a bit late, but I'm afraid we can't keep telegraph wires up in the Territory more than a day before some son of a bitch cuts them down."

The sergeant told the group what his corporal had found in the Choctaw Nation. He also related the story of his brother and family, and how he would not return to Fort Gibson until Six Claws was either dead or in custody.

Valentine Morgan slammed his hat to the floor. "I'm tired of that savage ruling the roost around here. I want to get him once and for all. He needs to be found and brought to justice."

Bob Johnson was amazed. Not only at the fact that Morgan was a black liar and was probably hindering more than helping the posse work, but also at Valentine's ability to keep from getting out of control and using cuss words when he expressed a determination in grave situations. He had been so on several occasions over the past few months since he had known him. But Bob was not so inclined.

"I agree," he said. "That son of a bitch needs to die, and die slowly. With his liver in my hands."

Everyone agreed and thought in Bob's terms even though their admiration for Morgan's composure was solid—especially since the deputy had the best record in the Territory for swift and sure justice to the men he tracked.

"Marshal, I'd like to go out for a day or two alone and see what I can find. This will give you time to get Tyler's posse ready for the trip. I'll be back with some leads by the time they are ready," Morgan said.

Hainey asked to assist. "Valentine, why don't I ride with you and give you a hand?"

"No, Jack, I believe I can travel faster alone."

"I trust your instinct, Val. We will be ready when you return. Jack, you can go along with the group also. We will need all the help we can get," John Law said.

Bob thought very deeply about John Law's remark. When did he need to confide in the marshal about what he knew? It was becoming serious. He and Will Tyler both wished that they had the counsel of Two Snakes now. If Two Snakes had been there instead of dead or captured or a dozen other things discussed daily by the deputies, he would have stood in the corner of the room and listened intently. He would have been troubled. Sure enough troubled by two things at once. First, the Indian had a distinct hesitation about Morgan. From the moment they had met, he felt in his spirit that something was wrong. He just could not see it clearly yet. Perhaps he felt the man was a blow-hard, he had tried to reason as he pondered the deputy on many occasions. Bob Johnson knew this about his friend, as he thought about him during the briefing. He knew also that Two Snakes would have been very disturbed at the mention of Six Claws. That killer was more than a mere acquaintance of Two Snakes—he had said so that night in the ravine—he was part of his life—a childhood hero, of sorts, but still an evil killer. Bob knew enough about Kiowas to know the old tribal belief that a killer, and his evil spirit, would take your reasoning powers, and a man was never the same. Perhaps Six Claws would just kill Two Snakes, as he would any other Indian. *If he had captured their friend.* Or maybe the killer would remember him and keep him safe, or as a damned pet. And then just kill him anyway. Bob Johnson pondered this during the sergeant's report and Valentine's comments. He would think of this a great deal more. The Indian had become very important to him, almost as important as Will.

Will, too, was thinking a great deal. But not about Two Snakes, or killers or anything of the kind. His love affair with Katherine was like a whirlwind. He had spent every moment possible in her company and hated the thought of a long assignment that would take him away from her. After the past months of *coveting your neighbor's wife, diddlin', or taking the hickory stick for a walk,* as Bob had called it along with a dozen other expressions, he did not relish leaving on any assignment. Whatever it was called—a sin in the eyes of many for sure—but a pleasure, for *damned* sure, of the heart and every other part of the body and soul—he did not want to leave her. Not for any outlaw. Especially Six Claws, who was no ordinary killer. This would take some time. He was still disturbed about the whole situation as they met that evening after the posse decisions had been made.

"It will be a while before I get back. We will be leaving as soon as Valentine has it checked out and we are planned and ready. This time we've found the remains of Buck Thomas for sure," he said to Katherine as they strolled down the street. This is what she had feared. She knew that Will was a consummate professional about his work and would never shirk an assignment. Still her heart ached to ask him to not go this time. She had heard all the horror stories about the Indian killer and his gang, and even though she knew Will was capable, she still feared for his safety. Besides, they had only begun discussions about the wedding. It was to be the event of Fort Smith. John Law would stand up for Will and Judge Parker had agreed to give her away, if need be, in her father's absence. She had thought about setting a date far enough in the future so her family could make arrangements to come west to Fort Smith—or even more perfect, convince Will to go to Boston for the wedding. She knew, however, that he would never take the time to do that, and she didn't want to wait that long in any event. She was ready to marry him for her own burning passion and out of a building insecurity and impatience. She imagined the worst every time he rode out. This time her spirit was screaming for her to stop him. Since their first night together—when he had accepted her, and her *imperfections*, without even a second thought—she now had a foreboding despondency of losing him.

    She was reserved, however, in her response to his news, determined not to let another demon overtake her every mood and action. "Be very careful," she said. She tried her best not to show her concern. "You almost died at Younger Station in December—or have you forgotten?"

    "No, I haven't forgotten. And I remember who saved my life, too." He kissed her gently. She began to cry. Sadness mixed with happiness. It was a strange emotion.

    "Please. Please be careful."

    Will felt helpless to ease her anxiety. "You know I always am," he said reassuringly. "Besides with Bob, Two Snakes, and Colbert, who could be in better hands?"

    She thought immediately at his mistake of mentioning Two Snakes. Will's face turned ashen as he looked at her.

    "Don't worry, Will. You'll find him." That was still no comfort to her, but she smiled, tried to lighten the conversation that had taken a dark turn. "No, it is *they* who are in good hands."

    They kissed. Each time they embraced, she ached for his touch. Since she had first experienced physical love with him, two and a half months before, and seemingly, to her at least, countless times since, she desired him as much as human emotion could surface. Will felt the same. He had experienced other women, but these feelings were something so deep and profound that he could think of nothing but the warmth of her body. He relished the anticipation and dream even more than the fact that soon they would be married.

She broke the embrace and smiled. "It is going to be a good life with you, Will Tyler."

"I expect it will be better for me than for you," he said.

"How gallant," she said. "I was afraid that Bob's strange ways would affect your sensitivity, but I expect that you're safe if you keep talking like that."

"Oh, he's not so bad. He just has a curious way of filtering life, I guess."

"You just stay the way you are and don't let him influence you too much," she said. "If you ever up and ride off from me like he did his wife, well...just imagine someone more fierce than Six Claws after you," she said with a mischievous laugh.

"You'll never have to worry about that," he said, kissing her again.

"Now, when do you leave for the Nations with the sisters?" Will was so self-absorbed with his pending trip he had forgotten about the short missionary journey into the Choctaw Nation. *It was damned selfish of him*, he thought. Not to have even mentioned it. He knew it was important to her, and he had to start thinking about life from her perspective and not just about himself. He was embarrassed by the inexcusable absence of any thought of her work.

"Oh, we will leave early in the morning. We should only be gone five days or so, but I won't be back before you leave," she said with a sad look. He made small talk about her trip with Father Boles and the *Sister sisters*, but his thoughts kept coming back to the posse adventure in a couple of days. Again, he had to put himself in check.

"Don't you worry about me," he said. "I'll be fine. You just take care of yourself. I worry about you out there." He really meant that. For the first time it sank in on him. Even though that was the safest part of all the Territory, there was still some danger there.

"Anyway, it is probably safer there than here in Fort Smith," she said with a reassuring tone. She liked that he was concerned for her safety, but she was a veteran of two years of ghastly Civil War campaigns. She could take care of herself. Still, it was the type of words she liked to hear from him.

"Still," he said. "Maybe I should go with you."

"And just who would keep Bob Johnson and those other surly types from getting themselves lost?" she replied with a laugh.

As they walked along, she talked about the McGready sisters and their excitement over the trip. And since he was going to be gone with the posse, she would convince Father Boles to stay even longer if need be. The trip was planned to establish a teaching program, some basic medical care, and should take no more than a week. She looked forward to the outing. It would be the first since she had arrived, and it would help take her mind off his absence. He reasoned that he should be gone no more than a two weeks himself, and was already looking forward to their reunion kiss. If their parting kiss was any indication, it would be something he would look forward to immensely. And the wedding. In Boston. In Fort Smith. In the back of a wagon in the Cherokee Nation, she didn't care. She just wanted it. So did Will. All was good.

Chapter 19

▼

February 11, 1876
Six Claws' camp in the Choctaw Nation
The day before the capture of the missionaries

Nelson Creekmore waited impatiently as the sun began to sink lower on the horizon. His informant was hours late. He did not tolerate mistakes nor incompetence; however, he tempered his anger as the man rode up. He was the most valuable asset that he had. He was the source of all his information that allowed his entire operation to succeed.

"You must have had some trouble," Creekmore said.

"I didn't expect the news on Thomas' posse to be brought in by a personal rider from Fort Gibson. All the trouble it stirred up caused everything to fall behind," Valentine Morgan said.

Morgan had disguised his larceny well in the past and still did so. He befriended everyone and most men counted him a close companion and supporter. He had been the driving force behind the corruption in Fort Smith for years. Until Parker and Singleton came, he had stolen and embezzled from the court. Now because of the reforms, he was down to selling information to Creekmore. He detested Creekmore, but he detested trying to support his lifestyle with the meager wages he managed as a deputy even more.

"Your goddamn savages sure did their job on Buck Thomas," Morgan said. "One of these days they are going to get caught and swing from the gallows in Parker's courtyard, and I will be there cheering louder than anyone."

"Cheer all you want, Valentine. Just remember that the actions of that goddamn savage pay you a handsome amount of gold. We don't want to see him hang too soon, do we?" Creekmore asked. "I'll see him later today and I'll be sure to relay your wishes to him," he sneered.

Morgan was ready to conclude his business and leave. He had no remorse for selling out his fellow deputies. In fact, he felt a perverse gratification for being able to sell them to their deaths. They were a bunch of ignorant bastards. The pompous fool Bob Johnson and that Will Tyler, with his special treatment, could just cease breathing as soon as possible as far as he was concerned. And the town would be better off with those missionaries gone. He remembered his advice to Will Tyler—just love her. *Love her in the grave*, he thought with a smirk. Goddamn religious. He detested them. He quickly detailed the posse plans to find Six Claws and the plan for the missionary trip into the Choctaw Nation. He did not relish spending any more time with Creekmore than was necessary.

As he rode off, Valentine Morgan reached into his saddlebag and retrieved the heavy bag of fifty twenty-dollar gold pieces. He liked the feel of the coins. It was the only reason he tolerated Creekmore.

"Someday, I'll put a bullet in your eye, you son of a bitch," he sneered as he looked back at Creekmore, riding in the opposite direction. "Maybe, I'll put a bullet in both eyes!" His head began to twitch involuntarily, as he thought of Creekmore, then Johnson, then Tyler, then Singleton—all dead. His mouth pulled back and the taut grin allowed saliva to run down his chin as he thought of the nuns with bullets through their hearts. He was insane. He knew it. He liked the feeling.

Six Claws and his collection of killers were camped on the south side of the Canadian near its confluence with the Arkansas, in the Choctaw Nation. They had been waiting since yesterday for the gun trader. This area of the Territory was wide open to bandits and any outlaw who had the grit to enter and stay. Many entered but few stayed, because there was always someone meaner and deadlier just over the clearing. Six Claws had no problem camping there or anywhere else for that matter. Everyone gave him wide berth as he entered any part of the Southwest. He knew it and he expected it.

They had stolen a cow, butchered it, and were gorging themselves on a roasted hindquarter. They had not had any beef in a while and were hungry for it. A couple of stolen horses, and four or five wild Arkansas boars they had fattened on dead men's flesh had been their fare for about a month. They were ready for a change. Six Claws preferred beef to horse or dog, which had been the staple of his tribe for as long as he could remember. The aroma wafted far in every direction and scores of wolves, coyotes, wild dogs and varmints of every description were licking their mouths. One thing was evident though, be it animal or human, no one disturbed the outlaw's feast.

Six Claws had nine men riding with him. The number changed frequently, given the fact that they were constantly in life-or-death struggles with other Indians, outlaws, Army patrols, Texas Rangers or U.S. Marshal posses out of the Territory. Six Claws himself killed someone almost weekly, either in a raid or by his own hand. It did not take much of a reason for him to kill one of his own men— and he frequently did just to keep that thought in their minds. He ruled by savage fear and it worked. The outlaws and renegades that joined him knew that if they survived, they could enjoy the fruits of some good raids. It was worth the risk; the rewards could be great. Because Six Claws never had trouble finding a new killer to ride with him, he liked to keep the number at about eight or ten. It was just the right sized gang to be effective and feared, but small enough to travel fast and unencumbered by the necessities of a larger group. He did, however, have at the ready twenty or more riders in each of his hideouts in the sand bluffs near the Boggy River in the Territory, and at Ram Horn Canyon, south of the Red River in northern Texas. He had learned this tactic from Apache and Comanche bands who had been so successful in Texas and New Mexico.

Traveling with him were long-time members, Killing Tree, so named because he had killed a bear as a youth by jumping from a tree onto the back of a black bear and killing it with a knife; and Small Long Knife, named for his five-foot, two-inch stature and his preference for an old cavalry officer's sword as his weapon of choice. He kept it sharply honed and had taken the head off of a victim, more than once, with one swift stroke. Both Killing Tree and Small Long Knife were Comanche. This was unusual, because Six Claws was Kiowa, and the Comanche and Kiowa had been at war for generations. The gang also included an Apache named John Birdsong, a Creek killer named Russell Elk Horn and three Mexican brothers, Juan, Pelido, and Julio Marquez. The Marquez brothers had robbed and killed in South Texas and all over northern Mexico, until being chased out by the Texas Rangers, under Captain Tobias Johnson. There were five brothers, but the troop west of Fort Worth killed two. Axehead Smith, named because of a small pointed head that sat atop his two hundred and fifty pound body, and Henry Salmon, a half-black, half-Cherokee murderer who slaughtered his entire family in the Territory and two deputy marshals who were tracking him, were the remaining two that made up Six Claws' group.

"Killing Tree," Six Claws said. "What did that farmer say when you stole this cow?"

"He said nothing," replied the Comanche, whose right eye twitched constantly due to a scar down the right side of his face. "I had his tongue in my hand

and his ears shoved down his mouth in its place. But, his old woman said plenty as I raped her."

"What did she say?" Six Claws inquired, almost with disinterest, sporting a dead expression spread across his weather-beaten face. Even though he was just forty years old, his face looked much older. His body, however, was fit and muscular. He walked high on his six-foot frame.

"She said, 'Please, no more'," the Indian answered with a sneer. "So, I said, okay, and used my knife to finish violating her. After that, she said nothing more. Perhaps she preferred the knife to me, because she stopped complaining."

The Marquez brothers thought that was very funny. Julio, the youngest, especially thought that Killing Tree had a good sense of humor and often tried to entice him into conversation that would show the Comanche's wit.

"Hey, Killing Tree," Julio said. "How many Mexicans have you killed?"

"One less than I should have," Killing Tree replied.

Julio laughed with boyish abandon. "Kill Pelido here, he smells and snores. I can't sleep around him." He smirked loudly at his remark. Pelido, however, did not like it at all. As he did with similar remarks, he reached over and slapped Julio on the face. "Shut up, goddamn you."

"Such stupid Mexicans," Killing Tree said to Six Claws. "Why do you keep them around?"

"I keep them in case we get caught without food. We can make a meal out of them, or at least use them to fatten the pigs," Six Claws said.

Julio, again, thought this very funny. However, Six Claws kept Julio around for another reason. Julio was also born with six toes on his right foot. It was never spoken of, especially since Six Claws broke Julio's nose once for just mentioning the similarity in a joking remark. Six Claws did not joke about anything. He did not know how.

He was now forty years old. In the nineteen years since leaving his people, he had killed over two hundred men, women and children—Indian, Mexican, black and white alike. Often times he killed with such excessive cruelty that the details of the crimes had gone unreported by lawmen in fear of panicking the settlers and travelers through the Llano and into the Territory and even into the States.

His perfect companion in the raids was Killing Tree. Although Six Claws had dedicated himself to fear, he was guarded around the Comanche. Killing Tree had grown with savage brutality on the Llano plains. Since he was a boy, his life had been a daily struggle. His people's war with other tribes, Mexicans, and the Texas Rangers had been a nursery of horror in which the young man was nurtured. He had killed his first Kiowa at the age of eleven, and his thirst for human blood and the look of death in the eyes of his victims had never been sated. He especially reveled in raping his female victims. Not one woman had survived since the first offering to his savage desire some twenty years ago when he was sixteen. Only one had come close to stopping his vengeance. A young farmer's wife, caught in a raid of the family's small wagon train, managed to grab a knife from the floor of the wagon in which she was being ravaged by Killing Tree and cut into his face the eight-inch gash from the top of his right ear to his chin. She died, as she knew she would, as all eight of her family had, but she died knowing that she had almost killed him. From that time, Killing Tree was more careful in his attacks. He would drag the victims into the open so that there was no chance of a hidden weapon.

Six Claws never violated women, captives or otherwise. The memories of his mother, Hand Over Mouth, were heavy on his black heart. Even though he never complained or stopped Killing Tree, he himself would not torture women. He would kill them quickly. His cruelty toward men, however, far surpassed Killing Tree—who was very cautious around Six Claws. He would never go to sleep until the Kiowa killer was asleep, and then he would sleep at the ready. Seeing sights like the two deputies' parts being eaten by the wild pigs made him aware that Six Claws was more bestial than he was. That made him cautious.

The renegades camped on the Canadian were comfortable in the late afternoon sun. A good meal and a satisfying murderous raid of the old farmer and his wife had put them in a contented mood. All were asleep except Killing Tree and Six Claws. The Comanche was grooming his horse; Six Claws was on guard, as always. He was looking to the north. There were thousands of Indians and settlers and stupid farmers in the Territory, and he had no one to kill. He walked to the bank of the river. It was near flood stage. Wide as a giant lake where it joined the Arkansas.

He was restless. His black stare looked in the direction of the sleeping gang. He put his rifle to his shoulder and took aim. He pulled the trigger, and Juan Marquez died in his sleep as the bullet exploded his head.

The riders approaching the Indian gang heard the rifle shot. They stopped on the north side of the river and looked across at Six Claws camp.

"What's they shootin' at?" Moses Brown asked. He had the heavy reins of the wagon team wrapped tightly around his hand. He was a skittish man who jumped at every noise—especially around Six Claws. He was deathly afraid of the Indian. Brown was a former slave who had seen every type of torture that could be inflicted on a human being, but that killer did horrible things to people. It occupied every moment of his thoughts on their frequent trips to the Indian's camp.

"Oh, the son of a bitch is probably shooting one of his men again," Nelson Creekmore said. "Let's go, and be by-God careful crossing here. I don't want one damned bullet to get wet. You hear?"

"Yessir," Brown replied as he prodded the team into the river.

They came into the camp just as Six Claws was beginning to feed Juan Marquez to the wild pigs. Creekmore dismounted as if nothing seemed out of the ordinary. His men, however, especially Moses Brown, were spellbound at the sight of the Mexican's torso being ravaged by the frenzied boars.

"You are a day late, *Holcomb*," barked Six Claws.

Creekmore was incensed at the Indian. He had told him on countless occasions, in the clearest terms possible, to never call him Holcomb. The Indian, however, reveled in the opportunity to do so.

"Goddamnit, Six Claws, never call me by that name," he said. "Someday you will regret doing so."

Colonel Josiah Holcomb had fled Arkansas and had found fertile grounds for his hatred in Kansas. Stripped of his land, his fortune, his name, and forced to live a life in hiding, was just the fuel needed to make an already hate-filled man more so. Everything that had happened was the fault of the damned Yankees and the carpetbaggers who had plundered away the last parcel of dignity left to the Southern culture. His only reason for life was the daily vengeance he could exact upon those who had destroyed his way of life and all he had loved. He often thought of Franklin Tyler, who fueled his determination to destroy anything the Union Federalists protected. The killing of that Yankee bastard was the highlight of his life. Even though the son of a bitch Singleton had led a crusade against him, which finally had him flee his beloved country, his only regret was that he had not killed John Law and the entire family that night. *A moment of extremely poor decision making*, he had said myriad times since that night. With Little Rock captured and Helena taken, Holcomb disappeared from Arkansas late in 1863. John Law had helped Grant defeat Vicksburg and was back in Helena looking for Holcomb, determined to arrest him and to hang him for the murder of Franklin and Dora Tyler. With his farm confiscated and his political base gone, Holcomb fled to Missouri and into Kansas.

For all purposes, Josiah Holcomb had died in Arkansas, and Nelson M. Creekmore was born in Kansas. Creekmore arrived in Coffeyville, Kansas in October of 1863 with one hundred thousand dollars in gold, six loyal men from the old Phillips County command, and two former slaves. He bought a ranch in southern Montgomery County, near Coffeyville, and rebuilt his base to carry on his private war with the United States. By 1875, he was a powerful force in the Indian wars, but not an ally to the Army and law authorities. Eighty percent of all guns and ammunition sold to the Indians came through the Creekmore operation right at the travel routes of the Army at Fort Gibson in the Territory. He operated out of a hideaway base in the Brushy Mountains only twenty miles from Fort Gibson. This was particularly satisfying to him. "Right under their stupid Yankee noses," he liked to say. He sold and traded to any renegade or outlaw group that openly waged war on the Army and the settlers—especially Yankee settlers. He aided those groups with information on payroll shipments, wagon train movements, and land sale details. Troop deployment plans were bought by Creekmore from his valuable informant in the Fort Smith Court and sold to the gangs to assist them in raids on farmers and settlers. In taking his revenge upon the Union, he was becoming very wealthy. Wealth bought powerful friends and corrupted officials who, for a price, would turn their heads. Creekmore now had the needed sphere of influence and power to battle the North; a fight he had only dreamed of as Colonel Josiah Holcomb.

No one suspected Nelson Creekmore of treason. He was a stern man by reputation, and a powerful man who wooed power brokers in Kansas, Missouri and the Indian Territory. No one questioned his motives; he covered his tracks well.

Creekmore was not satisfied with just the planning and administration of the war against the United States. He participated in selected raids, often leading them. Anytime Yankee settlers or a group of wagons were heading into the Territory, they were in danger of being attacked by Creekmore himself. He reveled in killing settlers from the North, and then making it look like an attack by Indians. This accomplished more than just a method to satisfy his blood lust: it kept the Army in a quandary about which renegade group was responsible. Washington officials, local authorities and citizen groups west of the Mississippi railed against the Army and their inability to stop the blood bath in the Territory. This delighted Creekmore.

His greatest source of pride was the alliance he had forged with Six Claws. Creekmore would travel often and meet with Six Claws in the outlaw camp south of the Canadian. Information, guns, ammunition, horses and captives were traded for the gold and valuables the gang had taken from their many raids. It had perplexed the Army and lawmen for years as to how Six Claws had a seemingly inexhaustible supply of the newest repeaters and ammunition. His knowledge of payroll and supply movements was equally mysterious.

Six Claws was Creekmore's favorite client, but he had his hands full trying to keep the killer from randomly attacking settlers outside the planned raids. On several occasions, Six Claws' gang had slaughtered good Southern families. This was totally against Creekmore's agenda—only the Yankee families were to be targeted. There were plenty of those—enough to last Six Claws a lifetime. However, he continued to raid and kill any group that was available. Six Claws was amused with Creekmore's angry outbursts about Southern families who had fallen victim to the Indian. Six Claws considered any white person, regardless of political or cultural affiliation, an appropriate target.

There was one other factor in the relationship that amused Six Claws. Creekmore, in his personal raids in Kansas, Missouri and the northern part of the Territory, had begun cutting a toe from each victim. Creekmore explained that this would further confuse the lawmen and the settlers into thinking that Six Claws was in their area. This would make the legend of Six Claws grow stronger, Creekmore explained to the Indian. People would say he was so powerful he could be in two places at one time. Six Claws thought this was good. Creekmore would regularly bring the toes that he had severed to add to the Indian's collection. This put the Kiowa killer in something close to a good mood. He would lecture Creekmore about the proper way to cut a toe. It was an art to him, not a butcher's gash. Creekmore would always sever the toes in a jagged manner, just to keep the Indian going.

"Their badges," Creekmore shouted, looking through the sack of guns and bloody clothing from the dead deputies. "Where are their goddamn badges?" He was, as always, an impatient man. He could not tolerate sloth in anyone, not even Six Claws.

Six Claws stared at Creekmore. He knew the value of his relationship with the old man. He knew, too, that soon he would not be able to control his impulse to put a bullet through his heart for such insolence.

"I am not one of your captives," Six Claws replied. "Don't speak to me that way."

Creekmore swallowed hard and looked away for a brief moment. He knew how dangerous the Indian was, but still, he was enraged. "The badges are very important. We've discussed that. There were two and you did not get them."

"I guess the pigs ate them," Killing Tree said.

Julio thought that was very funny. "They was snorting and grubbing at everything else on them deputies, I 'spect that they did eat those badges," he said, all the while looking at the vanishing corpse of his brother Juan.

Creekmore was not amused. The U.S. Deputy Marshal badges would be valued trophies in his collection of Yankee spoils. He had required Six Claws to take any insignias, badges, corps flags, swords or warrants—especially warrants signed by Parker—from all soldiers and lawmen that they killed.

Creekmore decided to let the matter drop. He turned his anger toward Julio.

"Where are the two brothers of this Mexican?" he asked, looking around the camp, finally deciding to broach the subject of the sight of the boars and the half-eaten human.

"One is no longer with us, he's pig meat," Six Claws replied. "The other one is off maybe hiding under a rock. He probably thought he was next."

"Yeah, my mother has only two sons," Julio said with a perplexing laugh. "Juan died in his sleep."

"Six Claws, how can you expect to continue to raid if you keep killing your men for no reason?" Creekmore asked. "And you'd be better served if you didn't recruit these stupid Mexicans, they are unreliable at best, and their loyalty is always in question."

"We will ride with who we want to," interjected Killing Tree. "Besides, we only have two more to go."

"Let me know when you are ready, Killing Tree," Julio said jovially. "So I can get a head start."

Creekmore just sat and shook his head in disgust. His operation was in the hands of fools, he thought. He changed the subject.

"I guess you heard that Parker hanged six men in Fort Smith and one of them was Smoker Mankiller," he said.

"Mankiller was a good raider, for a Cherokee," Six Claws said. "After he left us and married that fat wife in the Nations, he got lazy. He deserved to hang."

"Still, that's a terrible fate, breaking your neck at the end of a Yankee rope," Creekmore said. "I always liked Smoker, he was a pleasant fellow, for an Indian." He lit up his cigar. "The whole damn thing was political," he continued, pulling a cloud of smoke from his fine southern stogie. "It was just a grand-standing move by Parker to show those Washington bastards how he has everything under control out here in the Territory. It's our job, by God, to prove him wrong. Dead wrong."

The Indians looked on without saying anything. They were used to letting Creekmore ramble.

Six Claws' men unloaded the case of Winchester rifles and the store of two thousand rounds of ammunition. Creekmore had also brought five gallons of whisky, some tobacco, and some staples such as sugar, coffee and salt.

"We don't need your white man's food," growled Six Claws as he tore the food sacks and spilled them on the ground. "If we want things like this, we will steal from some farmer and kill him for it," he said.

Julio scrambled to scoop up the spilled sugar. He loved sugar, and Six Claws, knowing this, would never allow it to be stolen in raids while the Mexican was around. Julio was stuffing it into his pockets and fighting off a wild boar who had begun rooting for the sweet treat, when Six Claws knocked the Mexican over, held his mouth open with his fist and began pouring handfuls of sugar down his throat. Julio choked and spit out the dry sugar as he broke away and ran to the river for water.

This amused Creekmore's men. It was a needed respite in the constantly tense mood of Six Claws' camp. Their laughter was short-lived. One look from Creekmore reminded them of the nature of the business. They continued their work of loading the wagon with stolen goods, which the gang had taken on raids during the past month.

Creekmore, surveying the booty, again found fault with Six Claws. "This is fairly worthless," he said, sifting through items of silver and some jewelry. "It sure the hell is not worth a case of Winchesters."

"Is this worthless?" Six Claws asked. The Indian then proudly produced a fifteen-inch, gold, diamond and emerald encrusted crucifix. Some of the stones were the size of a fingertip. Its beauty astounded the normally unflappable Creekmore. He took it from the Indian and held it up to the bright sun. Its faceted refractions showered the ground.

"Where did you get this?" Creekmore asked.

"I traded a Cherokee woman we had caught to some Comanches. They took it from a big raid in San Antonio," he said. "Is it worth a case of Winchesters?"

"No, hell no, it's just a trinket," he lied. "But I'll take it. Just keep your attention on getting more gold. That's what I need."

He walked over to his horse and put the cross in his saddlebag. It was difficult to conceal his elation. He couldn't wait to get away from the camp and examine the relic more closely. It was ancient, probably Spanish, and the diamonds alone were priceless. Creekmore felt generous. He pulled a small bag from his saddlebag and took it to Six Claws. "Three of the toes in that bag are from niggers, and one is from a Chinaman. They ought to go nicely with your collection." Six Claws poured the half-dozen toes into his hand. The black toes were always welcome. He did not get an opportunity very often to get his own. He did not know what a Chinaman was, but he put aside the one that Creekmore indicated as such. It would be powerful, he reasoned.

"Now, let's get down to business," Creekmore said. "I have some troop movement information, and one payroll shipment coming in from Colorado. You need to plan that one well, it is said to be thirty thousand in gold."

The Indians, Creekmore, and his men sat and talked for about an hour going over details of raids and distribution of rifles to other raiding bands; deciding which group would be able to do the most damage to the Army. He was not concerned so much with the Texas Rangers. He wanted damage inflicted upon the United States Government. He cautioned Six Claws to be wise in his trades with the guns. Whatever Creekmore considered wise, however, was not necessarily considered wise by Six Claws. Sometimes he traded on impulse never thinking of the larger plan, as did Creekmore.

"I want to speak with you and Killing Tree alone," Creekmore said.

"Throw that Mexican in the river," Six Claws said, pointing to what was left of Juan Marquez. "And finish the meat from that cow. We will be ready to ride soon," he said to his men.

"Help them eat that beef, men, and then we ride out of here," Creekmore said to his group.

"I want you to do something special for me," the old man said to the two Indians after the rest had begun attacking the remains of the hindquarter on the coals. "This is so important that I will pay you twenty cases of rifles and fifty thousand rounds of ammunition. We need to take care of this before we get that Colorado payroll." Six Claws listened intently. Creekmore had always doled out the rifles a case or two at a time, no matter how big the raid or trophy. Twenty cases would make Six Claws the most powerful force in the Territory and Texas combined.

Creekmore told them the story of his defeat in Arkansas and the poison in his heart for John Singleton and the Tyler family. The Indian knew some of it, but it still interested him. So, he listened.

"Now, that son of a bitch is the United States Marshal for Judge Parker, and his bastard grandson has joined him as a deputy. They've already brought in the Crabtree brothers, and that hurts me in my business in Missouri," Creekmore continued.

"The Crabtree brothers are stupid and lazy," Six Claws said. "I should have killed them in the New Mexico Territory."

"Never mind that," Creekmore said. "I'm talking about those bastards in Fort Smith. And I want them dead. I want that goddamn Judge Parker dead, too; but most of all, I want that son of a bitch Singleton dead. I want them all dead—Singleton, Tyler, Parker and his goddamn church-going wife and bastard children, too," he said, his mouth quivering with anger. "I'm working on a plan for you to make a raid and cause a diversion in order for me to get all those bastards at one time. Goddamn, that's my hope. To soak Fort Smith in Yankee blood," he shouted. He looked down and closed his eyes. He began to speak slowly and softly, almost painfully. "There is a chance," he said, looking up slowly with his dark eyes wide. "There is a chance that U.S. Grant, President of these United—goddamn—States of America will be in Fort Smith visiting Parker. My sources tell me that he is coming to go deer hunting with his old friend," he said. "I want that son of a bitch to be the one hung up and gutted. I don't know how it is going to work into the plan exactly, but I am not going to miss this opportunity to get them all. All the Yankee bastards at one time."

Six Claws, to the astonishment of Killing Tree, began to smile. He had never seen the man smile. Six Claws continued to smile as he looked silently at Creekmore.

"To kill Parker, who hounds me like a dog, would be a great thing," Six Claws said. "To kill the leader of the whites would be a greater thing. I would do this for no rifles, but I will take your twenty cases anyway."

"I'm glad you see the importance of this," Creekmore said. "I have information now on posse plans and I need something to stir them up good. I've been working on this idea since I heard from Morgan. I'll give you the details after you capture the missionaries. But remember this. No goddamn killing on this raid. I need the captives held, the situation stretched out, and the public outcry to be so loud that I can maneuver those Yankee bastards into my trap. I'll send a rider back and tell you when we are ready. Wait here until then."

"How long?" Six Claws asked. The smile had left his face.

"For as long as necessary," Creekmore barked. This was to be a very intricate plan, and he didn't need useless questions from anyone. "And remember, no goddamn killing. At least not until I tell you it's all right, then you can do with them as you wish."

"Who will we raid?" Killing Tree asked.

"If my plan works, it will be a group of missionaries from Fort Smith. That ought to make them all stop in their tracks and pay attention."

"But missionaries do not carry gold. Why attack them, unless I can rape the religious women?" questioned Killing Tree.

Creekmore was livid. "I don't know how to communicate with you any more clearly. Do not kill or harm anyone, especially the women, until I have my plan in action. What is so goddamn hard to understand about that?" he shouted, clinching his fists in anger.

Six Claws grew tired of the discussion. "Just let us know where and when to attack. We will take care of the rest," he said.

"All right, I trust that you can keep your men in line. This is very important and we will have only one opportunity. I've got it all set out. Just wait on my word." Creekmore looked to the river and saw Julio acting the fool in the water. "I'm just damned glad you haven't killed that stupid little Mexican," he said with a slight smile.

"What's the Mexican's part?" questioned Six Claws.

"Not much. He's too stupid to do much. But I have always had it in the back of my mind to someday use to my advantage the fact that he has six toes like you," he said to Six Claws. "I will use him to cause all sorts of hell and draw that lazy bastard Singleton himself out on a posse for you. Then we will have him. Goddamn, then we will have him."

Creekmore was silent for a moment, relishing the vivid scene of Singleton tied up somewhere for torture. He continued as he threw his cigar butt into the fire. "And then, maybe, one of these days, we may need that Mexican to lend us one of his feet, for proof to make people think you are dead for some reason or another. Of course, he won't be getting it back."

The three laughed simultaneously. This was a remarkable day. Killing Tree had seen Six Claws smile and laugh in the same day. It was a good prophecy, he thought.

Julio came walking up from the river where he had been washing the sugar out of his mouth and ears. He had also tired of his playful activities to catch a big catfish stuck on a shallow sandbar. As he walked past Creekmore and the two Indians, sporting his usual hapless grin, they burst out in laughter again. Julio started laughing with them. Perhaps they had seen him wrestling with that catfish. He continued to laugh as he walked on.

Part Four

The Capture of the Missionaries

Chapter 20

Dawn, February 12, 1876
The Choctaw Nation in the Indian Territory

Will and Bob rode across the Poteau River at dawn. They accompanied the missionary wagon for two miles and then paused before turning back east to Fort Smith. Will had a longing feeling of depression as he saw Katherine and her group continue west. He arched himself high in his saddle and watched her wagon until it was only a dot on the horizon.

"Damn, boy, you are the most love-sick animal I've ever witnessed," Bob said. "That is truly a sad sight."

Will ignored him and sighed loudly as he whipped his horse and turned back to Fort Smith and left Bob in his dust, almost as a statement of his inability to do something about the doom he sensed looming over the horizon. It was there. He just did not know when or where. But it was real and it was eating at his soul.

"A truly sad sight," Bob repeated as he whipped his mount to catch up with his friend. He was sorry for the remarks to Will and he was determined to be more sensitive on the subject of Katherine.

Six Claws and his men lay in wait for the missionaries. They were hidden under a small rock ridge that fell along a dry gorge that cut across the dusty flat lands. Bored as usual when there was no immediate action, arguing and testy natures were reaching a fever pitch among the men. Six Claws also disliked the prospect of waiting any longer for the quarry. Holcomb and Valentine had laid out plans in the past that were well timed and usually planned out to the hour as described. But this was no consolation, as he hated waiting for anything.

John Birdsong vocalized the shrill signal from his hiding place atop the ridge. The long-awaited dust on the horizon was a welcome sight. Scrambling down the small hill, he reported to Six Claws that there was a wagon, maybe two, approaching from the east.

"Four, maybe five miles," he said. "Looks like some cattle, too."

"Cattle?" Six Claws wondered aloud. "What would they be doing with cattle? Must be some damn settlers or someone. Too goddamn bad for them," he said, pursing his chapped lips.

"Sure ain't their lucky day," mused Julio. A wry little grin spread across his dusty brown face.

"Shut up, damn you," snapped Six Claws. "Or it will not be your lucky day." He decided to wait on the wagons and positioned the men behind the ridge. They were disgruntled at the assignment because most of the fun was the riding, hollering, and scaring the hell out of the prey before killing them. Waiting was no fun at all.

Alton and Henrietta Pritchard were on top of the world. A fine, healthy family of three boys, two wagon loads of good solid possessions, eight head of cattle, over five hundred dollars in gold pieces from the sale of their South Carolina farm—and the promise of new adventure in the Territory was plenty of reason to think life was grand. Newton and Willard, the six-year-old twins, and Tubby—his given name was Hammond, but he was never called that—their four-year-old brother, were rough-housing as usual in the back of the wagon driven by their mother, when Alton slowed and stopped the lead wagon.

"You boys settle down back there while I see what your pa wants," Henrietta said.

"See that small ridge over there, Henny," he said, pointing to the south as she walked up to his wagon. "Why don't we cut over there for a while, have a little early lunch, and let the boys play in the cool air to get their restlessness worked out. Besides, I been craving that last piece of peach pie you stuck back last night," he said with a wide smile.

Henrietta Pritchard loved her husband of seven years. She loved her boys. She loved her life. "A rest would be appreciated," she said, returning his smile. "Besides, I put two pieces of pie back. I might join you while the boys are off chunking rocks at lizards or something."

"A piece of pie and a little cuddle—just right in the noon-day sun," he grinned.

"We'll see about the cuddle," she replied with a glint in her eye and wave of the head.

"You boys stop that or you're going to scatter the cows," Alton said sternly as he watched Tubby chase his older brothers with a rattlesnake carcass he had found on the ground as they followed their mother from the second wagon.

Tubby was two years younger but twenty pounds heavier and by the same measure more aggressive and fearless than his brothers. Newton and Willard had been running away from their chubby little brother for one reason or another since he was two years old. He was the most curious and happy child Henrietta and Alton had ever seen, and a delight to watch.

"You see that little outcrop of rocks over there? Why don't you see who can be the first one there while your ma and I bring up the wagons." They were already in the foot race before he could shout to them. "Pick us out a good picnic spot."

"Be careful," Henrietta shouted to the fast moving little bodies.

"I sure wish I had that much energy again," Alton said as he watched his three sons with pride.

"You got plenty of energy for me old man," she said as she climbed upon the wagon spoke and kissed him on the cheek.

"Henny, I'm sure glad I took that five dollars your pa gave me to marry you. I was going to hold out for ten, but it was a pretty good deal, I guess." He laughed with the jolly humor that was his trademark—his bright white teeth shinning through his full, black beard. She responded with a blush and a slap on the back of his head as she always did when he made that remark. He made it often. She loved it.

Newton and Willard could outrun Tubby, but not his rocks. He pelted them with small stones all the way to the ridge. He would shriek with laughter every time one would find its mark. So would they.

The twins had just taken cover, laying in wait for their little brother when Killing Tree grabbed their heads from behind and crushed their small skulls against the rock wall. The loud dull thud masked their stifled whimper.

"Newtie, Willie, where are you?" quizzed Tubby with a laugh as he approached the ridge stealthily with a rock in each little hand. Suddenly, he jumped, startled from the sound of the rifle as Six Claws put a single bullet through Alton Pritchard's heart. Tubby had turned to run toward his father's approaching wagon when Killing Tree swept him up and slung the boy over his shoulders.

"Damn, this is a fat one," he said with a grunt as he tried to contain the struggling boy. The Comanche watched as the rest of the men converged on the second wagon. His experience could sense the danger, but before he could shout to them, Henrietta had pulled a pistol from under the seat and fired at the group. A bullet grazed Small Long Knife in the right hip just before he leapt to the wagon and thrust his sword through her. Killing Tree threw the boy to the ground and ran to the wagon.

"Why did you kill her?" he shouted with vehement anger. He grabbed Small Long Knife by the throat and began choking him. The wounded Indian broke free and bellowed to the crazed Comanche. "She was going to kill me. Look," he said, pointing to his bleeding hip. "She shot me."

"She should have killed you," Killing Tree said. "This was a fine woman. I would have raped her many times."

Tubby Pritchard ran up to the group of outlaws, and sensing that something was wrong with his mother, but unable to see her lying back in the wagon, shouted to them in his childlike but strong voice. "Don't you hurt my ma."

With a swift kick from his little boot, he landed a solid blow into Killing Tree's left shin. "Don't you hurt my ma." The Indian instinctively backhanded the young boy across the face and sent his chubby body sprawling on the ground. The other men broke out in laughter, which further infuriated Killing Tree.

Tubby, bleeding from the mouth, jumped up and sunk his teeth into Killing Tree's bare calf.

Six Claws, who had been watching the events, shouted to stop the Indian as Killing Tree drew his knife to rid himself of the boy once and for all. Tubby turned and faced Six Claws.

"Are you a Injun?" he asked with determination in his voice.

"He is a Kiowa killer, you little pig," Killing Tree said, wincing in pain. "And I am the Comanche who is going to eat you for dinner."

Tubby started again toward Killing Tree swinging both fists. "Where's my ma and pa and Newtie and Willie, you dirty Injun?" he said with as much anger as a four-year-old could muster. Six Claws grabbed the boy by the back of the neck before he could reach Killing Tree, who was beginning to be humored by the boy.

"This I believe is a real warrior. You cowards should look at him," he said to the outlaws still laughing at the events. "Twice he has attacked me without fear. Which of you would do that?" He waved his knife at the men. The laughter stopped as Killing Tree's cold eyes looked at each of them.

Six Claws quickly jumped into the wagon as if reminded of unfinished business and cut one of the toes from Henrietta's left foot. He added it to the silk bag holding the other ones he had taken from Alton and the twins. He returned to the ground where Killing Tree was holding Tubby back by the top of his head. The youngster was flailing wildly at the Indian.

"I'll see how brave he is," Six Claws said. He grabbed the boy, threw him to the ground, put one knee on his chest and pulled off his right boot. There was dead silence from the men, even Killing Tree. The only voice was that of Tubby, subdued yet amazingly strong for a four-year-old.

"Don't you hurt me mister," he said defiantly. "My pa will get you."

Six Claws showed the knife to the boy and slowly moved the blade to his foot.

"Don't you cut me, mister," he repeated bravely with his jaw set squarely.

With a quick, decisive pull of the knife, Six Claws cut the middle toe from the boy's foot.

Every man was watching the boy as he let out a muffled, but controlled cry, pursing his small lips together; unwavering in his refusal to show any fear.

"Don't you hurt me no more mister...I'll get you," he said bravely. Breathing hard and squinting his blue eyes as if expressing hate for the Indian, he passed out from shock. Every hardened face in the group looked away, showing an expression of respect for the lad, no matter how hard they tried to mask it.

"You're right, Killing Tree. This is a little warrior," Six Claws said. "Which of you bastards' toes can I take and you not scream for your mother?"

The men looked at each other in fear that the insane Kiowa would try this game. Even Julio had lost his usual jovial outlook. They had all seen many cruelties at the hands of Six Claws, and from their own hands—why, they had just committed four murders—but this business with the boy was different, somehow. No one understood it.

"I will keep this one," Six Claws said as he looked at the unconscious boy. "Now you bastards pull these wagons behind the ridge before the missionaries come. Take the valuables and leave the rest. We cannot carry too much. We will need to travel in a hurry."

Six Claws lifted the boy up onto the horse of a small skinny outlaw. "Tie him down," he said, returning to the cover of the rocks. They did not wait long. In less than an hour, John Birdsong spotted the missionaries' wagon on the horizon. They rode to intercept it. Six Claws, his gang, and little Tubby Pritchard.

Father Albert Boles was dedicated to his work and mission, but he often questioned whether God could just as easily have left him in Boston, or at least in some civilized colony on the Eastern Seaboard. Fort Smith and the Indian Territory would not have been his choice for ministry. He did, however, accept his assignment without hesitation and saved his doubts and apprehensions for his nightly talk with God. It was easier than talking to the bishop. Nevertheless, he went about his work with a zeal and energy, which everyone admired.

This particular journey into the Territory had bothered him more than usual. The bitter cold was bad enough, but for some reason, and to his mind a half-dozen more just as good, he was uneasy from the moment that he, the McGready *Sister sisters*—the name *Sister sisters* always amused him—and Katherine O'Reilly set out from the church in Fort Smith. It was more premonition than fact, but this mission trip was different. He felt anxious. He could not put a finger on the feeling, nor its source. If the three women had any like feelings, they did not show them. The trip had been carefree and optimistic, especially for Katherine. After endless self-doubt and torment, she was not only in love, but moreover, she was loved—and accepted. Without regard or care for her inability to ever bear children, she was loved and accepted. It was like a dream. A wonderful dream! Her husband-to-be and his posse had accompanied them across the Poteau River and had disappeared over the horizon. She and the two sisters had sung songs, huddled in warm blankets, and talked all the way, enjoying the trip in the wagon as if they were on a church hayride back when they were best friends in Boston. The *Sister sisters* were also especially happy for Katherine. It was a good trip, except for Father Boles. They had tried, to no avail, to bring him out of his restless mood. His cautious feeling preoccupied him.

The rifle crack rang out and the four looked in the direction of the sound before they saw that old Zebediah, one of the two horses pulling the wagon, had been shot through the neck. He stumbled and fell among his rigs. The other horse panicked and began to bolt, and the body of the dead horse tangled in his footing, causing the wagon to overturn.

Six Claws and his men were at the scene before the disoriented missionaries were on their feet. The first spectacle the four witnessed was Axehead Smith being shot in the face by Six Claws' double-barreled, ten-gauge shotgun.

"I told you not to hit the horses," an enraged Six Claws said as Axehead's bloodied body fell to the ground. The dead man's massive frame rolled repeatedly as it slid down a small ravine.

"You did say that to him," Killing Tree said. "He did not listen."

"Take his guns and money and put them in the bags on his horse," Six Claws said, pointing to the Marquez brothers.

"You mean, *your* horse now, don't you Six Claws?" Julio asked. "He won't be needin' it now for sure. I 'spect he don't need nothin'. That double-naught buckshot done turned that Axehead into a melon-head," he quipped, laughing at his remark.

"Just do as I say or you'll get the other barrel," the killer said.

The priest interrupted the outlaws. "I'm Father Alfred Boles, and this is Sister Mary Anne McGready, Sister Mary Margaret McGready, and Dr. Katherine O'Reilly, a surgeon. We are on a short mission trip to some of the villages here in the Choctaw Nation, and we come in the name of the Lord and mean no harm to anyone. Why in God's name did you kill that man?" he asked, in a loud and exaggerated voice.

"Because it was his time, Padre," answered Pelido Marquez as he walked back up the ravine with Axehead's pistol and goods. "Just like it's yours now." Pelido raised the pistol and shot the priest. The aim was errant, even at that close range, and the bullet struck Albert in the right ear, severing it from his head.

Killing Tree, without hesitation, thrust his six-inch, razor sharp, flint rock lance deep into the chest of the young bandit. With eyes agape in surprise, Pelido reached for his brother Julio, and then fell dead.

"We will tell you when to kill hostages," Killing Tree said as he quickly dismounted and drew his lance from the dead man's heart. Killing Tree liked the old weapons. He used his lance and knives every chance he got. And this lance was a particularly good weapon. He had worked for two days honing and shaping that piece of flint, which he had found down on the Brazos River. Six Claws had sat and watched him the entire time, as if giving approval to the enterprise. But who knew what Six Claws was thinking—at any time?

"Damn, my mother's got one son left," Julio said, looking at the bloodied corpse of his brother. "She always told us to be kind to the priests and nuns, didn't she, Pelido?" he whimpered, kicking his dead brother with a perplexed grin on his face. "Well, you should have listened to her, goddamnit." The young Mexican bandit continued, looking at Killing Tree. "He didn't like priests. The old padre in the village would beat us when we did something wrong. Pelido did not like that."

The savagery so occupied the gang that they seemingly had forgotten the missionaries. Katherine was holding a bandage to Father Boles' ear to stop the profuse bleeding. The *Sister sisters* were standing in shock, clutching each other. Two of the bandits, John Birdsong and Henry Salmon, were scavenging through the wagon to find any valuables the missionaries had brought, while Small Long Knife butchered two large slabs of meat from the dead horse and laid them across the remaining wagon horse he had unhitched.

"What do you want with us?" screamed Katherine toward Six Claws. "We are no threat to you." She then noticed a young child, no more than three or four years of age, who was bleeding from the foot. He was tied to a horse, mounted by a scraggly, small-framed individual. His weather-beaten long coat failed to hide the filthy and tattered pants and shirt that looked several sizes too big for him. The rider had more the look of a bum than an outlaw killer. "Who is the child?" she asked. "Have you hurt him also?" she pleaded, looking at the strange individual.

The bum looked up and said nothing. His thin, oblong, bony face gave no expression.

Ignoring her comments about the young white boy, Six Claws turned to Katherine. "Bandage the priest's head and stop your shouting," he said. "If he cannot walk, we will kill him here."

The gang headed toward the south. They tied Father Boles, the two sisters and Katherine behind the horses and forced them to walk along, in almost a running gait. If anyone fell, they were dragged along. Katherine struggled with all her strength to keep everyone afoot. Although she was exhausted, she kept struggling with the *Sister sisters*, trying to keep them afoot. In the distance, buzzards had begun to feast upon the two dead bandits.

Chapter 21

February 13, 1876
The Choctaw Nation near the Canadian River

"May your soul rot in hell," Katherine screamed to Holcomb. It had been a day of horrors for her, matching those she had seen at any of the Civil War battles. For the safety of the others, she had tried to hold her anger in check. Now, however, that Holcomb had joined the gang only a few miles from the capture site and began to detail the plan to Six Claws, she could not restrain herself any longer. She was tied to the wagon with the other captives within earshot of the group and had overheard their plans. She had also heard Six Claws refer to Creekmore as Holcomb, as he often did out of spite.

"May God damn you to hell," she repeated, glaring at the group, especially Holcomb.

"Katherine," Father Boles said with blood still running from the side of his head. "That should never be said, no matter how degenerate they are. They are still in reach of God's grace."

"On the soul of my father, that is my cry to God," she said, still staring at Holcomb with her jaw set so firmly that her head was shaking. "How can you be so stupid to believe you can get away with this, you ignorant Southern trash? You dirt-farming bastard."

"Katherine, for God's sake, please hold your tongue," pleaded Boles.

"Shut up, damn you," Holcomb replied. "Both of you."

He walked over to the wagon that held the missionaries. The strange-looking bum accompanied him. "I don't care what you've heard, there's nothing you can do to stop it."

"You're Josiah Holcomb," she said steadily with her lower lip twitching in anger.

"Well, since that damn Indian is dead set on letting the whole world know, I won't deny it. Yes, I'm Colonel Josiah Holcomb, and goddamn proud of it."

"You murdered the Tyler Family and caused great anguish to their children," she said.

"I should have killed them all that night. It was a big mistake not to have finished my business. But mark you well, Missy, I will finish my business this time," he said, slapping Katherine hard across the face. "I will soon see that old bastard Singleton and his grandson dead and picked apart by this heathen's pigs," he said, pointing to Six Claws. The Indian was looking on with some interest. Though he seldom interfered, the abuse of women got his attention.

"I might even let you live to see it," Holcomb continued, slapping her again across her already bloody mouth.

She spit the mouthful of blood and saliva into his face and held her head straight in defiance as if asking him to hit her again. She did not have to wait long.

"You Yankee bitch," he said with a fury, hitting her with the full force of his fist. She responded with another mouthful of blood forcefully projected toward his face. "And you are demented if you think you are capable of killing John Law, Judge Parker or any of them, much less the President of the United States. It is almost comical that you could imagine such a ridiculous thing. You aren't even worthy to be within sight of Ulysses Grant, much less close enough to harm him. His security will cut you down, and I hope I am there to see it."

Holcomb pulled his fist back with a vengeance to strike her again, but the bum stepped in. "Let me do it."

"All right, Belle," Holcomb said. "Be my guest."

Katherine felt the stinging slap from the small, calloused hand across her face. She looked up. *Belle?* It was a woman. Her open coat gave evidence to a bosom, ample in size. The Bum, now exposed as Belle Shirley Reed, smiled, exposing her crooked teeth. "You're the woman of the deputy. The friend of the goddamn Texas Ranger Bob Johnson." Here is another one for him," she said, slapping Katherine across her bloodied and swollen face. Belle balled up a mouthful of saliva and spit it full at Katherine. "You prim Yankee bitch. How does it feel now?"

"Don't you hit her again, mister," came a small voice from the wagon. Little Tubby Pritchard had risen up from the wagon with his fists clenched in protection of Katherine. "I'll get you," he continued with a weak voice. He had lost a lot of blood in spite of Katherine's best attempts to bandage his foot.

Holcomb thought the boy's actions almost humorous. He stepped in front of Belle Reed and began to lecture the lad.

"Damned, if it isn't the little Carolina boy with all that Southern spirit. I do apologize, boy, for the loss of your family at the hands of these savages. I'm sure they were a fine Southern family. Hell, I saw a Confederate-issue rifle and with captain's insignias carved on it that they took from your wagon. I must say, boy, that did sadden me. But, young man, don't ever defend a Yankee bitch like her," he said, holding Katherine's jaw in his hand and shaking it back and forth.

"Don't hurt her again," the boy repeated with a high-pitched voice.

"They've done corrupted your mind," Holcomb said as he started toward the boy.

"Holcomb," shouted Six Claws. "Enough. Let's get on with our work."

The Indian's tone brought the old man back to reality. He glared at the wagon full of captives and returned to the group. Belle swaggered close behind, sneering at Katherine. *I used to be that pretty and refined,* she thought. *Bitch*!

The plan was simple. Six Claws would head on to his camp in the sand bluffs near the Boggy River some one hundred miles southwest of Fort Smith. He would wait there with his full gang. Two men would go into Fort Smith immediately and raise the stakes of the outrage by killing some fine citizens in their homes. Julio Marquez was to be one of the riders because of his ability to leave six-toed tracks. Moses Brown, Holcomb's man, would accompany him and, in Fort Smith, they would meet up with Valentine Morgan, who would supervise the event. Traveling in a wagon disguised as laundry delivery workers, the two could steal into the town unnoticed. Word would be spread that the missionaries had been captured, and with the outrage in the citizens' homes, this would surely draw out Marshal Singleton himself in pursuit. Holcomb and his men would be riding from their stronghold in the Brushy Mountains, just north of Fort Smith. He would flank Singleton and the original posse, led by Will Tyler, and wipe them all out, once and for all in the trap at the sand bluffs.

Belle Reed interrupted the talks. "That Texas Ranger bastard is mine. That is all I ask. I want him."

Holcomb waved her off with a move of the hand and an almost disinterested nod. Like the Mexicans, he failed to understand why Six Claws tolerated this woman. She revolted him. *Goddamn*, he was dealing with some poor-quality individuals. They continued to talk. Holcomb continued to conjure his plan, even given the inept array of perpetrators he had assembled, he knew it would not fail. *By God, even Parker would be dead, and without Singleton and a good portion of the Deputy Corps, the rest of Parker's family would be easy.* The only problem he saw was how to get to Grant. Surely, the President would not join the posse, and if he did, it would only raise the odds with all the extra protection. Holcomb was working overtime to finalize that part of the plan. It had to be good. It had to be bloody, and it had to be sweet revenge. Of the last thought, there was no qualification. "Why, this would start the war against the Yankees all over again," he often swore in a high-pitched, almost squeal-like voice under his breath. "And this time, I will be the victor." Then he reckoned, he, Six Claws and their forces would settle down in the plains below the Red River and take West Texas and New Mexico Territory. They would rule the West. Let the Yankee Bastards' have their burned-out shell of the East and the ghost of his beloved South—only now, she could rest in peace knowing that her faithful son had avenged her slaughter.

Every detail was worked out, and the plan was unveiled to all members of the gang. With the promised prize of a portion of Holcomb's wealth and a vast supply of guns already in the process of being shipped by rail to the nearest site in the Llano Estacado, each man was anxious to get started on the adventure.

"Remember," Holcomb said to Six Claws. "Don't harm these hostages until I tell you so. If you follow the plan, it will work and every man will be rewarded. I'll follow behind the posse and we will crush them at the sand bluffs in a less than a week."

"Why do we need the hostages?" Killing Tree asked.

"Goddamnit," snapped Holcomb. "All you think about is raping these women. Why don't you engage Belle Reed there if you are so goddamn randy?" Belle looked at Killing Tree with a devilish smile, as if to say, *come on—try it.*

"Six Claws, you've got to keep this under control. I want Singleton and Tyler to see these hostages die before they do. I want to see them suffer one last time at the death of loved ones, just like I've suffered at the death of my homeland and my Southern life," he said in exasperation.

"We will follow the plan," Six Claws said, losing patience with Holcomb.

Killing Tree just stood and shook his lance at Holcomb with two short jabs. Six Claws knew what his warrior meant. Holcomb also knew what it meant. Holcomb made a mental note to see that one of his men would kill that Comanche during the battle. He smiled as he turned to leave. Seeing the hostages tied to the wagon, he remembered the fine black riding crop that he had lost to that Tyler boy a dozen years ago. How he wished he had it now. He gripped the substitute whip he had taken from a Yankee Colonel at Helena. With a strong downward blow, he summarily struck each person tied to the wagon, including Tubby Pritchard.

"That's the last strike I want placed on these people until I return," he said, mounting his horse.

Chapter 22

▼

February 14, 1876
Near Fort Smith, Arkansas

"Valentine Morgan, Valentine Morgan, Valentine Morgan," Julio Marquez was saying over and over. He was amused by the sound of the name. "Don't that sound funny for a name, Moses?" he asked.

"Shore does, Mista Julio," Moses Brown replied.

"Don't call me 'Mr. Julio', just call me Julio."

"Okay, Julio," Moses said. "But you right, that is one peculiar name for a man."

"What's all your name?" Julio asked.

"Moses Brown," he replied.

"That's a good name. Moses Brown. I like that. Moses is like all them Bible people like Mary and Jesus that the priest would talk about. Moses. Yep, I like it," he quipped.

"Why, thank you, sir. What's your full name?"

"Juan Antonio de Vincentia Sanchez Marquez," he replied.

"Now that's a mouthful," Moses said. "How they get Julio outta all that?"

"I dunno. That's what my brothers would call me. Julio. Only Julio," he said with a nostalgic tone. "My mother only has one son left," he added softly.

"All my family's done gone," Moses said. "So, I guess we both alone."

"Hey, Moses, I'll be your brother. Then my mother will have two sons left," Julio said with a broad smile.

"I'd be proud, Julio. I'd be proud," Moses said as he whipped the reins and hastened the wagon team on toward Fort Smith.

"Where have you been? I am supposed to be on the trail to the Buck Thomas killing. I can't be caught out here waiting on you two fools," snarled Valentine Morgan as he approached the wagon at the designated meeting place. He almost laughed at the sight. Both Julio and Moses were dressed in white dusters with short-brim hats pulled tightly on their heads. The wagon was filled with burlap laundry bags. *Holcomb is one thorough bastard*, he thought.

"I look more like a monkey's asshole than you two look like laundry men," Morgan said.

"I dunno. I ain't never seen a monkey or his asshole." Julio laughed. "If you say so, but I dunno."

"Shut up, goddamn you, you filthy Mexican!" roared Morgan. Moses Brown could hardly contain his laughter. He had been on the receiving end of the man's abusive nature countless times, and to see Julio get the verbal best of him was a treat.

"I asked you where you've been. We are behind schedule."

"*Por favor, Senor*, we stopped for a nice siesta or two," Julio said, smiling broadly.

"Mista Morgan, we got here as fast's we could. We didn't stop for nothin'," Moses said in an attempt to calm Morgan's anger.

"All right, Moses, but you keep the reins in on that little bastard or I'll cut his liver out."

"I will, Mista Morgan. I promise, sir. Now, where does we go?"

"Go to the church rectory on Garrison Street. Go to the front door and say that you are bringing some old clothes for the poor. As you bring a load of sacks in I'll come in from the back."

"Then what?" Julio asked.

"Never mind, by God. You don't say or do anything until I tell you."

"We understands," interrupted Moses.

"Okay then, I'll go ahead a little and you come on. I should see your wagon there in about a half-hour."

"Yessir, Mista Morgan," Moses said.

Morgan turned and headed east into town.

"Yessir, Mr. Morgan. Mr. monkey asshole," Julio said softly. Julio and Moses laughed loudly. It was funny. Funny out of simplicity to Julio. Funny out of rightness to Moses.

Father Cafferty answered the door and gratefully accepted the donation offer of clothing from the two men. At first, he had been apprehensive because they looked so unlikely to be bearers of such good and welcome news. Conversely, they looked the part of ones needing the clothing. But he put aside his reservation and gladly accepted the generosity they offered.

"Well...if it isn't the good father himself," Morgan said as he walked from the back of the room.

Father Cafferty was startled, and turned to see who it was that had come from the back door.

"Why, Mr. Morgan, you surprised me. It is good to see you, however. You are just in time to help me thank these good gentlemen for their marvelous gift of these bags of clothing."

"Oh, I'm sure you have thanked them properly, Father. You do everything so proper," the deputy replied sarcastically.

Father Cafferty caught his tone. He had always felt uneasy around Valentine Morgan. He felt that there was a dark and disturbing side to his character that lay just beneath the surface. Not that Morgan had ever done anything overtly wrong around him, but the priest's training in human nature signaled a fault. Morgan himself was aware in some sense of the priest's sensitivity and was cautious around him. It deepened his hatred for the man.

"Yes, I have asked God to bless them greatly for their good deed," the pastor said, trying to ignore Morgan's tone.

"Good," snarled Morgan. "Why don't you lead us in a prayer?" He grabbed Father Cafferty by the back of the neck and forced him to his knees. Moses Brown and Julio Marquez looked on with astonishment. It was inconceivable to them that Morgan would kill the priest. Moses especially, was taken by surprise. He knew that someone was going to die tonight, but to kill the priest shocked him. But he said nothing; just swallowed hard as he looked on.

"You, Mexican, what is one of your Catholic prayers that the good priest could pray for us?" Valentine asked, as he held the priest tightly around the neck, bending him over hard.

Julio was less amazed than Moses because of the constant butchery he was accustomed to. "I dunno no prayers. I did not pay too much attention to the priests and nuns."

"Surely you know one by name or something, I want this good man to bless our souls for us."

"Okay...we always had to say a *Our Father* at the mission," the bandit replied. "But I dunno it."

"What were you doing?" Morgan asked. "Playing with the little Mexican girls behind the church when they were praying inside?" Julio smiled. That statement was truer than Morgan knew.

"All right priest, say that prayer that the Mexican said."

"Our Father who art in heaven," Father Cafferty said with a labored voice. His breathing was severely restricted by the heavy hand around the back of his neck.

"Our Father who art in heaven," mocked Morgan. "Now isn't that a comforting sentiment. I had a father, but he sure as hell is not in heaven. I personally dispatched his drunken ass from this earth with his own pistol. Sorry son of a bitch. Goddamn him."

"Hallowed be thy name," the priest continued.

"When you get to heaven, father, hallow my name a bit if you would. And round up any of them other bastards I sent up there and you all just sing a hymn song about the man who made that choir possible." He drew a large skinning knife from his boot and tightened his grip on Cafferty's neck. "Go on priest, pray."

"Thy kingdom come, thy will be done on earth as it is in heaven," he said, choking out the words. Moving his right hand free, he made the sign of the cross on himself.

Moses Brown looked away. This was very difficult for him to watch. He had seen many things in his life, but this he could not bear to witness. Julio strangely looked on without any expression.

"Give us this day, our daily bread. And forgive us our trespasses, as we forgive those who trespass against us...." Father Cafferty was interrupted in mid-sentence by Morgan, who was now tiring of the game.

"Forgive this trespass, priest," he said as he pulled the razor-sharp knife deep across the cleric's throat. Blood poured onto the highly polished pinewood floor, splattering and beading up across the room. The priest fell to the floor, lying in a pool of his blood. His eyes were wide open and had a look of great serenity, or so Moses Brown thought as he looked and then looked away again quickly.

"Damn," Morgan said. "I should have thought of this," as he pondered on the blood not soaking into the floor. "There's no way we can get a good footprint here. Mexican, take your boots off, tramp in this blood, and walk across the floor. Then step outside on the stone steps."

"What for?" he asked. One look from Morgan convinced him not to ask again. Julio pranced in the priest's blood almost play-like as Morgan watched. Moses Brown was praying silently. He had not prayed much since his family died. In a sense, he had died with them. But this sight made him search for some answer to the embodied evil he was witnessing as the deputy cut a toe from the priest's foot.

Following Morgan, they proceeded to Fourth Street and to a small road behind the Parker home. Morgan could see the catatonic state that Moses Brown was in, so he motioned for Julio to follow him with the special bag of clothes brought from the Six Claws' camp. Moses sat in the wagon as the deputy and Julio entered the back door.

Judge Parker was at the courthouse. He often held sessions until late into the night. Mary Parker was away at a school board meeting that had run overly long. The children were asleep in their upstairs bedrooms, and Ellie Faulkner, the housekeeper, was dozing on the parlor sofa. She died there and a perfect six-toed footprint was left on the white area rug in the middle of the room. It was fate. Had the judge and his wife been home all would have died. But just the housekeeper tonight—while the children slept unmolested—had about it an urgent sense of imperceptibility, reasoned Morgan. It would certainly disorient things for the judge and his perfectly ordered mind. Morgan sneered as he pondered the scene. To make the scenario look real, and in some part to satisfy his envy and greed, Mary's fine silver, jewelry, and the judge's gun collection, including his fine English muskets, were taken. Also stolen was Parker's ancient coin collection, which he proudly displayed on his study walls. Since he was a boy, the judge had been diligently collecting silver denari minted for the Caesars of Rome. Morgan had seen them many times, beautifully polished and displayed in the fine cherry-wood cases lined on the wall. He hated Parker for having such things. Now he had them.

They left after Morgan emptied the bag of clothes he had brought in. A bloodied dress with the monogram *K.O.* on it; a nun's habit and a blood-soaked cleric's shirt and collar were all placed in a corner of the room. Valentine was giving orders about taking the wagon back across the river, leaving it and continuing on horseback as fast as they could to the sand bluff rendezvous. Moses was impervious to the man's clamoring. Julio just smiled and shook his head in acknowledgment, not comprehending anything that had taken place.

"Now, go, damn you," he shouted to the men. He dismounted and took his pistol butt and hit his horse with a crashing blow on the right front hoof.

"Why did you do that?" Julio asked with a puzzled look. "Why did you do that?" repeated Moses.

"Because I have to have some excuse to come back in, you idiots! My horse went lame," he said, smiling. "Now, I am not going to say it again—go."

When Mary Parker found Ellie Faulkner an hour later, it was almost another hour before she could ascend the stairs to check on the children. In shock and with a sense of doom at the fate of her children, she sat on the sofa at the foot of Ellie's body, unable to move. Over two hours had passed since the murder before she took her carriage to the courthouse with her children bundled tightly at her side. Valentine was in the marshal's office complaining of his bad luck with his horse on the trail when Parker burst through the door.

"Come," he said, gasping for breath. "Come."

John Law Singleton shook his head in disbelief at the sight of Ellie Faulkner with her throat cut. He had not felt and tasted the salt of tears since the arrival of his grandson, Will Tyler. Now he had to hold that emotion back again. He had liked Ellie. In fact, he had been her constant escort to town social functions and had even fancied that some day he could settle down with her by his side as he sat on his retirement porch drinking buttermilk. She seemed to be agreeable to the notion herself, and had said so more than once—maybe she would just sit with him on that porch, if she couldn't find a stout young cowboy to finish her life with, she would joke. At fifty-five years of age, Ellie had acted and lived like a woman half her age. She was full of life and John Law liked her company. Portly and friendly, she was loved by the Parkers and everyone who knew her.

"Dear God, who could do this to her?" he asked in a low voice.

"It was a robbery from the looks of my study wall and gun case," Parker said. "My coin collection is gone."

"But why?" the marshal repeated, his eyes wide in shock. "Why not tie her up? Or just knock her unconscious for just a few guns and some goddamn coins?"

"Marshal, look at her foot," Valentine Morgan said. "It's bloodied like the toes have been cut."

"Six Claws," exclaimed Parker. "It can't be. Not right here in Fort Smith."

"And here," Valentine said as he moved over to the rug. "Look at this foot print. It has six toes. It is Six Claws. I was hesitant to say anything until we discern the meaning of this," he said, walking to the bloodied clothing in the corner. "I noticed this when we first came in."

"What does it mean?" Parker asked, almost in a daze as he bent down to pick up Katherine's dress.

"It looks like a message from the killers that they have also killed or captured the missionaries," Morgan said sternly. "If I were to guess from a gut feeling I would say that they are not dead—yet."

Singleton was in too much shock to assimilate things. Everything was moving so fast. He was impressed by Morgan's cool nature and professionalism at this moment. The deputy had remained calm and found important clues. He should have done that himself, he thought. After all, he was the marshal and the town depended upon his judgment and professionalism. He was acting like a damned amateur, he deemed, as he returned to his senses. But Ellie's death hurt. It hurt bad.

"Good work Valentine, as usual. I don't know what we would do without you," he said, finally, trying to hide his emotions. "It seems so impossible, but that savage has come into our town and laid us a heavy blow."

"A damned heavy blow," the judge said. "I shudder to think what would have happened if my wife and I had been home. What do you think, Val? Why this? And why weren't the children harmed? You have such good reasoning gifts about you. What is your read on this?"

Valentine Morgan basked in the compliment. *You haven't seen anything yet*, he thought to himself. He had to grip his fist to keep from laughing.

"It is difficult to say, Judge. Maybe they thought the house was empty except for Miss Faulkner."

"I wonder," Singleton said. "That son of a bitch was too careful for that."

Just the confusion that Valentine had hoped for. He deferred to Singleton's thought. "You're right Marshal. Maybe it is a message of some sort. Like these clothes," he said, handing Katherine's dress to the marshal.

John Law had avoided any thought about the missionary's clothing. It was too difficult for him to imagine. Morgan was making sure that he realized the full impact.

"Dear God. Will...Dear God," John Law said.

The three stood looking at the dress, and at Ellie's corpse, and said nothing. Finally, when he thought the time was right, Morgan spoke up with his voice full of compassion and concern.

"Marshal please allow me to start making arrangements for a posse, while you stay with the judge and his family for a moment."

Singleton nodded his approval. "I want a full group. Completely outfitted. I will lead it myself. We were almost ready anyway, just awaiting your return." He paused. "And make sure Jack Hainey is with us. This is in his jurisdiction now, and I'm sure he is ready to go."

"I'll be going also," Parker said. "The President's visit is delayed a day or so. I have time." It was unheard of for the judge to accompany the posse, but no one would argue his right to do so. Especially now.

Morgan was ecstatic. Things were working out just as Holcomb had planned, except for President Grant's delay. But Morgan never figured Holcomb could pull that part off anyway. *Trying to get Grant would have gotten us all killed. It will be a lot easier now,* Morgan thought. He put that thought out of his mind, and reasoned not to even tell Holcomb anything about it. It would not be worth the problems it would cause with the old colonel.

"It will take until dawn to get everything in order, but we can ride at first light," Morgan said in an official tone. "And, Judge, I will go by the church and ask Father Cafferty to come to comfort Mrs. Parker and the children, if you'll allow me." *Wait until you see what I find!*

"Thank you, Deputy Morgan. That is very kind of you to think of them. Your unshaken presence is needed in this crisis. Thank you. And tell Father Cafferty to hurry."

He'll be fairly slow, I suspect.

Chapter 23

▼

Late Evening, February 14, 1876
Fort Smith, Arkansas

9:30 PM February 14, 1876
Major Sam Westcott, Cmdr.
Texas Ranger HQ
Austin, Texas
STOP. Maj. Westcott. Six Claws and sizable group raided Fort Smith area killing and capturing many. Even local priest slaughtered. STOP. Believe headed for Red River area. Unknown at this time. Posse in pursuit. STOP. Help of Ranger troop from south to assist greatly appreciated. Contact Tobias Johnson. Son Robert in posse. STOP. Rendezvous above sand bluff area Lawson Fork below Pine Mountain no less three days. STOP. Reply Immediately. STOP.
Isaac C. Parker
Federal Judge, District Court Western Arkansas/Indian Territory
Fort Smith

* * * *

9:40 PM February 14, 1876
Col. Julius Dixon
Fort Gibson Indian Territory
STOP. Six Claws on rampage. Posse with Sgt. King believed to be in area deputy bodies found. STOP. Dispatch rider immediately to route Deputy Capt. Wm. Tyler to this posse at Stone Ridge. STOP. His posse continue under Deputy Robert Johnson to rendezvous at Lawson Fork at Pine Mountain. STOP. Reply Immediately. STOP.

Isaac C. Parker
Federal Judge, District Court Western Arkansas/Indian Territory
Fort Smith

* * * *

10:35 PM February 14, 1876
Isaac C. Parker
Fort Smith, District Court
STOP. Rider dispatched to posse by your instructions. STOP. Also squad of six with supplies to join group at Lawson Fork. Godspeed. STOP.
Col. Julius Dixon
Fort Gibson

* * * *

12:10 AM February 15, 1876
Federal Judge Isaac Parker
Fort Smith Indian Territory
STOP. Judge Parker. No help from Austin or other troop at this time. Telegraph sent to Capt. Tobias Johnson near Buffalo Gap. Closest help to you. Availability of most his troops in area. STOP. Can assure his response. STOP. Kill Indian bastard before he enters Texas again. STOP.
Maj. Sam Westcott.
Texas Rangers, Austin Texas.

The loud banging on the door brought Tobias to his feet. He had been sitting by the dining area hearth and had fallen asleep with Bob's letter in his hand. It had been a habit to read it every day. Sometimes several times a day.

"Cap'n," the voice shouted from the porch. "Cap'n, it's me, Caleb Jackson."

"Corporal, what the hell do you want at this hour? Are you drunk?" Caleb assured him that he was not drunk and that he had an important message from Austin.

Tobias read the telegraph message from Major Westcott and almost smiled at the turn of events. Action! A chase! With Bob! Again! He read the message again. "Thank God all the telegraph lines were up between here and Austin, Fort Smith and Fort Gibson. That in itself is a miracle. Just plain bad luck for those murdering sonsabitches that they took the day off cutting lines," he said, now smiling.

He could not hide his glee, even in this dire situation. "Pick up Noah at the bunkhouse and you two ride to every man's house. All four of them. And tell them we are riding to the Territory to kill that red bastard Six Claws. If they have any feeling for the old troop tell them they are all sworn in again at two dollars a day. I don't care how much time or money they lose at their spreads. This is Rangering business, by God. We will meet on the ridge of my north pasture at dawn."

"Sure as shootin' Cap'n," Caleb said, hopping up and down as if on a bed of hot embers. "Hot damn. Hot damn," he shouted with a wide grin.

Six of Tobias' original eleven-member troop had followed him to north Texas and into a life of families and ranching. Most were successful. All were content, except for a pain of restlessness upon each occasion of news about the exploits of Rangers around the state. Tobias was certain that Caleb Jackson, Noah Parnell and the others would be at the north ridge at dawn.

"Hot damn for sure," he shouted to the rider disappearing into the night.

Elizabeth and Rebecca had been awakened by the ruckus and were standing at the dining area door when Tobias walked back into the house. They had heard most of it and guessed the rest.

"I'll get your pack ready," Elizabeth said.

"I expect two, maybe three weeks," Tobias replied, looking her straight in the eyes.

They communicated that way. He knew her feelings. She knew his. In the eyes. And though her heart was shaken with fear, she tried never to show it in situations like these. He knew it though and loved her for the unspoken words.

"Is Bob involved?" Rebecca asked. Her voice was quivering.

"Yes, darling," Tobias answered, in an assuring tone. "And if that scamp gets into any trouble, I'll be there to get him out of it."

She grabbed him and hugged him as hard as she could. "Oh Papa Toby, bring him home. Bring him home."

"If I have to hog-tie and drag him all the way, I'll do just that, darling. I'll do just that."

"You mind yourself too, old man," Elizabeth said. "There's going to be a lot of work piled up around here for you when you get back and Rebecca and I don't intent to do a lick of it."

"You two just keep yourselves beautiful for us Johnson men when we come riding in here in a few weeks. That's all the work you need to worry about."

He knew just what to say at just the right time. Just like Bob. That's why they were loved.

CHAPTER 24

▼

Dawn, February 15, 1876
Six Claws' camp in the Choctaw Nation

The outlaw camp was dirty, dark, and cold. A putrid smell hung over the camp and assaulted the group as they rode in. It was the smell of home to Six Claws and his men. It was the smell of hell to the captives.

Hidden behind a row of trees and brush and at the bottom of an old riverbed, the camp was a series of old sod-huts and corrals with the ground littered with an array of bones and discarded items. Five impregnable stone and log storehouses lined the west end of the parameter. Surrounded by a group of twenty five-foot embankments for guards and sentries, it was a perfect fortress, from both the north and south. The east and west venues were protected both by rocky outcrops and rows of piled tree and stone buttresses. A natural spring from the south supplied an ample amount of fresh water and fifteen-foot mountains of firewood, supplied by the labor of many past captives, outfitted the camp. The design was Holcomb's. He had spent thousands of dollars and months of preparation to build and supply the camp for Six Claws and his men. Built by captives, there was no evidence or proof that it even existed. And if anyone stumbled upon it, usually it was their last stumble. It just added to Holcomb's inflated ego that he could keep such a place a secret for so long. He felt invincible. Six Claws however, although agreeing to camp there, much more preferred the open plains and the ability to flee than to be caught in a closed camp. But it had worked well for several months now. Dozens of captives had been brought in and the bounty from hundreds of raids was well stored and supplied. So, for now, Six Claws deferred to Holcomb and tolerated the place.

Smoke lifted from the half-dozen outdoor campfires and the chimneys in the dwellings. The corrals were full with the several dozen horses that served as mounts for the more than thirty bandits who came into the open area to greet the riders. A series of messages had been relayed for over two miles as sentries along the way had allowed the group to pass. News had reached the camp that their leader was returning. Mostly with fear, but also with anticipation for what he brought. The bounty. The guns. The captives.

Odell Skaggs and his brother, Treewell, looked at the approaching group with interest. Even though they had seen dozens of captive groups arrive since they themselves were taken and imprisoned months ago, each new group brought a mixed feeling of hope and sadness. Joy that there would be new people to meet and talk to other than the ignorant bandits that suppressed them, but also a deep sadness that these new people were about to endure unspeakable horrors.

The Skaggs brothers were coming from upper Ohio to the dream life in the West when Six Claws' riders attacked them. Their wives and four children had been traded or killed over the past weeks but the two men kept hope no matter how bitter they became.

Odell was especially hopeful. It was his spirit. A kind and gentle man that would go out of his way to dissipate any combative situation, he was the consummate peacemaker in all his family. Some say he took after his father, Jester Skaggs, who was a peacemaker and lawman in the Ohio area for many years, before being killed by a drunk in a fight. Jester, as always, tried to talk the man in, but the murderer pulled a pistol and shot him down without warning. Odell was there and responded by wrestling the man down, disarming him and taking him to jail. The loss was devastating for the family. Only three months later, they had pulled up and left for a better life in the West. Now, a scant six months after the death of their father, Odell's wife, two children and the family of his brother Treewell were dead, or worse, sold into who knew what kind of evil and horror. But Odell remained hopeful. Hopeful that somewhere there was a good life for a good man.

Odell and Treewell were the only two captives allowed to roam free around the camp during the day. Their honest and gentle natures had in some unrealistic way found the respect of the captors. They were believed when they promised not try to escape, and would help keep the other captives in line if all were treated with some dignity. Several had been spared harsh treatment at Odell's pleading.

"Skaggs, here are some more for you to beg for," sneered Killing Tree as Odell approached the group.

"I surely appreciate that there are no dead in the wagon, Mr. Killing Tree, I thank you for that," the tall, muscular gentleman from Ohio said.

Standing over six feet and weighing over two hundred pounds, Odell was a formidable figure; a spectacle that did not escape the bandits. Even though they believed him to be genuine in his passivity and gentle nature, they were all aware that his strength could more than likely snap a man in half. If provoked. The question was, what would it take to provoke him? He was a perplexing individual and a wary Six Claws always had his eye on him.

Treewell stood by, as usual, and said little if nothing at all. An identical match to his brother in size and stature, Treewell was even more of an enigma to the group. He not only was non-combative, he did not interact with anyone at all. Even Odell. He seemed to take his commands from his brother by some mystical inner-voice that he listened to. A look, a smile or even a frown from Odell would send Treewell along his way with duty in hand. "Never did talk much," Odell would say of his brother when questioned by other captives. "Ever since we was boys, he would just seem to look to me and know when and what to do without much talk. It has worked out pretty good, I suspect. We are twins, both of us is thirty-five. We are both still alive. So, it works, I guess." Odell would often add his best remark. "I even had to ask his Deborah to marry him. That boy is shy. But I didn't have anything to do with the rest of it. They worked out about their two babies all by themselves." Odell would always smile when he said that. Treewell would smile also. One of the few times that he did. But both men would slip into a secluded dark place in their connected minds as they soon remembered Deborah and the two boys, and Odell's wife Esmaralda, and the two girl babies she gave him. The sadness was pervasive. Nothing needed to be said. One could feel it. But as usual, Odell would break the spell of sadness that inevitably fell upon the group. "Let me tell you about Treewell's name," he would interject. "He got that about the age of six when we would go out hunting with my father and his brothers. And little Treewell would run ahead with the dogs and almost without fail, he would beat them to the game. He could almost tree any animal as *good* as any hound dog. So, my ma, a beautiful and educated woman from Vermont, would say, tree *as well*, not tree as *good*. And to this day we call him Treewell. If you asked his real name, I couldn't rightly say, because it's been so long, I don't remember." He knew the name to be Obadiah, but he kept it a secret for the sake of the story.

That would always lighten the mood. As well as it could. Every time Julio Marquez was in camp, he would always ask Odell to tell him about Treewell's name. It was the height of the Mexican's day to hear that story over and over again. Today, however, Julio was on other business.

Odell quickly surveyed the group. That was his way. To see if anyone needed help immediately. Two Catholic nuns, a priest, a resolute-looking woman and a small boy. All were bleeding. "If you'll allow me, sir, I'll get these folks settled and give them the outlay. So, come on now, and be quick about it," Odell shouted sternly to the captives. Six Claws rode away in seeming disinterest and Killing Tree and the others quickly dismounted and headed for the nearest open fire and roasting spit with meat on it.

Katherine and the others did not know what to think of the Skaggs brothers. Were they part of the group, or captives themselves? They were hard to figure, especially as they dispatched the group to one of the back corrals with a small hut. Not a word had been spoken in the hundred-yard walk. But Katherine seethed in her anger as they arrived and were closed inside. "We need some attention to these wounds," she shot out in halted tones. "And we haven't had food or water in two days." She glared at Odell and looked at Treewell, who shifted his gaze nervously to the ground. "What's the matter, don't either of you understand the plight of these people?" she questioned impatiently.

Odell smiled and tried to reassure her with his conciliatory tone. "Yes, Ma'am, we are gravely aware of your situation and of ours, but please keep your voice down and don't be hostile in your tone."

"Hostile. Why, I'll show you hostile!" She lunged at Odell.

Tubby followed. "Yeah," he said as he kicked at Odell with his one good foot. Odell, nervously acting to stop any attention that the scene might be causing, looked back at Killing Tree and the others occupied around the campfire.

"Please. Listen to me. It is imperative that you listen to me."

"Why should we listen to you? Do you have any idea what we have been through?"

"I expect I do. I expect I do," he repeated. His voice trailed as he again looked to Killing Tree and any of the dozen guards in view. "Still, you must trust me. We are your only friends here. Don't even trust any of the other captives yet. This is a dangerous place. So, again, please listen to what I have to say."

Father Boles moved to Katherine's side and extended his hand in friendship to Odell. "I am Father Albert Boles from Fort Smith. We were on a journey into the Nations when we were violently and without warning attacked by those men," he said, pointing to Killing Tree and his group. "This boy's family was slaughtered and who knows who else was killed back there," he said, putting his arm around Tubby's small frame. "And then we were privy to a gathering of evil men who evidently plan these atrocities and have unbelievable plans in motion for further aggression against the law officers who will be coming for us."

"That would be Colonel Josiah Holcomb, I suspect," Odell said with a sudden change of expression. His face became very drawn. "I guess we will be seeing him before long now."

After introducing himself and Treewell, Odell gathered the captives around the small hut and told them of their experiences. Father Boles related all that they knew and what they expected. The *Sister sisters* had not say a word. Like two deer frozen in step by a bright light, they huddled and looked straight ahead. Motionless.

Katherine also had not said another word since Odell's plead for her to listen. Now she finally spoke. "I am sorry, Mr. Skaggs, for my behavior. I am sorry also for your family. But what can we do?"

"Nothing but stay alive, Dr. O'Reilly," he responded with a smile and clasping her hand with his. "Your value as a doctor will be beneficial to us all, and unfortunately also to the raiders. But that may work to your chances for staying alive."

"I'll not lift a hand to help even one of those bastards," she said with a stern glare, jerking her hand from his comforting grasp. "Not even to save my own life."

"But what about the life of the boy and the others?" he asked, looking at Tubby and the nuns.

Katherine looked away. She knew, of course, that she would do anything she needed to help the group. And to stay alive herself. She had Will Tyler to think about. It was just her nature to be stubborn and self-assured. A tear fell down her bruised cheek. That would have to change and she knew it. She was determined to listen to Odell's sage counsel. She was, after all, a doctor. Maybe if she were honest to herself, she pursued the career out of the despondency over never being able to have children. Just something to prove she was tough and capable. It was now time to use her skills for the good of all.

"Just tell us what to do, Mr. Skaggs and I promise to keep my temper in check."

"You can start by calling me Odell, and this is Treewell, or Obadiah, if you refer to him by his given name." Treewell looked sharply at Odell and at Katherine. She smiled. "Treewell will do fine," she said, reaching over and gently clasping the hand of an embarrassed Obadiah.

"The first thing we must do, after everyone is bandaged and fed, is start a work program so everyone will look busy. That is very important," a relieved Odell said. He had won Katherine over. That was a victory. But his nature was such that it was a one-sided fight. He won most of them like that. A good man trying to be a good man in a bad world.

The little stray dog, a small Mexican breed that ran around the camp begging for scraps, scurried into the lodge. He looked around and growled at Father Boles.

"What a little Mexican devil you are," he said.

"Diablo," Katherine said. "That's a good name for him."

The dog suddenly went to Tubby and leaped into his lap. Contented. Boy and dog. Katherine was pleased that Tubby had something to help him find a smile. It helped her, also.

Immediately Odell set about getting food and supplies to the group and then groveled before Killing Tree that all would be ready to get to work very soon. Killing Tree just grunted and continued to gnaw on the piece of deer meat he had torn from the carcass on the spit. The Indian was confident that Odell knew what to do. And if he didn't, he could just kill him, rape the women and have a good afternoon sleep. It was of little consequence, Killing Tree mused as he squatted on the ground for a more relaxed meal. It was then that he remembered the special captive in the far hut by the stockpiles of firewood. "Bring me the Kiowa," he said with a shape tone. "It has been a while since I had the pleasure of skinning him."

A bloodied, beaten and half-dead man was led to Killing Tree. "My good friend. How are you doing today? Still alive I see. Too bad; but good luck for me. Now I can amuse myself after all the work today."

The man looked up from his stooped position.

Katherine immediately screamed. It was reflexive. She could not stop herself from the horror of the site. "Two Snakes!" she shouted, running to him from the hut.

"You know this coward?" Killing Tree asked.

Katherine did not know how to answer; she was so appalled to see her friend in this place and in this position, after the astonishment wore off, her anger rose. "He's no coward," she shot back.

Two Snakes turned his face toward Katherine's voice. His eyes were swollen shut, his body was bruised and his skin had been literally cut and slashed from his body. His wounds were open and infested with filth and maggots. The sight horrified her. Two Snakes nodded to her and bowed his head again, weak and beaten.

"He was a gift from our friend, the bitch, Belle Reed," Killing Tree said with a wide, proud smile. "He is my amusement, as long as he lasts. It has been longer than I thought, and I am weary of the game. Maybe I will just cut his head off now and be done with it," he said.

"No!" screamed Katherine.

"She likes you, Kiowa dog. Maybe she would like to have a game with you. Maybe she will take you to her bed and see if a Kiowa dog can satisfy a fine woman like her." He looked at Katherine. "It will be a hard task. I have whittled on his manhood a little bit. I am afraid he is not ready for the pleasure you need. Maybe I can take his place," he said, standing suddenly and looking at Katherine with his cold, dark eyes.

Six Claws approached the scene. "Killing Tree. I have warned you about the women. Leave them alone." He stared at Killing Tree with his look of death that every outlaw killer in the group feared would be given in their direction someday. Usually it was the last thing they saw. Killing Tree kicked the dirt and walked away. He spat on the bowed Indian as he left. Six Claws looked at Two Snakes. "My friend of boyhood. Are you still alive? Maybe your Snake Spirits have been watching you more than I thought," he said in a low and non-threatening voice. There was maybe some truth to what he had just said. The memories of the Kiowa's bravery were as fresh in his mind as they were a quarter-century ago. Six Claws had no time for belief in the stories of spirits and fate at their whim. He forged his own destiny. But still, even in his non-belief there was a kernel of doubt that maybe the Old People, if not correct in their spirit language, still possessed some knowledge that he did not. In that sense, he respected Two Snakes, even though he had allowed the savage treatment at the hands of Killing Tree and others.

"Take him," Six Claws said, much to the surprise of everyone. "I am tired of him and the way he looks at me."

Odell and Treewell quickly helped Two Snakes to the lodge that was given to the missionary captives. They put him on an old buffalo hide. Katherine quickly went to his side. "Two Snakes, do you know who I am?" she asked softly.

"Katherine," he said. He was motionless, making no attempt to move or speak unless spoken to.

"He came in about a month ago," Odell said. Pretty bad shape. He had been shot by Belle Reed and her beau back in the Nations and they brought him when their gang hightailed it here with some posse after them."

"He was part of that posse; brave men," she said with tears welling up again. The very mention of the posse brought back vivid and painful memories of Will Tyler and the last time she saw him in the distance as the missionary wagon pulled out of sight.

"Two Snakes, what happened? We've been looking for you for a month."

He tried to speak as best he could. Physical torture and privation of food and water had left him weak and even unsure of his speech, but he nonetheless tried to speak.

"At the cabin, I killed two sentries," he said slowly. "I walked to cabin. They heard me...woman shot through the wall and bullet hit my body." He pulled back the waistline on his tattered pants and exposed an open bullet wound, untreated and badly infected. "They brought me here and I have survived."

Katherine was already working with the few supplies salvaged from the wagon. She cleaned and dressed his raw skin, evident that it had been ripped with a knife. From his neck to his lower torso, strips as long as eight inches had been cut and pulled from his body. He had multiple contusions and she found that his right upper arm had been fractured in two places. She worked for hours removing the bullet. It had caused a great deal of damage, given the fact that it had passed through the wall of the cabin, flattening out and then causing a larger than normal hole in his intestinal area. The infection was rampant, but she rendered the best possible aid she could, in the flickering light of the lantern. Odell and the others watched with open amazement. Even Father Boles was amazed by her skills. It made him wonder whose work did more good in the outcome. His work was that of a philosophical, even theoretical nature; her work was that of saving lives and the practical. He thought about that a great deal.

After three hours in the hut, Odell was brought back to reality. "They will be looking for us. It is about time for the whisky to wear off. We must get to our work. Dr. O'Reilly, you stay here with your friend and the rest of you come with me."

"Surely you don't mean me and the sisters," Father Boles said.

"Father you have a lot to learn. Please do as I say or it will be a bad learning experience," Odell said.

"Do as he says, Father, and don't argue with him, or me for that matter until we get our bearings," Katherine said with a tone of irritation.

Father Boles and the *Sister sisters* followed the Staggs' brothers out of the lodge into a new and frightening world.

After the group had gone, Two Snakes looked at Katherine. He had waited to ask. *Not in front of everyone*, he thought. "Will and Robert?"

"They are all right, probably riding hard as we speak to come and get us out of here," she replied with a smile. *I hope so, God I hope so*, she thought.

She sat by his side and told him of all the events of the past month.

After she had finished, Two Snakes spoke. "Katherine, I have had a vision. About you and Will."

Katherine was astonished—happily so. She did not believe in the mystical-magical ways of the Indians, but this astonished her and intrigued her. She wanted to hear more.

"I was taken by the Spirits on a journey not many days ago when I thought I would join them forever. My wounds were about to have victory over me. But my vision was not about me. It was about you and Will, and Robert and his wife, called Rebecca. I saw your lives as one. Together in one valley of fertile growth. I saw a meadow, rich with flowers, each a happy time and event to be your lives. I saw thorn bushes; there were many. But the Great Spirit avenged them and they soon died and were consumed by the rich blooms of flowers.

I saw a pine seedling by a vision of Rebecca's face, very young and fertile. I then saw a young, strong oak sapling, nearby you. That I do not understand, for the pine seedlings grew and strong pine trees lined the forest, one after the other, season after season. But the oak sapling also grew, and next to it grew a bigger tree and then a bigger tree until there stood in the forest meadow of happiness a giant redwood tree, towering over all others and all the pine trees encircled it and paid homage to its greatness. And, at the base of this giant tree stood you and Rebecca, showered by its shade in the sunlight of the meadow. Will and Robert stood nearby and gazed upon the forest but upon the giant tree, they wept, not in sadness but in joy. I do not understand this. I have tried, but my strength is failing." He turned to Katherine, whose face was aglow. "I do know that the young pine seedling is Bob's daughter, and you will live to see the other pine trees come and sprout. But it is the oak sapling, strong and alone, that I do not understand." He closed his eyes and rested, comfortably perhaps, for the first time in a month.

I know who it is, she thought, looking over at a sleepy little boy, clutching his dog.

Two Snakes awoke and called Odell and Katherine over to the side of the hut. He could hardly move from the wounds but he had to act drastically. "I must escape," he said to them. "I must get to the posse and help them get in here."

"How can you do that when you can barely walk?" Katherine asked.

"I can manage. I have to. This is the first time they have not had me under guard. And now that I am in your care, they have forgotten about me," he said in such a determined way that they believed that he could. Not understanding how, but that somehow he could.

"The Spirits have given me the way," he said. "Odell, has the young Mexican man died? The one in the next hut?"

"Yes, just today."

"Bury him tonight and tell everyone that I died and you have buried me. I will be gone before you tell them."

"That might work," Odell said.

"The Spirits have told me so," Two Snakes replied. He turned to Katherine. "I will get you all out of here. I will bring Will Tyler to you. I promise."

She believed him. Her heart soared with hope for the first time. "Hurry then, Two Snakes. Hurry," she pleaded.

Two Snakes slipped out of the hut. The Spirits guided him. He was not seen.

Odell's announcement of the death and burial of Two Snakes went without very much concern. "He was a brave Kiowa. Too bad," Six Claws said. But there was a dread that fell over Six Claws that he had not felt since boyhood. He remembered vividly the brave acts and offer of friendship from the boy, Two Snakes. He also felt the presence of the Old People, suddenly and fully. He suppressed it. It meant nothing to him, he told himself. That life was gone. No more Old People and their talk from the dead.

Chapter 25

Dawn, February 15, 1876
The Choctaw Nation, Indian Territory

They rode as fast as they could. Almost too fast; the horses were soon exhausted. But the posse would not slow for even an instant. It was hard to tell who was in the lead. Will Tyler, Bob Johnson, Marshal Singleton, Judge Parker—all whipped their horses with an undaunted ferocity. The rest could barely keep in stride. They were on a mission. Every man knew it and every man had nothing else on his mind. Except Valentine. And unknown to him, he was on the thoughts of the two deputies.

"Marshal, we will be in a fix if we kill these horses. We need to pace ourselves and do this right," he shouted at the top of his lungs, trying to be heard over the thunder of horse's hooves. Of course, Valentine did not want to catch Julio and Moses' wagon before it had a chance to be out of reach.

"Marshal Singleton signaled for the group to stop.

"What the hell is the matter, John Law?" shouted Will.

"It seems that Valentine is again the voice of reason," he responded, trying to catch his breath.

"To hell with Valentine and anyone else who waits. Ask him why he wants to stop all the goddamn time. What is he trying to hide?" barked Bob, as he started to resume the ride.

Morgan shot back a dagger glance at the Texan. "Bob, I know you are tired and feel a sense of urgency about your friends, but I will not tolerate any accusations of that sort. What the hell are you trying to say," he said, pressing his luck. He lived that way at all times—pressing his luck.

"Never mind, by God, I'll have my time. It's coming," Johnson shot back. His tone and determination shocked Morgan more than the words. He felt, for the first time, that something was wrong.

"Hold on, Bob," Will said as he grabbed Bob's horse's reigns. He quickly changed the subject. This was not the time or place. "What are you thinking, John Law?"

"It's just that we need to be clear-headed here and not go off and ride into a trap," he responded. "My mind has been pretty clouded for the past few hours and maybe we ought to step down for five minutes and collect our thoughts." He looked at Judge Parker for affirmation. The judge dismounted and bent over, trying to cough up the dust that had filled his throat. He was not used to a forced ride. In fact, this was as intently as he had ever ridden in his memory. "Cool the horses down and give them water," he shouted to the two rear deputies.

Bob walked in circles. He could not fathom stopping. He looked at Valentine, who returned his glare. "What's your problem?" he asked in a gasping voice.

Bob did not reply but just re-mounted his horse. Morgan's time was up. He felt he ought to tell the judge everything he had heard that night on that lonely road from Fort Smith. But Will was right as usual, this was not the time or place. The group just stood around for a moment and not a single word of plan or strategy was voiced. Then as if one body, they mounted and resumed their furious trek.

Valentine's worst fear was soon realized. The wagon was moving slowly just a few hundred yards ahead of the posse. His mind reeled with scenarios of what he was going to do. *How in the hell could that nigger and that Mexican be so stupid to still be in that wagon. Goddamn, they should be long gone on the horses.* His eyes began to widen; his mouth began to draw back and he began his trademark twitch with every breath. As the posse arrived and circled the wagon, he looked sternly at the two men and moved his head stiffly to the side with his mouth clenched as if to pass a signal to them. *Don't open your mouths.* It didn't work. Julio stood on the front board and smiled at Morgan.

"*Buenos Diaz*, Mr. Valentine," he slurred the words slowly. "Mr. Valentine. A monkey's asshole. What are you doing here?"

Moses looked down in resignation. He knew that he was about to die. He closed his eyes and waited on the report of Morgan's gun. Deputy Bass Reeves looked at the man with a twinge of sorrow. Moses was almost a dead-ringer for his father, old and broken by the years and the injustice of the culture. Bass almost wished he could help the man. But skin color did not change the fact that he was with the rabid killers and may be one himself, though, for some reason he doubted it.

"Eyes up, Mister," Bass said to Moses. "I want to see what you are looking at."

Moses just looked at the young deputy. Amazing to see a black man in such authority, he thought. He smiled and nodded his compliance.

Julio, still wearing the blood-soaked duster, looked at Morgan with a half-silly smile. "Mr. Valentine. This is not the plan, remember. Remember, Mr. monkey's asshole?"

Morgan drew his revolver and shot Julio squarely in the chest. The blow knocked him completely out of the wagon. As Valentine turned his gun toward Moses, Bob Johnson adeptly brought his gun down across Morgan's head.

"*Godamighty*," Bob said. "I never thought you were in it this deep, Morgan. We got to figure this out."

Will Tyler and Bob went over and propped Julio up from the ground. "Can you talk?" he asked.

"Ain't you one of them bean-eatin' brothers we chased all over Texas? Marquez? Why, you're the young silly one, Julio," Bob said.

"Yeah, you right, Ranger, and now my mother don't have no sons," he said weakly. He looked up at Will and smiled. "Do you got any sugar, *mi jefe*?" he asked. "*Madre de Dios*," he said, crossing himself—a practice long forgotten but now it was important for some reason. "*Adios*," he said with a grin, then closed his eyes, smiling to the end. Mrs. Marquez had no more sons.

Judge Parker grabbed Valentine Morgan and pulled him up from the ground. "What is this all about, Morgan?" He shouted in a dazed amazement. He yelled the question repeatedly as he shook Morgan into a semi-conscience state.

"I'm sorry, Judge. That smart-mouthed Mexican made me lose my temper. I could not control my self. I just shot him out of instinct."

"That's no excuse, man. He was the only witness we had," Parker replied, in a tone of exasperation.

"I can tell you what it is all about Judge," Bob said with a scowl. "Will Tyler and I have been trying for more than two months to put this together and it looks like a *slow* wagon has solved all the mystery." He told the judge what he heard that night on the road and how he and Will had been watching Morgan's every move. Will added his suspicions of all the delays and the Morgan's insistence to go alone and scout ahead of times when nothing turned up and it always was found out to be some grisly crime or slaughter involved.

"I'm afraid that's all circumstantial, but very damning none the less," Judge Parker said, his eyes crimson red and his face beginning to pale with anger.

"What about the Negro?" Singleton asked. All eyes suddenly turned to Moses Brown. He had almost been forgotten in the unfolding scene. There was a moment of dead silence. In an instant, Morgan wrestled himself out of Parker's grasp, grabbed his gun from the ground and leveled it toward Moses. Again, Bob Johnson brought his pistol down across Morgan's head with a loud crack.

"I said we've got to figure this out Valentine. Try that again and I swear I'll kill you right here before God and the judge," Bob said. All of the group stepped to the wagon to hear the damning verdict come from Moses Brown.

"Please, Deputy Johnson," Parker said. "Let me sort this out."

"Now sir, tell me everything," Parker said sternly to Moses Brown. "Who is that dead man in the duster?"

"That's Mista Julio," Moses replied. He worked for Mista Six Claws and Mista Morgan, there on the ground."

All eyes shot toward Morgan, who looked up at Moses with a sneer of hatred. His mouth foamed with his insane twitching. His neck jerked uncontrollably. "Shut up you stupid nigger. I'll have Holcomb skin you alive and feed you to the hogs."

The name *Holcomb* stunned the group. Eyes locked between John Law and Will Tyler. They did not say a word. There was fifteen years of anguish and torment in that moment. No words were needed.

Parker was enraged. He shook violently as he walked over to Morgan. "Stand up," he shouted. Morgan struggled to his feet. Parker looked at him sternly. "You've been properly tried and by the authority of the Federal Court of the Western District of Arkansas, you are found guilty of malfeasance of office, murder and other heinous crimes and are hereby condemned to death. May God have mercy on your soul, because I will not."

Valentine jerked his head back and forth, eyes wide and glaring. He balled up a large amount of spit and blood streaming from his mouth and sprayed the judge. Isaac Parker did not blink.

"That's for you and the rest of these goddamn sonsabitches that ride with you," Morgan rasped. "To hell with the District Court. And to hell with you. I only wish I was there with Six Claws and his men right now. I'm sure your pretty little women are having a real good time with that bunch."

Parker pulled his Navy Colt and, without flinching, shot Morgan between the eyes. "Sentence carried out," he said. No one said a word. In turn, each man walked by the body and shot Morgan, resolving the matter in his own mind. "A goddamned firin' squad," Bob had said.

After what seemed like an eternity of time, the group returned their attention to Moses Brown. He told them everything, honestly and without hesitation.

The group sat around a campfire and sipped some of Jesse Allen's coffee. It was decided that Morgan was to be buried right there. Parker said he did not want Morgan's rotten body in the same city with the souls of Ellie Faulkner and Father Cafferty. All agreed and short straws drew the burial detail. Bob Johnson and Sheriff Jack Hainey decided to make it shallow—*very* shallow. "Damned if I am going to waste one drop of sweat over that son of a bitch," Bob said. "Maybe the coyotes will be hungry tonight. We'll make it easy for them," he said to Hainey as they walked back to the coffee.

Will Tyler, John Law Singleton, Jesse Allen, Bass Reeves and young Bennie rode north with Moses Brown to intercept Holcomb. Bob Johnson, Benjamin Colbert, Sergeant King, the Fort Gibson troop, and the rest of the posse rode south to join up with the Tobias Johnson posse from Texas and then to pursue the missionaries. Judge Parker rode east to Fort Smith, accompanying the John Law posse as far as that point to cross over the Poteau. He had an honored guest arriving in two days, a day later than expected: his old friend U.S. Grant, a person Colonel Holcomb would never get to meet. It was a different world, for everyone.

The bishop paused to wipe the tears from his eyes and then continued, in great distress, to address the parishioners at the Church of the Immaculate Conception. It was a very emotional and trying time for the cleric, attempting to retain his dignity at this special Mass for the missionaries, three days after the capture.

"Is there one hearth, warm and inviting, in one home that has not been assailed by the cold, icy hand of death, its bony fingers reaching in and snatching from there a loved one? Is there one hearth where not a vacant chair sits, still awaiting in vain the return of its owner? Is there one little hearth in this fair land that has not been visited by the evil so a part of our visage? When, oh when, will Heaven hear our cries to lay lifeless these vile hearth-snatchers? Has death and sorrow so become our lot that tears flow torrents from every doorstop and not one home is left with a smile? Oh, Lord, where is our delivery from these days of cruelty and desolation? Where, Oh, Lord, is our champion of victory? Where, dear Father, is our hope?"

"We are doing our very best, Bishop," Parker said as he exited the church following the Mass. "There is not an hour passes that I have not had the full weight of the tragedies heavy on my heart. Just yesterday, with my own hand, I executed one of the conspirators. The very killer of Father Cafferty."

"I know, Isaac, but Satan has struck at me personally here. It has been three days since *Hell* visited us. A priest murdered in his church; missionaries at their place of service; and the murder in your own home—obviously intended for your family. This is not a matter where I can merely hold the hand of a parishioner and offer my prayers and sympathy. I, personally, need the consolation. And the consolation I need is swift justice and resolution," the bishop replied. His eyes were dark and sunken into his large wrinkled face. He was finding it very difficult to mask his anger at the outlaws and killers running rampant in the Territory. "Never in my life would I have ever thought that I would wish God's damnation upon a living soul, but upon these ruthless snatchers of hearth and home and life, I wish God's hard retribution," he continued in a strained voice, tears streaming down his corpulent cheeks.

"I will resolve it, Excellency. I give you my word of honor." Judge Parker strolled down the church steps with Mary, who had also attended the special Mass for the captives. As they walked down Garrison Street toward the courthouse, Mary, normally reserved, genteel and prayerful, broke the silence.

"Isaac, you've got to do something. This must stop. It is well enough a tragedy when no settler, farmer or traveler is safe from these killers. But now, even nuns, priests and missionaries suffer the same fate. And blood in my own home!" she said, her eyes puffed and red. "It must stop!"

"Mary, it will stop. We have very competent men on their trail. I have already killed Morgan, and if that is proved to be insufficient I will find and kill the rest of the sonsabitches myself," the judge said, his jaw set squarely.

"I take that as a solemn oath."

"It is Madam. On my love for you and the children and all I that hold dear in this life, it is."

Chapter 26

February 16, 1876
Yellow Wolf Creek Canyon, Choctaw Nation

"They be comin' up this draw and pass around this canyon," Moses Brown said as the posse surveyed the trail. "If you can draw him in there, just a bit, you can get him from the rim and get him good."

"Maybe he will stop to water the horses in that stream in the canyon," speculated Will.

John Law looked the situation over. "Brown, that seems like a good plan to me. You wouldn't be setting us up, would you?"

"No, sir. I shore ain't. I want you to get that ol' bastard and get him good. He has done the last thing he ever gonna do to me," he said, balling up a wad of saliva and spitting it on the ground.

The deputies took positions on the ridge overlooking the canyon with Yellow Wolf Creek running through the gorge. It was never more than three or four feet deep and twenty feet across at the height of the wet season. Now, it was a more shallow than that, except it was very cold. Ice had begun to form on its rocky banks. The lawmen could see more than ten miles over the canyon to the flats approaching the high ground. It was a good view. The sun was high and the beautiful cloudless day was a preview, they hoped, to some good luck. According to Moses Brown, they were supposed to meet Holcomb at the mouth of the creek at two o'clock with information on the raid and reaction in Fort Smith. They waited.

Will Tyler and Singleton, at first, avoided the obvious—information about Holcomb. But they could not wait any longer.

"Tell us about this man called Holcomb," John Law said.

"Yeah," Will said before Moses could speak, almost wishing that he had been the first to make the point of facing the question.

"Mista Holcomb is a mean, crazy man. He kills anybody anytime, just for the killin'," Moses replied. "He been going by the name Creekmore, Nelson Creekmore. But he the same mean man no matter what he call hisself."

"Creekmore, you mean the landowner and businessman from Kansas?" John Law asked, puzzled. "I've never seen him in Fort Smith."

"Nor have I," Will said.

"Yessir, that's him. Same ol'sumbitch. He stayed outta that town. Didn't want to be recognized."

"Why do you call him Holcomb?" Will asked, almost afraid to hear the answer.

"That is who he is, Colonel Josiah Holcomb, from Helena, or used to be that is, afore the Union Army chased his skinny ol' ass clear outta the country," Moses replied with a laugh. His humor did not settle on Will Tyler and John Law. They were stunned and silent. Dark memories invaded their thoughts and old hatreds took hold of their hearts. Moses Brown saw their reaction immediately.

"You folks know that man?"

"Yes, we know him," John Law said. "We know him well."

"Where from?"

"Helena," Will replied. "He killed my father and mother and stole our plantation and everything we had. Every good memory I would ever have. Every good thing in my life."

"When was that?" Moses asked reluctantly, seeing that this was a perilous situation, maybe for him. He had a lot to do with Holcomb's murdering, and he hoped that he was not a part of whatever dark thing was in the deputy's past.

John Law just looked off. Tears began to roll from his eyes, but he held back. "May 7, 1861. The Tyler Plantation," he said, labored and drawn-out.

"The Tyler Plantation, dear Lawd," Moses said. "That was a terrible thing. I wasn't there. But he shore did laugh and talk about it some after the raid. He hung the father and mother and shot dead the old granddaddy and little boy."

"Not quite," John Law said. I did not die and neither did Will here," he said. "And Dora…" he could hardly finish. "Dora was kicked by the bastard's horse. He did hang a beautiful old man and his granddaughter, though. Old Joseph and sweet Bessie. Sweet Jesus."

"Are you sure you were not there, Moses?" Will asked again.

"No sir, I just heard about it as he laughed and hooted about it to all his friends. If'n I had been there I woulda', I woulda'…."

"You would have what, Moses?"

"I dunno, sir, but I woulda' not liked it for shore."

"That was my family," Will said. "And if I thought you were there, I would kill you where you sit."

"No sir, Mista Tyler, if'n I was there I would own up to it. I would deserve a bullet, I 'spect. Yessir, I 'spect," he said, looking intently at Will.

"I believe him, Will," John Law said. "I believe him."

Moses did not say a word for a long while. Neither did John Law or Will. Finally, Moses spoke. "I have to ask you sir. I have to ask you. It has hainted me ever since I hear'd about that. Did you whip them horses to hang your pa that night? Did Mr. Holcomb make you do that? He shore got a powerful kick outta tellin' that part. Or was that one of his lies, too?"

"No, Moses, I whipped the horses! *Goddamn me to hell*, I whipped those horses."

"That ol' sumbitch," Moses said. "That ol' sumbitch."

A dust cloud from about a dozen riders appeared on the horizon. "That's them," Moses Brown said.

The group, as expected, rode into the canyon and began watering their horses. John Law and Will Tyler surveyed the group. "I count thirteen, and a heavy wagon," Will said. "There are four of us not counting young Bennie. I have seen enough young men kill a man. I won't have it here, today."

"John Law, you can count on Bennie, if we need him. He is a good shot," Bass Reeves said.

"No sir, by God, no sir. Not today. Maybe later in life he'll have to kill a man, but not today." He looked and smiled at Bennie, who was wide-eyed and taking the whole scene in, not knowing if he would have to take a gun or not. He wanted to. He sure wanted to.

"Bennie, you just keep us loaded, if we need it. That will be a big help, son. A big help."

"Mista Tyler, I can handle a rifle real good. I'd be honored sir, if'n I could bear down on that ol' sumbitch," Moses offered.

Will looked at John Law.

"It would give us five against thirteen," Will said.

"Bennie, give this man a carbine," John Law said.

"When they have all dismounted we will all take a man and the man next to him. Shoot true and shoot to kill. If we are lucky we can get eight to ten on the first shots," John Law counseled the men. "I'll take the left two. Will, you take the next two. Jesse and Bass take the next two each in line and Moses you take the last two. That will leave three in the line. Then we'll see what happens. For damned sure don't let them back on their horses." He pondered a minute, remembering Bob Johnson and Palo Duro Canyon. "On your next shots, if any man still alive tries to remount, shoot his horse out from under him." Every man nodded. It was ready to commence.

"Bennie, keep the cartridges ready, in case we are not the good shots we claim to be. By all means, we don't want them to get in those rocks behind them. I want this over with so we can get on to the posse and go after Six Claws," John Law said.

"And Katherine," Will said.

"And Katherine," John Law said.

"When I say *now*," John Law said, waiting for the last man to dismount. It seemed like forever, but it was only a second later that the group heard, *now*! The rifle volleys were instantaneous and deafening. Young Bennie plugged his ears as forcefully as he could with his fingers.

Seven men fell dead from the first two shots from the lawmen. The remaining outlaws scrambled for the cover of the rocks on the canyon wall behind them, using their horses as cover. Five horses were killed by the next series of shots.

Holcomb and five of his men were behind the rocks and had managed to grab their long rifles and ammunition as they scrambled.

"Who the goddamn hell is that?" he shouted, gasping for breath.

He shouted across the canyon. "Who are you sonsabitches, and why did you open up and cut down my men like that?"

"I'm a goddamn specter from your past. I am going to kill you and then burn your rotten corpse. This day!" John Law replied with a voice of hatred that sent chills down Holcomb's spine.

"That old bastard Singleton," he said as he looked around wildly. He pulled his best sarcasm up from his wit. "You mean you're not even going to offer to arrest me, in the proper judicial fashion that is the cornerstone of your Yankee law?"

Will Tyler responded. "We did not come here to arrest you. We have come here to kill you, Holcomb."

"And, who the hell are you?"

"I'm the one you handed a riding whip to fifteen years ago in Arkansas."

"Oh, my brave little Yankee bastard. I hear you are all grown up. And a big lawman now. And, sweet on that Yankee bitch doctor in Fort Smith. Unfortunately, for you, Mr. Tyler, I have met her just recently—in the capable hands of

Six Claws and his randy-dandy men. I *trust* she is all right. But I must be honest to say that by now, she is no longer the sweet virgin you knew three days ago."

Will jumped up immediately. Rage overcame his better judgment.

John Law immediately pulled Will back down, and was likewise enraged beyond the ability to control his actions and the call for good sense. He stood up and fired as fast as he could with his repeating Winchester at the rocky outcrop that sheltered the outlaws. As he stood, immediately, one of the outlaws with a Sharps long rifle took a bead on the Marshal and fired. The puff of smoke was visible before the report was heard, but by that time John Law was on the ground with a massive hole in his chest.

"That's one," shouted Holcomb. His cackle echoed across the canyon. It trailed off as Will was at the side of John Law.

"I believe he's finally killed me, Will," John Law said softly as he lay in Will's arms.

"Bennie, bring some water and get a blanket off the horses. Make a pillow for his head, cover him up and don't leave his side," Will shouted to the boy. "And take his sidearm out. Have it ready in case you need it. Can you handle that, boy?"

"Yessir," he shouted. "I can sure handle that." He jumped and did as he was told.

"Jesse, we are not about to have a stand-off here. You and Bass make your way around the rim and come up behind them. Moses and I will keep firing here until we see that you are in position. I'll wave a white cloth as a signal, and then you wait on me and open up after I do. We will fire heavy on them if they try to leave the rocks."

"Okay, Will, be careful. Don't anybody else stand up."

"We won't, Jesse. And, don't kill Holcomb if you can help it. I want to see him face to face before he dies."

Jesse Allen and Bass Reeves crawled behind the rock ledge and made their way around the rim of the small canyon. Will Tyler and Moses Brown fired relentlessly on Holcomb and his men, not allowing them to raise their heads to return fire. Bennie, with the marshal's Colt in his waistband, was watching John Law and reloading as fast as he could.

"Go ahead. Waste your ammunition," shouted Holcomb. "We have plenty—a whole wagon full. What about you?" He laughed as he asked.

Will figured that they might not be hitting anyone, but they were sure splattering rocks above their heads and keeping them honest.

Finally, Jesse and Bass were in position. Will tied a white cloth to his rifle and raised it high.

Holcomb saw the flag. "Why, by God, is that a surrender flag I see?" he shouted across the canyon.

"No, it's your funeral flag, Holcomb," Will replied. He and Moses then laid down a rapid volley of fire, as Jesse and Bass blasted away from their position and took deadly aim on Holcomb's men. As they tried to leave the rocks, Will and Moses dropped them. Will Tyler waved the flag again. "How many left, Jesse?"

"Just one that's moving. I believe it's Holcomb, but he's wounded," the deputy replied.

"Hold your gun on him. We are coming down. Kill him if he moves."

Will, Moses, Bennie, and John Law were all on the flats of the creek when Jesse and Bass led Holcomb to them. John Law was losing a great deal of blood, but he stood proudly as Holcomb appeared.

"Moses, you *traitorous* son of a bitch. I never thought you would have betrayed me. After *all* I have done for you," spewed Holcomb as he saw his former slave with the deputies.

"What you ever done for me, but kill my family and now done killed me? I suppose they expect to hang me too." Moses answered.

"You nigger bastard! What more should I expect?"

"Shut your goddamn mouth, Holcomb. This has been a long time coming," Will said. He told Jesse Allen to bring two horses and put a rope around the neck's of Holcomb and Brown after he had them mount up. They were then led to a stand of trees at the edge of the creek.

Jesse threw the ropes over a strong elm limb, and waited to see what was going to happen next. In all his years as a lawman in Fort Smith, no deputy had ever hanged an outlaw on the trail. That was Judge Parker's job. Jesse was apprehensive, but he would do as he was told.

Will propped John Law up against an adjacent tree. John Law stared at Holcomb for a long time. No one was saying a word. Holcomb became nervous at the awkwardness of the long silence.

"What the hell are you looking at, old man?" Holcomb asked, finally. He was leaning slightly from the bullet wound in his side.

John Law did not respond. He just pointed at Holcomb and began to speak as if relinquishing the thoughts that had been on his mind for the past several minutes.

"This bastard was at Helena when it fell on July Fourth. It was his incompetence that lost that battle for the Confederacy. I've studied it for years. The Rebs outnumbered us but they lost 1,600 men because of misplaced battery on the hills. He was in command of the battery assault," John Law said. "You were there weren't you, you stupid bastard?"

"Hell, yes, I was at Helena," Holcomb said. "It was a gallant fight."

John Law continued to address Will. He ignored Holcomb.

"I was down river at Vicksburg when Helena fell on the same day. Holcomb and his men escaped over into Mississippi and then up to join that devil Nathan Forrest in Tennessee," John Law said. "He was assigned to the west side of the river defense of Memphis and in April, he moved up and set up in trenches near Osceola." John Law drew a heavy breath. "I know the bastard was in command of the battery that was engaging the gun boats moving from St. Louis. He was at Fort Pillow. I know it."

Will stared at his grandfather. The subject was painful to the old man.

"I chased him for a year after the massacre," John Law said. "He's the murdering son of a bitch that gave the order to fire on those poor bastards as they were surrendering. Then he fired on those trying to cross into the river to reach the gunboats—men, women and children. We both know that if anyone said, 'there'll be no nigger prisoners', it was Holcomb. If he was there, he said it. It was said, and he was there," John Law grimaced. "That settles the matter for me."

"I suspect you are dead right, John Law," Will said. "But he can only die once. And in my purpose, he needs to die for my daddy and mother, before he answers for killing three hundred black soldiers. The Almighty can discuss Fort Pillow with him. That's what is in my heart."

"Mine too, son. Mine too. And it has eat out our souls long enough. Let's hang the bastard."

"Fort Pillow?" Holcomb questioned. He had been listening with pride as John Law recounted the eyewitness reports of the battle. Those reports were national news in the Congressional investigation that followed. It was the most controversial battle of the war. "Why, I wish I could take the credit for that. But that was all Nathan Bedford Forrest, the greatest general officer in the whole goddamn war. All I did was give the order to shoot those niggers as they swam to hell. No Quarter! No Quarter!" He laughed as he shouted again. "No Quarter! They sank straight to hell in that river. Damnedest thing I ever saw. I never knew a nigger couldn't float."

"You are a heinous bastard," John Law said. "Even at the moment of death you have no remorse." His voice was failing. He had lost a lot of blood and was losing more by the minute. "Hold those horses steady," Will said. "I don't want him to kick, and cheat us of the opportunity."

Bass Reeves and Jesse Allen held the mounts tightly by the reins. They were seasoned deputies, and did as they were ordered. Bennie Reeves looked on—wide-eyed and attentive, holding tightly to his father's gun satchel.

"It was war," Holcomb said. "It was war."

"It was murder, you maniacal son of a bitch, it was murder," John Law said, his strength fading. It was hard for him to even focus his eyes on the men sitting on their horses with ropes around their necks.

"You can't hang me," Holcomb cried. "You're a goddamn Yankee lawman. You must execute the warrant, not the accused."

John Law ripped the badge from his chest and threw it at Holcomb. He was dying and his vengeance was the only life force left in his body. "I'll not give you the pleasure of seeing me dishonor that badge. I am no longer a United States Marshal. I am now a man who will enjoy this last act, more than any in life. The only thing I ask of the Almighty is that I be sent to hell, so that I might have the chance of killing you again in that place."

Will Tyler picked up John Law's badge, took off his own and placed them in his pocket. "I am that same man," he said. There was no moral decision to be made. Will Tyler was determined that nothing would stop him from seeing Holcomb die.

"Then, goddamn your soul, if you must hang me, then don't hang me with this nigger. That is an affront to God," Holcomb said, gritting his teeth and spewing saliva as he talked. He looked over to Moses with hate in his eyes, and then glared back at John Law.

"You, sir, know nothing of God," John Law said. "And in a moment, God will know nothing of either of us. But seeing you die like this is worth an eternity in hell."

"Don't hang me with this nigger," he shouted even louder.

Will looked at the outlaw beside Holcomb.

"Mr. Brown, I owe you a debt today, but I must ask you this. Why are you riding with Holcomb?" Will waited anxiously for an answer that would allow him to spare the man.

"I came from Arkansas with Mista Holcomb, sir. I pretty well done what he said all my life. If he say *kill this man, or kill that man*, well, I kills him. If he say *fetch this thing or that thing*, well, I fetches it. He's *Mista Holcomb*."

"How many men have you killed, Moses?" Will asked.

"As many as I was told to," he replied with a low, sad voice. "I guess the good Lawd is plenty mad at me, but I just couldn't stop doin' what he said, just like my daddy had to."

"Moses, I reckon you deserve to hang, too, no matter your help today." Will said.

"Yessir, I reckon so. And I'm tired. My daddy's gone, my mama's gone, my wife and children, they all dead. It's time I guess for me to explain all this to Jesus."

"Don't hang me with this ignorant, whining son of a bitch," repeated Holcomb. "You can't do that to a white man no matter how much you hate him."

"You did it to my father, and thought nothing of it," Will said, his eyes welling up. He thought again of Old Joseph and Bessie Rison.

Holcomb looked at Tyler and then at John Law with his body shaking from anger. He was in a losing proposition and he knew it. All his life he had been in control, able to command anything and have it come his way. The flight from Arkansas during the war, even though bitter, had allowed him to set his determination and rebuild to a life of even more power. His pride had always found a way to overcome wounds and setbacks. This day, however, he was in a box with no way out. All he could do was die with some part of his dignity intact. Die with some sense of honor, no matter how perverted. It would do no good to bargain with Tyler and John Law. He would not consider it in any event. His vainglory would not allow him to beg or make deals with these Yankee bastards. All that was left for him was to be able to die knowing that he fought for the cause to the bitter end. He would not die with this heathen, though; he had been desperately trying to reason with Tyler. No more.

"Your father was a fool," he said finally. "There is no changing that fact. It will be the last thing I say. I hope my words ring in your ears until you meet me in hell. Your goddamn Yankee bastard daddy was a fool." Holcomb winced as he shouted. Blood was pouring from the wound in his side.

Will stood at the side of Holcomb's horse and looked into the man's red and swollen face. Turning slowly, he walked to his horse and retrieved the black leather whip that he had carried with him for fifteen years.

Holcomb looked at the whip incredulously. For some reason, he was now feeling fear for the first time. His heart pounded and he began to sweat profusely.

Tyler walked over to the black man's horse. "Moses, I have decided not to hang you with this bastard." Moses looked nervously at the whip. He remembered it vividly from his days at the Holcomb plantation. He had seen it used on his daddy.

"I'm going to let you ride out of here," Will said, motioning Bass Reeves to take the rope from Moses Brown's neck. "Holcomb has no more control over you."

Moses Brown was shaking when Bass Reeves walked up, helped him off his horse and put an arm around the old man. "I don't understand, sir," he said, overwhelmed.

"Just say that it is for your family," Will said. John Law looked on with a smile. He had raised the boy well, he thought. He caught Will's glance and they locked eyes. They were thinking the same thing. Perfect justice. Perfect closure.

"Mr. Brown, there's one thing that I ask of you," Will said, looking at Holcomb. "Take this whip and give his horse a lash."

There was dead silence in the grove. Bass Reeves and Jesse Allen looked on with astonishment. John Law smiled, even though the pain in his chest was unbearable. Holcomb stared in unbelief. His most unimaginable fears were crashing to a ghastly reality.

Before Holcomb could utter a sound, Moses Brown grabbed the whip from Will's hand, and looked Holcomb squarely in the eye. "This is for my daddy and my mama and for my Ruby and the babies, you rotten ol' sumbitch." Saliva flew from his mouth through his tightened teeth as he spoke. His neck veins bulged through his dark, cracked, skin.

Moses brought the whip down with a vengeance. The horse bolted out of Jessie Allen's grip and Holcomb fell with a violent snap, but his neck did not break. He struggled and gasped for air as he swung, kicking and jerking. His face began to turn blood red, then a dark blue. It took him eight minutes to choke to death. In the end, his urine was running down his left pant leg to his boot, and dripped to the dry dust beneath his feet. Bennie Bass dropped his father's gun satchel to the ground. He couldn't breathe at that moment. He had seen a lot of violence in his short eleven years, but this would carve a deep impression on his memory.

Will Tyler looked at the dust absorbing the drops of urine falling in rhythm. He felt a sickening satisfaction. Not so much for what he had done, but for the fact that all his hate and dreams of vengeance for fifteen years had only one short, swift, conclusion. He wished somehow there could have been more. This was not enough to satisfy and repay him for half a lifetime of nightmares and loneliness.

John Law sensed the same emptiness. He just stared up from where he was propped at the tree, bleeding and breathing hard. He looked at Holcomb's lifeless body, and strangely felt no relief.

"It's over, son," he said. "But I'm afraid he's killed me as well."

Will had known since the bullet tore into John Law that the wound was more than likely fatal. He could not, however, face the reality of it. He tended to other matters as if this were not real.

"Moses Brown," he said. "I want you to take your horse and go. I don't ever want to see you again in the Territory. Go back home. Go back to the delta and find whatever family you can." He looked at the man sternly. "If I ever hear that you've killed another soul, I'll track you down and hang you myself. Do you understand?"

The man handed the whip back to Tyler. "Yessir, I understand. Thank you sir. I really means it. Thank you, sir."

"Go on now, and keep that whip. It will remind you as to what will happen if you every kill anyone again," Will said.

"Thank you, sir," he repeated. Will put him on his horse, and whipped his horse as he turned east, to Arkansas.

"Jesse, you and Bass ride as fast as you can without jarring him too much and get John Law back to Fort Smith," Will said. "I'm going South and catch up to the other posse."

"Will," Bass said slowly, looking up from his position, kneeling over the marshal. "He's dead."

Will walked over to John Law and returned the marshal's badge to his vest. He then pinned his own back where it belonged. "Take him...." Will could not finish his sentence. "Take him to Fort Smith," he said finally, with a failing voice.

Jesse looked up. Tears were falling down his dirt-caked cheeks. "I'll take him on to Fort Smith. Bass and Bennie can ride with you on to the Canadian."

"No," Will said sternly. "John Law deserves a by-God honor escort." He looked at Holcomb's wagon loaded with twenty cases of guns and ammunition that Six Claws would never see. "I want all three of you to go. Put him in that damned wagon full of guns, comfortable like. And stop outside of town at Solomon Nobel's place and put him in a proper wagon. I don't want him brought into town slung across no goddamn saddle or in a wagon full of stolen guns. And have Solomon take that flag he flies over that place and put it over John Law in that wagon."

He turned to Bennie. "I suspect you've seen enough today." He looked at the boy's father. "Bass, get this boy back and put him in school. He has seen enough. By God, he's seen enough." Will was red-faced and sullen. The boy reminded him of what fifteen years of death and dying would do to a person. "Do you hear me, boy?"

"Yessir," a shaken Bennie Reeves replied.

Will, softening his tone, reached over and shook the boy's hand. "You did good today, son. You did good."

Bass walked over, picked up his gun satchel, and took the boy by the hand. "Yes, you've seen enough. Your ma would not have liked the way I have raised you."

"But, Pa," Bennie interjected.

"No buts," Bass said. "I won't have you ending up like that," he said, looking at Holcomb's lifeless body. You have seen enough." Bass looked at Will Tyler. "What about that bastard hanging there?"

"Cut him down and take him, too. But when you get to town, I don't want him in the wagon with John Law. Take him in dragging behind his horse," he said with a dark stare. "Send a detail back to clean up this mess," he said, surveying the carnage. "And tell Judge Parker that I will settle up with him about all this when I get back." He mounted Sky to begin his journey. He turned and looked at John Law again. "And don't forget that flag. John Law always took pride in that flag."

Solomon Noble and his wife Judith operated the livery, blacksmith shop and the river ferry at the Poteau crossing for most of twenty years. It was the only civilized outpost before the Nations. Outlaws, lawmen, good citizens and just about everyone else making the trek into the Territory had to pass through the post. It was the last chance for anyone to get supplies, whisky, and a pile of Judith's peach cobbler before heading into *hell* across the river. Of course, buying whisky and guns was off limits to the Indian travelers, but most ate a considerable amount of that good lady's pastry concoctions. Many times Bob Johnson and Benjamin Colbert would make the ride from Fort Smith to satisfy a late night sweet-tooth craving.

The identifying sight at the post was a very large Union flag flying high in the wind. Any approaching rider could see it for two miles. It was the pride of Solomon Noble. He had it sent all the way from St. Louis and was always on the look for a larger one. To his dismay, one could not be found. But he was proud of it immensely in any event, lowering it every evening, cleaning and folding it with great care, and waiting for the sunrise so he could raise it again on the hundred-foot mast, he had hewn from a slender, straight pine. His one other treasure was Judith. His wife for the last thirty-five years. Why she agreed to marry him was a constant question—not only to him but everyone who encountered her. At fifty-two, she was a striking woman. Beautiful, intelligent and infectiously friendly—anyone who arrived at the post was her friend within a few minutes.

Solomon, although amicable, went about his business and work without much fanfare, a man of a few words but solid and dependable. Everyone liked him and knew they could count on a fair and prompt service. He was short, stout and portly, heavily bearded but clean. They were an odd couple, but there was not a doubt in anyone's mind that they were loving and dedicated. John Law had been especially fond of them.

Any arrival at the post was usually an event looked forward to. The approach of Bass Reeves, Bennie, and Jesse Allen was to be a very different occasion as they rode in with John Law and the murderer Holcomb.

The flag was lowered and tenderly laid across John Law's body in a brand new wagon, just in from Wichita. It was also laden with early flowers that Judith had painstakingly grown and protected from the frost. The ferry and stable were closed and the procession headed into Fort Smith, a town unaware of the meaning of the sight as it entered Garrison Street. Watching were Judge Isaac C. Parker and his friend Ulysses S. Grant, President of the United States. John Law was adorned as a statesman with the highest honors, and Holcomb was tied to a rope and dragged behind his horse, raising a dust cloud as he went. Just as Will Tyler had said.

Chapter 27

▼

February 16, 1876
Six Claws' camp

Life was hard in Six Claws' camp. Doubly so for the captives. Each hour was a horror. After Holcomb's departure at the rendezvous two days before, both nuns had been beaten and threatened with rape. Restrained by Father Boles, Katherine screamed and fought as they were led away by some of Six Claws' men.

"You were told not to harm anyone, remember? Holcomb said not to harm anyone," she shouted. Killing Tree lunged toward her and hit her hard enough to knock both her and the priest to the ground. "Holcomb is not here. And if he was, I would kill him, too. No one tells me who to rape or kill and who not to rape or kill. You will be next," he said as he kicked her violently in the side.

Tubby cowed in the corner with Diablo, the little stray dog he had adopted. The boy wanted to help, but he just sat holding his dog.

Six Claws was losing interest in the whole matter. If it were not for the wagonload of guns that Holcomb had promised, he would ride out then, without hesitation. He agreed that Holcomb was not in charge. He only thought he was. And when they got their hands on the twenty cases of rifles, they would feed Holcomb to the pigs. He was tiring of the stupid white man. He waited impatiently for the inevitable posse and Holcomb's men to flank them from the rear. It was a good plan, but Six Claws had a premonition, perhaps given by the Old People, that it was going to be a disaster.

Katherine struggled to her feet. "Do something, Father," she screamed to Boles. "Do something!"

"What do you want me to do, Katherine? I don't know what I can do."

"Be a man, damn you. Be a man!"

The words stung. Boles was a passive man. But even he knew that the situation was at an end for doing nothing, or even praying. Before Odell could stop him, Boles ran toward Killing Tree with his arms flailing like a schoolboy in his first playground fight. The Indian turned and shoved his knife deep into the priest's body. Father Boles looked surprised, then smiled as he fell to the ground. "I *am* a man," he muttered. I *am* a man."

"You are a dead one now, priest," Six Claws said with a passive glaze in his eyes.

"No!" screamed Katherine. "No!"

"You wanted him to be a man. Then, here is your man." Killing Tree said in a loud voice as he looked to Katherine and kicked the priest.

"No, no, no," Katherine cried as her voice lost its intensity. She cradled the priest's convulsing body in her arms.

The scene was interrupted by the screams of the McGready Sisters. They were in the middle of the square with a half-dozen men gathered around them. Odell Skaggs ran from the hut to help. He was stopped by the strong swing of Six Claws' rifle butt. "Stay out of this, Skaggs. I am getting very tired of you and your whimpering brother," the Indian said. "You get on with your work or you will be next, right after the loud white woman."

Odell stumbled back to Katherine. "I'm sorry Dr. O'Reilly, but I pleaded with you not to cause any trouble. Please, there has been enough dying. If only Two Snakes has made it. I hope he has not died out there."

Katherine stared coldly at Odell. "When is enough, enough?" she spewed. "Even if Two Snakes is alive, who says he will get here in time?" She left Father Boles and reached for Tubby who, though not crying, was trying to hold his tightly pursed lips in place and not betray his desire to scream. Katherine cuddled the boy and gently kissed him on the head. "You said there has been enough dying. When is enough, enough—for them?" She continued to stare at Odell.

She was viscerally sorry for having caused Father Boles' wound. He was a kind and gentle man. She wept not only for him but for her actions, also. She had to get control of her anger and start figuring out as to how to stay alive, how to keep the boy alive, and somehow hold on until Will came. Will Tyler. Her despair fell to a deeper trance as she thought of him. How she loved him. God, how she loved him.

"Let me have Father Boles," Odell said. "There is nothing you can do. He is dying. I'll bury him as soon as he dies, before one of these goddamn bastards remembers that it is time to feed the pigs," he said. "Pardon my language, Ma'am."

"I am the one who needs to apologize to you," Katherine replied. "I know you are doing all that you can to keep people alive. I promise that I will not give you any more trouble. Just get us out of here—please!"

"That is my every waking thought, Katherine, I promise. And if that fellow of yours is anything like you said he is, I suspect we will be getting some help in no time at all. I pray to God so."

She looked again at Albert Boles, his eyes pleading for help, trying to pray.

"I have to do something," she said. She had been able to bring only a few of her medical supplies from the wagon. Precious few. "Bring me what ever I have. *We will not* bury this man!"

She worked feverishly to save his life. The wound was deep and he was losing a great deal of blood. She prayed for the first time in a long time. She meant it. Any bargain with God. Anything that he would do. She prayed, Saving Father—Healing Father. She applied all she knew through the night. She prayed for the intercession of the Virgin and every saint she could remember. She prayed with every movement of her hands. Every bandage. Every thing she could do to stop the hemorrhage. She looked out of the hut, frequently, at the *Sister sisters*. There was nothing she could do. They, like Father Boles, were in the hands of God. With every ounce of her resolve, begged that she not doubt God now. *God, let Two Snakes get through for help. Please let there be a God!*

At dawn, sitting with her head bowed into her raised knees, she heard a soft, weak voice. "I *am* a man." Albert Boles had survived the night—by her hand or the hand of God, he had survived.

"Yes Father, you are a man. You *are* a man," she whispered softly to him. She wrapped him securely in blankets and bowed her head. She thanked God, earnestly. She asked to be delivered from her anger and her hatred. She knew, however, there was opportunity for both, at anytime.

She asked Odell to gently lift Father Boles to the rear of the hut, and she bowed her head again and pleaded to God for assistance. That prayer was violently interrupted by the renewed screams of the *Sister sisters*. They had been tortured through the night. Katherine returned to her prayer, now dark and possessed. "But…" she said to God—in the hearing of Odell—in a low and determined voice, tightly holding on to little Tubby. "But, if I get the slightest chance, I'll kill that goddamn Killing Tree."

She had her chance, a few moments later. A loud scream—louder than the cries of the *Sister sisters,* came from the group outside. Killing Tree had forcefully pulled Half Scar, a Kiowa killer, away from Mary Anne McGready. Remarkably, the nuns had not been raped, even once. Only threatened and beaten.

Their torture had become a game for the drunken bandits. They would toss the dice to see who would have the turn at the *game*. One by one, they would wager for the chance to approach the women with their sordid play. Each would drop his clothes around his boots, and terrorize the nuns by moving closer and closer, exposed, without touching them. It was the game to see who could elicit the greatest scream. There had not been a great deal of screaming throughout the bizarre event. It had declined and this infuriated the marauders. Either the nuns found courage in their faith, or they had lost the power and ability to scream, and even react, anymore.

But now, Killing Tree had enough of their stupid game. He felt the waiting was over. *Holcomb be damned.* He would not wait any longer. Half Scar, sensing that the time was finally here for what they had been working themselves up to all night, wanted his turn, first. He pulled his knife and plunged it deep into Killing Tree's left lung. The pink-colored blood bubbled from the gash. Six Claws walked over to the crowd. "There is nothing but trouble when you try to rape these women. Are you alive, Killing Tree?" he asked angrily.

The fallen Indian could not talk for the pain and the gurgling of blood from his side. He tried to get up but fell back to the ground in anguish.

"Get the woman doctor, here," Six Claws said. I cannot lose any more men today." He looked at Half Scar. The Kiowa brave was drunk, but he realized that he was in a bad situation. He backed up and brought his knife toward Six Claws. "Are you stupid as well as drunk?" Six Claws asked. "Put that knife away. I will not kill you today. I will let Killing Tree do that—if he lives."

Odell and Katherine were shuttled to the group and surveyed the ghastly sight. The *Sister sisters* were sprawled on the ground covered in blood from the beatings with knives and sticks. Three drunken bandits, passed out from whisky and various blows to the head were lying around Killing Tree's bleeding body. In the confusion, Treewell was able to get the nuns to their feet and move them to the safety of the captives' hut. Odell quickly moved to help him. Katherine, sensing that the brothers needed a diversion, spoke up loudly. "Well, I see that someone finally opened you up like the pig that you are," she said, looking at Killing Tree. John Birdsong reached over and struck Katherine in the mouth. She reeled from the blow.

"Stop it," shouted Six Claws. "I ought to kill every last one of you stupid bastards and ride out of here. There is a bad spirit about this place. You, loud mouth woman. What can you do to fix Killing Tree?"

She took a deep breath as she wiped the blood from her lip. She wanted to kill John Birdsong, who looked on with a stupid smile. "Get him into one of the huts that has a table and some light. Bring me some boiling water and the rest of my medical supplies from our wagon, if your men haven't destroyed them with their ignorant plundering," she said, staring at Six Claws with a stern and defiant voice. She could not help the 'ignorant plundering' remark. To her mind that had been excessively reserved.

"Do as she says," Six Claws said.

She knew, now, there was no need for threats. She would do as she was told. If she harmed Killing Tree, she knew well enough what would happen. She did not want to take any chances with them hurting the boy, or throwing away any chance of ever seeing Will Tyler again. She took a deep breath as she turned toward the nearby stone storage house where Killing Tree had been taken.

Katherine looked at Killing Tree's badly wounded body. She was delighted at the pain he was in. But she was determined to remember her station as a doctor and to do what she could to help him. He was, after all, a human being. Only barely, but still a human.

It was cold and dark and the dim lantern provided just enough light to see, not perform surgery. "I'll do what I can," she said with a quick, stern glance toward Six Claws. "But there is one thing I want you to understand." She quickly put her temper in check. "There is one thing I pray that you will consider," she re-phrased. "I will help this man and any of your other wounded. But, please give me access to the needs and injuries of the captives." She paused, her eyes flashing with anger. "And, don't harm the boy. *Please*, don't harm the boy." Her tone was tenacious, but pleading.

"The fat, little pig is my best warrior," Six Claws said in an almost conciliatory tone. "I wish all my men were as brave."

Tubby stood in the shadows, silent and staring. He clutched Diablo tightly.

"I am sure his parents would appreciate your compliment," she said sarcastically. She checked her temper once again. She opened her medical supply bags and took out some clean, cloth strips. "Bring me the hot water," she said.

Staring at Killing Tree lying on the wooden table, she saw a pitiful figure. An unclean, ignorant savage who had never known anything but killing and death, now put his life into the hands of someone who had sworn to God in prayer that she would kill him. Perhaps it was fitting and just, in some perverted way. He glanced at her and she saw fear in his eyes. Perhaps for the first time in his life, he now knew fear. He saw the unknown. His life was in the hands of someone who possessed a greater power and spiritual magic than he could imagine. Several outlaws stood in the room to watch, perhaps as a warning to Katherine to do her job right; but somehow she believed that it mattered not one way or the other whether Killing Tree lived or died. In fact, every man in the room would more than likely have killed the man if they had the chance. A slip of the knife on her part would have been appreciated. Nonetheless, she was duty bound and sworn to do her best to save his worthless life. As she approached him with her scalpel to make an incision at the wound over his lung, he glared at her in obvious fear.

"I have to cut away the damaged tissue so I can better see the wound," she explained to the killer.

He looked at her with resignation, somehow sensing that it was time to die. He sneered and with his last breath, uttered a curse, grabbed her hands and forcefully thrust her scalpel into his heart.

"Goddamn," he shouted, and died.

Katherine was stunned. As she stood there, shaking, the outlaws just filed by the table, looking at the dead killer, and left the cabin. It was of no matter to them now. Katherine returned to her hut, walking in a daze.

The entire camp was awaiting the attack of the lawmen. They were in disarray. There was an air of defeat before it even began, mostly because Six Claws had given up, not out of any lack of courage, but more than that. Since the news of the death of Two Snakes, He felt a strange presence. A presence of the Old People all around him. From the time he was forced to leave his village, as a boy, he had no use or respect for any leading of the Spirits. Now, it was if they had returned and cashed in on decades of absence to do their bidding in his life. He felt powerless. Strangely, he did not fear them anymore than he feared the posse camped on the distant ridge, waiting to attack at sunrise. His thoughts about the Spirits were more of anticipation. An anticipation of a power over which he had no control. He welcomed the battle with them. He certainly realized the superior power of the lawmen he was up against. That never concerned him. He owed nothing to Holcomb and intended to give him nothing. The wagonload of rifles held no interest anymore. It was just that he had lost the will to fight *this* fight. He felt the leading of the Old People, strongly now, that his fight was now a new fight and it was somewhere else. It was with a new foe. It was unknown, but promised to be powerful. This fight was soon, and would be worthy.

He decided to leave. He had the feeling from the Old People that all here would die because they were stupid, ignorant, and unworthy to live. But he must live to face the new foe, the new fight. So, he would just take his mount and his weapon and leave. He would be guided as to where. There was always someone to kill. He must go and find them. But first, he must face the woman. She had power and strength that he admired. She must come under him in the sight of the Old People. He must take his prize.

Six Claws walked to the lodge occupied by the missionary captives. He looked defeated and drained. His countenance was more sullen than any had seen before. The battle will go decisively against him and all his men, and he was not only to be defeated by firepower, brute force and determination of the posse, but moreover and implacably, he was defeated in spirit. A rare if not impossible event, most would say. He looked on the horizon for the coming foe. He felt it in his spirit. Six Claws entered the lodge.

Father Boles was lying against a wall, looking at the ground without any expression. His wounds did not kill him, but in some sense, he wished that they had. The *Sister sisters* were lying prostrate at his feet intertwined in an embrace that made it difficult to tell one from the other. Their bodies were only wounded, but their spirits were almost destroyed. All were bleeding freshly and wore the dark-red, blood-soaked and caked bandages of earlier atrocities. The nuns were finally asleep, or so it seemed. In any event, they were absent from any more activity around them. They were like soldiers fresh from many battles for the Lord, who had mercifully been allowed by the commander-in-chief to finally sheath their swords and retire to the rear of the camp in rest. Father Boles, too, was among that retreating and limping band.

Katherine sat in the middle of the small hut next to the single lantern on the floor. Tubby Prichard, jettisoned beyond his age of four, was tightly embraced in Katherine's lap; he and Diablo wrapped in a tattered blanket. His small foot stole a view from beneath the blanket and gave witness to the ghastly wound from Six Claws knife.

Six Claws looked at each of them, pausing to look—for what seemed an interminable amount of time to her—upon Katherine with his pitch-black eyes, emotionless and empty, before he spoke.

"I am leaving," he said in a terse, low, command.

"By God in Heaven, you will go alone. We will not set another foot with you—anywhere," she said with lip-biting vehemence. Her jaw was set and her head shook as she glared intently at the Indian.

Tubby stirred and looked at Six Claws. He could not mask his terror no matter how brave he had been. Katherine quickly pulled his head back to her body and stroked his hair, comforting him as best she could.

No other Indian was present, so no other witness would ever be able to tell the tale in the villages and campfire sessions around the reservations strewn across the

Plains, but Six Claws was moved. Perhaps it was that childhood memory of his own mother, Hand Over Mouth, trying so desperately to protect him from the insane rages of his cruel father. He paused for a moment in the silent hut.

"Don't you hurt Miss Katherine," screamed Tubby as he leapt from her embrace and threw his portly little body into the Indian. The move broke the lock of the moment and caught Six Claws off guard. He instinctively delivered a heavy blow to Tubby's face. The boy reeled violently and fell back against Katherine. The dog spun around in frenzy, barking and growling, as if seeking the best angle to attack the Indian.

Six Claws kicked the small dog and sent him flying across the lodge with a shrill yelp.

"Goddamn you," Katherine spewed. "Leave us alone!"

Father Boles looked up from his trance, and then sensing that all his fight was gone, he slowly returned to his death-grip gaze upon the ground, silent and dejected. Powerless, he awaited his death. It was overdue he summarized.

Six Claws seemed energized by his attack from the small boy and the snarly little dog, and was jolted back to the matter at hand.

"I have come to take my prize," he said as he drew his bone-handled knife.

Katherine knew exactly what he meant. "Take my toe!" she shouted. "Take two of them, but leave the others alone."

"No!" shouted Tubby. "Don't you cut my *mama*. Cut my other toe. Don't you cut my *mama*."

Katherine looked at the boy, with his teeth set and his fist clenched as he stood between her and the Indian. *Mama? Mama?* Her mind reeled with the instinct to grab the youngster and squeeze him with all her strength. There was no stronger light of joy that could possibly have entered the hut at that moment, than that little four-year-old, who had just a few days ago witnessed his parents and two brothers brutally butchered, and then have his own toe severed in some insane ritual—that little boy—brought such joy to Katherine, that she cried again. She cried even more now, but for joy. *This is my oak sapling and the start of my redwood tree.*

"Be quiet, you little bastard, or I will cut your head off, and your dog's head, too," barked Six Claws.

"Cut my head off, but don't cut my *mama*." He hesitated a moment as if finally correcting that slip of the tongue. "*Miss Katherine*, I mean," he followed sternly, if not embarrassed a bit. As much as a four-year-old could be.

Diablo stood his ground, limping from the blow of Six Claws' foot. He snarled, and barked with all his might at the Indian.

Katherine grabbed Diablo quickly from the looming stance of Six Claws, and held the boy, with his dog even more tightly. She gently rubbed his small head with her cheek and kissed it tenderly. "*Mama* was right, my little soldier. *Mama* was right. I am your mama now. And don't you forget it." Tears flowed to his dark brown locks of curly hair.

Suddenly she looked at Six Claws again. "Take my toe if you must satisfy your cowardly, barbaric lust. But leave the others alone. They have been through enough, even by your standards." She then spoke in a less stern and more conciliatory voice. "I will *do this* for you. If you will leave the others alone and just go, I will sever it myself. That should be very powerful for you to have such a prize." It was perhaps a divine stroke of inspiration that she uttered this compromise. Not only would it possibly intrigue the Indian, but also with her surgical skills she could amputate the appendage in such a manner that would cause less permanent damage than having it hacked off by the savage. She waited for his reply.

He pondered the amazing offer. Of the hundreds of toes in his collection, not one had been cut off by the owner. The bravery of such an act would be very powerful and pleasing to the Spirits. He nodded at Katherine and handed the knife to her, handle first.

The *Sister sisters* and Father Boles had stirred and were now watching in horror. "No!" all three shouted in unison. Tubby tried to grab the knife and in his haste grabbed the blade, gashing his hand. Blood poured. Father Boles, as if infused by some mystical energy, jumped up and grabbed the boy.

More concerned with Tubby than the impending drama of losing a toe, Katherine screamed and prayed at the same time. "Father. Dear God. Is Tubby okay?"

"I'll get some bandages from your kits and take care of him," Boles responded moving as best he could. His life was still in jeopardy from his wounds.

"Hand me the small surgical bag," she said. Retrieving it from the priest's hand, she reached inside and drew out a surgical scalpel. "I will use my own knife. That will make it even more powerful," she said, looking straight into the eyes of Six Claws. She held the small razor sharp implement up and twirled in briefly to catch the low light from the dim lantern. It sparkled like a fine jewel. Six Claws was captivated. He picked up his knife, bloodied from the small hand of Tubby Pritchard, looked at it curiously, and then re-sheathed it into his deerskin scabbard. Again, he nodded at Katherine.

Katherine had the room at her full attention as she meticulously unhooked each eyehook in her black ankle boots, bought by her mother in Boston as a gift for the trip to Fort Smith. Katherine thought of her mother, surely sitting in the parlor of their fine Boston home with friends having tea and her trademark lemon cake. She removed the boot and the soiled white linen sock from her foot. She looked deeply into the face of Six Claws, crossed her legs in a squatting position, and brought her right ankle to rest upon her left knee. She lowered the scalpel to her middle toe—It seemed to be the one that Six Claws preferred for some reason—and she brought it sharply and with all her force across the flesh and through the bone. She never released her look with Six Claws and he never looked away.

A hot, searing jolt raced through her body. She leaned forward in her squatting position as if she were losing consciousness. Quickly, with great inward struggle and determination she regained her composure and offered her bloody toe to Six Claws like the head of a vanquished foe, ceremoniously handed to a conquering potentate.

Six Claws took the prize from her hand and looked at her with what she deemed as some perverted look of respect. He reached over for the medical bag containing the bandages, and just as ceremoniously as she had presented the toe, he handed the bag to her. She accepted it with a nod and half-smile of affirmation of understanding that it was over. She had faced the bear, given him his bite of flesh, and now the beast would retreat, satisfied.

Six Claws returned the nod. He saw courage and respected it. Strange as it was to understand by the others looking on, she understood.

Six Claws left the hut to prepare his men for the battle, but it was now of no consequence to him. His heart was no longer in the defense of the camp. At least, he would keep the men sober and alert. He would leave, but not until they were ready to die like the killers they were.

With the vengeance that made his reputation, he went from outlaw to outlaw barking final orders and breaking every whisky bottle in the camp. He promised that any man not willing to fight to the death, he would kill then—at that moment. One renegade, too drunk to comprehend, made a surly remark to the Kiowa leader. Six Claws took the man's pistol and forced it into the bandit's mouth and pulled the trigger. His head exploded. At that moment, the thirty or so killers were ready for the task. They gathered to their places and waited. Katherine huddled in the corner of her hut with Tubby snuggled in her lap. The nuns and Father Boles lay nearby. She waited.

Six Claws mounted his horse with his bag of severed toes and his weapon. He rode out of camp and left them to their destiny. He never looked back, only forward to the future fight promised by the Spirits.

Chapter 28

Dusk, February 18, 1876
The Choctaw Nation near Six Claws' camp

Will had rejoined the posse. He and Sky both were sapped of all physical energy, and he was devoid of emotional energy, as well. He had ridden at break-neck speed to reach the posse and had arrived at dusk. It was a sad reunion. The news of John Law's death sobered the group and there was a deep sadness, even among Tobias Johnson and the Texas Ranger posse, and the Army patrol that had joined up with the group that day. They had never met John Singleton, but he was a legend. And the mutual respect among lawmen transcended any colors or territories: black or white, blue or gray; Texas or the rest of the world, small as it might be to the Texans' minds.

Will now recounted the details of the Holcomb battle and the swift justice that befell the hated man. Every man listened with a dead silence, as if reliving the fifteen years of torment suffered by Will Tyler, John Singleton and the entire Tyler family. With every word, Will kept looking at the horizon, remembering Katherine and her plight.

One of the deputies caught a glimpse of a campfire far on the darkening view. "I think I saw where one of the scouts is camped," he said.

"Let's go," Bob said as he reached for his saddle.

"Hold on," a cautious Tobias said. "We don't know who they are or how many there are. Let's send a scout to look at it."

"I'll go by foot," Bob said. "I can make it in half the time and I'll find out what we are up against."

As much as Will Tyler wanted to ride out with the brash Texan, guns blazing, he saw the soundness in his friend's intervention. "Go, friend. Go. And be careful."

Bob ran as fast and quietly as his feet would carry him. Each stride was calculated with every instinct that his heritage and training could muster. When he reached the base of the ridge, he climbed without notice and broke the neck of the bandit with one swift turn of his clenched hands. As much as he wanted to unfetter his Colt, he thought the better of it because of the noise and the dozens of the bandit's companions who would respond. This way, the scout died with a muffled crack of his spine.

Upon his return, carrying the dead man's rifle, Bob reported that the man had been alone, but that another campfire a mile farther south indicated there was another sentry in waiting. He was unsure how many were at that spot or where the main camp was located. They might even be in pursuit of them at this moment. That revelation made the group even more edgy. So, they agreed to bed-down and wait until first light for a better chance to get at the situation.

They needed a diversion. Bob would have been the first choice for the comic relief, but just having killed a man took the edge off his humor. Colbert rose to the task.

"This reminds me of a fix that I was in up in Montana Territory," Colbert said as he stroked his beard and stared into the fire. He paused. There was silence, except for the cracking and popping of the dry oak wood being consumed by the fire, and the occasional distant gunshot from Six Claws' camp. The group looked at him as if wondering when he was going to continue. Finally he spoke. "Yeah, I was trappin' for some beaver and I stumbled onto some sacred burial ground. Before I knew it, a band of Crow braves was coming at me out of the hills and was they mad," he said, shaking his head in confirmation. "They was still a distance away but I felt a musket ball whistle by my ear and I decided that the wise and reasonable thing was to ride without hesitation. The main thing I was thinking about was my scalp, so, I didn't even bother to load up my packhorse and supplies—including about a dozen big fat beavers. I just grabbed my Henry, jumped on my mount and beat the hell out of there—cussin' the son of a bitch that ever gave them Crows their guns."

Tobias was completely absorbed by the mountain man and his tales. A good story always took the sting out of a perilous situation on the trail. He had used the tactic many times himself, as had his son, Bob, who likewise was enthralled by Colbert and his story. Will Tyler, standing guard away from the campfire, was in hearing range but impervious to the story. He was totally lost in his thoughts of Katherine, looking into the night and surveying the dark horizon for movement.

"Now, I was ridin' low and getting all the gallop I could out of my horse," continued Colbert. "I looked back and I could count nine Indians on some swift ponies. They was gaining fast on me. I didn't really have time to do much shootin'—I may have got off three or four shots, but didn't hit anything, so I just concentrated on gettin' the hell out of there. Every time I looked back they was gettin' closer and closer. I could now hear the rifle reports. Then somethin' damn near knocked my Henry out of my hand. I looked down and saw where one of them balls had done hit my stock." Without missing a breath, he lifted up his rifle and showed the men a smooth hole in the rifle butt about the size of a quarter dollar. They all gazed at the Henry being held in the air as Colbert continued. "Then, before I could think about my gun much, I felt a powerful burn in my leg." Pulling up his pant leg, he displayed an old scar on his left calf. Some around the fire got up to move in closer and get a better view.

Sheriff Jack Hainey, who had heard the yarn before during his many drinking jaunts with Colbert at Birdwell's Saloon, bent over to look at the wound. He was helping Colbert add to the suspense. "I bet that hurt like hell," Hainey said, shaking his head at the sight of the scar.

"You're right there, friend," Colbert said. "It pained me considerably. So, there I was ridin' as hard as I could, outnumbered nine to one, and them red braves was closing in by the second," he continued. "They was no more than a hundred yards behind me, when my horse started stompin' and skiddin' and fell to his front knees." Colbert paused again and looked at the fire. There was not a sound from the group—their mouths agape—as he slowly shook his head and resumed the story. "Right there, no more than five yards ahead, was a deep gorge—probably two hundred feet deep and five hundred feet across. It went straight down. A sheer cliff. There was no way to go anywhere. Nine savages, close enough that I could taste the dirt from their dust cloud were whoopin' and hollerin' and throwing them lead balls and arrows and lances at me like a spring gully-washer. And in front of me a drop so far that I couldn't see the bottom. My Henry shot to hell and my leg bleeding like a gutted bear." He paused again, reclined slowly back on his bedroll, and pulled his big black hat over his eyes. He made no indication that he was going to continue.

Bob Johnson was exasperated. "What the hell happened?"

"Yeah, by God," shouted Tobias. "What happened?"

Colbert pushed the hat up to his forehead, and continued with a matter-of-fact tone. "Why, they kilt me, of course."

"Goddamn! I sure fell into that one," exclaimed Tobias as the group burst out into laughter.

"Oh hell, anyone could tell he was leading us on a chase," Bob said with an air of smugness. "Shit, I heard Jim Bridger tell that same yarn."

"Hell, boy, you was took in just like the rest of us. Just admit it. This man is a great story teller," laughed Tobias.

"Yep, they kilt me, of course," repeated Colbert as he smoothed out his blanket. "And you know," he said, sitting up on one elbow, rubbing his beard, and shaking his head slightly. "It ain't so bad—being a ghost. You don't have to worry about performing any of the body doin's. Hell, I don't even have to eat if I don't want to."

Bob Johnson stood, looked at Colbert, dusted himself off and ambled over to join his father. He ignored the whole matter. Or at least he tried to seem as though he was.

"When we get through with this business you know we will be heading back to Buffalo Gap," Tobias said with a stern but hopeful voice. Almost a request as much as a statement.

"That's for sure, Captain." That was his favorite thing to call his father. Tobias liked it. He loved it. "That's for damn sure. I want to get back and build. For Rebecca and me. And us," he said, putting his arm around the old Ranger. "And, I will be talking to you about bringing a friend or two to help with the building."

Tobias nodded in approval. He was not sure what his son was talking about, exactly, but just to be talking about it was a welcome sound. Both to his ears and to his heart. He thought of Elizabeth and Rebecca. *Damn, I hope I don't cry here*, he thought. That possibility shocked him. He smiled and walked away as quickly as he could back to the campfire.

Sensing that it was important to let him go, Bob set out to walk down to where his friend Will Tyler had settled himself. The laughter from the campfire group continued and followed him to the edge of the scrub brush line where Will was.

"Hey, amigo," Bob said. He had referred to Will by that term ever since that day on the Mississippi when they had met. He did it sometimes to goad Will, thinking it was a source of irritation, reminding him of the events of that day. But mostly he did it out of genuine affection and friendship, especially when Will was in one of his gloomy moods. Will Tyler knew that, and he appreciated it.

"Evening, Bob," Will replied. They looked silently into the night. Will stood and looked at Bob. "I have something for you." He reached into his pocket and took out the note for the ranch, won in the now infamous poker game. "I want you to take this."

"William, how many times have I told you? I deliberately put that in the pot so you and Katherine and Two Snakes and Colbert and whoever-the hell-else tags along, will come on down to ranch with me and my daddy. It will be a good life. That's my last word." Then he pondered. "Except, of course, if you want, we can split some of those other notes you won."

Will Tyler laughed for the first time in a long while. He looked at the Texan. *Life in Texas with a good friend. That is beginning to sound more and more like a great idea. A damned great idea.*

The few moments of silence that followed gave way to more somber thoughts. Like a cyclone that twists and turns without any seeming plan to its direction, Will Tyler's mood was a rag being blown about in the winds. Once again and without warning, he became increasingly anxious to the point that his good judgment was being affected. Tears—now more and more common—welled up in his bloodshot eyes.

"I'm going down there after her," he said suddenly. Bob looked at him with a blank stare. Johnson knew that it was the thing to do—*at least the Texas thing to do*. And if he were in Will Tyler's place that is exactly what he would do. Go down there and get his woman. It fact it was getting to the point that it was far too late. It should have been done sooner. A lot sooner, with guns blazing and fate be damned. The Texan thought about it anxiously. It spun through his mind. *Let's do it by God*, he thought. But before he spoke and gave way to the passion of the thought, better sense grabbed his mind. He was being tossed in that same cyclone.

"I'd do it in a minute, Will. I'd go in right beside you, but I'm afraid it would do Katherine no good, and we sure as hell would wind up dead." His rational thought surprised himself. It wasn't like him to be the voice of reason; that was Will Tyler's job. But his flight into good sense did not last very long. "Of course, if you want to, then by God let's go."

Will Tyler looked at his friend and his mind became a swirling storm of contradiction—good judgment against a strong desire to rescue Katherine from danger. He was breathing hard and grasping for any decision that would make him just grab his guns and ride in blazing away. At least it would satisfy the pent-up fear, anger, and vengeance that seized him from every direction. He jumped from thought to thought. Bob could see his torment.

"Goddamnit Will, you're right. Let's go. I'm ready. By God, I'm ready." His jaw was set and his brows rose high on his forehead. The deep scar on the left side of his face, dug by Belle Reed's Spenser ball, seemed darker and meaner as he contorted his face, which seemed to say *I'm ready—even ready to die. I'm damned good and tired of this shit!* He grabbed his Colt and shook it toward Will as if to emphasize his rage.

Will Tyler was ready also. No matter the cost, at least he was going to try. Colbert's stories and the campfire chatter seemed as far from the task at hand as he could imagine. It was time to go. He locked eyes with Bob Johnson and did not say a word, but they both knew that a decision had been made. Life or death, win or lose, a decision had been made. It was made out of passion, frustration, and years of death, killing, and seeing the dark, shadow-side of human nature far too often. The decision was made. They turned to go.

"My friends," came the voice suddenly out of the night.

Both deputies drew their guns at the shadow approaching up the brushy hill.

It was Two Snakes, bloodied, bruised, half-dead, but it was Two Snakes.

The entire posse gathered and listened at the horror story that Two Snakes relayed about his month of captivity. Every detail was absorbed so the plan to attack in the morning would not be in doubt.

Will asked repeatedly about Katherine and her every move, her every action, her every torment. Two Snakes told him the truth; he held back nothing. Will took heart at her courage, which Two Snakes praised. For an Indian to speak in such reverence about a person's courage was a rare thing.

"What about Belle Reed and Sam Starr? Are they there?" Bob asked. It was a personal matter to him.

A truly disappointing answer awaited the anxious Texan. "No, they left three days ago. Killing Tree had enough of her and would have killed them both had they not left. So, like cowards, they packed up and rode off into the night."

Another time, another place, Belle. You can count on it. The Texan was determined so.

Two Snakes told them about a sheltered gully that led to the back of the camp. Riding from the ridge and down into the draw, an entire troop could come in by surprise. But there was one problem. A big problem. Holcomb had supplied Six Claws and his men with the new model 1875 Gatling gun with a cyclic rate of spewing up to 800 rounds a minute, and every man in the posse knew of its deadly prospect. Two Snakes related scenes of the practice sessions he had witnessed—captives used as targets and ripped into shreds by the hundreds of deadly slugs it unleashed.

They talked for hours about plans and the method of attack. It was decided, out of no clear decision—too many different styles between Texas Rangers, Army Cavalry and Deputy Marshals—that they would just by God go to the gully, and *charge like hell*, shooting anyone with a gun, bow and arrow, knife or "even an angry look," Bob had said.

The group settled around the fire and each man was occupied with his own thoughts. Wives, sweethearts, revenge—even fear invaded their minds. Two Snakes had made it perfectly clear that the killers below in the stronghold were prepared to die. They were men of no plans, no future and no other thought but to kill or be killed.

Sergeant King, reflecting on Two Snakes' report and the fear that had settled in the minds of some of the men—especially his young Cavalry troops—looked up at the night sky almost ablaze with the full moon. "It's a digger's moon tonight, boys. A digger's moon."

The men looked up at the sky, wondering what the sergeant had meant.

"When I was a young corporal in the war, I was often chosen by my First Sergeant for burial detail after a battle," he continued, still looking at the moon. All necks were likewise cranked back. "And often, a full moon night, like tonight, was chosen to light the way to the grave digging." He paused and stirred a stick in the fire. "Yep, it's a digger's moon tonight."

Each man now had another thought to occupy his mind. Who'd be digging graves—and for whom?

Chapter 29

Dawn, February 19, 1876
Six Claws' camp

As planned, one hour before sunrise, Two Snakes and Bob Johnson ran toward the sentry outposts overlooking the camp. They reached the first outpost where the dead bandit lay with a broken neck courtesy of Bob Johnson a few hours before. Two Snakes found a waiting rattlesnake, donned the dead man's serape and hat and they continued to the last outpost. Two Snakes walked toward the man on duty and swaggered in the cold wind.

"It's cold back up there. I need some company and some coffee. I believe them damned lawmen done lit out," he said, distracting the man. In the darkness, the outlaw was caught off guard just long enough for Two Snakes to offer his rattlesnake poison to the man's waiting veins. He died, as most had, with a surprised look of horror. Quietly and quickly.

Bob Johnson walked out of the shadows in time to see the man take his last agonizing breath. "In all my life, I'm never going to get used to that, my friend," he said as Two Snakes secretly released the snake. Two Snakes picked up the dead man's rifle.

"I suppose I'll need to take up the white man's weapon. My snakes have served me well. But I think they'll need some help."

"Never too late to improve," Bob said. He was relieved that those damned snakes would not be crawling around in the scrape about to commence. After all, they would not be too particular as to which man to bite when things got confused. "For my part, you can just turn 'em loose right now. Give 'em a rest," he said hopefully.

Two Snakes smiled, as he pointed to the retreating snake. "Don't worry, Bob. They are particular as to the caliber of man they bite. You don't qualify."

Bob Johnson did not know quite how to take that. He was just glad he didn't qualify.

The plan was on schedule as the sun began to show its red glow on the eastern horizon. Two Snakes and Bob slid down the hill, which the Indian had dragged his bloodied body up from the camp just hours ago. As they hid in a stand of thorns, they surveyed the camp. It was very quiet, and they could see that the thirty or so men were stationed and ready. The Gatling gun was on its stand about ten feet off the ground. It was pointed north toward the main embankment and was ready as Henry Salmon had his hand on the crank. He was looking around, nervously, but alertly.

The two men slipped past the edge of the camp as Two Snakes led toward Odell and Treewell's lodge. Odell looked wide-eyed at the Indian as he walked in. He recognized him even in the bandit's clothes. Treewell looked on, as usual without saying a word.

"Two Snakes. God, you are a welcome sight. And this must be Katherine's fellow," Odell said, looking at Bob.

"That is absolutely not the case, but he will be here shortly."

"This is Deputy Bob Johnson. My friend," he said, looking at Bob and emphasizing the word, friend.

Bob felt strangely good, and honored.

"There is no time to waste. We have only a few minutes. The posse of eighteen men is on the ridge at the end of the gully," Two Snakes related. "I need for you and Treewell to help with an important move."

"You can count on us," Odell said. "We are ready." He turned and took a knife from under a log in the corner. It was the knife of Walking Bear, which Two Snakes had been able to bring in when he was first captured. "Here, this is yours."

Two Snakes took the knife. It was powerful. It would bring the Spirits to help against Six Claws. It was a part of Six Claws' life that would be used to end the killer's life, Two Snakes reasoned. Even in the urgency of the moment, he held the knife and chanted to the Old People to help with the end of the terror by this Kiowa killer who had once been his friend. The three men looked on. They did not understand but they also did not interrupt.

As quickly as he had begun his spiritual journey, he stopped and brought the group back to reality.

"Odell, go to the west ammunition storage lodge. Treewell, you go to the east storage lodge. Bob will go to the main corral." He paused to make his point and drew the plan in the dirt floor with Walking Bear's knife. It was the plan that would symbolically cut into the body of Six Claws. "We must do this at the same time."

Bob took over the briefing. "Odell and Treewell. You both are able to walk freely in the camp. Get some cups of coffee and take one each to the guards at the front of the ammunition lodges. As you distract them—kill them! Then set the charges to blow those lodges to hell with a short line of powder. As soon as I've unleashed the horses to start them runnin', I'll fire three shots. When you hear those blasts, light the powder and run like hell. Set it for no more than five seconds. Then run like hell! Can you handle that?"

"I can run, and in five seconds Treewell can be clear across the camp," Odell said with a smile.

"Well, get down when you do, because there will be more fireworks," he said. "Two Snakes is going to have taken that Gattlin' and open up on any thing that moves—and then the posse is gonna ride in like General Pickett in that great charge—different results though, bless his fine Southern soul—so you'd better hug the ground. Got that?"

"You bet, Mr. Johnson. I will definitely be huggin' mother earth and so will Treewell." He looked at Two Snakes with a frown of concern. "Mr. Two Snakes, you know where the captive lodges are. Please be careful with that devil gun."

"Don't worry, Odell. If you remember, I had to help load that gun for them during the last month. I know exactly how and who to shoot." Two Snakes silently began to chant. He prayed for the souls of those he would kill so quickly. Too many spirits loosed at one time against him. *Old People, help me.*

"What about the posse?" Odell asked. "Will they be careful with the captives?"

"Every man has the map of the lodges burned in his head," Bob said. "No one got bacon or coffee this morning until he could draw it out." Still, Odell had a good point. It was something to consider. "Two Snakes. How long would it take Odell and Treewell to make the rounds of all the captive lodges and have them keep their heads down and take cover as best they can?"

Odell answered before Two Snakes had the chance. "We can do it, and have the coffee cups at the ammunition lodges within five minutes." He wanted to do that. The possibility of someone coming out of their lodge when all the firing started worried him.

"All right. Here is each of you a pistol to kill the guards. Aim for their heads. Don't take a chance with a body shot. Kill the bastard before he can take his next breath. I want him on the ground before he drops that goddamn coffee cup." Bob was turning red. His anger and passion was rising again. He felt as ready as he did a few hours ago when he and Will contemplated going on in alone, and just blaze away.

Odell and Treewell took the guns. They were not killers. Neither man had ever taken a life. Even in the war, they had both been spared that horror. The brothers looked at each other. As always there was silence between them, but this time there was a deadly determination.

Treewell took the lodges on the East Ridge, stopping to get a cup of coffee for his quarry. Odell went to all the west lodges, stopping at Katherine's lodge last before heading to the ammunition dump. As he walked in, he saw the bodies of seven dead bandits. Katherine was as far as she could get against the corner with an empty revolver in her hand, snapping the empty cylinders at Odell as he entered.

After Six Claws left in the hours before the attack, some of the men left in the camp had come and attempted to rape Katherine and the *Sister sisters*. Katherine had fought them off one by one. Killing the first with her surgeon's scalpel, she took his pistol and shot the next six that entered the hut. No one else had tried to enter after the last man fell. She had lost count of how many she had killed. Tubby was her ally and suffered greatly from the abuse. He had suffered a broken arm and many other bruises too numerous to count. Even Diablo had valiantly defended them, but he was also beaten into a state of final submission.

"Katherine," Odell said as he took the pistol from her bloodstained hand. "It's me, Odell."

He tried to explain the sequence of events about to happen, but she just stared into the darkness.

Odell turned to Father Boles. "Father, whatever happens, don't anyone come outside." Boles nodded as if he understood. He was in semi-conscious state himself. Odell hoped for the best and went to the ammunition hut. It was time.

Treewell's guard fell dead only a second after the guard killed by Odell had fallen. The shots were almost simultaneous. Both men scrambled inside the lodges, opened kegs of gunpowder before the other guards and sentries in the camp could figure where the shots had come from.

Bob Johnson cut the leads and hobble ropes to all forty horses after he had cut the throat of the renegade guarding the mounts. The Indian had been asleep. *Too bad*, Bob had thought. *I'd liked to have seen your damned eyes*. He looked toward the Gatling gun emplacement. Two Snakes waved from the stand, as planned.

"Here we go, you sonsabitches!" Bob shouted as he fired his Colt three times into the air.

Exactly five seconds later, amid the thunder of more than three-dozen scattered horses running through the camp, both ammunition lodges exploded with such a violent blast that the ground shook. As the roar of the explosions quieted slightly, the deadly sound of Two Snakes firing the Gatling gun filled the early morning mayhem.

Will Tyler led the charge as the troops rode the parameter to avoid Two Snakes' shower of .45 caliber lead. The long-awaited battle had come. No Quarter. No thought of surrender on either side. Every outlaw, killer, renegade, and murderer was running for cover.

Two Snakes had to abandon his position with the Gatling gun. It was too dangerous to everyone else for him to continue firing. He dismantled the firing crank so no enemy could fire it and grabbed his carbine. He had a good position from which to fire and he began by killing a bandit hiding behind the north side firewood stacks. Another outlaw beaded in on Two Snakes and shot him in the fleshy part of the right underarm. He dropped his carbine and struggled to climb down, now armed only with Walking Bear's knife. He was determined that before he died, he would return the knife to Six Claws—blade first. He took the serape off and ripped it into shreds to bandage his arm. Although the slug did not hit a bone, the wound was bleeding freely. He was becoming weak.

The posse had dismounted and taken positions all around the camp. Each man had one extra advantage. Sergeant King had thought through the plan in their camp in the early morning and envisioned a great deal of confusion. He had taken his prized white cotton sleeping roll and had cut it into twenty-five two-foot by two-foot squares. Each man had then cut a sapling and affixed the white flag at its top. When a posseman reached his firing position, he would hoist his flag to keep from being fired upon by friendly forces. All others, without a flag, were open game.

Bob Johnson, of course, disliked the idea and came without his flag. He now was pinned downed, firing and yelling alternately to everyone as to who he was. One bullet took his prized sombrero, which Two Snakes had risked his life to get at Younger Station. That made Bob mad. Young Corporal Jones had fired the shot.

"Goddamn man, it's me, Bob Johnson," he yelled.

"Where's your damned flag?" the corporal yelled back.

"You dern fool, the flag tells *them* where you are," he yelled back.

"Maybe, maybe not. But you almost got it because you didn't have one."

"Well goddamn if you can win any argument with a *bluebelly*." He grabbed the white sombrero, still stained with the blood of Two Snakes, tied it to his carbine and lifted it up onto the rock pile he was behind. "There you go, Yank, there's your damned flag. Now, don't shoot in this direction anymore."

A bullet tore into Corporal Jones just as he rose to see Bob's sombrero flag. He screamed as he fell out from behind the barrels where he was hiding.

"You hit, Yank?" Bob shouted.

The young corporal screamed again.

Bob jumped from behind his rock pile and ran to the fallen soldier. Bullets pocked the ground as he ran. He dragged the corporal behind the water barrels. The wound was mortal. His stomach had been cut in half.

"Am I dying, Deputy?" he asked in a whisper. Bullets struck above their heads and water poured all around them.

"Yeah, I'm afraid so, son. I hate to tell you straight, but I think they killed you here. What's your name, son?"

"Jones. Corporal Roscoe Jones, United States Cavalry," he answered proudly.

"Well, Corporal Roscoe Jones, you did good. You served your country good today. You can be proud," Bob said as he cradled the young man.

"Looks like that flag got me killed after all," the boy said.

"No, son, just bad luck. Just bad luck," Bob said as he shot back at the assailant crouching behind a row of oat sacks.

"I'm sorry I made you mad about the flag," the corporal said. He was almost gone. "My pa was in the war. He was a Yank. I don't mind being called a Yank. Makes me proud," he said with his eyes flickering.

"Makes me proud, too, boy. Makes me proud, too, boy," he repeated. "I ain't never served with a better Yank than you. You did yourself proud." Bob began to tear up. *Goddamn, he had seen enough dying. He was tired of it.*

"I ain't ever served with a better Reb than you, either," he said. He died in Bob's arms.

Bob sat for what seemed like an hour holding the boy. In reality, it was only a few seconds. The bandit behind the feed sacks fired and grazed Bob's hair. The smell of singed hair filtered to his nose.

"That's it, by God" he said as he rolled over and jumped into the sacks and put three slugs into the bandit's head. He looked back at Corporal Jones. "That's one for you, Roscoe. That's one for you."

Sergeant King saw the corporal fall and began to crawl toward him.

Bob saw King coming and shouted him back. "It's too late, Rupert. Get back to your cover. He's dead."

As Bob finished his warning, Small Long Knife jumped from a tree and landed on the back of Sergeant King. He took his cut-down cavalry sword and severed

King's head. The sergeant died never getting to see the face of Six Claws. It had been his obsession for two years. Now, it was just another unfulfilled dream on the border, where so many dreams were smashed and crushed. Small Long Knife screamed a warrior's yell as he stood above the sergeant's body. Shots from a half-dozen guns riddled the Indian. Tobias Johnson, Will Tyler, Bob Johnson, Two Snakes, Jack Hainey and one other possemen fired at the same time. The bullets lifted the small Indian off the ground and turned his body in the air before he fell on top of Rupert King's body.

Bob Johnson voiced his thoughts aloud. So loud that everyone heard him, even over the gunfire. "Goddamn, I am tired of this. I am tired of this!" He tore the Sombrero off his carbine and emptied it into the riddled body of Small Long Knife. "Goddamn, I'm tired of this," he screamed.

Tobias worked his way over to Bob. "Robert! Listen to me! Snap out of it!"

Bob's hot, flashing eyes shot toward his father. It was evident he did not know him. Tobias took his hand and slapped him hard back and forth across the face.

Bob went limp and dropped the rifle. He looked up at Tobias and whispered. "Goddamn, I'm tired of this."

"I know you are, son. I am, too. When we get out of here we are going back to Texas where we belong. That's a by-God *Red River Promise*." He smiled at Bob. Bob smiled back at his father. Like a twelve-year-old boy, still in shock over the site of Jake Standing Owl's body with a Hawken ball through the heart, he smiled. He was soaking in the promise that everything would be all right. Everything would be okay. Somehow.

"Now let's get this over with. I promised Becca I'd have you home in time for supper. And oh, by the way, she's about four months pregnant. I thought you'd like to know and start trying to get out of this alive."

Bob wanted to cry. He smiled as wide as he could to keep from doing just that. If he ever got back to the ranch, to home, to his Becca—then by God he'd never go north of the Red River again. Now, *that* was a by-God *Red River Promise*!

The possemen killed the outlaws one by one. No Quarter!

One additional man had been killed: Sheriff Jack Hainey, a friend to all, was shot through the neck. He was one of the most respected men in Fort Smith and had been studying at night, under the tutelage of Judge Parker, to become a lawyer. He wanted to make the law his life, not just as a sheriff. It would not come to be. He had died as Will Tyler tried to stop the profuse bleeding from the neck wound. Two slugs had ended his life. He had lived long enough to get a promise from Will though. "Please don't let them plant me here under no digger's moon. Please!"

"There won't be anybody buried under no digger's moon except these bastards who belong here," Will had promised. "You don't worry Jack...." Hainey had died before Will could continue to assure him.

It was almost eight o'clock in the morning—just three hours since the posse entered the gully—when the last outlaw was dead. Twenty-seven bandits and three possemen had been killed. Three other members of the posse suffered wounds—one bad enough that he required surgery in Fort Smith the following day. One captive, a small child, had been killed when she ran from her hut terrified at the noise, and six others had been wounded by gunfire. The usual bragging rights about the number of kills went unvoiced. No one had reason to feel particularly proud about all the deaths that they had seen. It was never officially tallied, but by accounts later given, Benjamin Colbert had killed nine bandits on his own. A remarkable feat, but not one ever spoke of it again in the following days.

Six Claws! It took several moments of decompression before anyone realized that Six Claws had not been seen.

"Oh, he lit out last night, early," Odell said. "He just didn't seem to care about the fight for several days. He kept talking about the Old People and such, and he just lit out. Hard to understand. After all this hell, it is sure hard to understand," Odell said, shaking his head.

Two Snakes understood. And he knew that his fight was not over. He still had to confront Six Claws and the Old People for one last time at the table of destiny.

Will Tyler did not care. His mind was on Katherine. He asked Two Snakes where her lodge was. He really needed to know, but his feet felt like blacksmith's anvils as he tried to run toward the hut. Bob and Two Snakes ran with him. Bob Johnson entered the small lodge first. He held Will back. Love for both of them, and concern for what was inside made his point.

Will struggled with him—half-heartedly. He did not want to go in at all. Out of fear, out of a sense that his life hung in the balance upon what would be found, he let Bob go inside first.

Bob was overcome by the stench of urine and feces. It was very dark inside and only the light from the small opening of the door shown through, illuminating the suspended dust particles and the swarm of flies, even in the cold February morning. Bob covered his face with his neckerchief and placed his arm on his forehead to shield himself from what the small lodge held. It was then that he could see the figures of bodies littering the room. Stumbling over the corpses of the dead men—he counted seven—he saw a woman, at least he thought it was, lying in a fetal position against the far wall. As his eyes adjusted to the light, he could discern that it was a woman, clutching a small boy and a small dog. "Please God, don't let it be Katherine," he said, slowly bending over the lifeless form.

It was. The long auburn hair, once lying radiantly upon her shoulders, was matted and tangled, yet just familiar enough to make his heart sink. He sat next to her and lifted her head in his arms.

"Katherine, dear God," he murmured. "What have the bastards done to you?"

Will Tyler shouted from the outside. "Bob, for the sake of God, tell me what you have found." Will began to weep openly. He fell to the ground and sobbed, knowing that if his *love* had been lost, then his life was over. Wretched life. Good goddamn riddance!

Tobias Johnson and Odell Skaggs joined him at the outside of the lodge. Neither said a word. There was nothing to say.

"Just a minute, Will. I'm still sorting it out," Bob replied with a broken heart himself. He thought of Rebecca, his wife, at home with his mother. He was gripped by an overwhelming sense of relief almost, and he felt guilty about it. He missed his wife, and he was overcome with the emotion that she was safe and secure away from horrors like these.

Katherine stirred and turned her head to the voice calling her name. She had just enough strength to whisper to him. "Bob?" she asked. "Is that you, Bob? Bob?" She coughed up some fluid resembling a blood and water mixture, gasping for her next breath.

"Katherine, don't try to talk. It's me, Bob, and you're safe now." He shouted. "Will, Will, God in heaven, she is alive!"

"Bob. Bob, please don't let Will see me like this. Please." She coughed again and gasped more violently. Will Tyler was already in the room, stumbling and falling over the dead assailants.

"You're all right darlin'," Bob Johnson said. "He's already here."

Will Tyler grabbed her from Bob's embrace and held her until he was in fear of stopping her breath. They kissed and embraced in that dirty hut with Bob Johnson, Father Boles, the *Sister sisters*, Tubby Prichard, one feisty Mexican dog and seven dead bandits as witnesses.

Bob and Will lifted her outside as Tobias and Odell were taking Father Boles and the nuns to a wagon. Tubby held close to Katherine. His eyes set squarely on the two deputies. He eyed them with defiance. Diablo bared his little teeth at Bob.

"Who's the boy?" Will asked, as if not knowing what to say first, or at all.

"Don't you hurt my mama," Tubby said with a dark, pouting stare at the deputy. Will sat there motionless and without expression.

"Let it be for now," Katherine said with tears falling from her eyes. "Let it be for now. We'll all have a talk later. Ask Two Snakes, he will tell you."

Two Snakes walked over, took Katherine from Will's arms and lifted her into the sunlight of the beautiful February morning. He chanted a prayer of thanksgiving. He gently laid her on some blankets and covered her from the cool morning air.

"Katherine I must tell you that I have never met a stronger and more courageous woman in my life. And the Spirits have told me that I never will. Thank you, and love my friend William. Love him with all your heart."

"There will be no problem with that my good friend," she said. She reached up and hugged him with what strength she had. "But don't be so sad. We will have a big party and a wedding when we get back to Fort Smith. You will be the life of the party, showing off your half-skinned body," she said, trying to laugh. Then she noticed the wound to his arm. "You're bleeding again."

"It is just another scar. It will heal soon enough," he said stoically.

"When we get to Fort Smith, I'll look at it," she said—always the doctor.

"I can't," he said sadly. "I must ride on after Six Claws. Just as I have told you your destiny in my dreams, the Old People have told me mine. I must go and find him," he said as he clutched the bone-handled knife that had tasted the heart of Walking Bear, so many years ago.

"And I am going to depart with him also, Miss Katherine," Colbert said as he reached over to hug her. "I would not miss this for the world. I have spent my entire life studying man and his destiny and I trust I will be a witness to a meeting where true destiny meets. I must witness that. Even at the expense of missing the most important wedding that I have ever been invited to." He bent over and hugged her again. "Would you do me the honor of giving a wretched old reprobate, of dubious character, a parting kiss that I may carry a memory of Will's Juliet, peering from vaulted window; his Aphrodite, atop the Athenian hill; his Guinevere; his Mona Lisa with eyes and smile that have melted his stone heart; and his Helen of a thousand ships; his…."

"Oh shut up and give me a kiss, you old bear cub," she said, crying. "We will miss you both. You will both be a part of our lives. I promise we will not forget you."

Will grew despondent at the thought of their farewell. It suddenly amazed him that after the happiest moment in his life—finding Katherine alive, he again became engrossed in his shadow-side with depression over the loss of his friends, Two Snakes and Colbert. He could not hide his incongruity from her. She saw it plainly.

"Two Snakes will always be a part of you and your future. He had a dream, and lifted my heart by telling me about it. This little boy will be the one who plants our happy forest. He is our legacy. I want to build something—to grow a vision, a future. I want to stop your restless spirit in its tracks. Whatever has plagued you since that night in Helena; whatever demons you battled in Andersonville, we are going to bury, right now. I have buried Gettysburg and my uncertainty." She began to tear again. "And together...together," she said erratically, trying to catch her breath, squeezing Tubby and Will. "Together, we are going to forge that vision. Two Snakes gave me, and us, hope. Just believe what I say," she said with a look of pride and happiness that he could not imagine from her face.

"Just believe what I say."

Will sat and looked at Katherine, and he stroked the boy's bloodstained face. *Whatever she says. For the rest of our lives. Whatever she says.*

"Who's the dog?" Bob asked, as Diablo snarled at him.

There was a wedding in Fort Smith on the first day of March in 1876. The President of the United States attended it. Also attending were Judge Isaac C. Parker, 200 United States Deputy Marshals, a priest and two nuns on stretchers, and a snarly Mexican dog, held by a tubby little boy. Also, there was an ex-Deputy Marshal, headed for his one-quarter-ownership ranch in Texas. The new bride and groom would soon join him. And coincidentally, the groom was also an ex-United States Deputy Marshal. After a short wedding trip to Boston, and a train ride to South Carolina to take care of some legal matters concerning an adoption of a tubby little boy, the couple planned to head to Texas with all their belongings, including a parting wedding gift in a glassed-in frame. Two poker hands, with proper descriptions, of course.

Epilogue

Forty-Three Years After the Capture of the Missionaries

September 12, 1919
Fifty Miles Northwest of Abilene, Texas
(Known Formerly As Buffalo Gap)
Cattle Drive from the *Circle J-T* Ranch

"Will, get your ass up; you planning to sleep all day?" barked the familiar and irritating voice of Bob Johnson. Will Tyler had never been particularly fond of that Texas drawl anyway. But at four in the morning, cozy in his bedroll, it was a damn sight more irritating than most of the thousand times he had heard it for the past forty-three-plus years.

"Bob, those damn cattle can use a few more minutes' rest before they start another dusty day's walk. And I can use a few more minutes myself, for damn sure."

"You ain't never going to get that slow startin'—Arkansas—attitude corrected, are you? Why, hell, as long as we been together here in Texas you ought to know we don't wait for nothing. Everything waits for us, or chases us to catch up. That's the by-God Texas way. Not that Philadelphia or Boston, Arkansas-Tennessee wherever-way of figuring out things you been doing since I known you. Hell, fellow, it's time to burn some daylight."

"Bob, if you don't leave me alone for a few more minutes here in this bedroll the only thing that's going to be burning is your jaw when I relieve you of a couple of your teeth. Now, go bother one of the other boys and see if you can start some ruckus with them. I damn sure am done on the deal. I am definitely one crazy son of a bitch for letting you talk me into this damn drive. By God, it's the twentieth century. The railhead at Abilene is no more than seven miles from the ranch. Hell, we are going to have to stop and wait a dozen times at train crossings while the damn train that our cattle should have been on, goes by. If that ain't the dumbest thing. Why in hell I let you talk me into this I'll never know as long as I live. In fact, I don't want to ever remember it again. Ever!"

"You sure are a bowl of peaches and cream in the morning, ain't you," Bob replied, in his usual sarcastic, witty manner that drove Will to the edge sometimes. "Damned if a fellow can even talk to you without getting his head bit off slick as if by one of old Two Snakes' rattlers. And you sure have taken up a lot of that by-God cussing over the years. It could be a bad influence on a fellow of my tender nature. Go ahead, lay there. Damned if I care if it's the twentieth century. As for me, that is more of a tragedy than a blessing. And you sure didn't have to come on this drive to Kansas City. If you admit it, I couldn't a kept you from it. Hell, boy, you wanted this one more time as bad as me. I'll just find someone civil to talk to. Someone with a little of that old-time spirit left in them, like we had in the Territory. Hell, you'd think you was a hundred instead of eighty."

"You know I ain't eighty yet."

"Well...you sure act like it. Spirit sucked right out of you, old man. I'll find someone who enjoys my talk at daybreak," he said, his voice trailing off as he strolled to another bedroll at the camp. "Hey, Tubby, you awake? Tubby?...Tubby?...Hammond!"

Tubby Tyler rolled over and sprayed an honest-to-god three-second fart in Bob's direction. "No I ain't awake, and if you ask me again, I'll give you a more solid answer—if you get my meaning. And don't call me Hammond!"

"Oh, I get you, you little four-toed shyster. And that's your real name by God, if you like it or not. I don't care if you are some high-tone Harvard doctor. And by the way, wouldn't your mama be proud of you, fartin' like a cowpuncher on a Saturday night. My God, ain't nothing sacred or genteel any more?"

"I was a cow-puncher before I was a doctor. I guess old ways are hard to die. Besides, living around you, and Pa, and all the rest of the old deputy corps for all these years, I guess she's heard her share of farting. More than her share. And as for sacred and genteel, the only things in your whole life that you ever seen genteel is Aunt Becca, Callie and Ma and Mama Elizabeth. You don't know nothing about genteel. And as for farting, you sure do your share. Eating those damn campfire beans ever time you get a chance. You'd eat 'em three times a day if they'd let you."

"Beans is one of the good Lord's greatest gifts to the cowboy. It is a damn sight better for you that that fancy stuff your ma and Becca cook up all the time. Like salmon croquettes. Hell, I can hardly say it, much less spell it. The good Lord never intended a man to eat anything he couldn't say or spell."

"I never noticed that you left even a forkful of anything they cooked—especially salmon croquettes."

"Well, as you get older you'll learn that etiquette and such, and polite behavin' like not offendin' the cook, gets you a lot farther in life," he responded with his usual quick wit.

Tubby was enjoying the banter with Bob Johnson, but he continued as if he was as tired of it—as usual. "Now let me sleep a bit more, Uncle Bob, or I'll put some drugs in your coffee that will make your old dried-up pickle just fall right off."

"In your most fanciful dreams you only wish you had a pickle like mine you little snake oil pusher," Bob said, spitting his first morning tobacco juice on the ground near Tubby's feet. "And go near my coffee and I'll make our sweet Callie a widow and Willard an orphan before you get back to your potion bag. Sleep on, hell, you're as lazy as your old man. I'll go see if Corporal Parnell wants to get this drive started today before you old men and smart-assed kids sleep the day away."

Tubby rose up on one arm and looked at his favorite hero—outside his dad. "Uncle Bob, when they finally put you in the ground, I am going to make sure that no one says a word. Why, you would argue half the day from that box at anything we had to say."

"Words of wisdom, as old Ben Colbert used to say. Words of wisdom. Living or dead! And you'd do good to listen to a few. It might just learn you something," Bob said with a half-grin and a squinting eye.

Will Tyler rolled over and barked at them both. "If you two don't let me get a few more winks, I'm gonna get out of this bedroll and walk back to Abilene—in my bare feet if I have to."

"I'll go with you, Pa," Tubby said. "My ears are hurting like hell from all his jawing."

Bob grinned widely. At least the boy was learning the Bob Johnson art of verbal comeback. *Yep, he was learnin' it well*, he thought. The old Texan loved Tubby like his own son. Not just a son-in-law, but also his own flesh and blood. Ever since he met the lad at age four some forty years ago, he liked his spunk and solid honesty. When Will and Katherine saved him from the horror that began his young life and then adopted him as a son, he knew their lives would be inseparable. Bob had helped raise him in the needed ways of the West, a damned sight more than Will. Absolutely, by his reckoning, Will had lost some of his old ways in the Territory at the end. But Bob had not. Hell, he was as game as ever. And, as destiny would have it, Tubby and Bob's daughter Callie had grown up together, fallen in love, married, and produced him with the best son-in-law and grandson—and soon to be a great-grandson—that a man could want, or ever hope to be blessed with. Yes, sir, Bob was proud of the training and direction that he had been able to give Tubby. Why, hell, Will and Katherine would have had him stay in Boston as some damn surgeon to the rich if it had not been the background of love for the frontier and pioneer spirit he helped, to a great deal, instill in the boy. He felt that Tubby reckoned the same way. Bob was bursting with pride and elation as he approached the next body under blankets.

"Well, hell-fire," Bob said as he passed Noah Parnell's bedroll with a loud snore coming from inside the blanket. "Ain't a single soul to talk to. Or even start breakfast. Hell, I'll go on down and sit on that knob with the oak stand on it, check on Odell and guard the place for a while—if it won't put you fine gentlemen out to much for me to be gone." He grabbed his ancient Hawken rifle and headed toward the trees on the hill overlooking the thousand head of peaceful, contented cattle. If they could think and reason, they, too, were not ready for another hot day's walk. Another hour or even more was fine with them.

"Guard this place," Will Tyler shouted after him with a smile and a muffled chuckle. "Guard against what? The last rustler died in prison at the age of one hundred and ten. All the Indians are on the reservations, sleeping in their cozy beds, with their houses with gas cooking stoves and electric lights. If you see one of them Indian houses, go in and ask if you can use their telephone and call my Katherine to send the Ford after me. This ground is killing my back. Guard this place my ass!" he continued even louder with Bob Johnson standing near the oak trees looking back at him. "Guard against them automobiles on that gravel and cement road we got to drive these damn cows across without any of us getting killed. Or guard against them lions and tigers over in that circus up in Lindley, ten miles over that way. I'd sure hate for a clown in war paint or a trained gang of dogs, rolling barrels, to attack us in the night. Guard away you old fart. Wake me when the clowns attack."

"If them clowns do come, I'll sure as hell put a frown on their face with this Hawken," Bob replied with a grin.

"Hawken, hell. Just talk them to death. It will be more painful," Will said. "And I bet they by-God deserve it with all that smiling and laughing. No one deserves to be happy tonight. Not as bad as my ass hurts on this ground. Talk them to death," Will whispered to himself. "That Texan is a dead-eye shot at that." He shouted toward Bob again. "That old Hawken might not be enough fire power for all those desperadoes waiting on you out there. You need one of those army machine guns."

Bob walked back a bit toward Will. "Why, by God, William, you've been reading my mail. I got one on order from that Sears and Roebuck outfit."

"Sears don't sell machine guns, you dern fool."

"Why, they ought to. I tried to convince them of it in my letter."

"Rebecca will have your ass if you bring a machine gun on the place."

"She'll have to stand in line. There has been a lot of people out to get this ass. None yet, by God. None yet."

Will pondered the idea with a half-laugh, still unsure if it might not be true. That was an unsettling thought. That old fool out on the range, firing away with a machine gun, scaring half the cows in the county. *I hope he's just being Bob.* Who knew, with Bob? Will Tyler had not strapped on a gun in twenty years, and here that damn Texan had an arsenal that General Pershing would be interested in—and, always on the look out to expand it.

Bob Johnson settled in under a big oak and looked into the still-moonlit sky. "Digger's moon," he said softly. "Digger's moon." He began to think of the strangest things. Of course, that was one of his trademarks. Strange thoughts. And one of the strangest things about Bob's mental ramblings was the way one thought or memory was just in line with a half-dozen more waiting to take its place. *Zelda Pine Needle. Hell, I ain't thought of her in years,* he thought. Zelda was a whore who lived in the Territory just inside the Choctaw nation. Bob was a regular customer in his days in the Territory. He grinned as he thought about her dark tan skin and her coal black hair that fell around her shoulders. He only dreamed, fleetingly, of whores now. Rebecca had seen to that for almost half a century.

It was nearly five o'clock when Will Tyler walked up the knoll where Bob Johnson was sitting under the large oak tree in the middle of the small grove. Will stood and watched as Bob sat motionless, evidently in the middle of a deep sleep. The morning sun was trying to emerge on the eastern horizon with just a hint of red-orange breaking through the star-lit sky.

My God, he thought as he looked at his old friend, *he looks just like the young man he was when we met those almost forty-four years ago—riding and hollering and raising hell all over the Territory. He hasn't changed a bit. Sitting there, holding that old Hawken on his knees. I wonder if I still look that young and vigorous when Bob looks at me?* Certainly, Will would never admit something like that to him. The Texan was hard enough to be around without fueling his arrogant pride anymore.

Odell Skaggs rode up the crest from the valley below. He had been riding night watch over the herd since evening, and was weary in the saddle. But he never showed it. Odell was another one that never changed. He was always constant. Always faithful—never complaining. He completed his duty with a smile and a refreshing outlook. He had been an inspiration to the group ever since the capture of the missionaries all those years ago, and the hell that followed with Six Claws and Two Snakes. He was an unsung hero of those events, but everyone knew they owed their sanity, if not their lives, to him for his actions during those dark days and months. Everyone was grateful. He had become a part of the family over the years. He also proved to be a valuable asset to the ranch operation with his even and pleasing attitude. Many times over the years, he proved that patience and a civil tongue and attitude was the right mix at the right time.

"Looks like old Bob gave up on his lookout duties," Odell said with his slow, quite voice. "He's sleeping like a baby."

Will looked on and nodded his agreement, just as Bob raised his head from its bowed position. "You two gents better hope you live long enough to catch me sleeping on guard duty. It just ain't gonna happen."

"Hell, Bob," Will replied. "You were sawing logs enough to fuel the fireplace all winter. You were slap-dab asleep."

"I'd have to agree with that assessment," Odell said with a smile.

"Hell, Odell, you'd agree with anybody, about anything at anytime. You are the most disagreeable, agreeable fellow I've ever met. Just once I'd like to hear you say 'hell no, that ain't so', or, 'you damn fellows is out of your minds', or, 'kiss my ass', or any damn thing that's to the contrary point. I'll say it for you—I was not asleep. I heard every twig snap on your way up the hill, and Will made enough noise to wake up them circus clowns over in Lindley he's so scared of."

"Bob, you are so full of shit, I don't know how we can stand to be around you for the stink," Will said. "You were asleep and Odell and I both know it, and you know it."

"Gentlemen, if you don't mind I'll let you two settle this point. I'm going on into camp and get me some coffee and about a half-hour's shut-eye before we move out," Odell said diplomatically, as he edged his horse down the other side of the hill toward the campfire.

Will sat down beside Bob and looked silently over the cattle visible in the twilight of the fading moon.

Bob looked on also at the scene. He liked what he saw. It was a glimpse into the distant past, when times were hard but life was good from the adventure. What he wouldn't give to be back in the Territory half a lifetime ago.

Will broke the silence. "I guess we better get moving here in a minute. We can get a good twenty miles in today if we stay at it."

"By God, I'm delighted to hear you say a positive word," Bob replied, in a surprised tone.

"You're not the only one who still has a twinge of nostalgia every once in a while."

"Yeah, but your twinges have been few and far between lately. I thought I was gonna have to tie you up and drag you along on this adventure. But I knew, by God, you was really for it. Just as much as I was."

"Maybe so." Will said with a slight smile. "Maybe so." Will Tyler knew that Bob was completely right. He did want to come. He did miss the adventure. He did long for the days of saddle sores and cold baths in some creek and hardpan biscuits and bitter coffee after a restless night on a posse assignment chasing some black-hearted bastard that had transgressed the law. He missed the smell of gunpowder and strong body odor that comes from the sweat of sheer fear. But after four and a half decades of disagreeing with Bob Johnson—even when that Texan was right—was a hard habit to break. He loved it. Bob Johnson loved it. They wouldn't have it any other way.

"Twenty-five."

"What?" Will questioned.

"Twenty-five," Bob replied with that trademark, *what the hell is so hard to understand about what I'm saying* look. "You said we could make twenty miles today. Any fool can tell we can do at least twenty-five, maybe thirty if we push it."

"You're right, Bob. As always, you are right."

"Damn straight."

They walked down the hill toward the camp. The coffee aroma filled the air. Odell had roused everyone from their warm blankets, and the camp was alive with noise and action. Another day was about to begin on this, yet another grand adventure.

"You ever think much anymore about Two Snakes and Six Claws?" Bob asked. He paused a moment to stomp out a cigarette butt.

Will did not answer. He just looked toward the camp. *Think about them—and Colbert, and Judge Parker—all the time.* John Law, his family, even Bessie Rison's sweet dark face with her shy grin invaded his thoughts sometimes after half a century. He could see her hanging from that tree at Helena, beside his father and old Joseph Creed. He thought about the past a great deal.

"You know, Will, after we got Katherine back, and that old bastard Six Claws escaped and all the hell that happened after that. All that hell! My God, all that hell!" He looked at Will, begging for some response. "You ever ponder on that much? You ever wonder if it could have been different? I mean, hell, that spree is hard to forget. You ever regret any of that, Six Claws and Two Snakes and Old

Benjamin?" His voice trailed off and his face showed the pain of the subject. "Does it keep you up late at night sometimes like it does me?" Bob continued to question a stoic and unresponsive Will Tyler.

Two Snakes and Six Claws and Big Benjamin, thought Will, in a detached, disjointed, yet emotional twinge.

"Yeah. Yeah, I do," he responded softly. "I think about all of that, a lot."

Two Snakes, Six Claws, Colbert and the rest. But, that's another story.

THE END
Digger's Moon

Watch for *Red River Promise*, the exciting sequel to *Digger's Moon*.

About the Author

John W. Heird writes from Little Rock, Arkansas where he is a research historian. Having advanced degrees in Biblical Archaeology and Theology, Dr. Heird also writes a nationally syndicated newspaper column, *Dr. Dig Uncovers the Bible*. He is a member of The Western Writers of America.

0-595-28387-X